THE ADOW

CHAD MICHAEL COX

The Adow

5-Ruby Edition: February 2024
First Edition: February 2014

Published by Yellow Suit Publishing
Ankeny, Iowa

yellowsuitpublishing.com

Cover Painting: Eric Wilkerson
Map and Interior Artwork: Chad Michael Cox
5-Ruby Drawing: Ron Wagner

ISBN 978-1-7356718-1-9

For Jessica—this world would not exist without you;

and to Breanna, Sean, and Heath
who complete my stories.

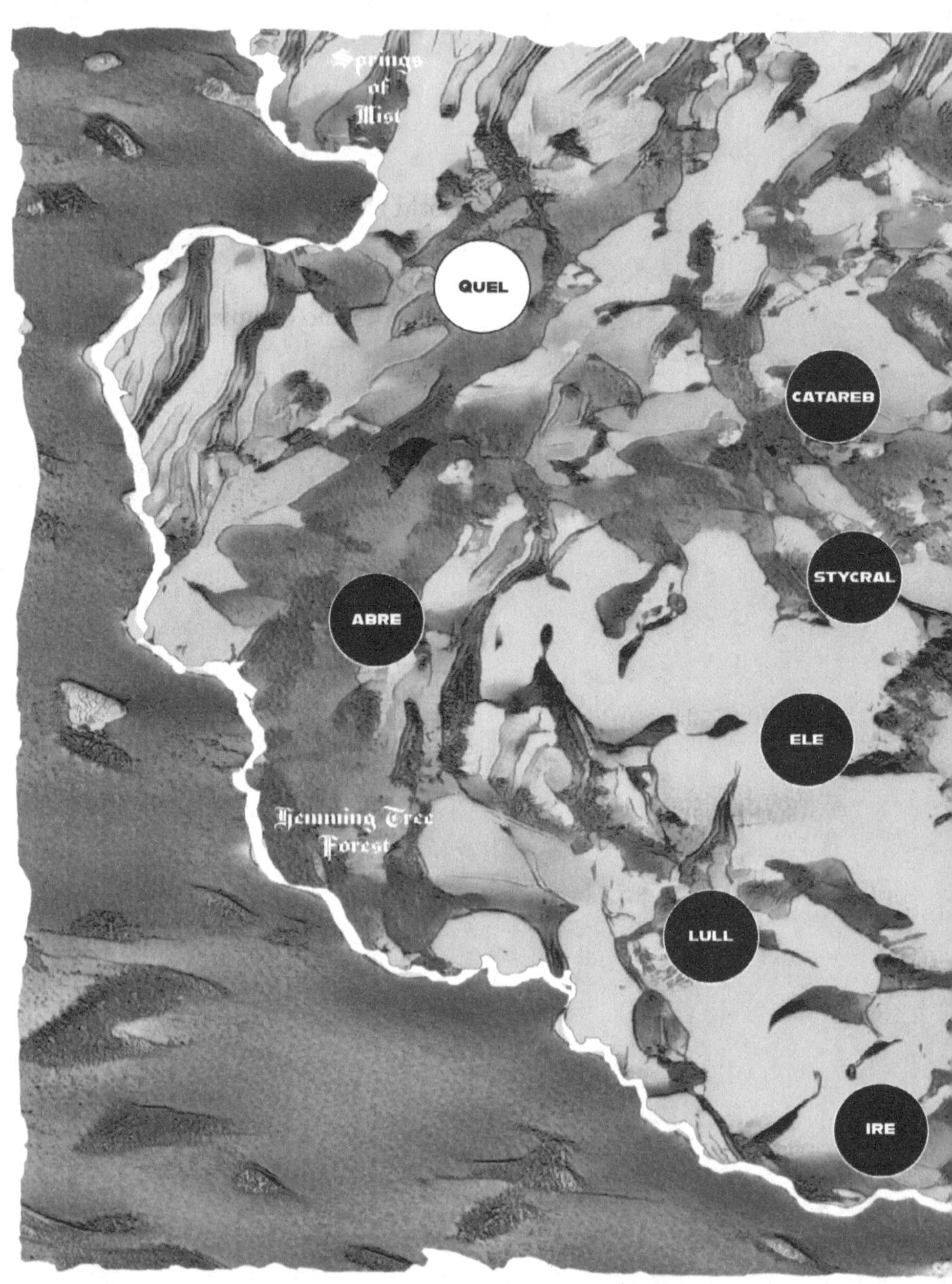

Springs of Mist
QUEL
CATAREB
STYCRAL
ABRE
ELE
Hemming Tree Forest
LULL
IRE

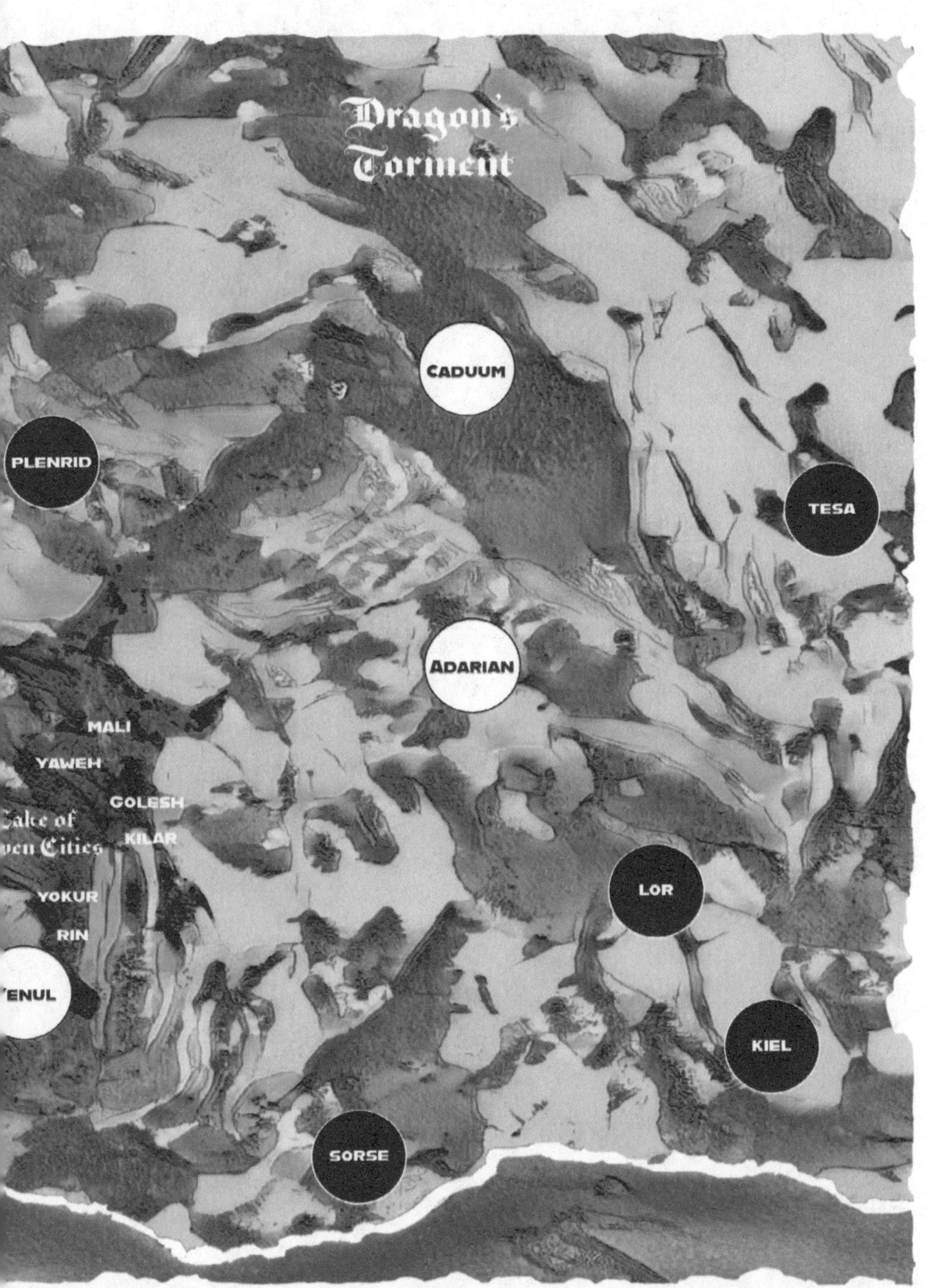

Dragon's Torment
Caduum
PLENRID
TESA
Adarian
MALI
YAWEH
GOLESH
Lake of
Seven Cities
KILAR
YOKUR
RIN
ENUL
LOR
KIEL
SORSE

QUEL

remember a goat tied. A knotted rope held it to the broken remnants of a wooden cart where it stood with one hoof upon half a head of cabbage. Several purple leaves hung from its mouth, twirling with every exaggerated and twisted chomp of its crooked brown teeth. Splatters of wet blood coated its white fur, but it stood there as though untouched by the battle, unbothered by the chaos that surrounded the two of us in that moment. And I knew, I knew, whatever we had achieved—for at that point we had completely overtaken the city—whatever we yet attained would prove just as senseless as that damned goat.

from Recollections of a Survivor of the Battle at Quel

a taggle's tale

I first encountered this tale in Lor. The storyteller, a near-naked taggle boy who stood amid a downpour and in the middle of a rain-sodden street, spoke with uncommon maturity and a surprisingly deep voice which I found pleasing to hear. I told him as much, afterward; also noting several faults in his delivery. For one, his green eyes displayed only one emotion: sadness. His weakened posture teetered on the verge of full collapse, leaving the audience to wonder after his own well-being and more than slightly distracting them from the spoken word. Fortunately, timely gestures helped him to compensate, and the forgiving audience remained attentive.

I implore you, speak his name. Speak of Lucen, for he spoke in the manner of all taggles. He told stories, and his words still linger. He lived and we heard his voice. May the Sphere forgive our mother and remember our father.

- DK Vel

A nameless taggle boy tells a familiar story as he slowly strikes an iron skillet with a wooden spoon. Repeatedly. Creating a source of audible irritation which culminates in a final *clunk* as the taggle reaches the end of his tale. Before the boy began his performance, dozens of topi warriors spun their discolored silver spoons around the edges of an altogether unsatisfying breakfast consisting of a single white glob of grits, silently wondering if this would serve as their final meal—wondering if they, too, would fall upon the now seventeen-day-old battlefield ¬that surrounds what remains of the city of Quel. Whatever their thoughts, however, whether silently cursing the Adow for leading them into this war or going through mental repetitions of sword movements, they offered the taggle boy little more than a distracted audience in no mood for a story. No different from any other interaction between topi and taggle. Yet, the taggle persevered long enough to garner their interest; and with the final strike of his wooden spoon, as though serving as some prearranged signal, every topi warrior within earshot of the resounding clunk stands in solidarity, replacing tin plates with steel swords. They raise them to the smoke-covered sky and collectively chant, "For Adarian! For Adarian!"

Adarian. Their ancient champion. The warrior after whom they named a city. The oft repeated story always ends with Adarian's death. His final breath always taken while held in the arms of his Adow. His life given. Her life saved. *Protector of the Adow.* For this, the warriors from Adarian remember his name. Indeed, the Adarians honor him because more than anyone he brought meaning to the title of First Etabli. Protector of the Adow. Those who served prior to Adarian did so with the grace and eloquence a formal title demands, but Adarian defined the role. He died in battle so she might live. Protector of the Adow. A trumpet beckons, silencing their chant. The Adarians quickly sheath their swords and march with organized haste toward the front lines, eager to find the same eternal glory of their acclaimed champion. Eager for immortality.

The invigorated topis forget about the wan taggle boy who rallied them to battle. The taggle takes no offense, for taggles live as slaves, easily identified by their mutilated ears. As with all taggles, a guard stood watch over this boy's mother until she gave birth, then he promptly hacked off the top of the boy's ears, forever marking him as a cursed taggle. Rumors suggest some newborns have escaped the ritual, claiming these unmarked taggles live freely among the topis, but most taggles only find freedom only after they fulfill their assumed role as keepers of story and teller of tales. Though not truly free, the taggles who live long enough to become storytellers, whether deemed novice or great orator, share their tales across the land and with everyone willing to listen. And they always listen…except the Adow—never the Adow. Though a select few taggles serve her directly, they may not speak in her presence or die in the attempt.

Fortunately, this taggle boy does not serve the Adow, nor does he have reason to bow before her. He may freely ensnare any gathered audience. He may boldly speak of Adarian's champion without fear of death. But when the story ends and the topis leave even this taggle must kneel in desperate hunger. He snatches the nearest plate, digging his cracked fingers under clumps of poorly mixed grits. A less than appetizing meal, for certain, but the taggle hasn't eaten since his master fell in battle five days ago. He knows he shouldn't touch their food, for it isn't allowed, nevertheless he devours three plates worth. Then he feels the broad blade of an Adarian sword pierce his chest, held firmly in the smallish hands of Birate, an aspiring topi warrior eager for advancement.

The brutal punishment of the taggle's offense, Birate's first kill, fails to elicit a single reaction from any of the warriors who maneuver past him; and though Birate pauses to listen for the cheers…though he seeks the visual affirmation of a raised fist or even a head nod, none of the passerby acknowledge the kill. In their eyes he has dealt with nothing more than a squawking chicken or a chittering squirrel. Someone had to act, but the act does not in itself bring any semblance of honor. Thus, the now crestfallen young warrior, who arrived at Quel two days ago, withdraws his sword and continues along the route with his customary short stride and unorthodox march, praying to the Sphere, rather, pleading with his god for an opportunity to slay a rebel this day; that his god would grant him honor.

Behind him, the taggle boy lies with his face in a glob of grits, eyes vacantly staring at a series of tattooed markings upon his knuckles. Like his mutilated ears, the tattoos identify him as a taggle. In life, they spoke when he could not. In death, they serve as his final words. They represent every taggle's prayer:

Remember our father
Forgive our mother

Thousands of Adarian warriors march by the taggle's body. Formed and reformed after five years of war, the Adarian divisions that remain, 161 in total, accounting for over half of all the warriors in the Adowian Army, have suffered sweeping losses including the most devastating of all, that of the Adarian 6th division, completely wiped out three days prior. Yet, their banner hangs proudly over the entrance of two separate, if vacant, large green tents. The Adarian warriors purposely steer toward the tents on their way to the smoke-veiled city of Quel, and as they pass, they kiss the backs of their silver gauntlets in remembrance of their fallen brothers.

These warriors then form the front lines of the greater Adowian force, each division led by a Rovet, a warrior who has proven himself in battle. A respected warrior and one with honor. Still, Rovets cannot purport themselves as *formal* leaders of each unit, deferring instead to the otherwise detested Madars—a blood-inheritance. The Madars, as custom dictates, quietly hide within luxuriously decorated, maroon-colored tents…far removed from the chaos of war.

Every Madar except Maldinado, Madar of the Adarian 45th.

Maldinado refuses to hide or retreat.

"May the Sphere protect you," he says quietly to his lifelong friend, Hintor.

"And keep you in his light," Hintor responds automatically. Once a farmer from Plenrid, Hintor now dons the disguise of an Adarian warrior. His relationship with Maldinado allows him to serve in the Adarian 45th, usurping his lack of Adarian blood. He is thin and short in stature. A poor disguise, really, but his black hair blends in with the Adarians gathered around him…and, well, he can match their considerable sword skills which by itself removes any lingering doubts and denotes him as one of their own.

Maldinado, in contrast, is pure Adarian with his black hair and gray eyes and sculpted jaw line. He stands tall, thick in the chest and shoulders. Serious. Focused. The Madar is slightly older than Hintor; even so the two of them resemble a pair of yearlings, not warriors. And neither truly belongs in this battle. One an imposter. The other a perceived craven.

"Why do we fight this battle, Maldinado?"

"For Adarian…and for Decrome." Maldinado points toward the Rovet of the Adarian 45th, a flat-nosed warrior with overly long arms standing a good distance in front of them. The true leader of the Adarian 45th. The one not named Madar. "And because I refuse to die in my tent a coward, like my father."

Decrome raises his sword and shouts, "The battle ends today!" The roar in response surges through the gathered warriors.

Then, in accordance with Adarian tradition, Hintor and Maldinado exchange swords with a promise to again exchange them at battle's end, a promise to survive. All around them, stalwart warriors of the Adarian 45th make similar exchanges, though not everyone follows the tradition. One of the taller warriors, Halcromb, bare-chested under a gray beard that drips with sweat from a two-day fever, refuses to exchange weapons with his son, Shamlon, a red-haired warrior standing beside him.

"No, yearling, I'll keep my sword. I've no intention of surviving another day."

"Father!"

Halcromb pats his right thigh, blood-soaked bandages concealing an infected wound, "I'm already dead."

Shamlon nods his head in resignation, "May the Sphere protect you."

"And keep you in his light."

Several other Adarian divisions surround the highly decorated Adarian 45th. The Adarian 8th, generally considered brutes. Adarian 29th, known to capture and torture prisoners regardless of age or gender. Adarian 11th, strategists. Indeed, every remaining Adarian unit stands behind their Adow except the Adarian 41st, an embarrassment to the city ever since they mistakenly shot a barrage of arrows into the ranks of the Yokur 3rd at the Battle of Ire. Beyond the Adarians, warriors cluster and shuffle and twitch, representing every city in the land including Lor, Abre, and Kiel. Only Quel stands in opposition to the Adowian Army. Quel, homeland of the rebel Yenen. A city at least twice the size of Adarian. Quel, known for its fine weavers and silversmiths. Quel, the enemy.

The Adow arrives and assumes her place as leader of her forces. She rides along the front lines, claiming this army as hers. Her warriors. Her war. *And the war ends today!* She inspects the ranks of the Adowian Army, greatly dwindled as compared to the mammoth host she led out of Yenul five years earlier. *It can't be helped*, she convinces herself.

Ayson rides before the Adow. Her chosen First Etabli. Undeniably, the most polarizing figure to ever assume the title. He wipes the sweat from his bald head and, once more, secures a golden helmet snug against his brow and the nape of his neck, sliding it down over his ears. Behind both Adow and First Etabli ride a fearsome collective known as the Adowian Guard, twenty elite warriors chosen by the First Etabli to protect the Adow whether in periods of peace or times of war. This war. Her war. The royal detachment settles into position at the front of a now restless army even as the eerie scream of a dying warrior rises from the battlefield, unseen behind a wall of smoke.

"Warriors shouldn't sound like that," Ayson says. His black horse shifts closer to the Adow.

"They're calling my name," she slowly wraps her black hair around her finger, listening to the stuttered moans of the dying. *My Adow! Save me, my...my Adow!*

Ayson takes her hand, pulling it away from her hair. She's shaking, "You don't have to do this."

"The walls have fallen. I won't give Yenen another day."

"I meant you don't have to lead the charge."

"You know that's not true."

The Adow raises the First Etabli's hand to her lips, kissing his moist palm, "I'm fine. Yenen will be dead soon, and all of this will be over." She clings to his hand, stares at it with absent intensity, seemingly unwilling to release it. Ayson gently pulls his hand away. He draws his sword, thus signaling the march to begin.

The Adow's sword, known as the Sword of the Sphere, remains sheathed. Never drawn. Never used. Not by any of the Adow, not ever. One of the Adow—she who reigned During the Changing of the Blue Moon under the seal of the Crowned Warrior, when Fael served as First Etabli—practiced swordplay in her early years. But even she never drew a sword in battle, and this Adow—she who reigns During the Completion of the Green Moon under the seal of the Crown Between Swords, while Ayson serves as First Etabli—never received instruction on such maneuvers. A sheathed sword and not a pound worth of armor, choosing instead to wear a traditional white linen blouse with gold doublet and matching trousers. *I'm not here to fight*, she reminds herself.

No, she will not fight, though she longs to end this battle. Instead, she will judge or be judged, and all the warriors whether friend or foe must abide. Not her judgment, specifically. Her god will judge. Indeed, her body will serve as a vessel for the Sphere's verdict. Let him speak, yes, she too, wants to know his final decree. She needs to know she rightly chose Ayson over Yenen as her First Etabli. All the land needs to know. For this reason and this alone she leads the march, kicking her horse forward into an unhurried walk and into the smoke. One of her Adowian Guard, Teyo, lifts a polished trumpet and quickly blows a five-note tune. The pace quickens to a trot.

The Adarians lead the rest of the army as the full force follows their Adow into the smoke, unaware of her misgivings and altogether unconcerned for they represent Adarian! They fight for honor, not the Adow. Even Brink, the stout banner bearer of the Adarian 45th, he who received his position merely due to his status as brother-in-law to Gan, Overseer of Adarian, marches proudly into battle. He too, like his Adow, has never drawn his sword—a fact disguised, if not completely concealed, by his duties as banner bearer; something for which he garners respect from all those unaware of the political ruse. The lucky bastard. He basks in the admiration of the entirety of the Adowian Army without having ever wielded a sword in battle. Though, not everyone gives Brink such respect. In fact, within the ranks of the Adarian 45th he endures constant ridicule.

Halcromb, on the other hand, does not. Lesser known than their famed banner bearer, and altogether hidden behind his gray beard, he nevertheless draws attention as he defiantly limps forward on an infected leg. He refuses any assistance offered by his red-bearded son, Shamlon, or that of any other warrior. His eyes are wide with the expectation of battle. Shamlon drifts slightly behind his father, capturing to memory the last details of Halcromb's life so he can later describe the moment to his mother and sister. He notes his father's altered gait...the mud splattered about his boots...the naked torso, his armor too badly damaged to wear any longer. Instead, sweat turned black by the smoke now coats his back and arms. The last remains of his father.

In contrast to Halcromb's labored steps, another warrior further back in the battle lines of the Adarian 45th hops like a locust from muddy footprint to muddy footprint. Short in stature with even shorter legs, Birate searches for a glimpse of the city walls. Instead, he finds leather and armor and a general mass of warrior ass blocking his view. The story of his life. *Little Birty* they call him, for he stands shorter than some yearlings, but what he lacks in stature he compensates for with ambition. So, what if killing the taggle boy gained him nothing? Today, at some point, he will finally earn the respect of his fellow Adarians. At the moment, however, those around him audibly voice their annoyance and threaten to trample him down if he doesn't keep pace, offering him no mercy despite his father having once served as division Rovet.

As for their current Madar, Maldinado and his friend, Hintor, bring up the rear of the Adarian 45th, all but forgotten in the pre-battle maneuvering.

The Adow does her best to ignore the screams of the dying warriors who litter the battlefield, remnants of the previous day's struggle. Somehow, remarkably, still alive. *Save me, my Adow! Bless me, my Adow! Have mercy, my Adow!* She moves her horse over their swollen and mutilated bodies, refusing to look at them even as they grab for her. They plead with her. *Help! Please!* But what can she do? She reaches for Ayson's hand.

The First Etabli sees images in the smoke. Ghosts. Shadows. He strains his brown eyes, desperate to navigate a path. He motions for the Adowian Guard to fan out, fearful of an ambush. *Where are you, Yenen?* Ayson moves closer, allowing the Adow to shift onto his own horse. She sits behind him and wraps her arms around him; buries her forehead into his back. To the side of them, her white mare wanders away, disappearing into the smoke.

A hulking figure emerges from the haze, a lone warrior who, at last, reveals the enemy's position. Two Adowian Guards, Teyo and Yla, instantly converge upon him. Ayson raises his sword to warn of the impending attack, but quickly lowers it as the warrior comes more into focus. One of their own. Tesha from the Rin 9th. Wounded and badly burned, his eyes swollen to blindness, and left to wander in pain and agonizing madness.

"What lies ahead?" Ayson asks, but Tesha only hears a deafening ringing in his ears. He groans like a damned mule, and blindly walks past the First Etabli into the ranks of the Adarian 45th.

Decrome, realizing the severity of Tesha's condition, mercifully buries his sword into the wounded warrior's belly. Tesha's life fades with a gasp and a whispered *thank you*. Decrome dutifully lowers Tesha to the ground. Then he pulls his sword from the body. This act of mercy from a Rovet known more for his courage than his compassion serves as his last and perhaps his only good deed, for in that moment a large stone descends upon him with such velocity as to leave nothing visible save his elongated sword arm. Shot from a catapult, the stone, or rather a remnant of Quel pulled from the crumbling city walls, severs arm from body with a sickening thud. Where once stood the Rovet of the Adarian 45th, now sits a chiseled boulder half-buried in the ground.

Brink stumbles backward from the resulting shock wave, nevertheless, he manages to maintain his grip upon the fiercely rippling banner of the Adarian 45th. He stares at the remains of the Rovet with noticeable alarm, but quickly gathers himself enough to slowly rotate the banner in a wide circle. He repeats the motion five times, thus alerting everyone of a change in command. Everyone except Little Birty who cannot see for want of height.

"Decrome is dead," Maldinado points to the circulating banner.

"May the Sphere be with him," Hintor responds.

"And keep him in his light."

"Hey!" Hintor pats his friend on the back, "That leaves you in charge."

"No, another Rovet must be chosen. Adarians will never follow a Madar."

"They will follow a Madar if he also serves as Rovet," Hintor insists.

Maldinado and Hintor march past Decrome's arm, pausing long enough to register his death. The Adarian 45th selected him as Rovet during the battle at Stycral after he beheaded the Rovet of the Stycral 12th. Proven in battle and oldest amongst them, Decrome outlived four division Madars and personally killed Maldinado's father while he lay asleep in his tent.

For that, Maldinado will forever remain grateful.

All around him the Adowian Army continues to march through the smoke despite a barrage of boulders catapulted into the air, mostly unseen until they strike. Crushed. Flattened. Left dead or maimed. Warriors across the battlefield either fall victim or they grow wary of what may descend upon them. Ayson, too, navigates his horse cautiously through the smoke while raising the shield of the First Etabli skyward. The shield, with its engraving of Erin's head, fully covers both Ayson and the Adow behind him, offering them protection against the assault—if a feeble defense.

Worse, Ayson can no longer see the Guards, "It feels like we're all alone."

The Adow kisses his back, her own sweat blending with the coolness of his armor upon her lips, "I am never alone."

Still, Ayson searches for the Guards. *Where are they?* He strains to see past the smoke to the larger army. *Where are they?* But wherever he looks, however long he stares, Ayson finds neither form nor shadow. The gray haze swirls around them, and though he feels the trembling gait of his horse, the smoke creates an illusion of suspended movement.

Far away from the Adow and her First Etabli, Hintor hears the wisps of arrows soaring past him. He draws closer to Maldinado. The smoke seems thicker with every step until, suddenly, it clears, and the city rises before them. Hintor stares at the mighty wall surrounding Quel and finds it…surprisingly, unscathed! *Where is the breach?* Far as he can see, in both directions, Hintor finds large yellow square stones neatly stacked and grouted. He and Maldinado and those around him stare at the site in stunned wonder. Indeed, the assault grinds to a halt as the Adarians await orders or guidance…or a single word to point them in a new direction. Nothing. Hintor searches across the landscape behind him. *Where is the Adow and her First Etabli?* Gone. Unseen. Only the raised banner of the Adarian 45th truly stands out amidst the sea of silver helmets—always the banner…and the mounted banner bearer!

"How is it he never dies?" Hintor asks. "Brink's been carrying that banner all over the damn battlefield for three weeks—you'd think someone would use him for target practice."

"Right now, we're the target," Maldinado points upward. "We need to move."

"There's no breach!" The anonymous shout echoes through the Adarian ranks. "Retreat, Adarians! There's no breach!" It's coming from above.

Maldinado doesn't retreat. Instead, he yells, "Ignore the enemy! Find the breach!"

Hintor beams with satisfaction, "Does this mean you're finally taking command?"

Maldinado shrugs his shoulders with feigned indifference, "Decrome is dead. Someone has to give orders."

The Adarian 45th responds en masse, shuffling and blundering their way back through the smoke. They can't see their enemy above. They can't see the arrows loosed upon them, or the boiling pitch poured overhead. Death sweeps across their huddled ranks with ferocious frequency, only to have their peril worsen as the rest of the Adowian Army reaches the point of attack, thus merging with the Adarians. Confusion turns to turmoil and Maldinado's opportunity to seize control of his division suddenly collides with the real danger of completely losing command of his warriors amid the panic. Strangers from other divisions mingle helplessly. Warriors crush together, shoulder-to-shoulder and chest-to-chest. No one can move. They gather and huddle and squeeze around the Madar. Maldinado can't walk. *There are too many bodies!*

"Find the breach!" Maldinado yells again.

"I'd love to, just as soon as I can move!" Hintor shouts back, unable to see past the dour face and straw-colored hair of the noble looking warrior pressed against his chest. "Pleasant day under the circumstances. I don't believe we've ever met. I'm Hintor of the Adarian 45th."

"Gilvan of the Adowian Guard," his breath smells of candied walnuts.

Another volley of arrows. Gilvan stiffens as one of the arrows pierces his clean-shaven throat, splattering warm blood all over Hintor's face. Worse, he can feel the sharp tip of the arrow tickling his own throat. The warrior's body slackens in death, but it doesn't fall. Supported by Hintor and those around him, Gilvan's remains continue to stand in defiance which means the protruding arrow continues to nestle in Hintor's beard even as blood now trickles down and pools at his lips. Unable to wipe it away, he spits in the face of the recently departed. "Well, Gilvan of the Adowian Guard, I suppose this marks the end of our relationship. For the record, you were a piss poor friend?"

"There it is, Hintor!" Maldinado declares with renewed vigor.

The breach is real! Maldinado catches a glimpse of it through the thinning haze. Unfortunately, he can't breathe. The crowd presses tighter against him, bodies crushing him from every direction. Hintor grabs at his arm but quickly loses grip as the surge pushes the Madar away from his friend. The strain proves too much!

"May the Sphere be with you!" Maldinado yells.

"Maldinado!" Hintor fights to move forward, but the mass of flesh and steel renders him helpless. The Madar disappears as Hintor finds himself steered violently toward a wall positioned further down and well beyond the breach. The relentless pushing threatens to sweep him underfoot, and though he manages to keep his feet, he hits the wall with such impact that it knocks the wind out of him. He tries to push away, but the warriors of the Adowian Army persist in their inadvertent attempts to kill him. He can't breathe! Then help arrives from those inside the city as its defenders hurl a fresh brew of pitch down upon the armored pack, scattering, flattening, or scalding their attackers. Hintor gasps for air.

Unfortunately, his lungs fill with smoke. "Tasa Ro!" He coughs.

He searches for Maldinado, spotting him in the breach. The Madar stands face-to-face with his enemy, neither able to effectively use their sword in the paralyzing crush. Hintor watches in disbelief as the two foes pass one another without engagement. "Our mighty Rovet," Hintor chides, but the Madar, now lost behind the walls of Quel, does not hear or, at any rate, does not respond.

East of the breach and a good distance removed from the chaotic assault, for they inexplicably strayed off course, Ayson and the Adow ride with noticeable haste toward a limp black banner only just visible through the smoke. The disreputable emblem of the rebellion. It hangs overhead like a flayed carcass from atop the city walls, awaiting the butcher. The stilled banner enables Ayson and the Adow to regain their bearings, drawing them ever closer to the distinctive sounds of warriors clashing. The Adow looks down at her faintly glowing skin to assure herself of what lies ahead: An end to the battle. The nearly white light now bursting forth from deep within her inner being shines brighter with every step the horse takes toward the city. A sign. *The* sign for which she has so desperately awaited. A sign to signify the Sphere's approval of this endless bloodshed! For five long years she has wondered. Waited. But now, all her doubt fades away. The final battle approaches. At last, this war will end. *Everything will be alright!* "Hurry, Ayson!"

Maldinado and most of the rest of the Adarian 45th spill over the breach like fish jumping upstream, and the enemy beyond greets them with the desperate enthusiasm of a starving beast. Though initially repelled, Maldinado courageously leads the Adarians into a wave of silver-armored warriors. He kills two of the rebels and searches for another, eventually working his way to an oddly empty cobblestone street where he discovers the toothless face of a city attempting to hide behind the impenetrable mask of a towering wall: Burned thatch roofs. Shattered carts. Here, a row of bodies dutifully collected and gathered along one side of the pitted street; a gruesome task left inexplicably unfinished for some of the dead still lie where they must have fallen, neglected or forgotten or abandoned, regardless, having never made it to the street to take their place along the macabre path. There, a still bleeding yearling lies in the middle of a small garden. His lifeless hand clings to a rope tied about the neck of a much alive, black-spotted goat. Life paused. Death interrupted. The street resembles a tomb set apart from the conflict just west of the main gate now visible beyond the line of corpses.

To his right, Maldinado finds a mess of wagons, broken crates, and bulging bags of grain positioned at the top of a slight incline to form a makeshift barrier for a group of archers so intently focused on the battle beyond they fail to notice the Madar. He could take them by surprise and eliminate the threat. To Maldinado's left, however, he sees a torrent of rebels eagerly racing to join the fracas, and more of them run along the city walls. *You're late in shifting your defenses, Yenen! Victory is ours!* Maldinado ignores the entrenched archers and rejoins the surging Adarian 45th. Soon after, he fights alongside the red-haired Shamlon who struggles to keep pace with his gray-bearded father.

On the other side of the city wall, Hintor once again rushes into the sea of warriors that surround the city. With some effort, no, with a great deal of effort he manages to navigate his way toward the breach and finally makes his way into the city. Once freed from the pack, Hintor raises his sword, or rather, he raises Maldinado's sword and quickly finds someone to attack. Some he leaves humbled and moribund, a clean wound given by the better swordsman. Some he slaughters with the practiced force of a farmer hacking through the beast he means to eat. Another warrior attacks, but Hintor grabs his sword arm, slick with sweat, even as he buries his own sword into the now exposed gut of the defiant defender of Quel and Yenen and all who hate the Adow. He holds him until the life fades from his brown eyes, leaving Hintor with only the weight of death. He forcefully discards the body, freeing his sword, and continues his search for Maldinado.

Several moments later, Little Birty, too, finally enters the city. He stands like a morning rooster atop a pile of crumbled stone. He surveys the scene, searching for a fight, but the rebels have already started to retreat deeper into the city. The honor he seeks continues to outpace him. The validation he needs as a member of the vaunted Adarian 45th has once more escaped his tiny grasp. Undeterred, he waddles along in pursuit of the rebels, eager for the kill.

Outside the city, Ayson guides his horse along the red stone walls, again holding his shield above his head to protect the Adow against any stray attacks. There is little chance of any direct attack, not with the Adowian Guard now maintaining a much tighter perimeter around the Adow, more than a little panicked at having lost her in the first place; but the task of keeping track of her has grown much easier. They need only look for the white light emanating from her skin. The heat-less light reveals all, even the drops of sweat pooling at the base of Ayson's neck as he strains to hold the shield aloft. Despite his physical exhaustion, however, Ayson feels a welcome sense of relief, for he has long wondered if the Adow chose wisely when she appointed him as First Etabli; long questioned his place in her world. But now the Sphere has spoken! Let all who question finally know the truth. He straightens his back and lowers the shield, proudly presenting his Adow to those who will bear witness to future generations. *Yes, I am your First Etabli, and this is your Adow!*

The battle falls silent. Warriors on both sides follow the Adow and her First Etabli as they travel through the jumbled hive of the living and the dead. They reach the breach and move into the city. Those who don't follow watch from their positions along the walls as Ayson leads his horse through the housing district and further still toward the city gates and finally into the market square. He weaves between and around several dozen misaligned rows of red canvas tents, an impromptu extension of the city caused by the influx of rebels, damaged homes, and the pride of a rebel leader in need of the makeshift rebel camp complete with a golden tent at its center to serve as his headquarters—an obvious symbol of defiance. Only Yenen would dare adopt the royal color.

"Here," the Adow says.

She releases her grip from around Ayson's waist, and slowly ascends from the horse. She looks below at all the faces raised in worship, all those who followed her light through the city; those who have maintained their faith in her. She floats high above the rebel camp for all to see, for all to know the Sphere approves of this war! *And it ends today!* She smiles, silently acknowledging her own doubts. When she chose Ayson as her First Etabli over Yenen, she went against tradition—but she knew it was the right decision. She *knew* it was right! Now the Sphere emanates his approval, using her body as proof she acted with his blessing. She can feel his presence, his warmth. *I was right!* She looks down upon her warriors who fill the market square. She looks down upon the rebels beside them. They all await her final judgment, and she does not delay the moment, boldly declaring, "The Sphere is with us!"

"And we are in his light!" The Adowian Army roars.

But the rebels from Quel respond with trepidation. Those who value honor immediately drop their swords, refusing to fight against the Sphere regardless of what they think of the Adow. The more intellectual ones reassess where their loyalties lay, though, curiously, perhaps due to sheer stubbornness or a refusal to admit defeat, most of these rebels again choose to side with Yenen. Others strike anew, having long since abandoned both the Sphere and his cursed Adow in favor of Morlac, the god of another world; Yenen and his rebels serving only as a convenient disguise. Still others, those filled with rage and the blood lust of war, hasten to engage with those who oppose them.

The killing resumes.

Ayson dismounts and moves into battle with the confidence of a champion. Though many questioned his status as First Etabli, none have ever questioned his ability with a sword; or that of any Adowian Guard. The rebels nearest him die with a bitter sigh and a final curse of the Adow. His sword sends fierce and vast ripples through the gathered forces. Soon, even the most ardent to the cause begin to yield rather than face the First Etabli in combat. They cower before him. They gather by the dozen and kowtow.

Yenen watches with disgust from where he stands atop the city walls, his mouth slightly agape, adding to the general awkwardness of his facial features. A familiar hatred fills his mouth. *Wench! I loved your mother. I brought comfort to her in her dying days. I was chosen by her to succeed Cidal as First Etabli! I was chosen! But this…this new Adow, this obstinate bitch has taken everything. Everything! And still the Sphere aligns himself with her!*

"So let it be known," He pulls a red-feathered arrow from his quiver. The color of Quel. The color of Morlac—his new god. *The only god with any sense, it seems.* The one who has delivered her to him in this moment. He nocks the arrow to the string of his heavy bow. He holds it at the ready with thickened arms, and then he moves toward the woman he despises with little regard for the battle around him.

The Adarian 45th, Brink still holding the banner high within their midst, pushes through a line of defense hastily assembled upon a set of stairs leading to the parapets above the city. "If they had more discipline, they would present a greater challenge!" Halcromb yells, adrenaline fueling his assault. His son, Shamlon, fights proudly beside him. They continue their bloody advance until they gain the parapet along with most of the Adarian 45th.

Yenen runs past them.

Warriors from both armies rally at the appearance of the rebel leader. "Kill him!" Halcromb yells. "For Adar…" But the old topi's rally cry ends with a mouthful of blood and a sword through the back. A sleep-deprived and badly sunburned warrior pulls the same sword from Halcromb's body, sending him over the edge of the wall. He falls away from his final unseen foe…away from his son…to his death below. But Shamlon does not mourn his father's death. His own wounds have left him dying and slumped against the parapet. Unaware of his father's death, he searches for Halcromb amidst the closing darkness. *Forgive me, father…*

Shamlon and Halcromb die even as Maldinado continues to hack through shield and sword and limb. In the city below, still chasing his friend with reckless abandon, Hintor charges into every hazard like a hawk piercing the water with its talons. He swings his sword. He maims. He thrusts. He kills. He stands in the shadow of the wall and—*dammit all!* He remains several feet away from the stairs which Maldinado ascended moments ago. For all his effort, Hintor has yet to overtake his friend, and worse, he has now lost sight of him. *Tasa Ro!*

He has never witnessed such chaos and desperation. Quel and Adarian and Adowian warriors fight alongside him in the street below. The street funnels onto the stairs ahead. The stairs spill out onto the ramparts above. Bodies lay about him in pieces or in loosely gathered piles, threatening to trip him with each step. Everything, everywhere, exists in a perpetual state of fighting, or surviving, or dying…even the walls bleed. Hintor again searches for his friend, but he only finds the banner of the Adarian 45th raised high atop the parapet. Brink, at least, survives.

"Lucky bastard!" Hintor shouts.

A not so lucky Little Birty chases his newest foe into an empty tavern. He follows at about fifteen paces behind, far enough away to force a clumsy search for the rebel upon entering the musty darkness. Little Birty proceeds to upturn every wooden table and stacked set of chairs. He looks behind a cracked marble bar top, presumably imported from Adarian, and swings his sword at every deformed shadow, but he finds nothing of substance to strike. Then, a broken window signals the rebel's whereabouts and Little Birty charges up the stairs—one at a time lest he stumble—to the rooms above.

A different and much more capable rebel stops running. Yenen stands atop the eastern wall which spans the length of the market square below. He raises his bow and takes aim at his target. The Adow still floats above the fray, arrogantly judging him—judging everyone—glowing like some ancient relic. *Damn!* He struggles to find her physical form beyond the blinding light.

Maldinado finally escapes the horde and closes the gap between he and Yenen even as the rebel leader takes his aim. *Nooooo*! Suddenly realizing Yenen means to kill the Adow, Maldinado raises his sword in a charging if mostly panicked attack.

Yenen releases the arrow.

Maldinado brings his sword crashing down, severing Yenen's body at the shoulder and neck with enough force to send his remains over the wall to the city below. But Yenen's arrow flies true, striking the unarmored Adow near the heart. Maldinado, desperately shifting his weight in time to keep himself from taking a fatal plunge, then must watch in helpless horror as his Adow falls from the sky, her body limp. She crashes to the ground with shocking violence. Tents, both red and gold, collapse around her. The Battle of Quel ends abruptly.

The Adow lies dead.

5-RUBY
SPECIAL EDITION

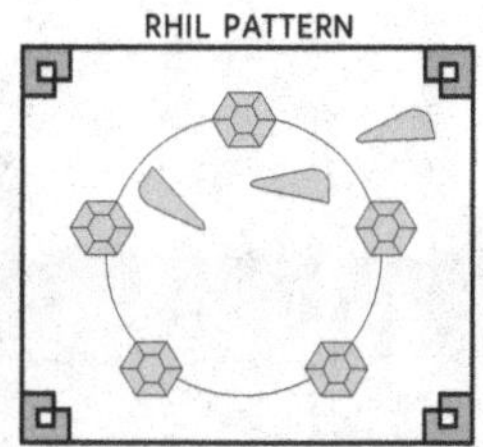

<u>A Record of—she who served as—The Adow:</u>

Moon	Seal
Completion of the Purple Moon	Floating
Completion of the Purple Moon	Hemming
Shadow of the Purple Moon	River un
Shadow of the Purple Moon	Sword th
Completion of the Red Moon	Broken (
Completion of the Red Moon	Crown o
Changing of the Silver Moon	Five Cro
Completion of the Yellow Moon	Sword wi
Changing of the Blue Moon	Crowned
Completion of the Green Moon	Crowned
Completion of the Green Moon	Crowned
Completion of the Green Moon	Crown ov
Completion of the Green Moon	Two Cro
Completion of the Green Moon	Crowned
Completion of the Green Moon	Hammer
Completion of the Green Moon	Sun Risi
Completion of the Green Moon	Crown b
Dark Moon	Tiger an

Months: Erog | Utine | Cil | Flatine | Joone   Date Format: (

Periods: Year = 5 Months | Month = 5 Weeks | V

The Adow

oon, Official Seal, and Chosen First Etabli
First Etabli
ver Sphere   Erin, the First Etabli
bove Crown   Anine
n   Aul
wn   Taggle, the cursed
              Ylaf
              Erbohn
              Ig-poy
n, on Hilt   Adarian, hero of Ire
              Fael
              Irloore
              Cintyge
sed Swords   Lio
              Enyure
              Athoyen
Crown   Ferya
rown   Cidal
words   Ayson, of Quel
              Ayson, of Quel
uring the Red Moon | (Specific) Erog 23, Completion of the Red Moon 51
Days | Day = 5 Hours = Spheric Hour | Hour = 300 Minutes

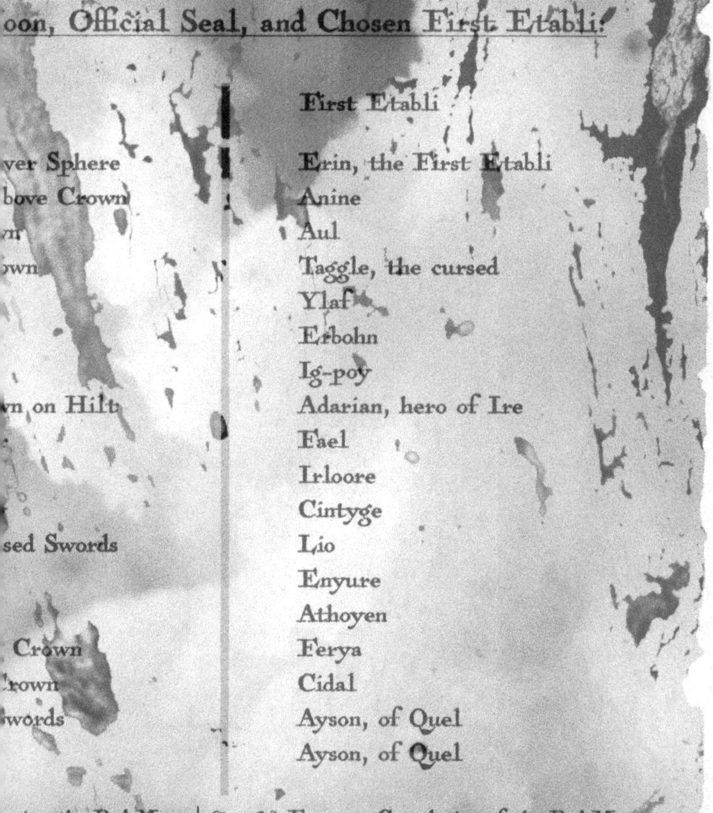

he Battle at Quel changed everything. My mother is dead. Now I reign as Adow and my First Etabli, Ayson…Ayson, my father. My ever-present, burden of a father is like moss clinging to my every pore!

"Call off the Guard, Ayson!" And leave me the hell alone. A fierce rain coats my face as I walk toward a clearing in the forest, adding weight to my already too long hair.

I wish Troq was here. Troq, my guardian before I became the Adow, before Ayson, before everything. He called me Ovda, short for Daughter *of the* Adow. My caretaker. Each night he would hold me close and tell me a story, his crinkled fingers warm upon my back, his quivering voice caressing my ears as I fell asleep.

I wipe this blasted rain from my face.

Troq is gone. He isn't coming back. I woke up one morning to find him dead, and I was given to another guardian, Faunride. That's how it is—the First Etabli protects the Adow, and the next best warrior protects the Daughter of the Adow. When they die, they're replaced. Troq just happened to live long enough to serve as my guardian. It could have been anyone. He was part of a tradition, nothing more. We all have our duties.

Tasa Ro!

So much has changed. Now I'm the Adow, the youngest to ever assume the role, and Ayson is my First Etabli. I barely knew my father two years ago. He was a warrior like any other warrior. But after my mother died, Ayson replaced Faunride just as Faunride replaced Troq. Without a word. He simply entered my room, slid into bed beside me, and assumed his role as my First Etabli…always beside me. My protector. My guardian.

My moss.

Again, I wipe the rain from my face. I prayed for sunshine, but apparently the Sphere doesn't bother with the weather, or maybe it's just me he doesn't bother with. Either way, I'm drenched. Aiya, my enduring maidservant, made a valiant attempt to dress me in a more weather appropriate cloak, but I stubbornly chose a simple blue vest instead. Dammit! I hate it when she's right.

Towering pine trees surround me, completely concealing twenty of my guards, including Faunride, now returned to his former position as guard from afar. No doubt, they scan the forest for any sign of danger. I suppose it's a comfort knowing he's…that *they're* there, but right now I just want to be left alone. Every second of the day, I'm surrounded by warriors whose sole purpose is to keep me safe. An assassin killed my mother, so now they assume someone will kill me. For two years, now, they've checked every room before I enter, tasted every meal. They scanned this same forest, yesterday, for an enemy who wasn't even there. It's not like I don't make this trip every day!

"Call off the guard!" I yell again. But Ayson ignores my request, same as he did yesterday…and the day before. I will never be alone again.

Thanks to Yenen.

I don't have any memories of my mother's assassin. When she appointed Ayson as her First Etabli, Yenen disappeared. My mother, as was her way, assumed it was the last she would see of him, but twelve years later the Overseer of Quel was murdered. Yenen reappeared and seized control of the city. He led his newly formed army from Quel to Stycral. Then he conquered Ele and Lull, effectively closing the northern trade route. Predictably, my mother was caught completely by surprise. Two more cities, Plenrid and Catareb, fell before she finally, if slowly, mobilized her forces and began a march on Quel.

Five years of war followed.

Now my mother stands as a marble statue, sculpted by Beaug. That's it. That's all that remains of her life. It stands like a giant, towering above me as I enter a large, grassy clearing almost completely covered with yellow and blue flowers. Of course, the flowers sag in the rain.

Fitting.

I've come to hate this place. I hate that it's become this hallowed ground. A shrine to my mother. If anything, there should be a statue of Troq. This was our place! His and mine. This is where he taught me to fly a dragon kite, and later how to use the forbidden sword. Yes, he taught an *Adow* how to use a sword! It was our secret, of course, but the fact is I don't need a First Etabli. I don't need Ayson or Faunride or any of the rest of them. Hell, I'm a better swordsman than my father has ever been!

Still, my guardians surround me. They surround this clearing. They surround everything.

I came to this clearing when Troq died. Quickly, before they could assign me another guardian. I didn't want another guardian. I wanted Troq. They searched for me. They searched for hours. It is the only time in my life I've ever been alone. It was Faunride who found me. It was Faunride who served as my guardian after Troq. But he stepped aside when my mother died, dutifully allowing my father to take his rightful place as First Etabli.

Ayson stops halfway into the clearing, unwilling to come any closer to the statue of his dead lover, a reminder of the Adow he failed to protect, causing the physical gap between us to widen. With any luck, he may soon refuse to enter the clearing altogether, but for now I'll take what little personal space I can get, which isn't much; so I hasten to widen the gap, eventually reaching the statue of the mother I despise.

Unfortunately, I look just like her. I mean, identical. We're remarkably similar in facial structure, with soft cheeks that highlight our green eyes and then fade into a rounded jaw line. Our nose is the width of a finger, and our lips are thinner still. It's not just my mother, either. All of the Adow look alike. It's how we're identified as the Adow, confirmed as the Sphere's chosen ruler. The Sphere is our god. The Adow is our duty. This statue is all of us.

"Why don't you look upon your Adow, Ayson?" I ask with relish.

"It's enough I come to this place," he turns his back to me.

No, actually, it's not enough, "One day it will be *my* face on this statue. Who will come to see *me*?"

"I won't do what you ask! I can't!"

Of course, he can't. He doesn't *love* me like he loved my mother.

I look back to the statue. Her face. Our face. I close my eyes and pray that when I have a daughter, *if* I have a daughter, she never has to experience such hell. It's not like I want to do this any more than my father does, but we all have our duties. Yes, Ayson, tradition trumps love.

Love, it seems, died with my mother.

I open my eyes, ending my prayers. *Dammit*! I don't know why I'm praying to a god who isn't there. I suppose it's because Troq taught me to pray like a good little disciple, or because Faunride taught me to follow every useless tradition without question.

I hear the arrow as it slaps the rain. Too late. It strikes me just below the collarbone. The stabbing pain resonates all the way to my throat. It's hard to breathe, and I'm on my knees before I can steady myself using my mother's statue. Yes, I'm bowing before my mother like a damn taggle, and yeah, maybe struggling to regain focus.

I hear Ayson yell, "Assassin!"

I can't see my attacker. I can't see my guards. Everything is a blur. I think I hear another arrow. It lands off to my right. They're trying to kill me. Why are they trying to kill me? I'm not her! I'm not the one who chose Ayson over Yenen! You idiots. I'm not my mother!

There is blood, my blood…my blood is dripping onto a yellow flower that lies crushed beneath my hand. I pull away from the flower, willing myself to stand and confront my unseen enemy even as my guards rush into the clearing. Stand! Troq would want me to fight.

There is someone there in the distance. He is wearing a red robe and I'm certain he's running toward me, fumbling to nock another arrow. But Faunride and the rest of my guardians close in on the would-be assassin. He's dead before he can reach me. *Bastard*! I clutch my arm.

Then, Ayson is beside me. He holds me like he once held my mother, shielding her too late…shielding me too late. My blood travels the length of the arrow shaft, large drips of red life tainting the rain…and swallowed by the earth below. I'm dying. *Why would someone do this to me?* I need the healers. Walk! Walk, dammit! I need to leave this blasted clearing. I pull away from Ayson. Every step brings pain, but I have to keep walking. There's no one left to carry me to the healers. Not anymore. Troq is dead. Faunride and his traditions—he wouldn't dare touch me now. And Ayson…my father doesn't care.

"Tasa Ro!" I can't feel my arm, anymore.

I leave the clearing, retracing my steps through the now-spinning forest. I scan the wavering trees for anymore assassins come to finish the kill, come to silence the famed Oracle of the Sphere. I spit blood, but still it fills my mouth. Some oracle. If they only knew the truth—the Sphere doesn't talk to me. He never has…

I'm actually dying! I can't breathe! Is this how it felt, mother?

I must have stopped walking because Ayson catches up to me.

"Take it out!" I garble a yell.

"You'll bleed to death."

"Take it out!"

The arrow didn't penetrate completely, so of course, Ayson has to push it out my back. He might as well be driving it through my brain. The pain brings a blur of spots and blinking lights. It's all I can manage not to pass out. He snaps the arrowhead off the shaft, then pulls the blood-laden shaft back through my chest. I grab at a handful of my blue vest and press it against the wound, resisting the impulse to pray to a god who doesn't listen.

Ayson tries to support me as I continue to walk, but I push him away. "It should have been you!" *Why are they trying to kill me?* "Why didn't you protect her?"

Because my father's never been good at that sort of thing.

Tradition.

Moon	Seal
Completion of the Purple Moon	Floating C
Completion of the Purple Moon	Hemming T
Shadow of the Purple Moon	River under
Shadow of the Purple Moon	Sword thro
Completion of the Red Moon	Broken Cro
Completion of the Red Moon	Crown of L
Changing of the Silver Moon	Five Crown
Completion of the Yellow Moon	Sword with
Changing of the Blue Moon	Crowned W
Completion of the Green Moon	Crowned R
Completion of the Green Moon	Crowned Sv
Completion of the Green Moon	Crown over
Completion of the Green Moon	Two Crown
Completion of the Green Moon	Crowned B
Completion of the Green Moon	Hammer St
Completion of the Green Moon	Sun Rising
Completion of the Green Moon	Crown betw
Dark Moon	Tiger and C

Months: Erog | Utine | Cil | Flatine | Joone   Date Format: (Ge

Periods: Year = 5 Months | Month = 5 Weeks | Wee

The Adow

on, Official Seal, and Chosen First Etabli

	First Etabli
er Sphere	Erin, the First Etabli
ove Crown	Anine
	Aul
wn	Taggle, the cursed
	Ylaf
	Erbohn
	Ig-poy
n on Hilt	Adarian, hero of Ire
	Fael
	Irloore
	Cintyge
ed Swords	Lío
	Enyure
	Athoyen
Crown	Ferya
rown	Cidal
vords	Ayson, of Quel
	Ayson, of Quel

ring the Red Moon | (Specific) Erog 23, Completion of the Red Moon 51
ays | Day = 5 Hours = Spheric Hour | Hour = 300 Minutes

eeches are the most disgusting aspect of a trip to the healers, but Scholars are the most annoying. Honestly, I don't see much difference between the two. After my mother died, almost immediately after I received the news, the Scholars came with their empty pages and open ink bottles. They waited and listened, breathing like horses, writing down every utterance I made. Every lip quiver sent shivers of excitement through the lot of them. If the guards weren't bad enough, now I had a brood of Scholars attached to me. I could feel them sucking the blood from my veins, so I told them the Sphere hadn't spoken to me. It was the truth, anyway, and there was nothing more to reveal, but they wouldn't leave. "Pray to the Sphere," they begged me. "Tell us what you hear."

"Nothing."

"Pray again."

Obviously, they weren't going to leave until I gave them what they wanted. I prayed again…nothing. The Sphere couldn't be bothered. The Scholars went so far as to watch me pray, ostensibly judging my ability to communicate with their god. Was I truly their new Adow? Was I really the new Oracle? I had to give them something or they would have never allowed me a moment's peace, so I told them a story, one Troq used to tell me about a tiger.

Thus, my first big revelation from the Sphere was nothing more than a retelling of the tiger and the hunter. It was easy enough. In Troq's story, the hunter disguised himself as a red cricket in order to kill the tiger, so I told the Scholars that the Sphere would one day appear, disguised in red, and he would destroy Morlac, the god of another world. The fools recorded the perceived prophecy with eagerness, and the lies appeased them for a time. They left me alone, off to study this new revelation; but then they came back. They always come back. Always wanting more prophecies. Even here among the healers, as I lie dying—maybe not dying, exactly, but painfully wounded—ink drips from their feathered quills; empty pages fully extended and awaiting my immortal words like a naked lover anticipating the first touch; or in this case, an orgy of Scholars. So, dutifully, I struggle to sit up from the bed, reluctantly grabbing Ayson's hand to steady myself. He's standing beside the bed, of course. Always there, always guarding me, but also waiting for me to speak like everyone else in the room. *Leeches*! In my current condition, however, the only story I can think of is about the tiger and the five wolves. It doesn't matter. Any story will suffice…any drop of blood.

I give them the summarized version complete with a rhyme, "When the Green Moon is complete, in Dragon's Torment you must seek. Five Arms of the Sphere will appear, five you will find." Names, they'll definitely want names, "Madic Baltin, Pel F'rute, Sol Pedantic, Disen T'lade, and Adelic Hon you will bring near."

I pull these names from Troq's past: his two brothers, his uncle, a cousin, and a nephew. I haven't thought about them for years. Now they'll forever be known as *Arms of the Sphere* because I designated them as such; because the Sphere refuses to speak, leaving me with nothing but these lies.

That's weird. The Scholars feast upon my words more than normal, quick scratches suffocating the ruffling sound of their feathered quills. They stop and stare at their pages. Do they know it's just a story? They don't say anything. They never do. Leeches don't speak, after all.

The Scholars leave the room. "You've given them a quest," Ayson says.

It's all a lie, Ayson, not a quest. Troq would've understood. I lie down even as the healers appear with a bowl full of leeches. *Tasa Ro*! Just leave me alone! Like some pathetic yearling, I pull the mass of blankets over my head—no more leeches! Please.

"The Green Moon is complete," Ayson continues.

The healers pull at my blankets, but my grip remains tight. Something inside me suggests this is probably irrational behavior for an Adow, that I should act differently, but I don't care. "No more leeches!"

The healers persist, tugging on the blankets, pulling them away from my outstretched hands. I immediately curl my head into my knees, "Kill them, Ayson!"

My First Etabli doesn't kill the healers. He's never killed anyone. He's good at *watching* people die, though, and apparently, he's good at watching me bleed. He's as useless as a prayer to the Sphere!

"Ayson!"

The healers wrestle me into position, eventually managing to remove my soiled bandages. One of the healers, his fingers like twigs, a wart on his thumb, reaches into the bowl of leeches and pulls out a brown blob of slime. The blob extends, dangling between the healer's thumb and finger. It's seeking blood. My blood.

"Faunride!" I know he is standing guard outside my room. He is always nearby.

The healer places the leech on my shoulder. Ugh! I'd rather feel the arrow again.

I close my eyes and conjure up an image of Troq's face: white beard and bushy eyebrows. Brown eyes, a shade lighter than his skin, and the uneven wrinkles that fell away from his nose.

I open my eyes and look at Ayson. Bald. Beardless. Gutless. "What did you say?" I've regained control, suspending my admittedly petulant fit, if only temporarily.

"Last night a new moon appeared. The Scholars are calling it the Spheric Moon."

"Why wasn't I told about this?" Why doesn't anyone ever tell me anything? Another leech touches my skin. I close my eyes. Troq's beard…

"You were sleeping, my Adow."

I open my eyes. The prophecy was just a story! A lie! The Green Moon has been around for 280 years, how was I supposed to know the moon was complete?

"We'll leave as soon as you are healthy," Ayson says.

"What?" It's all a lie!

The healers place another leech on my wound, a muted presence savoring my blood.

To my horror, I've become my mother. I'm leading my warriors into Dragon's Torment, leading them to their death because of a lie. They'll hate me just like they hated her. No! My mother is a statue in the clearing ahead. I'm not my mother. It isn't my face on that statue. We look alike, but it isn't me they hate. This will be a good thing. A quest is always a good thing—it unites the land, gives the warriors something to believe in…

…until they realize the prophecy is a story…find out I can't actually *hear* the Sphere. He's supposed to speak to me, but instead I'm telling stories about tigers that the Scholars have somehow turned into a quest! And someone is trying to kill me! Tasa Ro!

I stop to face my father, behind me as usual. "Why are you following me?" *Why are you even here?*

"I don't understand, my Adow."

I shove him backward. Wow! Did that ever feel good! I shove him again with such force that he falls over, lying there in an awkward pile of legs and sword and armor. What did my mother ever see in him? *Love?* He's a useless old horse! The only leech I can never remove! I start pacing, daring him to get up.

"Why do you always follow me?" I yell. Then I start walking toward the clearing because I can feel tears coming. Not now!

I focus on the leeches. Leeches! Leeches!—their slick bodies on my exposed shoulder. My mother. My father. The Sphere. That does the trick. No more tears. And just in time: Ayson catches up to me and turns me around to face him. He's holding me, his fingers biting into my arm.

"Forgive me, my Adow."

I slap him and break free of his grip, "How many times have I come to this clearing? You always *follow* me. If it's your duty to protect me, then *lead*! Enter the clearing before me! I wouldn't have been injured if you were doing your duty. Act like you actually *want* to protect me! Tasa Ro! We're heading to Dragon's Torment!"

This can't really be happening.

Ayson grabs my right arm, so I slap him with my other hand. Then he grabs that hand, too. I fight against his grip, but he pulls me closer to him, holds me.

"Forgive me, my Adow," but I'm his daughter, not his Adow. His Adow is dead, and she'll never forgive him!

I pull away and start heading toward the clearing, searching for assassins as I walk. Troq taught me enough. I don't need Ayson to protect me. Besides, I have Faunride. My faithful Faunride. And Teyo…and other guards. And the Adarians. *The Adarians!* Oh, they love a good quest.

But this isn't a real quest. I stop walking.

What the hell am I doing? I'm the last of the Adow. There's no Daughter of the Adow to take my place. We shouldn't even be going on this quest. Has anyone ever survived Dragon's Torment? Then again, will I survive if I stay here? Someone tried to kill me! Yes, the Adow has always been surrounded by the First Etabli and the Adowian Guard, but it was all for show. We were never in any real danger, but now—dammit! This is insane!

Ayson comes to a stop behind me. He motions to the guards who follow, and to the ones in the surrounding forest. Silently, they fan out in search of assassins. I watch them move through the trees, suddenly grateful that Faunride is nearby. All of them. I'm never alone because they are always there. But then I realize they'll all die if we travel to the Torment, every last one of my guardians. I can't ask them to do that. Of course, I can't tell them the prophecy is a lie, either. Admitting that means I'm no better than she was…or worse. To her only credit, my mother never lied to them. She was a fool, but she never lied. These warriors who so faithfully serve me would never recover if they ever find out I can't hear the Sphere. Not after she led them to Quel. I'll lose my guards, my army, all of them. Even Faunride. It would break his heart. They would all curse me and the Sphere…probably turn to Morlac. Already, too many of my topis worship the god of another world. I can't let that happen. Troq would never forgive me, and neither would my future daughter. No! I need them to follow me. I need them to follow the Sphere, even if he doesn't exist, or they'll never follow my daughter. I won't do that to her. At least in this way, I am not like my mother. So, I'm left with no other choice. If they die, they will die for me. They will die because I am their Adow.

My father moves to my side, scanning the forest. He's not fooling anyone. His protection is useless. He's an impotent warrior, unable to lead and incapable of inspiring others to follow. What I need are competent warriors. I need the Adarians. They've always done their own thing, though. They won't follow just because I tell them to…but maybe the promise of an Adowian Burial will inspire them. Yes! To whichever warrior finds the Five Arms of the Sphere. It won't matter that the Arms of the Sphere don't actually exist. The Adarians, and everyone else, will join the quest for that honor alone. It's perfect!

Faunride emerges from the trees, walking as he does—a familiar gait, his right foot turned slightly inward—his dark skin all but disappearing behind golden armor; he is always the most polished among my guardians. He's escorting an old topi with a face like a mole, no, seriously, like a mole with his small forehead, scrunched nose, and exposed front teeth; his yellow-stained beard, likely grown in a poor attempt to conceal his features, only adds to the depths of his unfortunate facial infliction. In that moment, I take a disturbing amount of pleasure in knowing my prayers aren't the only ones the Sphere has ignored. Unfortunately, I can tell by his purple robes that he's a Scholar, no doubt, come to record another prophecy. Great, more lies.

"Forgive me, First Etabli," Faunride says. "I found this Scholar in the forest surrounding the clearing. He says he must speak with the Adow."

That's right, Faunride, always address the First Etabli before the Adow unless she initiates the discussion. He's an absolute traditionalist, always has been, but it's annoying he never speaks to me directly. Annoying... and somewhat comforting. Faunride serves as constant reminder of how things used to be before Quel, of a time when he was my guardian— before all these lies.

"I'm listening, Scholar."

Ayson and Faunride turn to me in surprise, serves them right, but the Scholar speaks without hesitation. Indeed, he stands rather proudly, and with an arrogance I quickly decide I don't like. His knowledge has, obviously, inflated his ego, "Long ago, a prophecy was spoken..."

I knew I wouldn't like him. Scholars tend to speak in monotone, and in a language no one understands. He rambles on about the Green Moon and Dragon's Torment. There was a journey that he took. Failure. Death. I don't understand anything else he says for what feels like an hour.

"The Sphere has grown angry. Listen to my words! Your warriors..."

He is speaking, but I hear nothing...kind of like the Sphere—except there's this white substance on the Scholar's lips. It stretches and snaps as he widens his mouth, and I feel an uncontrollable urge to wipe it off.

"Some say there is a dragon caged within, that the winds are his breath and the rumblings are his attempt to break free of his chains, but I fear there is a creature in the Torment far worse than a dragon. When you find this creature, you will die." So, I have that to look forward to. I guess he doesn't realize the whole thing is a lie. Instead, he spent time studying my words, thinking himself divinely appointed, and he's reached this wonderful conclusion. I'll die. Thanks. Knew that.

Faunride draws his sword and lops off the Scholar's head. My traditionalist, unwilling to let anyone condemn his Adow. My true guardian. Our eyes meet for a moment, his dark eyes show a well of guarded emotion. He is concerned for me. It's the same look he held after Troq died, after he found me. I wouldn't eat, couldn't sleep. He was worried. He told me Troq's death should be celebrated, not mourned. He didn't understand, still doesn't, but I'll admit his insistence upon routine and tradition has its place. Back then he got me out of bed in the morning, forced me to face each day. Now he's the only person or thing that makes sense in this suddenly decapitated land. I watch the Scholar's body fall into a lump of purple robes. Serves him right—all of them. *Do they all want me dead?* Leeches! If it weren't for the Scholars, there wouldn't be a quest!

"Remove his robes and display his body in the market," I order. "Strike his name from the Chronicles of Yenul."

Faunride sheathes his sword.

Ayson, I can't help but notice, never even reached for his.

Traditions.

a taggle's tale

I stood just inside a tavern called The Bread and Stew. My voice consistently betrayed me as I spoke——a pitch too high, for I had not yet reached maturity, but the ale-raising, marginally interested and fully inebriated audience listened graciously. Looking back, I may have swallowed one too many sips, myself. My movements felt languid, and one of the gathered taggles later told me she thought my facial expressions lacked enthusiasm. Fortunately, the Sphere forgave my drunken stupor and blessed me with a metal bucket. I took it in hand, and I drummed. Deliberately. Sporadically. I beat on that bucket whenever I wanted to enhance a dramatic pause, and I beat on it with muted intensity during key points in the tale. I implore you, speak my name. Speak of DK Vel, for I spoke in the manner of all taggles. I told stories, and my words still linger. I lived, and you heard my voice. May the Sphere forgive our mother and remember our father.

- DK Vel

"*A*dowian Decrees don't concern you," the warrior growls. "No one is going to read it for a taggle boy."

The boy wipes the spit from his face, still learning his lot in life. He runs off to find his father. The warrior turns back to his task of posting the decree, then he leaves without glancing at the gathered crowd. One of the peasants approaches the posting and stares silently.

Someone in the crowd shouts, "What's it says?"

The peasant shakes his head.

"Find a herald!"

"There's one."

The herald approaches and motions for silence. The taggle boy sneaks back to within earshot.

> *Adowian Decree 1575*
> *We seek the Five Arms of the Sphere. All who are able*
> *must journey to Dragon's Torment—to death or glory. An*
> *Adowian Burial awaits the one who finds the Five.*

An Adowian Burial! The taggle boy lingers on the thought. He is a descendant of Taggle, the First Etabli who betrayed the Adow, identified by the scars given to all taggles—their ears carved into and made round at the tip as they exit the womb. The mark of their bloodline, the curse given to them by the Adow because Taggle had an affair with Koyo, producing a male yearling. Allowed to live because of their father, their ears serve as a sign to all that the Adow does not recognize their birth or their life; neither will she allow anyone to call them topis, for she has given them a different name: taggles.

But an Adowian Burial would change everything for the boy. Upon his death, a funeral procession would travel the land, stopping at every city for a five-day celebration of his life before returning to Yenul where they would burn his body in the Fire of the Sphere. Traditionally reserved only for the Adow, and for her First Etabli, only one other, Beaug, sculptor of

Adarian, has received such an honor. No one else. Yes, an Adowian Burial would change everything!

The taggle boy leaves the crowd…

…even as Hintor, disheveled and in a foul mood from a disturbing lack of ale, returns to Yenul after visiting his father in Plenrid. He leads his horse alongside Lake Yenul, the *blood lake*, as it's called due to Erin's Fire, a flower with red petals and a white center, which floats upon and nearly covers the entire surface. An overcast sky stretches downward in sheets of soft rain that evaporate before reaching the ground, as though not allowed to touch the hollowed expanse of the lake. Hintor follows the blood lake south to where it forms a river, and continues along this path until it descends into a waterfall. The entrance to Yenul.

The irritable warrior of the Adarian 45th passes behind the massive waterfall, entering into a tunnel that leads toward an enormous cavern. The heart of Yenul. And the most obvious display of magic, for inside the cavern a geyser erupts without ceasing, forming the underbelly of Lake Yenul. This vast amount of water remains suspended above the cavern with some sort of ancient magic Hintor has never understood. Cast and maintained by the Adow's sorcerers, travelers and passerby need only follow the geyser upward to see a selection of stunning fish, vibrant waterweed, and streams of sunlight sporadically penetrating the blood red petals of Erin's Fire. The constant roar reverberates with hypnotic allure, drawing Hintor's attention while his horse navigates the noticeably humid cavern.

"It's a wonder we don't all drown," he mutters.

The path he follows leads to a marketplace surrounding the geyser. From here, travelers can choose from any of twenty-three roads. Houses lay hidden along these shadowed paths. Houses and taverns! Specifically, Three Horns Tavern. Finally, he will have ale! Hintor's friend, Maldinado, awaits him there, no doubt, delightfully drunk already. The Madar and recently appointed Rovet of the Adarian 45th, stubbornly refused to take a well-earned two-month furlough, unwilling to return home; unwilling to leave the newly appointed Adow. Thus, and though every other Adarian unit returned to their beloved city, Maldinado insisted Hintor and his fellow warriors travel back to Yenul at the end of their allotted rest. So, Hintor returned to Yenul by way of forest trails, swamp covered lands, and bloody lakes, for unlike Adarian which boasts a paved road and many taverns along the way, Yenul forces all prospective visitors to search and scramble and otherwise seek out an all but hidden entrance, literally concealing itself from the world above.

"He better be drunk enough for all of us," Hintor grumbles even as he pulls on the reins, bringing the horse to a stop beside a posted decree. He reads the Adowian Prophecy announcing the quest to Dragon's Torment. He reads it again, "Tasa Ro! What, she doesn't have enough enemies? Now she wants to take us into the Torment?" Hintor tears the ludicrous decree from its wooden pole, and then spurs his horse toward the mineral caves, "She's as obstinate as her mother!"

Behind Hintor, far enough to remain unseen, a taggle boy follows. The boy maintains his distance, and he takes care to not look any topis directly in the eye. It doesn't matter. They don't notice his thin frame. Nobody makes mention of how his neck sinks into his collarbone, exaggerating and elevating his shoulders. His nose extends from his face like the handle on a pot, making his eyes look all the more concave and beaten. His short, black hair appears sawed-off rather than cut. He wears a black breech cloth and nothing more save the symbols which make up the taggle's prayer. These symbols mark both hands across each knuckle:

Forgive our mother

Remember our father

The boy freezes in his journey while Hintor exchanges gold for two pairs of emerald earrings and a loaf of bread. The taggle studies the warrior's features: eyes folded under a drooping brow, a scar that crosses his nose and down his right cheek, black hair pulled into a tight braid. A series of tiny scars dance along his right jawbone, interrupting the growth pattern of a fresh beard. He wears a green tunic and matching cloak.

Hintor places the earrings into his saddlebags. A journey to Dragon's Torment means they will pass through Adarian. Kaletine and Belur, Nataline's daughters, would never forgive him if he returned to Adarian without a gift for each, and he would never dream of disappointing them. He bites into the sourdough bread. A poor substitute for a tankard of ale, but he hasn't eaten for two days, having exhausted his food supply when, like a damned fool, he gave it to a beggar he found in the forest.

"Probably a thief," Hintor takes another bite, still cursing his act of kindness, but a two-day fast at least spared him the guilt he would have felt if a fellow topi had starved to death. He had his father to thank for the guilt, the result of a *proper* upbringing.

Hintor enters the mineral caves of Yenul, the crowds thinning significantly as he moves through the silver-speckled tunnel. Even so, the warrior doesn't notice the taggle boy who follows him. The walls of the cavern, rich with undisturbed silver by order of the Adow, offer a subdued glow as he approaches the well-constructed Three Horns Tavern; a favorite of the Adarians due to its status as the only structure in all of Yenul erected using timber—the only structure not carved out of or into the rock; even the Adow's palace, to hear the Adarians tell it, consists of a series of caverns and tunnels. "Why would anyone choose to live in this city?" Hintor dismounts, leaping from the horse while it still trots, and quickly tosses the reins to the nearest taggle boy; unbeknown to him, the same taggle boy who has followed him through the city. He enters the tavern, its main decoration a full-sized bronze sculpture of a three horned ram, and a moment later he finds Maldinado sitting at a wooden table along the back wall.

"She wants to die!" Hintor throws the torn decree at his friend with one hand, reaching for the nearest mug with his other hand.

Maldinado nods, "I've seen it."

Hintor takes two gulps—not nearly enough to improve his mood, "It'll be worse than Quel. I won't go!"

Maldinado stands to hug his testy friend, "How was your trip?"

Hintor drains the rest of the mug and slams it onto the table, "You've already enlisted us, haven't you?"

"I had to. I'm an Adarian," Maldinado grabs two more ales from a passing server, handing one to his friend.

Hintor grabs both, "Well, I'm not."

"That circle burned into your chest says you are," Maldinado reminds him of the mark he received when he joined the ranks of the Adarian 45th, matching the one on his own chest.

"Furmec Ro!" Hintor drinks more ale. Both mugs. All of it.

Maldinado sits down, and motions for Hintor to join him, "How's your father?"

"Mardtbren sends his blessing," Hintor grabs a passing mug, but he doesn't drink it immediately, "and something tells me we're going to need it."

"It's good to have you back," Maldinado says. "I've been drinking alone for too long."

Hintor can't help but notice Maldinado's beard looks as though he has spent the last two-months pulling at every hair on his face. Little remains of the ambitious yearling he once knew, replaced by the weathered features of a beaten warrior, "It wasn't your fault her mother died, you know. It was the will of the Sphere. There was nothing you could have done, and you sure as hell won't be able to protect this new Adow while we're busy trying to survive Dragon's Torment!"

But Maldinado can only see Yenen releasing that arrow. Again, and again. His sword slices through Yenen. The rebel leader falls from the wall. The loosed arrow pierces the Adow's heart. Maldinado failed, and for this, they anointed him Rovet. Now, he serves as both Rovet and Madar, but more importantly, he serves the Adow. He will not fail her again. Never again. "What do *you* know about the will of the Sphere?" Maldinado chides his agnostic friend. "You've never prayed a day in your life."

Hintor shakes his head, "Not true. I pray for your sister and those yearlings every day." He finishes the ale and signals a taggle girl to bring them more to drink, admittedly with slightly less enthusiasm than when he first entered the tavern. He can feel the ale in his stomach sloshing around as though it were a water skin hanging from the saddle, "Those yearlings have lived a hard life."

Maldinado lowers his empty mug, waiting for Hintor to continue, but his friend stares off into the crowded tavern. The scars on his face have greatly disfigured the farmer he once knew, the yearling who fell deeply in love with his sister, Nataline. Maldinado turns to the window beside the table, its blackness reflecting his own face…his gray eyes. He hardly recognizes the warrior staring back at him, a warrior far different than his father. Rovet *and* Madar of the Adarian 45th. No other Madar has ever claimed such status. "I have to go on this quest," Maldinado admits.

"I know," Hintor responds, his mood finally subdued, his attention momentarily distracted at the sight of Little Birty picking a fight with a much larger stranger. "And I'll be there fighting right beside you, like a damned fool." He takes another sip even as Little Birty takes a swing, "Please tell me we don't have to take Little Birty with us." The stranger sends Little Birty skidding across the floor, unconscious from the looks of it.

Maldinado turns at the commotion, "You've got to admire his

determination."

"Like watching a bleeding toad attack a horned-dragon." Hintor raises his mug in toast to the stranger, grabbing his attention, "I'll drink to that!"

At this same moment, outside the tavern, the taggle boy who followed Hintor spots a group of six taggles milling around the back door. All of them serve warriors in the Adarian 45th. The boy joins them and introduces himself as DK Vel, thus beginning his unlikely journey to Dragon's Torment, or rather, his quest for an Adowian Burial.

5-RUBY
SPECIAL EDITION

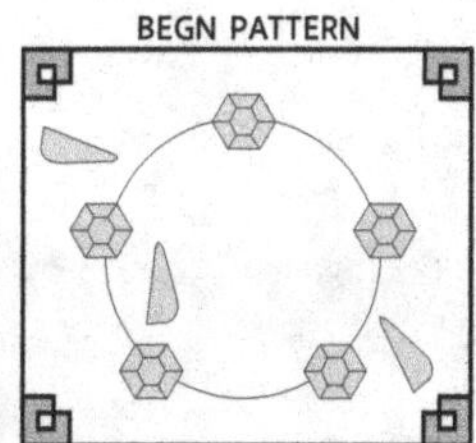

a taggle's tale

As spoken by Uncle Taggle of the Abre dallic. A thin white beard covered his sunken chest and swollen stomach, highlighting all 72-years of his awe-inspiring life. He spoke slowly and with great patience, allowing the audience to absorb both the rhythm of his voice and the meaning of his words. During his tale a fly landed upon his beard, another on his shoulder, but his voice so enraptured both flies they remained unmoving, as though caught in a trance. He offered his audience a perfect telling. In his younger days, they called him Treth, and though his sister once served the Adow, she could not have known all the details found within Uncle Taggle's story. Only the Adow knows the words spoken between herself and the First Etabli in moments of solitude. But I find this telling consistent with other stories which we do know for certain, thus I have preserved this tale. I implore you, speak his name. Speak of Treth, for he spoke in the manner of all taggles. He told stories, and his words still linger. He lived and we heard his voice. May the Sphere forgive our mother and remember our father.

- DK Vel

Ayson wipes his brow, interrupting images of Quel that flood his thoughts. The warm day has already caused him to sweat thru the tunic he wears under his armor. The Adowian Army marches toward the city of Adarian where thousands more will join the quest, and though Quel may have changed many things, he knows some things will probably never change: Adarian pride and their sense of honor. Adarians love a good quest more than they love battle, and Ayson knows firsthand they hold a great fondness for fighting, but a quest offers them much more glory. At least, for the one who completes the quest and, bolstering their triumph further, the one who completes *this* quest will lay claim to an Adowian Burial, a sacred honor previously given only to Beaug and to the beloved First Etabli, Adarian, hero of Ire.

First Etabli. Ayson absently mouths the name. A title. A great honor. Throughout history, the First Etabli have protected their Adow:

Erin, *the* First Etabli

Anine

Aul

Taggle, the cursed

Ylaf

Erbohn

Ig-poy

Adarian, hero of Ire

Fael

Irloore

Cintyge

Lio

Enyure

Athoyen

Ferya

Cidal

Ayson, of Quel

Ayson, first and only one to witness the death of his Adow. Even

Taggle, even *he* had enough sense to die in the arms of his Adow. *Ayson* lives. *Ayson* still rides at the front of the Adowian Army, having departed Yenul two days ago. *Ayson*, their infamous champion. He looks back on all those who follow him, but he finds them awash in a sea of shimmering, golden brilliance. All things have a purpose, even armor fashioned from gold. It shines with incredible force, a heavenly glow meant to exalt the Sphere. The golden armored warriors follow colorful, if listless, banners held high in the placid air. Once, Ayson recalls, these same banners flew with more purpose. Once, these warriors followed their First Etabli instead of focusing on their respective banners. Once…before Quel.

He shifts his gaze to the Adowian Guard. Faunride, Teyo, Valin, and Yla all surround their Adow. Others patrol the perimeter. Strong warriors. Capable protectors. He looks down at the shield secured behind his left leg. It boasts an image of Erin, *the* First Etabli. Then he turns back toward the glowing army. No, they no longer follow him. They have *never* followed him. He is Ayson, of Quel, not Adarian, hero of Ire. Not Cidal. Not even Taggle, the cursed. No, they no longer follow, and he no longer leads; she does. The Adow. He, too, follows her, trailing her like some starving orphan. She deserves more. His daughter has the right to choose her First Etabli, instead, she has what barely remains of her father. He wants her to know the joy of a union ceremony and the feel of a Leet Socno upon her wrist, binding Adow and First Etabli in marriage. But his presence prevents such a time-honored union. Ayson can't help but remember his own wedding day. The banner-like Leet Socno, specially designed by the Adow, served as the symbol of their love. After the ceremony, it hung above their doorway…until she died.

Faunride kicks his horse forward, rousing Ayson from his morose thoughts. The dutiful warrior quickly disappears into the tree line as part of a standard rotation of the guard. Right on time. He is a fine guardian of the Adow. Better than Ayson, certainly. His daughter could do worse than choose Faunride as First Etabli. Ayson motions to the remaining guards and, within moments, they have moved out of earshot, "You deserve better, my Adow. You deserve a wedding, and a Leet Socno, and a daughter and…I wish I could provide all those things for you."

"You can provide me with a daughter," the Adow says. "According to the Scholars, you're my *only* option."

"No," Ayson wipes at his brow. "I cannot. I will not." He is not her First Etabli. She never chose him. It wasn't supposed to be this way, of course. The Sphere never intended for him to outlive his Adow…his love.

"Then why bring it up?"

"I just...I wish things were better. You deserve more."

"I deserve what I have, Ayson. It's what the Sphere decided. There's nothing more to discuss."

First Etabli. Lover of the Adow. Only the First Etabli can touch her. Only he can give her a daughter, as declared by the Sphere. "Forgive me, my Adow," Ayson whispers, unable or unwilling to speak loud enough for her to hear. They ride in silence for the remainder of the day.

After dinner, Faunride enters the Adow's tent and gives a final report for the evening, careful to avoid looking at the Adow who, with help from a maidservant, undresses in preparation for her bath. He reports the army has completed camp preparations. Two warriors and their horses died when a cylen tree fell on them, unexpectedly. No deserters to report. The Stycral 14th arrived, and they joined what remains of the Golesh 47th where Eshion now serves as Rovet. And finally, "The sorcerers request permission to relocate further south due to the overly rocky terrain where they currently reside."

"This is turning into a nightly ritual," Ayson grumbles.

"Isn't that always the case with sorcerers, First Etabli? At least in my experience."

"Alright, let them move. Who's over there now?"

Faunride glances down at a scrap of parchment paper, "The Golesh 13th states a willingness to accommodate their request."

The Adow, now fully disrobed, slides slowly into a silver tub, "Give them my blessing."

Faunride starts to acknowledge the Adow, only to quickly turn away, "At once, my Adow."

"It wouldn't hurt my feelings if someone forgot to wake the sorcerers in the morning," Ayson adds. "At least, not until the rest of the Army has moved on."

Faunride gives an auspicious nod, "I plan to invite their leader, Galinor, to a game of 5-Ruby tonight. I'll make sure he drinks plenty of ale."

"How is the game progressing?"

"The Yowt Ruby lies naked, and four peach pits are aligned to the Rhil Ruby."

"Place a wager for me. The Unern Pattern will be rolled tonight," Ayson hands Faunride a pouch of gold coins.

"Of course, First Etabli, but I must warn you the boar tusks haven't rolled in my favor for two nights. Perhaps, you would rather place the wager yourself?"

"No, it is better if you do it. May the Sphere bless you."

"And keep you in his light," Faunride bows and exits the tent, leaving Ayson to his nightly prayers.

He kneels beneath a makeshift altar, suspended from the top of the tent, consisting of a single golden candle set within a glass aureole. His prayers become thoughts that mimic the drifting smoke of the candle: *When did you last kneel before the altar, my Adow? How does someone get crushed to death by a falling tree? Eshion will prove himself a fine Rovet.*

Behind him, Aiya, an ever-attendant maidservant, bathes the Adow, "Tomorrow, I think we put some hot oils in your hair. It will keep it healthy. You travel out in the open, too much. It's not good, so much dust from the horses and wagons."

"My skin feels so dry," the Adow says.

"Mine too."

"My arms are so dry they constantly itch. I scratched at them all day."

"I give you a cream I stole from my sister before we left. I used some this afternoon and already feel better."

"Aiya, you're such a blessing. I always miss you when you leave. Where did your sister find it?"

"It was selling in the market in Broken Tunnel. She got plenty, so she don't mind me taking it."

"How is she doing? Were the healers able to help her breathe?"

"She has good days and bad. I don't think they help much, but they give her remedies."

"Don't even talk about remedies! Ugh, leeches! I'm going to outlaw the use of those damned things. It's disgusting having them crawl all over you, sucking your blood. I can't even think about it!"

"You'll never get leeches on me. I die before they do that. And I wouldn't let them use leeches on my sister, either."

Ayson rises from beneath the altar, tired of their rambling conversation. Hair oils and creams? Leeches? He walks over to the gefor and relieves his bladder before continuing over to the entrance of the tent. He opens the flap to a chorus like greeting, "First Etabli!" The Adowian Guard rise from their game of 5-Ruby and bow in unison, awaiting orders. But he looks to the tents beyond them…at the row of torches and the night sky…the distant shadows where the horizon touches the stars. He once wondered what lay beyond the horizon. Now he knows. Emptiness.

Failure. Nothing.

Faunride moves forward, "First Etabli?"

Ayson stirs from his thoughts, "I placed a wager on the game. I thought I'd watch for a while to see if the Sphere will bless me, tonight."

Faunride bows respectfully, "The First Etabli is eternally blessed."

Ayson nods his head in response, effectively signaling they resume their game. They huddle together, close enough to cause a constant, almost harmonious, clinking of armor. Their mannerisms follow a simple pattern: a throw of the boar tusks and a drink of ale. Their laughter sounds genuine and hearty, but one of them roars more loudly than the others. Ayson and Faunride exchange a knowing grin at the sight of the black-robed Galinor, leader of the sorcerers, noticeably full of mirth. Beads of ale fall steadily from his long white beard. Not surprisingly, Faunride has performed his task admirably, ensuring Galinor will sleep well tonight and, likely, oversleep, thus delaying what will surely prove frantic attempts to arouse his fellow sorcerers in the morning. With any luck the lot of them will struggle to catch up with the rest of the army and, hopefully, they will ultimately decide to return home. Ayson found sorcerers amusing enough when they cast their spells—particularly the powerful spells like the one holding blood lake above Yenul—but he considered them generally useless in a fight and entirely too demanding for his liking.

His attention returns to the game. It proves entertaining enough, but less engaging than when he sat amongst them as a guard. *We shared more stories in those days...before I became First Etabli.* He shouldn't have joined them. His presence makes them uncomfortable. *I am no longer one of them.* Even so, he places a few more wagers, guessing at the pattern of the boar tusks. *I've missed this.*

Faunride deposits the three tusks—miniature marble carvings resembling boar tusks—into a wooden cup before throwing them into a small circle made of string. Two of the three land inside the circle. Teyo, serving as overseer of the contest, confirms the resulting Rhil Pattern. "Damn!" Ayson swore. He wagered all of them would land inside the circle to create the less common Unern Pattern, trusting in Faunride's practiced throwing technique. Nevertheless, he laughs at the chatter that arises from those who guessed the pattern correctly, glad for the respite and the ale.

Teyo passes him the wooden cup, "It's your turn, First Etabli."

Ayson fills his mug with more ale before taking the tusks and turning toward Faunride. "It's been a long time since I've thrown the tusks, Faunride. I recommend you wager against me."

"On the contrary, I've already changed to the Begn Pattern," Faunride hands Teyo a silver piece, completing the transaction. "I only need you to land one of the tusks, First Etabli."

Aiya emerges from the tent and works her way through the crowd of warriors, brushing past Ayson without a word. She is crying, or rather trying not to cry. She steps right into and through the circle, inadvertently kicking away half the game pieces. Then she disappears into her own tent.

Ayson stares, dumbfounded. He has never understood the handmaiden.

Around him, the guards scramble to retrieve every game piece, including three rubies and five peach pits. Finally reassembled, Ayson throws the tusks. As he predicted, all three of them land outside the circle.

Teyo confirms the result, "No pattern thrown."

"I fear you've misplaced your faith, Faunride. It seems the Sphere is not with me, tonight," Ayson turns to leave, "Thanks for the tales and the ale. Goodnight."

The Adowian Guard rise and bow and offer him a departing, "First Etabli."

Ayson re-enters the tent. *First Etabli*. Again, he lingers on the title as he stands in shadow, listening to the warriors. Listening for any comments about him. Curses. Innuendos. Disappointment. Ayson wipes his forehead and waits. Nothing. Not a single mention of him.

Within the tent, the Adow lies on her side, resting on a bed of animal skins. She faces away from him like she always does, but tonight she's wearing a red silk gown that exposes the skin along the length of her back. That's different. Her black hair, normally pinned into a bun for sleeping, freely cascades over several pillows. A taggle girl stands off to the side, fanning her with large green leaves, causing the remaining candlelight to flicker over her body. She resembles her mother. She is beautiful. But it's not enough for Ayson to forget the daughter who lies behind the alluring image. *I will never do that to you*. He removes his sword before climbing into the circular bed to lay beside her, and they sleep facing opposite directions.

The royal pattern.

5-RUBY
SPECIAL EDITION

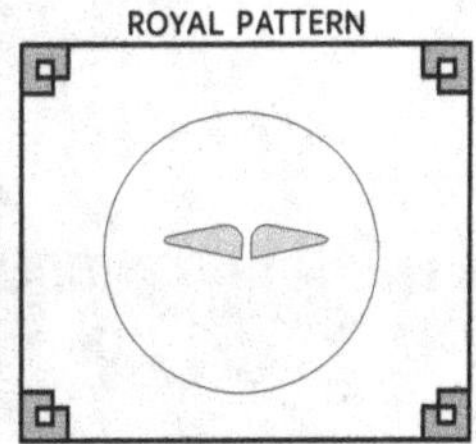

Moon	Seal
Completion of the Purple Moon	Floating C
Completion of the Purple Moon	Hemming T
Shadow of the Purple Moon	River under
Shadow of the Purple Moon	Sword throu
Completion of the Red Moon	Broken Cro
Completion of the Red Moon	Crown of L
Changing of the Silver Moon	Five Crown
Completion of the Yellow Moon	Sword with
Changing of the Blue Moon	Crowned W
Completion of the Green Moon	Crowned Ro
Completion of the Green Moon	Crowned Sw
Completion of the Green Moon	Crown over
Completion of the Green Moon	Two Crown
Completion of the Green Moon	Crowned B
Completion of the Green Moon	Hammer St
Completion of the Green Moon	Sun Rising
Completion of the Green Moon	Crown betw
Dark Moon	Tiger and C

Months: Erog | Utine | Cil | Flatine | Joone   Date Format: (Gen

Periods: Year = 5 Months | Month = 5 Weeks | Wee

The Adow

...on, Official Seal, and Chosen First Etabli

	First Etabli
...er Sphere	Erin, the First Etabli
...ove Crown	Anine
...n	Aul
...wn	Taggle, the cursed
	Ylaf
	Erbohn
	Ig-poy
...n on Hilt	Adarian, hero of Ire
	Fael
	Irloore
	Cintyge
...ed Swords	Lío
	Enyure
	Athoyen
...Crown	Ferya
...rown	Cidal
...words	Ayson, of Quel
	Ayson, of Quel

...ring the Red Moon | (Specific) Erog 23, Completion of the Red Moon 51
...ays | Day = 5 Hours = Spheric Hour | Hour = 300 Minutes

yson leaves the tent, a weed thrown from the garden. I laugh, causing Aiya to pause in her scrubbing of my back. "Have you grown ticklish, my Adow?" I shake my head, "No, Aiya." I look at my handmaiden with a new perspective; at her black hair held tight in a bun above her head, her green eyes, and that perfect skin—mine always feels so dry. Those adorable ears, "I'm just thinking how much of a blessing you are to me." More than that, though. I realize she looks exactly like my mother. Which means she looks exactly like me! And Ayson can't stand her.

Aiya starts scrubbing my back, again. "I'm only your servant, my Adow."

I pretend to be offended, "You're more than that! You've been with me since I became the Adow." But what does a handmaiden truly know? She doesn't know me like Troq did. I've never told her anything important—like the fact I can't hear the Sphere…that I question if he even exists. Still, I place my hand on hers, "You're my closest friend."

"I'm glad to be your friend," Aiya drops the brush in favor of a bucket which she dumps unceremoniously over my head. I watch the water drip from my hair, my eyebrows. Actually, she's my only friend. A handmaiden. Not much to brag about, really. She *has* to be friendly.

"What do you think about this quest?" It strikes me that Aiya has never given me her opinion before. In many ways, I suppose, she's not much better than a taggle, but she allows me to work out my thoughts and I have to admit I've missed her. She's been tending to her sister for far too long.

"What do *you* think about it?" Aiya pulls her white sleeves down and retrieves a towel offered by a nearby taggle girl.

Lies. They're lies, Aiya. That's what I want to tell her. Instead, I stand to exit the tub, my thoughts drifting to the pink scar below my shoulder. I press my finger against it. There's a void underneath, a piece of me the leeches sucked out. Is this what the Sphere wants? Am I destined to be the last Adow?

I finally reply, "I think a lot of warriors will die."

Aiya wraps me in the towel and helps me out of the tub. Then she lifts my chin, "It don't matter, I think. Those warriors are willing to die for you. More than what your mother could say, and anything that brings this land together is something worth doing."

"Even if it means going to Dragon's Torment?"

"Ask me again when we get there," Aiya smiles and pulls a sleeping gown over my head. It's red. I suppose I'm indifferent to the color, but Aiya always chooses red if it's available.

"Why do you like red so much?"

Aiya spins me around and guides me to a chair. She starts combing through my hair. It's tangled, but she has a gentle stroke, "I don't like red, but you look so beautiful in it. I could never wear red the way you wear it."

"Oh, but you do wear my gowns, Aiya. They always smell like you."

She stops brushing.

I turn to measure the impact of my words. *That's right, Aiya. I know your secret. Could you have been so naive?* She struggles to look me in the eye, a moment of fear.

"It doesn't bother me. In fact, it makes things easier. When we get to Adarian I want you to go into the marketplace. Try on everything, and purchase anything that fits."

She struggles to smile. I turn back around, and she resumes her brushing.

"Thank you, Aiya. You can go now."

She bows like a dutiful servant. A moment later she is gone, and I'm all alone.

I know *her* secret, but does anyone know mine?

I stand and walk to a gold-framed mirror leaning against a large wooden chest. The face of every Adow is reflected in my own. We are the Oracle of the Sphere, servant to a God who doesn't speak. Seventeen Adow came before me. At times I can see all of them, each face a slight alteration, layers of reflections composing my own. We are nameless, identified only in relation to our First Etabli. *She who reigned when Enyure served as First Etabli.* Or by our chosen Adowian Seal, variations of crown and symbol: *Crowned Rooster* or *Crown over Sphere*. Imperceivable differences! We have no identity apart from each other. I have their face. I speak with their voice. I wear the same clothes they wore…so why don't I hear their god?

5-RUBY
SPECIAL EDITION

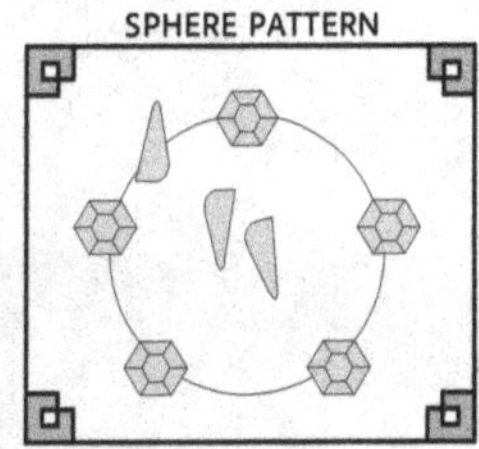

SPHERE PATTERN

a taggle's tale

As spoken by a taggle woman on the Mali coastline. It was windy, causing the Lake of Seven Cities to swell with great waves, but the woman's voice was hearty enough to rise above the distraction. Her pregnant condition prevented her from standing, causing some in the audience to miss several key expressions. All the same, her wide brown eyes sparkled and burned—indeed they conveyed vibrant emotions; and the violence of the sea offered a truly inspired backdrop for her tale. Her name was Jin. Her father served the Adarian 45th.

I implore you, speak her name. Speak of Jin, for she spoke in the manner of all taggles. Her father served the Adarian 45th. She told stories, and her words still linger. She lived and we heard her voice. May the Sphere forgive our mother and remember our father.

- DK Vel

(A)s the sun sets, and the sky blazes pink with streaks of red, Hintor sits upon a north-facing hill. He watches the bloodgrass move in waves out beyond the camp of the Adarian 45th. He sits with tunic untucked, sporadic patches of sweat visible across both his back and chest. Reluctantly, he drinks warm tea from a leather cup, wishing it tasted more like ale with every sip.

"I used to run through these fields as a yearling," Maldinado joins Hintor and hands him a bowl of warm, gray goop. He sits down beside his friend, skimming a spoon over the stew, "They say each blade of grass represents a drop of blood for all the Adarian warriors who have ever died in battle."

Hintor snorts, "Is that how you want to be remembered? As a blade of grass some yearling tramples?"

"I would die a thousand deaths if it meant the Adow was safe."

"You know she won't survive Dragon's Torment. And neither will we."

Maldinado shakes his head, "We survived Quel, didn't we?"

Hintor tastes the stew. Salty. Lots of beans and no meat. "I survived. You've never been the same."

"I guess I see things differently now." Maldinado raises his bowl, "Take this food. My mother used to go days without eating. She said her hunger fueled her prayers offered to the Sphere. I never understood what she meant before Quel. Now I understand. I've been praying ever since Quel. I've been faithful to the Sphere. Five prayers a day. Every cleansing. Every fast. So, the next time I have the chance to save the Adow, I know the Sphere will bless me."

"Oh, wise one," Hintor grins, "where would I be without you?"

"You'd be a blade of grass in that field. No doubt covered in horseshit!"

"That field is reserved for true Adarians," Hintor points out. "I still have Plenrid blood in me, remember?"

"Yes, I forgot all about that because you haven't reminded me for at least a week."

"It's all that praying you do. I can't get a word in."

"If you were a little more faithful, I wouldn't have to pray so much."

"That's what I like about you. You've always been able to overcome my faults. Besides, it doesn't matter how faithful I am. The way I figure it, with you and Nataline praying for me, the Sphere has no choice but to bless me."

Maldinado raises his bowl once more, "He already has blessed you. We have food to eat, don't we?"

"Is that what we're calling this? You know, the other Madars are enjoying their own personal feasts right now. We could be eating a roast with gravy, or warm biscuits. I like warm biscuits."

"Are you asking me to act like other Madars?"

"I'm merely pointing out the fact we could be drinking ale instead of this cursed tea."

"We?" Maldinado counters, "Need I remind you Madars don't share their meals with farmhands?"

Hintor shrugs and takes a bite, chewing uncertainly, "Have you heard from Nataline?"

Maldinado nods, "I received a note this morning. She's made tunics and gloves for both of us, and she'll meet us at the greeting rituals."

"Is she bringing the yearlings?" Hintor asks.

"She didn't say, but we'll be in Adarian for a month, so I'm sure we'll see them."

Hintor scrapes his bowl and forces down the last bite, "I hope she brings bread."

"Have you ever known her to not bring bread?"

"I should have married her when I had the chance."

"You never had the chance."

"Where did she learn to cook? Not from Breline. I can't remember your mother ever cooking a meal."

"I'm not sure. She was just born with the ability, I guess. She made her first pie when we were yearlings. I've never tasted a better one." Maldinado cocks an eyebrow, "Though I've never tasted a pie made by the Adow."

"The Adow doesn't cook. She has servants to handle that."

"True, but if she *did* cook, I bet it would taste better than my sister's finest bread."

"I don't think that's possible," Hintor stands. "I think I'll join the 5-Ruby game, tonight. You coming?"

"Not tonight. I need to pray."

"You're turning into your mother."

"Better her than my father," Maldinado stands and hands his empty bowl to a taggle boy standing nearby.

"Don't ever become your father," Hintor, too, gives his bowl to the boy. Then he turns to leave, "Do you want me to place a wager for you?"

"Place it on the Rhil to be the first naked ruby."

"Sure about that? Brink's aligned to the Rhil Ruby. And you know how lucky he isn't."

"I'm sure."

"Alright, it's your gold," Hintor departs with a shrug of his shoulders.

Maldinado retrieves his rucksack from the ground beside him before heading down the hill, passing Little Birty who walks hand-in-hand with a scarlet, one of a hundred or so who have traveled with them from Yenul. No doubt, more will join the caravan once they arrive at Adarian, all of them fully aware that these lonesome warriors receive weekly payments for services rendered. More importantly, scarlets know these same warriors only have two options for spending their acquired gold: gambling and female companionship.

Little Birty stops in his tracks upon seeing Maldinado, his efforts to sneak back to his tent suddenly thwarted. He quickly releases the hand of the scarlet, a disheveled blonde wearing a leather vest over her otherwise exposed torso, "My Rovet, I found this scarlet wandering the perimeter. I was escorting her back to the camp."

Little Birty's father served as Rovet of the Adarian 45th prior to Decrome. He commanded respect from his warriors and his city, so much, in fact, that Gan, Overseer of Adarian, personally attended Little Birty's First Cleansing as a favor to the Rovet. Adarians spent months gossiping about the reason for such an honored guest to the point most now believed the Rovet had betrothed his son to the Overseer. True or not, Little Birty never fully grew into a warrior's body, and Maldinado can't help but wonder if he has enough between his legs to satisfy his chosen lover.

He stifles a grin and wonders what Hintor would do in this situation? Well, something shameless if altogether harmless, and Maldinado felt an obligation to act in accordance, "On your way to relieve Gan-Pi from guard duty, then," Maldinado adopts an official tone. Little Birty stands there with his scraggly brown beard poorly disguising his youthful features, clearly relieved to discover his hastily conceived ruse worked.

Maldinado nods in approval, "In that case, I shall take it upon myself to escort this scarlet and leave you to your task."

"He did nothin' of the sort!" The scarlet turns on Little Birty, "This yearling wanted to keep things hush and quiet-like. Didn't want no one seein' me."

Maldinado turns his attention to the jaded lover, offering her an empathetic nod, "Truth is our Little Birty here has never left the nest. I trust you'll charge him extra for the education and, um, for your discretion?"

"I don't know what she's talking about," Little Birty stammers.

The scarlet pulls a bag of gold from her belt and smiles greedily at Maldinado, "I charged him three times the normal rate. Didn't like him bein' embarrassed about the whole thin', ain't right to be sneakin' around."

"Clearly, not everyone has experience in such matters," Maldinado lowers his head in apology. "I trust this doesn't sour the reputation of the Adarian 45th on the whole?"

She slides the coin pouch under her belt once more, "Of course not. Everyone knows Adarians be the richest warriors and they treats us..." She glances at Little Birty, "They mostly treats us proper like."

"Good!" Maldinado turns to Little Birty, "It appears Gan-Pi will need to stand guard a bit longer. You'll find a barrel of Stycral wine inside my tent. You are welcome to help yourself before you...eventually make your way to your own tent."

"Thank you, my Rovet!" Little Birty sighs with relief, and then takes the scarlet's hand into his own, but she's having nothing to do with it. She starts walking toward the camp, eager to be done with the whole affair. Little Birty doesn't move.

"Little Birty," Maldinado intimates. "Gan-Pi won't wait long." He watches with a chuckle as Little Birty stumbles up the hill with undisguised urgency.

Firelight from the camp illuminates the sky as darkness settles overhead. Maldinado continues his sobering descent. Soon, bloodgrass brushes against his knees, shimmering a deep red, almost black, in the moments before nightfall, offering him one final look at his Adarian brothers; at the warriors fallen in battle. He runs both palms over the sharply pointed vertical leaves, their serrated edges slicing skin; his blood mixing with past blood. He kneels, allowing the smoother lower edges of the bloodgrass to caress his face, breathing in their dusty leaf scent. He looks to the night sky, raises his arms, and begins to pray.

A rustling in the surrounding field draws his attention. Someone approaches. Little Birty, again? "Who's there?" Maldinado demands. Silence. Little Birty would have answered. An animal would run. But an enemy will freeze. "Who are you?" Maldinado reaches for his sword, "Show yourself!"

More rustling. Then a full rush. Maldinado rolls away and waits. Silence. The bloodgrass feels cool against his cheeks. He can sense the other's presence, but he can't see them. Movement! The outline of a figure appears less than three yards away. Maldinado charges. The figure straightens to meet his challenge, sword at the ready. He strikes desperately. Maldinado attacks with two strategic thrusts and one instinctive parry. The battle ends quickly. Blood splatters over bloodgrass as the stranger falls dead with a final, awkward wheeze.

Maldinado squats and waits, listening for other attackers in the field. *Are you alone? Just another misguided zealot or part of a coordinated assault?* But only the bloodgrass sways in the night. Another moment passes. Finally, Maldinado reaches for the body, lifting it into position over his shoulder. *Tasa Ro! You're a heavy bastard.* Slowly, silently, Maldinado works his way back toward the campfires of the Adarian 45th, fully expecting another attack on his way back up the hill, but no one else emerges until Gan-Pi spots him entering the camp.

He heaves the body off his shoulder, and though he doesn't recognize the stranger's face, the blood-stained red cloak immediately identifies him as a Worshiper of Morlac. "Assassins," Maldinado motions, but Gan-Pi has already started moving, so he instead turns toward the camp, stirring his warriors to action, "Assassins! Spread out and search the perimeter. If you find any more, I want them dead."

<u>A Record of—*she who served as*—The Adow: [</u>

Moon	Seal
Completion of the Purple Moon	Floating (
Completion of the Purple Moon	Hemming
Shadow of the Purple Moon	River unde
Shadow of the Purple Moon	Sword thr
Completion of the Red Moon	Broken C
Completion of the Red Moon	Crown of
Changing of the Silver Moon	Five Crow
Completion of the Yellow Moon	Sword wit
Changing of the Blue Moon	Crowned \
Completion of the Green Moon	Crowned I
Completion of the Green Moon	Crowned S
Completion of the Green Moon	Crown ove
Completion of the Green Moon	Two Crow
Completion of the Green Moon	Crowned I
Completion of the Green Moon	Hammer S
Completion of the Green Moon	Sun Rising
Completion of the Green Moon	Crown bet
Dark Moon	Tiger and

Months: Erog | Utine | Cil | Flatine | Joone

Date Format: (G

Periods: Year = 5 Months | Month = 5 Weeks | We

The Adow

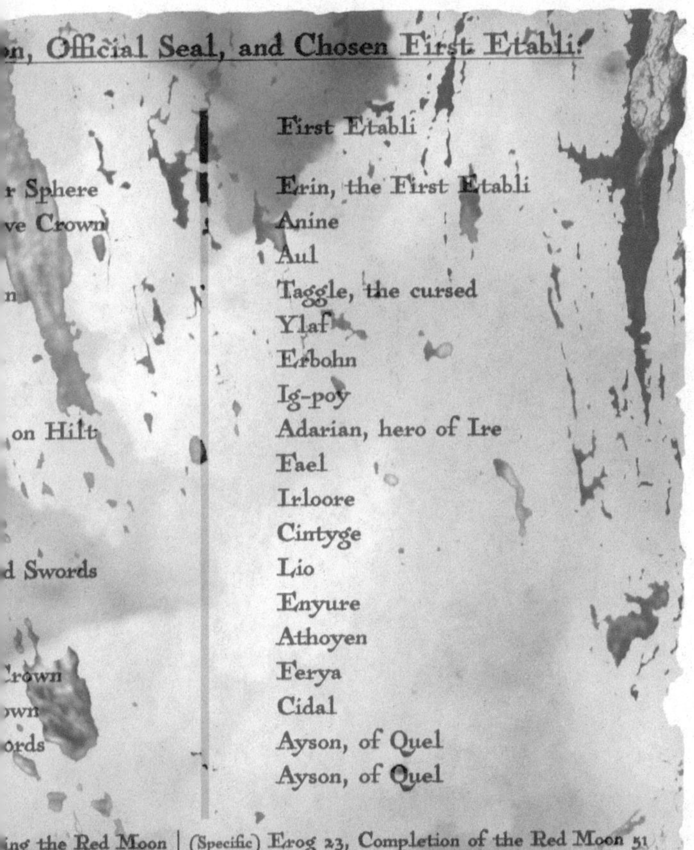

on, Official Seal, and Chosen First Etabli:

	First Etabli
r Sphere	Erin, the First Etabli
ve Crown	Anine
	Aul
n	Taggle, the cursed
	Ylaf
	Erbohn
	Ig-poy
on Hilt	Adarian, hero of Ire
	Fael
	Irloore
	Cintyge
d Swords	Lio
	Enyure
	Athoyen
rown	Ferya
own	Cidal
ords	Ayson, of Quel
	Ayson, of Quel

ng the Red Moon | (Specific) Erog 23, Completion of the Red Moon 51

rs | Day = 5 Hours = Spheric Hour | Hour = 300 Minutes

he warriors of the Adarian 45th have an overbearing air of confidence. Not surprising. I've heard all about their exploits. How they squelched the riots in Kiel. Broke through the gates of Quel. Captured Gubyer, the traitor, by tracking him down in the Nelic Mountains. Then there's Adarian, hero of Ire, who was a Rovet of the Adarian 45th before he served as First Etabli. But the stories only describe their adventures. They fail to accurately depict these warriors.

They're giants, every one of them, and they walk with an effortless, though calculated, gait. Their hands rest comfortably upon the hilts of their sheathed swords. Those who walk pass me bow without ever lowering their gaze, less a show of respect as it is a proclamation of their status within the Adowian Army. Definitely overbearing. But I must admit they do provide a sense of security. Even Faunride, walking in front of me, appears clumsy in comparison.

"I sent word to the Madar," Faunride reports, his dark eyes flickering from side to side watchfully, admiringly, as he walks. "He has made preparations for our arrival."

"Who is the Madar?" Ayson asks, walking behind me, as usual.

"Maldinado. He's young, but recently decorated and well respected by his warriors, many of whom owe him their lives."

"A *Madar?*"

Ayson voices my own curiosity. Madar is one of the few positions in the Adowian Army that honors blood over skill. The worst Madars, those stupid enough to give orders, are murdered by their own warriors. They're political figureheads ignored by everyone.

"From what I understand, Maldinado serves as both Madar and Rovet," Faunride adds.

Rovet? Impressive. I glance back at Ayson, "Why haven't you recruited him to the Adowian Guard?" But Ayson shifts suddenly to avoid stepping in a pile of shit, creating a timely distraction and delaying his response. I press the issue. "When was the last time a warrior from the Adarian 45th served in the Adowian Guard?"

"Not since Lio was First Etabli, my Adow," Faunride responds.

"Tasa Ro!"

Faunride cringes at my cursing, his traditions interfering with the reality of his Adow. He'll get over it. At this moment, I don't feel like coddling his expectations.

"No wonder we're in this mess." *This is your mess, mother. Are you listening?*

"What mess?" Ayson asks. I can't tell if he's serious or just clueless.

"Look at them, Ayson," I acknowledge the self-indulgent bow of three warriors, one of whom carries the banner of the Adarian 45th. Not carrying it as much as walking with hallowed purpose. "I wouldn't have to worry about assassins if these warriors served in the Guard!"

I can see the hurt on Faunride's face. I've said too much, "I'm sorry, Faunride." That's all I can manage. It will have to suffice. I know he needs words of encouragement, but I don't have any to give; nor do I have the time to spare now that we have arrived at our destination.

As with most encampments, we find the Madar's scarlet-colored, rectangular tent located in the center. Their division banner flaps tauntingly atop each tent post—six on either side with another three banners in the middle, these ones much larger in size than the rest. Fifteen total banners. No, these warriors aren't confident. They're arrogant.

Faunride announces my presence to the guards. I enter the bastion of Adarian pride, and quickly notice the rough and heavy canvas shows fraying along the edges. Probably the same tent they've always used. Arrogant, and also unrefined.

"My Adow!" I find their chorus-like greeting nothing short of striking—a greeting so perfectly timed by the sixty-two warriors who stand at attention on either side of a gold runner as to create a crisp echo; warriors adorned in their ornamental armor, as designed by the Adarian artist, Beaug, with silver plates attached to chain mail and black leather drawn tight around the body. Two emerald discs, one on the shoulder and one at the hip, serve to attach long strips of green silk that appear in constant motion, and their silver helmets boast an emerald carving of Adarian, hero of Ire. I've seen this armor before in Adarian parades, but I've never stood this close. Stunning. Still, the warriors bow without lowering their gaze, showing an annoying lack of respect! More than that, I can see them judging my escort, measuring them. No, none of them rose from your ranks. No, they aren't Adarian. Don't blame me!

Faunride continues with the formalities of my entrance, but I find myself distracted by the lack of decor. Though the outside of the tent resembles that of any other Madar, I have never known a Madar to live so modestly. More alarming, I can see several bedrolls at the edges of the tent! Does this Madar allow his warriors to share his tent? A large table of food, mostly eaten, would suggest as much, as do the barrels of wine stored between each bedroll, one of which serves as the tether pole for a black nelly goat who frantically nibbles at her rope. I don't blame her given the stories I hear about the Adarians having turned a yearling's game of *Blind Goat* into a much bloodier affair whenever boredom turns to drunken revelry.

Beyond the goat, at the end of the exorbitant gold runner, sits their heralded Madar, seated upon a surprisingly plain, wooden throne. *Dear Madar, don't you know a silver throne remains customary*. Hell, I've never even seen a wooden throne before.

Maldinado rises, "My Adow, I humbly vacate my throne. May it prove worthy of your presence."

If I want to sit on a piece of wood, I will climb a tree! But I hold my tongue, forcing a gracious smile. The Madar appears taller than Ayson. He has long, black hair and a growing beard; and a rigid facial structure. Gray, ice-like eyes. A thickened neck hints at the physique he hides behind armor. Wait! He's wearing armor? I've never known any Madar to wear armor. He approaches and kneels before me, somehow forcing my First Etabli, consciously or unconsciously, to take a step back. Interesting. He certainly carries a commanding presence about him, but he is not the only one with such demeanor, "Why aren't you wearing the customary dress of a Madar?" Not that I mind him wearing Beaug's armor. In truth, it fits him nicely, but well, we all have our duties. Something he's obviously forgotten.

"I find armor to be more useful in battle, my Adow," his voice resonates through the tent. Damn! No wonder he inspires these warriors. "If it offends you…"

"What's your name?" Why did I ask that? I already know his name. Stay focused!

"Maldinado."

"Does it have a meaning?"

"It means *wrath of the Sphere*."

Of course, it does. He serves with the Adarian 45th, after all. His mother wouldn't dream of naming her son something that meant *gutted toad* or *field of mushrooms*.

Ayson takes a step forward, "We have come to speak with the warrior who killed the would-be assassin."

Exactly! Yes, why am I even speaking to this pompous Madar?

Maldinado nods, "I am the warrior you seek."

Dam the river! Anyone but him. Anyone... But I draw my sword like an Adow should, and I touch the blade to his head, "May the Sphere be with you."

"And keep you in his light," he responds.

And keep you in his light. His voice lingers, brushing against my ear... one of them...both of them. Damn! I have the sudden urge to devour him as Faunride removes Maldinado's helmet because he knows I've never been a fan of kissing cold metal. Never more so than right now. I sheath my sword and take the Madar's head into my hands, leaning down to kiss him on the forehead. His thick hair feels soft like fine sand spilling out of my hands.

Sometimes, I hate being the Adow. Sometimes, I don't.

"May the Sphere be with you," I refrain from pulling his hair to my nose, a poor display in public let alone during such a ceremony. Instead, I taste the warmth of his forehead still on my lips, and then I force myself to back away. Damn these self-assured warriors!

"And keep you in his light," he stands...and now he towers above me.

That's it, time to leave.

"The Adarian 45th requests the honor of being the first to enter Dragon's Torment," Maldinado implores.

I've known a hundred Madars, but never one so eager to enter battle...to die for their Adow...to die for a lie. *Oh, hey, Maldinado, did I mention this whole thing is only a story about a tiger?*

"We don't know what we face in the Torment," Ayson responds.

"I've heard rumors we'll find Morlac. They say he's waiting for us."

I nod in acknowledgment, "I've heard similar rumors." It's about the only thing I hear, these days. *Oh, another thing you should know about me, Maldinado: I can't hear the Sphere.*

"Then it's vital to send your finest warriors with the first assault." The Adarian warriors salute with pride as their Madar continues, "We've already defeated one of Morlac's worshipers. We have earned this position of honor."

And you're just arrogant enough to make the request. It's decided, I don't like Maldinado. "Such an honor doesn't come at the request of a Madar," I say in my most elevated tone, one I learned from my mother. "It's *given* by the Adow. You would do well to remember your title, Madar! And even better to remember mine."

Maldinado bows deeply, again without lowering his gray eyes, "Forgive me, my Adow."

"The honor is yours."

Why did I say that? Tasa Ro! I should be cutting off his head, not granting this request. Dammit. Stay focused! Focused on his gray eyes...

I leave before he can make another request. The air seems much cooler once outside.

The figure of Dsal Tiger varies greatly depending upon the taggle and their respective dallic, ranging from the white and black figure of Kiel to the fully black, more panther-like, version found in Ire. This specific tale originated in Caduum where they describe Dsal Tiger as having two red eyes, white fur, and a single black stripe marring his left side—a scar that spans shoulder to hindquarters. I should also note this more traditional telling does not include the rabbit, a popular if recent addition.

The tales of Dsal Tiger, regardless of his physical depiction, serve as warning. Listen to these warnings and let Dsal Tiger guide you to the Sphere.

- DK Vel

Dsal Tiger

Dsal Tiger walks through a valley in Dragon's Torment where he has tracked the five wolves. Many have sought the wolves and never returned.

The bear is dead.

The lion is lost.

The owl has fled.

Dsal Tiger remains. He looks around. Sniffs the air. Continues carelessly; breaking sticks as he walks, sending echoes throughout the valley.

Overhead, a falcon draws near, drawn by the loud noise, "Flee this valley," it shrieks, "The Kul approaches."

"Have you seen the wolves?" Dsal Tiger calls, but the falcon flies away without another word.

Dsal Tiger doesn't flee. He's thirsty. The rain taunts him from a distance. He seeks a river, a lake, or even dewdrops suspended from leaves…but there is nothing to quench his thirst. Finally, at the top of a mountain, above the timberline, he finds a lake. He runs to its edge and lowers his head. The water feels cold as it travels through his body.

A fish appears, causing a smaller ripple in the already rippling waves created by Dsal Tiger's insatiable lapping, "Flee these waters. The Kul approaches."

"Have you seen the wolves?" Dsal Tiger asks, water dripping from the white fur around his mouth, but the fish has disappeared.

Dsal Tiger doesn't run. He's tired. He moves deeper into the Torment in search of a comfortable spot to rest, eventually coming upon a cave. He curls up and falls asleep beside a large rock.

Bats and more bats cover every inch of the cave. "Flee this cave," they squeak, "The Kul approaches."

Dsal Tiger awakens long enough to ask, "Have you seen the wolves?" But he resumes his slumber before the bats can respond.

A bear roars.

A lion roars.

But neither bear nor lion appears. Their roars echo from within the Kul, a creature of wind and shadow—a creature now standing at the mouth of the cave. The Kul has come!

Dsal Tiger no longer sleeps.

The roar of the bear fades. And that of the lion. Another sound emerges, barely perceptible, seemingly all that remains of the owl, "Who?"

Dsal Tiger feels his fur rise along the length of his spine. He growls at the Kul, raising his paw in warning, but the Kul is undeterred. Dsal Tiger roars before lunging at the creature, but he finds only wind and shadow. The Kul consumes Dsal Tiger. Mostly. A lingering echo remains, joining that of the bear and the lion and the owl.

Flee the Torment. The Kul approaches!

ADARIAN

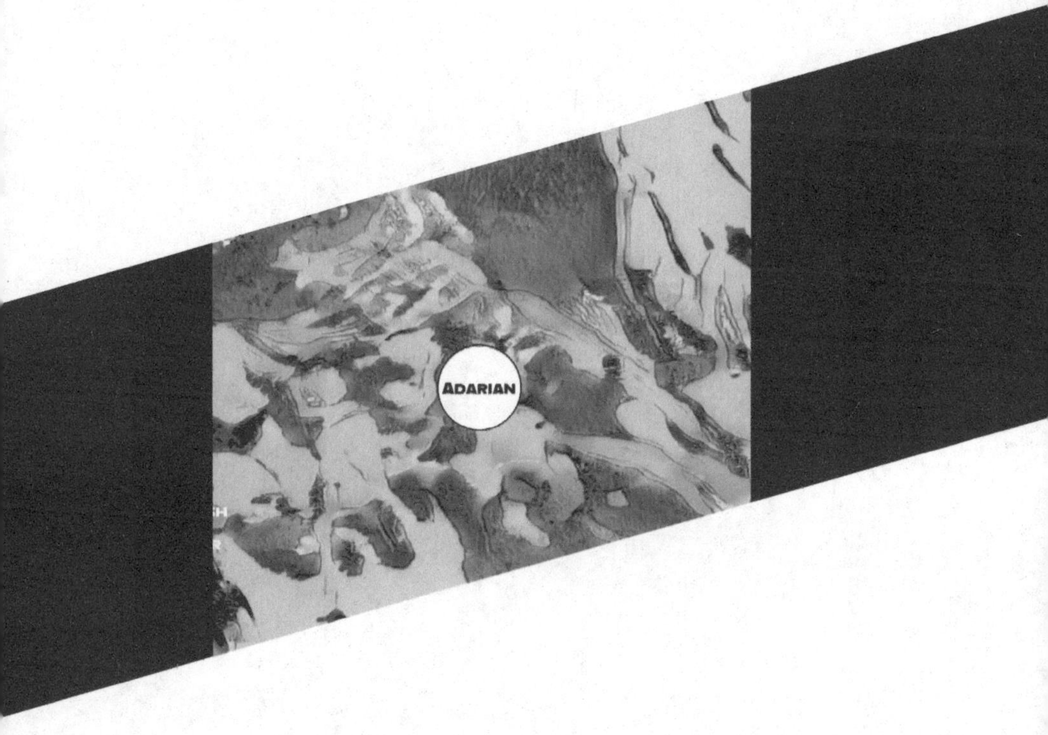

ou ask why I should endure such hardships. As a yearling,
my mother told me tales of giants tall as the tallest cylen tree, and of
large, horrifying winged creatures that would fill the sky on a cloudless
day. Fascinated by the tales she crafted, and soon enough exploring the
endless wonders of my own imagination, I determined to sculpt a city
filled with these behemoths. I wanted yearlings to not only hear about
them from their mothers, but to see them with their own eyes. Yes, these
sculptures bear faces of the ancients, these larger-than-life champions
of the Adow, but more importantly they stand above us. They give us
something to admire or fear. We are judged by these depicted figures
of our past, and haunted by the creatures that cling to the city walls or
those encircling a tower; and this grounds us, I think. We feel small and,
in those moments, we feel closest to the Sphere. That is my gift to the
Adarians. A moment of simple humility amid greatness. May they focus
on my craft, therefore, and never hear of my misfortune.

from *Collected Letters and Journal Entries of Beaug*

Moon	Seal
Completion of the Purple Moon	Floating C
Completion of the Purple Moon	Hemming T
Shadow of the Purple Moon	River under
Shadow of the Purple Moon	Sword throu
Completion of the Red Moon	Broken Cro
Completion of the Red Moon	Crown of L
Changing of the Silver Moon	Five Crown
Completion of the Yellow Moon	Sword with
Changing of the Blue Moon	Crowned W
Completion of the Green Moon	Crowned Ro
Completion of the Green Moon	Crowned Sw
Completion of the Green Moon	Crown over
Completion of the Green Moon	Two Crown
Completion of the Green Moon	Crowned Be
Completion of the Green Moon	Hammer St
Completion of the Green Moon	Sun Rising
Completion of the Green Moon	Crown betw
Dark Moon	Tiger and C

Months: Erog | Utine | Cil | Flatine | Joone   Date Format: (Gen

Periods: Year = 5 Months | Month = 4 Weeks | Wee

The Adow

he Adarian Greeting Rituals, my first as Adow, serve as a test—a rite of passage. I go over each stage of the ritual in my mind exactly as Troq taught them to me. The phrasing and delivery is critically important because the Adarians will perceive any hesitation as a sign of weakness.

The Adarians worship the Sphere, the Adow, and their traditions, Troq used to say, but *the Adow is the only one they criticize.*

I don't blame them. The Adow have given them plenty of reason for complaint. This road we travel offers the most obvious example, a lingering eyesore commissioned by my great-grandmother. We reached the Adarian Road nine days ago. One day it may extend all the way to Yenul, but the process of paving the road with marble has long since come to a halt. It seems my great-grandmother forgot to account for the preposterous amount of marble it would take to actually complete the road. She exhausted all the marble quarries surrounding Adarian before the third winter, and the search for a new supply source continues even to this day. Why *wouldn't* the Adarians criticize their Adow?

It's a fair exchange, I suppose. Their loyalty gives them the right to pass judgment. I'd rather they didn't whisper their accusations, of course, but we all have our secrets. I have mine. *Come, join me on an endless quest to find the Five Arms of the Sphere.* Endless because the Arms don't exist. In that sense, I'm building my own marble road. Great, I'm no better than my great-grandmother.

Faunride stirs me from my thoughts, his dark face highlighting the whiteness of his eyes, "A rider approaches, First Etabli."

"The Greeting Rituals," Ayson nods.

The rite of passage begins. Already, my hands are sweating. "I'll need Aiya."

"My Adow," Faunride bows and heads toward the supply caravan in search of my handmaiden. His galloping horse clamors upon the marble road.

"Who are you sending to Adarian as the Gift of Protection?" Ayson asks.

We've already had this discussion, but apparently, he wants to have it again, "Nothing's changed. I'm sending Teyo."

"Teyo is a strong warrior," Ayson agrees. "But I was hoping you'd reconsider and send Faunride."

"Faunride belongs with his Adow." The fact is, he's all that remains of my life before I became the Adow. I know it's selfish, but all the same I have no intention of allowing him to leave. Besides, he won't want to leave me.

"He'll be dishonored if you don't send him. He's earned it, more so than Teyo."

"You mean he's the only one capable of protecting me?"

"I didn't say that," Ayson adjusts his breastplate. His momentary silence heightens the clacking of hoofs against the marble. "Faunride deserves to go."

Yes, he deserves to go. So did Troq…but Troq is dead, and I can't go through the Rituals without at least having Faunride. He'll understand. "Protecting his Adow is a greater honor than taking part in the Greeting Rituals. Something you would be wise to remember."

"The worshipers of Morlac won't attempt anything with the Adarians nearby. They'd never make it through the city gates."

I'm not worried about assassins. Hell, I could use my sword against an assassin! Ayson doesn't understand. He isn't the one being judged; the one being tested with each greeting. I need the Adarians to follow me. They must join this quest. They must believe I'm telling the truth, or everything is lost. "I'm sending Teyo!"

"As you command," Ayson removes his helmet, runs a cloth over his bald head, absorbing the sweat. At least I'm not the only one sweating. Then he replaces the helmet and moves his horse behind mine so he can sulk, presumably, but I have other things to worry about right now.

Faunride arrives with Aiya, "Your hair!" She hands me a wet cloth for my face.

"We don't have much time. Make me beautiful, Aiya," I scrub around my eyes, my cheeks, my throat. The cloth turns brown by the time I'm done washing my face.

Aiya moves from her horse to the back of mine and begins pulling at my windblown hair. She braided it this morning, but it gave me a headache, so I took it out of the braid once I left her sight. It's not like she didn't know I would do it. We've argued about my hair for ages.

A rider appears on the road ahead. He carries the banner of Gan, Overseer of Adarian: a green sphere with three white stripes on a white background. Troq told me they always select a young rider, symbolizing hope and peace. He's escorted by two of my Adowian Guards, Pwax and Og, their golden armor diffusing the silver gleam of the yearling's shield.

Aiya finishes my hair with a sigh meant to inform me she's not pleased, but it's the best she can do from the back of a horse. Fair enough. I'm the one who took the braid out. Tasa Ro! Why do I always make everything so difficult? She brushes the dust from my gown, cream velvet with green braid, before returning to her own horse.

"Almost ready," she rummages through a knitted sack to produce half a lemon. "This'll revive those cheeks."

She holds the lemon out for me to bite into, a sour warmth that coats my teeth, spreads a dryness across the inside of my upper lip. Cheeks withdraw from mouth. Eyes squint. My throat tingles as I swallow hard, "Thank you, Aiya." Tasa Ro!

Ayson motions the army to a halt as the rider approaches. Faunride positions himself on my left, close enough to touch, close enough to grab his hand, but I resist the urge. He wouldn't let me if I tried. It's enough to have him beside me.

The Adarian rider appears younger than me. He sits tall in the saddle, however, the pride of Adarian already stiffening his back. He wears a white tunic paired with a brilliant green cloak decorated with silver thread. He bows with practiced grace, his eyes never leaving mine. Dammit! Everything about him is perfect!

"Gan, Overseer of Adarian, greets his Adow with a blessing," the yearling declares. "The Sphere is with you, my Adow."

Here we go, "Gan has greeted me with hope and peace. Return under the banner of your Adow." My mouth feels larger than normal. I over-pronounce every word, but I get them out without forgetting a single word. Are you listening, Troq? I motion toward Valin, who dutifully hands over the Adowian banner, a white sphere upon a golden background, in exchange for the banner of Gan.

The yearling bows, "May the Sphere be with you."

"And keep you in his light."

The first greeting complete, he leaves without an escort. Now, I'm sweating as badly as Ayson. Tasa Ro, this dress makes it hot! "Aiya, the next gown!"

I must complete twenty-four greetings but, thankfully, I have five hours between each one. Ayson gives the order to set up camp. By the time the second rider appears, Aiya has re-braided my hair to her satisfaction. Where would I be without her? A windblown disaster! She dresses me in a purple gown with exposed neck and shoulders, but I still can't breathe. Fortunately, I'm seated beneath the shade of a makeshift canopy, so I'm no longer sweating. Now I'm only shaking. Yeah, that's so much better.

The second rider looks older. They only choose the most decorated Adarian warriors for this task. I don't recognize him, but he wears his medals with seasoned arrogance. Adorned in full ceremonial armor with his long gray hair kept tight in a braid, he dismounts upon reaching the perimeter of the Adowian Guard. They promptly escort him to me. He unsheathes his sword and falls to one knee, fully embracing my gaze... judging me.

"Gan, Overseer of Adarian, offers you his sword, my Adow," he raises the sword hilt toward me.

My mouth feels so dry! "Gan has lain down his defenses, and I offer the protection of the Adowian Army." *...in return.* I meant to say *I offer the protection of the Adowian Army in return*, but it's too late. My first mistake. I motion toward Teyo, not Faunride. Teyo hesitates only a moment before exchanging swords with the warrior. Then he mounts the Adarian's horse and rides off toward the city.

That's when I realize my second mistake. Dammit! I've forgotten an entire portion of the greeting which, unfortunately, should have occurred prior to Teyo's departure. "What is your name?" I ask the warrior who waits on one knee, his face beaming with a look of self-satisfaction.

"Daden."

"I am honored, Daden. Join my Guard and protect me with your life." And water, get me some water.

"It is I who am honored, my Adow," he rises, sheathes Teyo's sword, and moves to join my guard.

I look up at Faunride. I want to tell him that I didn't purposely forget the order of the greeting, but he isn't looking at me. He stares resolutely at the Adarian Road extending from the front of my throne. He stares at Teyo who rides toward Adarian; a distant clatter.

I grab for his hand, but he avoids my grasp. Of course, he does. He won't permit himself to touch his Adow, not even when she needs him most. "I need you beside me, Faunride." *Please understand that's the reason I sent Teyo. I can't do this without you.*

"The honor is Teyo's, my Adow. He is a fine warrior," Faunride responds without lowering his gaze, his dark eyes vacant as a cave. He looks hurt. Perhaps I should have… No. He is *my* guardian. Still… No!

I dismiss him, "I need Aiya." Better not to look at him, right now. Besides, that should help him get over the disappointment. Faunride needs his duties. "And water!"

Faunride bows, "My Adow."

Ayson extends a perfunctory hand, but I stand without his assistance. If Faunride refuses to touch me, or rather, if no one can touch the Adow… I certainly don't need Ayson touching me, right now. What I really need is Troq! But he isn't here, so I head toward my tent. I need to prepare for the next greeting, and I need to bathe. I'm sweating again!

Ayson follows without a word. That's probably best.

Five hours later, my army sits mounted and waiting when the next rider approaches. Not just any rider, though. *The* rider. The only one I remember from my first trip to Adarian. She rides upon a horse of dark pink, almost purple, an inane color that, for her, seems majestic. Her white robe flows loosely in the wind. The color of her hair matches that of the horse, as though a natural extension of the horse's mane. Her features remain forever young, her skin pale and flawless. She rides bareback with hands resting peacefully upon legs, for the horse moves without bridle. Never a bridle. Not since the Sphere joined rider and horse. Not since the beginning of time. She never changes. Never ages. Every feature looks exactly as I remember.

She is Inindu, eternal sister of the Adow.

The horse speaks, "Greetings, my Adow." Her voice sounds like feminine harmony mixed with the slow deep breaths of a hardened warhorse. I'm fairly certain she is a goddess, or the next closest thing, but all I can think about is the sweat running down my arms and whether she will notice how much I'm shaking. It doesn't help knowing Inindu literally witnessed the beginning of time. How many of these rituals has she attended? She'll notice every mistake.

"Greetings, Inindu," I respond. "And blessings upon thee." I'm dripping sweat! I hate ceremonies!

Inindu is neither horse nor topi. She exudes the spirit of both creatures combined into one soul which sounds confusing, so I generally think of her as a divine presence. Unfortunately, she also loved Adarian, hero of Ire. The same Adarian whom the Adow chose to serve as her First Etabli. The same one who died in the arms of the Adow. It's kind of a big deal with her. Not that I blame her. If anyone has reason to despise the Adow, it's Inindu. But…it wasn't me, Inindu. So, just, yeah…don't blame me. Please, oh, divine one. I mean, I didn't choose Adarian. For that matter, I didn't get to choose my own First Etabli!

"I don't speak for Gan, though he would wish otherwise." Um, that's not what she's supposed to say, so this should go well. "I've never liked the Greeting Rituals," Inindu doesn't even attempt to hide her irritation with the ceremony.

I find her lack of interest more than a little jarring, and oddly calming. But acknowledging the fact I would rather be doing something else, anything else, doesn't strike me as something an Adow would freely admit. "It's an old tradition, Inindu. One that brings comfort to old souls."

"The words of one so young…one day you'll come to understand that loneliness is the only comfort for old souls."

Faunride moves his horse a step closer, realizing the ceremony has gone off course, his sense of tradition no doubt conflicting with Inindu's complete disregard for it.

"I understand loneliness more than you know, Inindu." Ugh! I didn't mean to say that.

She looks at Ayson, "So, the rumors are true?"

Ayson looks down at the road.

"Shall we continue with the greeting ritual?" I press.

"If you wish."

"I do." I don't, and I do. I wouldn't mind an honest conversation for a change, but we all have our duties.

"Very well. Gan, Overseer of Adarian, greets you with beauty; or rather he greets you with my beauty. As for Gan, he has not aged gracefully, or even well."

Then those rumors also prove true, but I dare not dwell on them, "Gan is blessed, regardless of his age. He has greeted me with beauty, and I offer beauty in return."

Ayson unsheathes his sword. Then, taking a single strand of my black hair in his hand, he lets it fall on the blade, severing it cleanly. At least he keeps it sharp. Not that he would ever unsheathe it during an attack. No, not for anything more serious than a ceremony. Still, he rides forward with a measure of decorum, handing the strand to Inindu, and noticeably avoids her eyes…both sets of them. My mother once told me Inindu has always made Ayson uncomfortable. I would think it painful to watch if I didn't find it so delightful. He quickly sheathes his sword and returns to my side. Oh, yes, weapons make him uncomfortable, too.

"Will you join us at the Greeting Feast?" I ask. I look forward to talking with her when ritual doesn't otherwise dictate our conversation.

Inindu turns to Ayson, "Will you be at the feast, First Etabli?"

"I go wherever my Adow goes, Inindu."

"Yet you are here, now, before us," Inindu smiles. "Yes, I will attend. And I will go wherever you go, Ayson. We have much to discuss: Quel, marriage, heirs to the throne…"

"I would be honored by your presence, Inindu," Ayson lowers his gaze.

"I'm sure," Inindu relents. "My Adow."

I watch her depart, wishing she would stay. But she disappears over the horizon, signaling the start of the next greeting ritual, "I need Aiya."

Faunride bows, "My Adow."

Travelers, detained in both directions by Adarian warriors, have yet another reason to criticize me. Seriously, whoever chose to inconvenience an entire city by conducting a five-day ritual in the middle of the Adarian Road also developed the ideal strategy for holding a city hostage. No one likes to encounter unnecessary delays when they travel, and I would gladly exchange this location for the inside of a much cooler palace. It's hot. Five days of ceremony hot. Five days of sweating and constant bathing. It's thirsty hot, too. I can't seem to drink enough water! Oh, turn your eyes from me, Troq! I can barely function despite all your training.

"A rider approaches, my Adow," Ayson announces.

It's noon of the fourth day. I set my plate down on the ground: seasoned boar with warm applesauce and greens, mostly untouched because my stomach has been burning since this morning's meal of pickled garlic, bread, and fried pork.

"I need a new cook," I take the last sip of wine before standing to face Aiya. She has me dressed in a yellow-and-green gown which she quickly adjusts and shifts before handing me a cloth for my face, then busies herself with my hair. "Faunride, find me a new cook."

"My Adow," he bows even as the next ritual begins.

My tongue sticks to my teeth, but somehow, I manage to get through each ceremony. The last ritual takes place in front of the city gates. It's a beautiful sight! Why must the Adow live in Yenul when there's a city like Adarian? *The city Beaug sculpted.* Its marble walls stretch the length of the horizon, every inch boasting another sculpted image. More impressive, giant warriors loom overhead from where Beaug placed them atop these walls, stunningly detailed depictions of warriors engaged in endless battle. One of the images, Adarian, hero of Ire, clings to the mast of a badly damaged ship. The sculpted hero leans out from the city walls as he battles a massive sea serpent positioned in the surrounding forest. Incredible! Never more so than on a windy day when the forest sways, seemingly imitating the look and sound of the sea; or at night, when the moon reflects off the remarkably smooth marble. I used to sit in Troq's lap atop these city walls, and I would stare at these figures for hours until I fell asleep in his arms.

The entrance to this city also leaves a lasting impression. Two towering marble figures sit upon bulky, though strangely unadorned thrones, guarding either side of an ornate silver-inlaid gate. The female guardian sits slightly turned, reaching to lift a large, open book. The male guardian leans forward in thought, allowing those who pass below to admire the intricate details of his full beard. Waterfalls frame each figure, pooling at their base to form two ponds which play an integral role in any visit to the city: Travelers, whether entering or leaving, throw a coin into the pools—one side for safe travel to their next destination, the other for prosperity during their visit to Adarian. Of course, Gan, Overseer of Adarian, has since placed guards at the gate to ensure this ritual continues; a not-so-subtle form of taxation the Adarians don't seem to mind paying. Again, I'm impressed! If I tried that in Yenul I'd soon face a revolt; or worse, in Lor! No, they'd never go for it in Lor.

The city gates open to reveal Beaug's masterpiece positioned just inside the entrance, a relatively small sculpture of Adarian, hero of Ire, made from black marble—the only black marble sculpture in the entire city. No longer battling a sea serpent, here he lies dying in the arms of the Adow, or rather, someone meant to represent the Adow. It's not my face. It's not *our* face. My mother's. My grandmother's. It's the only statue of the Adow that doesn't look like me and, for that reason alone, it's my favorite piece sculpted by Beaug. Here, Adarian's body lies draped over the Adow's lap, one arm hanging limp as he slowly slips away from her. Her cloak gathers around him in great swells of material that mimic his listless form. She cradles him in her arms as though willing him to live, but this Adow holds no power over death. I know. I've tried. But Troq died, anyway, and so did Adarian, hero of Ire.

Before me, a thousand or more Adarians have gathered here at the gate to greet me. They wish to judge me for themselves. Behind me, an army will soon celebrate—for at least the next several days. I can't help but forgive their eagerness. They willingly follow me into the Torment. I have effectively asked them to die for me, and for no reason. They deserve every ounce of joy the city can provide them. One last meal. A last drink. A final lover.

Faunride introduces the last greeting ritual in response to a cheer that arises from somewhere ahead, "The Overseer has arrived, First Etabli."

The Overseer, wearing a white robe, lounges in an open litter carried on the shoulders of eight muscular topis. Inindu did not lie. Gan is old, dreadfully old; even from this distance I can see evidence of his poor health. His face, pulled downward by the unseen hands of the grave, seems to dangle from his jaw. What remains of his white hair he leaves unkempt. His body appears bent and painfully twisted, made worse by an irregularly bloated belly. Despite his obvious discomfort, Gan leans, somewhat awkwardly, against the gloriously exposed and chiseled torso of Erisyte. He may belong to Gan, but I don't mind looking. Not that I have any chance of touching that torso, for although Gan is known to take many lovers, Erisyte remains his only true companion. Well, I suppose I could steal him like the Adow once stole Adarian, hero of Ire, but that seems overly cruel.

"Welcome to Adarian, my dear Adow," Gan calls out in a faltering voice.

"I am honored, Gan. It's good to see you in such good health," I'm lying, of course, but at least I'm playing to my strengths.

The caravan slows to a stop, "It took them an hour to get me onto this contraption, my dear, and I had to bring poor Erisyte along just so I wouldn't fall off. It will not take so long to get down, I think."

"May it take a thousand years," I respond.

He smiles, "You are too kind, my Adow, but death carries a blade that even I cannot avoid."

Honestly, I doubt he'll last another year. Then again, he may outlive me. Why shouldn't he outlive me? I'm heading to Dragon's Torment, after all. Hell, he's already outlived twelve previous Adow! I hope he does outlive me. Gan *is* the city of Adarian. He commissioned a young Beaug to sculpt the city. He developed roads and sewer systems, recruited warriors from all over the land, encouraged and cultivated discourse among Adarian philosophers, created public sport and organized games in the arena, and built a library to preserve the knowledge that will educate future generations. Nobody can replace Gan, and I don't want to replace him. Not now, anyway. I have enough to worry about, and we have one last greeting ritual to complete.

"You have greeted me with your presence, Gan. I offer my presence in return."

"I am honored, my Adow. Adarian celebrates your arrival." He gestures to his litter bearers, "I will escort you to your quarters, and then to the courtyard for the Greeting Feast."

The crowd erupts in celebration. That's it. Finally. I did it, Troq!

5-Ruby
Special Edition

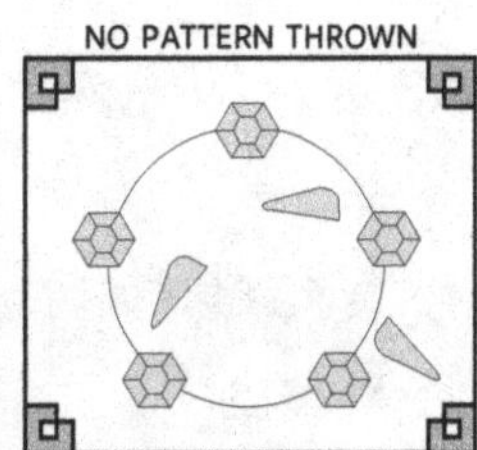

a taggle's tale

a taggle's tale

As told by a taggle woman at the base of a marble statue, the only known likeness of Hintor. The telling seemed well rehearsed, and she utilized the statue effectively, at times pointing toward it to emphasize the moment. In this manner, she turned an obvious distraction into a silent facilitator—a new technique which I must admit warrants further exploration. Her words did not carry as crisply as this old man may desire, but the audience seemed to respond well enough. Her name is Mistan. My granddaughter.

I implore you, speak her name. Speak of Mistan, oh cursed taggles, for she speaks in the manner of all taggles. She tells a story, and her words linger. She lives and we hear her voice. For this we have reason to pray: May the Sphere forgive our mother and remember our father.

- DK Vel

"It's been a long time, Nataline." Hintor twirls Maldinado's sister around in his arms, barely missing the heads of the two yearlings standing beside her, and soon enough, he kneels and turns his attention to them, "And who are these two beauties? Are you taking strangers in again?"

The tallest, Kaletine, drops the basket she is carrying and gives Hintor a tight hug around the throat. The other yearling, Belur, crashes into his side, causing all three to fall onto the worn marble of the Adarian Road. The warrior feigns a counterattack, roaring before scooping the yearlings into his arms, squeezing them until they giggle. Then he gives each of them a kiss.

"What did you bring us, Uncle Hintor?" Belur searches his cloak for hidden treasures.

"Belur," Nataline scolds softly, "It's enough that Hintor has returned from battle."

"No, it's not," Kaletine folds her arms and stares down at Hintor from atop the warrior's chest, daring him to refuse her a gift. "Uncle Hintor always brings us something, and he always hides it. So, where did you hide our presents this time, Uncle Hintor?"

"Hmm…It seems I've forgotten where I put them."

"See, Mommy?" Belur intones. "Uncle Hintor did, too, bring us something."

"Yes, Belur. It appears he did." Nataline retrieves the basket Kaletine was carrying, "And we've brought *him* something, too. Let him up. The bread is growing stale while the three of you tumble about."

Reluctantly, the yearlings allow Hintor to stand. They check under his cloak, and then run around him searching every pocket for their gift. Hintor reaches over them toward the basket, "Maldinado said you would bring bread."

Nataline positions herself between Hintor and the basket, "And where *is* my brother?"

"Praying."

"You could learn from his example."

Belur sneaks behind her mother, grabs a fresh loaf of bread, and hands it to Hintor. The warrior smiles broadly as he bites into the sourdough.

"That won't help you in your search, Belur," Nataline says. "Your Uncle takes too much pleasure in torturing the two of you."

"Give us a clue!" Kaletine pleads.

Hintor swallows and lowers himself until he can stare directly into the eyes of the two yearlings, "Where did I hide them last time?"

"In a barrel," the yearlings answer in unison.

"In a barrel…well, it's not there this time," Hintor takes another bite.

"You're hopeless," Nataline says, but her daughters are deep in thought, pondering the location of their treasure.

Hintor stands and resumes walking, "Your brother tells me the same thing."

All around them, Adarian warriors greet family and friends as part of the Tenth Greeting, the only one in which the Adow does not actively participate. Five hours reserved solely for Adarian warriors returned home. Hintor, Nataline, and her daughters travel through the crowd, eventually leaving the marble road in favor of the bloodgrass hills where the Adarian 45th has their temporary camp. Not just them. Tents, wagons, horses, and thousands of warriors await entrance to the city, casting shadows across the full expanse of the horizon.

"The wagons!" Kaletine guesses.

Hintor shakes his head, his mouth full of bread.

"Your tent!" Belur shouts.

"Not even close," Hintor shoves the last of the bread into his mouth and reaches for another loaf.

Nataline adjusts the basket, moving it out of his reach, "Save some for Maldinado."

Hintor leads them through the maze of tents even as the yearlings check behind every wagon wheel, bale of hay, and animal trough. The campground shows signs of heavy use and weary soldiers. Trampled bloodgrass. Open barrels of wine seemingly placed every twenty paces, a gift from the Adow. Naturally, a crowd encircles each barrel.

Hintor motions to a taggle boy who has followed him since leaving Yenul. DK Vel races to fill a goblet. He returns a moment later, and Hintor drinks the wine like a horse sloshing through a river. It runs freely and comically down his chin, soaking his black and red doublet.

"Manners, Hintor," Nataline reproaches him. "Adarians are nothing without our manners."

Hintor finishes the wine with a flourish, "Indeed! Thankfully, I am from Plenrid."

"Yes, but our children will be Adarians."

Hintor stops in his tracks, "*Our* children?"

"Kanbis has been dead long enough," Nataline says as she passes him. "You may court me if you wish."

Hintor wipes the wine from his mouth. The yearlings return from another fruitless search.

"Give us another clue, Uncle Hintor!" Kaletine demands. She does not possess the patience of her younger sister, Belur.

Hintor looks at the yearling with sudden apprehension. This could soon be his daughter. She waits for him to respond even as Belur hugs his leg, sitting atop his foot and hoping he will pick her up with each step. But Hintor looks beyond the yearlings, staring after their mother. This could soon be *his* family! He grins wider than the noticeably wide scar that stretches across his nose.

"Find the goat," Hintor finally replies.

The yearlings take off in a dash of delight, running past their mother who proceeds to tell them to, "Stop running!" Hintor forces his body to reengage vital life functions, taking one step and then another, eventually catching up to Nataline.

He falls in line beside her with casual flair. Then he proposes, "Will you marry me?"

"That is yet to be determined," Nataline states without a glance.

Hintor stops in his tracks for a second time.

Maldinado embraces Kaletine and Belur in a powerless bear hug. Then he pushes them back, abruptly. He looks at them sternly, "Have you been helping your mother?"

The two of them nod sheepishly, looking to their mother for confirmation.

"More often than not," Nataline offers. "Kaletine looks after the horses, and Belur has learned to cook."

"And your prayers?" Maldinado eyes them suspiciously.

Again, they nod.

"You should try my pudding!" Belur says excitedly.

"I can't wait!" Maldinado enwraps them again before standing to give his sister a kiss on the forehead.

"Maldinado," Kaletine asks, looking around the tent. "Where's your goat?"

The Madar flashes a look toward Hintor who stands just inside the tent. His friend holds his arms up in mock confusion. "You hid their gifts on the goat?" Maldinado shakes his head with mocking disapproval, then points beyond the mostly unlit back of the tent, "He's grazing in the fields with all the other goats."

The yearlings sprint away, screeching with glee as they run toward their hidden treasure.

Hintor turns to follow, "I better go with them. I may have tied the key around his neck a little too tight."

Maldinado looks down at his younger sister. She now keeps her black hair long and braided. Her warm, brown eyes remind him of aged wood, "You look more like Breline every time I see you."

"She wanted to come," Nataline hands her brother a loaf of bread before setting the basket down on a barren table.

"How is our mother?" Maldinado bites into the loaf, memories of home rising to the surface of his mind.

"Opinionated as ever," Nataline plops down upon her brother's wooden throne. "She doesn't want you to go on this quest."

"And you?" Maldinado takes another bite.

"I've never told you what to do."

Maldinado finishes off the bread, and then he rummages through the basket for another loaf, "Things are different now. I won't watch another Adow die."

"I know. I told her you have to go," Nataline watches her brother eat. Cooking is the least she can do for him, for he sends her every ounce of gold he receives in recognition of his service to Adarian. Not to mention he stepped in as father to her daughters after Kanbis died. "You're a fine warrior, Maldinado. And I know you must go—I won't even hold it against you."

"Dragon's Torment doesn't frighten me, but I'm worried about Breline."

"You should be worried! Six years have passed since you left home. And don't think she didn't notice how every other warrior came back after the Battle at Quel. If it hadn't been for your letters, we'd have thought you dead."

"I couldn't leave the Adow," Maldinado walks over to his sister, brings her to her feet, and then sits on the throne behind her with a ferocious grin.

She slugs him in the chest. Several times. He grabs her and twists her until she's pinned under his arms.

"Are you coming to the Greeting Feast?" He asks.

She struggles to free herself of his grip. Finally, he relents. She stands and adjusts her dark blue gown, "I haven't decided."

Kaletine runs into the tent waving a golden key, "Where's the chest?"

Maldinado stands with a smile, pointing to the wooden throne, "Under my throne."

Hintor enters the tent carrying Belur on his back.

"Did you find it?" Belur shouts.

Hintor lowers her to the ground so she can run to her sister's side. Kaletine lifts the seat of the throne and promptly removes a small wooden chest. Inside, the yearlings find two pairs of emerald earrings—one set for each of them.

Hintor watches their eyes alight with wonder, even as his gaze drifts toward Nataline.

a taggle's tale

As first spoken by a taggle man from outside the Adarian palace. The gathered crowd bordered on riotous, aggressively pushing and jostling for position until at last the taggle man sought an elevated platform. Thus, he told his tale from atop the palace wall, shouting so all topis and taggles below could hear. His position limited any movement, but the moment required little more than the words he spoke. As such, he garnered the full attention of his audience. When they finally settled and quieted, he began his tale. His name was Tuloo, chosen to serve Gan, Overseer of Adarian.

I implore you, speak his name. Speak of Tuloo, for he spoke in the manner of all taggles. He told stories, and his words still linger. He lived and we heard his voice. May the Sphere forgive our mother and remember our father.

- DK Vel

asks disappear and reappear as dancers turn their heads. The fixed emotions worn by the masqueraders shift and move like hunters among the trees. A flash of white disappears as grinning gold appears; a purple feather quickly conceals red glitter. Hands rise with the music and feet skip in rhythm. Diamond eyes wink at black-streaked faces. A painted stripe blends with a velvet tassel. Laughter mixes with conversation, and only the feast slows the wine.

The Greeting Feast.

Hintor stands in the crowd, searching for the mask of the Red Death; completely red, with no decoration. He doesn't know who wears the mask, but the identity of the topi doesn't matter. Hintor only cares what the mask of the Red Death will *bring* to the gathering: belladonna root. In small doses, Adarians favor this powder as their drug of choice. Of course, an overdose proves lethal. The victim breaks out in a red rash, their pupils dilate, they hallucinate, lose their sense of balance, and collapse. Their heart rate increases, then slows…then stops. The mask of the Red Death attends every feast and festival in Adarian. A simple exchange of gold for powder occurs, and the mask of the Red Death disappears.

Hintor moves through the crowd. He wears a full mask, white with gold stenciling and rustic creases at the eyes and nostrils; only his lips remain exposed. Jagged black lines give the impression that the mask once shattered, and then someone painstakingly pieced it back together. He spots the mask of the Red Death moving slowly through conversation circles. The exchange goes unseen, but Hintor watches the latest client discreetly pour white powder into his wine. The mask of the Red Death vanishes…only to appear again beside Hintor, as though simply seeing the mask attracted its presence; or the act of searching. Hintor hands the topi a pouch of gold and receives four tubes of powder, three more than the traditional purchase. The mask of the Red Death disappears, and Hintor knows he will not see it again.

His attention shifts as the Adow and her First Etabli enter the courtyard, their masks easily the most recognizable of the celebration, unchanged since the inception of the feast: She has paired a simple white gown with her mask of gold and white with the gold encircling the Adow's eyes as though she has donned a second mask. Gold lips, fashioned spikes, and dangling bells complete the disguise. The First Etabli appears as a sun god. He wears a black robe, leather gloves, and tight-fitting black coif under a raised cowl. His polished bronze mask reflects the light like fire, and painted flames extend wildly from his eyes. The mask, complete with molded lips and sculpted chin, fully covers his head. They struggle to navigate the immediate crowd of at least thirty heads deep, most of whom have political aspirations and dream of positions of power. The Overseer will soon die, after all, so the Adow will have reason to appoint an heir.

Hintor hides the tubes of belladonna root. A moment later, he dips his goblet into a nearby barrel. Wine runs and falls from his metal goblet like blood streaking a sword. He drinks the wine…slowly. An attempt to appease Nataline. She wants him to drink with manners.

Manners!

He refills the goblet, buries his nose into the wine in his haste to consume it. He's always wanted to marry Nataline, but now that she's given him permission… He fills the goblet again and surveys the crowd, spotting Maldinado a few yards away. His friend stands confidently if alone, dressed entirely in gold with a simple golden mask around his eyes and nose.

Hintor fills another goblet and joins his friend, "I feel the need to get drunk. Passed out in a pig sty drunk."

Maldinado raises a toast, "To the Adow, then!"

"No, to your sister!" Hintor counters, but Maldinado can't hear above the crowd.

They drink heartily.

Hintor lowers his mask and takes the Madar's cup, hands him two tubes of belladonna root in exchange, "A gift from a friend. I'll get more wine."

Maldinado conceals the drug in the pocket of his doublet. Then someone with a half-moon mask that lassos her exposed right eye pulls him onto the dance floor. His well-known partner's unmistakable magenta hair quickly identifies her as topi-Inindu. She does not say a word for her voice, Inindu-horse, stands off to the side.

Inindu-horse watches. Listens. She shamelessly eavesdrops on the conversations around her:

"...and now I have come to the conclusion..."

"...most of it began to surface..."

"...and take off this mask."

"...a new law that is itself a revision of the previous..."

"...children sleeping, but I guess I can't worry about the flowers, and in the morning it will all..."

"...cold night..."

The conversations linger and fade as the dancers move throughout the courtyard. Then all conversation abruptly ceases. Gan, Overseer of Adarian, host of this celebration, has arrived. He wears a mask of blue silk that forms a feathered wave at the top of his head. Blue beads—some scattered, some clustered—create the illusion of a rainstorm, all the more enhanced by a pair of large, raindrop earrings that extend downward in a shower of crystal and silver.

Hintor takes another gulp of wine. Waits for the moment to pass. Then he approaches Maldinado and slips between his friend and Inindu. The seamless exchange of dancing partners leaves Maldinado searching for another. His eyes fall on several topis standing beside Gan. His lovers, no doubt. But not all of them. One of them, obviously female, wears a full mask with gold leaves and blue jewels. Maldinado scratches his upper lip, considering how best to approach her. Finally, determined to make an impression, he moves forward, extends his hand to her, and bows.

She accepts his invitation. No, she grabs him, nails jabbing into his fingers. Her energy overwhelms him. They start dancing before either has the chance to speak. She moves her body close to him. Then away. She spins around him, raises her arms. The Madar embraces this unknown partner, her black hair brushing against the backs of his hands on her back. She collapses. Her arms move wildly around and about and over him. Maldinado presses his cheek to her skin, smelling the warm spice of the creams and oils she used to bathe, and the sweat that now coats her body like a summer mist.

He closes his eyes.

She stiffens. He pushes her away into a twirl. The gold leaves and blue jewels of her mask blur and stop and blur again as she returns to him. But he keeps her at a distance. Only their hands touch. He stares into her eyes, outlined in dark tones. Those eyes widen as she invites him to pull her closer. He wants to—he wants to feel her body against him once more, but their dance has come to an end. Their fingers embrace.

He holds her a moment too long.

The music stops.

The dance demands they should exchange partners.

"I hope you are not my sister," Maldinado says softly.

The stranger shakes her head, "I don't have any brothers."

The music resumes.

Maldinado brings her into his arms, "What is your name?"

"Don't ask."

"Ah! So, we play the roles of Tenush and Gieel," Maldinado leads her slowly, wraps her gently with his arm.

"*Misdeblue* is an ancient tale." She rests her head against his chest, "I've always hated the ending."

"You prefer tragic endings?" Maldinado asks.

"Life is a tragedy," she states with a sigh. "I've witnessed too many deaths to think otherwise."

"Whoever you are, you're definitely not from Adarian," Maldinado places his nose and lips against her sweat dampened head, a not unpleasant smell under the textured scent of spiced oil.

"Why do you say that?"

"Because Adarian is a city of hope and joy—look around you."

"I see strangers unwilling to reveal their identities."

"I'm not a stranger. Do you wish to know my name?" Maldinado pauses, "I'll tell you anything you want."

"No." She looks into his eyes, "I don't want to know your name. Not tonight."

The music changes tempo.

"Why do you grow a beard?"

"I'm headed to Dragon's Torment. It's a way to stay warm," Maldinado extends his partner to the right. Brings her close.

"It seems everyone is heading to the Torment."

"We follow the Adow."

"So does my father."

"Then he is honored," Maldinado guides her around him, and they dance back-to-back.

"He is *not* honored."

"What happened?"

She steps away. Returns. Their arms extend and lock, "You promised me hope and joy. Let's change the subject."

"You must come from Kiel," Maldinado closes his eyes. Embraces her movements. Feels the force of her body against him.

"Why do you say that?"

"I know the warriors from Kiel. They're all sad."

She seems amused, "You're trying to figure out who I am."

Maldinado opens his eyes, "I'm hoping you'll join me for the Toast of Sark."

"I have many suitors."

"A kiss from you is worth the pursuit," Maldinado counters.

"Then I'm yours to pursue," she changes with the music to another partner.

Dancers move in circles and lines. Crowds mingle around tended trees and barrels of wine. The courtyard resembles a painting full of colors that swirl and stop and blend. Inindu-horse turns from her study of the Adow to a topi who wears what must rank as the most absurd mask of the evening, mostly due to a fashioned tongue that sticks out. Chipped paint on the tip of the tongue adds an element of steadfast neglect.

"She's drawing quite a crowd."

"I've never understood this celebration," the tongued-one says.

"It gives Adarians a reason to drink wine…something I've noticed your mask doesn't allow you to do," Inindu-horse replies.

"It keeps me sober. As it's intended to do."

"It keeps you single, too. You don't have to worry about kissing anyone during the Toast of Sark."

"I have you to keep me company."

Inindu-horse shakes her mane, "My heart belongs to Adarian."

"Of course. I didn't mean to suggest…"

"This is the only place we were permitted to see each other after she took him from me. I'm sure you can figure out how we accomplished that."

The tongued-one nods in agreement, "The masks have many uses."

"Which is all you need to know about this ridiculous celebration," Inindu notices Gan in the middle of the courtyard. He raises his goblet, gulps down the wine. "Gan will find any reason to hold a feast."

"He's old. If anyone deserves to enjoy his last days, it's the Overseer."

"It won't be long," Inindu says. "He's the only living topi who knew my Adarian. But his mind grows weak. His memories are fading."

"He looks healthy enough."

"You're a poor liar. The truth is, Gan is dying, and he's grown rather boring," Inindu says. She finds the Adow in the crowd, "It's about time I leave this city. I think I'll journey to Dragon's Torment. Watching a thousand warriors die sounds more interesting than watching an old Overseer meet his end."

The assassin watches the taggles as they take food and wine to the Adow. His plan will work. She's the only topi at the celebration who doesn't supply her own wine. He imagines it has always happened this way. Worshipers flocking to her, making a mockery of themselves. He finds the masks suddenly transformed into fools bowing before the deceiver they call the Adow—seeking honor they'll never find.

Only Morlac can provide peace.

The assassin dips his goblet into a nearby wine barrel, empties a tube of belladonna root into the wine. Drinks it gone. Then he fondles the remaining four tubes he's saving for the Adow. Moments later, he follows a taggle out of the courtyard. The Toast of Sark draws near. The Adow will kiss her First Etabli, and drink from a golden goblet. The assassin follows the taggle through a dark tunnel. He can feel, or rather see, the effects of the belladonna root. Faces appear in the shadows. Strangers—twisted, mutilated faces shimmering in greens and blues. They all don masks, laughing. Whispering. Arms reach for him. The assassin waves them away. They disappear in a fog.

He, too, laughs, for he has not felt the effects of belladonna root for a long time. A taggle floats on the outskirts of these hallucinations, giving the Worshiper of Morlac a piece of reality that pulls him forward. He follows. He follows the taggle. Turn and follow. Walls liquefy. The assassin touches them only to discover his hand now drips with water.

The taggle seems so far away from where the assassin lay. Why is he lying on the ground? He pulls himself to his feet, follows the taggle. He seemingly falls toward a lit room. He clings to the walls, hoping to slow his descent. It's no use. He crashes full body into a wooden table. The room swirls. Blurred images of meat and fruit. Bread over knives mixed with flying pots and bowls.

He finds more than one taggle in the room; one of them, the boy he followed. The assassin can't make out their faces. He doesn't care. He leans on the table, waits for the effects of the drug to fade.

"Out!"The assassin shouts. "Leave me! Go away!"

The taggles leave with an eruption of commotion. The assassin stands alone, free to search for the bottle of wine reserved for the Toast of Sark. The best wine—served only to the Adow, only during the Toast of Sark. He finds the bottle on a shelf. He inhales the fragrant, sweet pear wine. He takes a drink. And another. Then he pours four tubes of belladonna root into the bottle before corking it once more. Moments later, the assassin vanishes.

Maldinado holds the long white ribbon that will allow him to choose his partner for the ribbon dance. He knows who he wants. He's lost her three times, already, but the Madar won't lose her again. He scans the masqueraders, pausing at every golden face. They mock him. They hide her. There! Their eyes make contact, letting him know she awaits. He wraps the ribbon around her waist.

"I've figured out who you are."

She laughs, "I'm a star above the clouds."

"No! You're both the storm and the rain."

She judges him—staring at the gold thread that encircles his gray eyes, "And you're a tree consumed by lightning!"

She spins away and out of the ribbon.

He wraps her again. The music starts. The dance begins.

Maldinado grins, "Maybe I'm a painter eager to travel the land. Maybe I'm a herald."

"If you could be anyone, who would you be?" The ribbon slides over her shoulder and around her back. She moves closer to Maldinado.

"The First Etabli." Maldinado looks at the sun-god mask of the First Etabli. He stands beside the Adow, always he stands beside the Adow.

"Why?"

"Wouldn't you want to be the Adow?"

"No," The disavowal sounds flat and convincing.

"Ah. Then who *would* you be?"

She smiles and turns, "The storm and the rain."

He kneels, maneuvers the ribbon over her feet. Curls it upward and around her body, "I can see you as Inindu."

"She's beautiful. I would gladly be Inindu."

"She's sad," he says. "Forever lonely, yet never alone."

She stops dancing, looking into his eyes. Then quickly resumes, "You never said why you would want to be the First Etabli."

Maldinado relents, "There is no greater honor than to die protecting the Adow."

She steps away. Returns. "And what if you failed to protect her?"

He holds her firmly against his chest, "I would not fail."

"Then you are a fool," She grabs the ribbon and wraps it around his waist. "The First Etabli has already failed to protect the Adow. Remember Quel?"

"I was there," he moves in step with her. "Adarian warriors have a saying: We cannot alter the path of the sun, but we can embrace its journey, and trust the ending will prove more beautiful than the beginning." He motions toward the Adow, "I failed to protect her once. I won't fail again." He takes the ribbon from her, wraps her wrists together.

She looks at the Adow, "I see a mask that can't be removed, a yearling who's lost her way."

"You're wrong," Maldinado says gently. He unwraps her wrists, "I've looked into her eyes. She isn't lost."

The music crescendos. Maldinado takes the ribbon in both hands. She grips the middle. They walk in a circle. She ducks under and up into his arms. Raises the ribbon and moves away. The music ends. Maldinado wraps the ribbon around her waist one final time. A gong sounds.

"It's the Toast of Sark. Where are your suitors?"

"Only one remains," she replies coyly.

"Then I'll get us some wine," he reaches for the tubes of belladonna root safely hidden inside his doublet.

"No," she pulls the ribbon from his hands. "I'll get the wine."

Maldinado watches her move through the masqueraders like a river flowing into the sea. Then she is gone. He starts toward the spot where she disappeared, frantically searching. She emerges once more, holding two goblets above her head, trying not to spill as she makes her way toward him.

The crowds huddle and separate as the dancers prepare for the toast. Taggles assemble a stage in the middle of the courtyard for the Adow and her First Etabli; Gan and Erisyte join them. A pause to fill each goblet. Whispered conversation. Random laughter. Growing expectation! Gan motions for silence. Erisyte holds forth two goblets, one of which he hands to Gan.

A commotion arises from the north corner of the courtyard, revealing Daden, honored warrior of Adarian, chosen for the Second Greeting, who bears the Adow's golden goblet.

Hintor is drunk. He sits on a tree branch, one of the many topis who climbed the trees to gain a better view of the Adow. Daden holds the goblet high so all can see it. He moves with measured step, and when he reaches the stage, he bows, extending the wine to the Adow. She takes the offering, and Daden retreats.

Gan speaks, "When I offered the first Toast of Sark, I gave a speech that was beautiful and lasted long into the evening. Now it seems I have grown dull, and my speeches are like gasping breaths. I welcome you to Adarian, my Adow, as Sark once welcomed me—with a kiss and a toast!"

The crowd cheers. The Adow turns to her right and lightly kisses the bronze lips of the masked First Etabli. She raises her goblet and drinks every drop of the wine. Gan turns to Erisyte. They kiss and drink. Every topi who has found a partner follows suit.

"Are you going to kiss me?" Nataline stands beneath the tree.

Hintor follows the voice, eventually finding the love of his life holding two goblets of wine. He promptly falls out of the tree, and into passed-out-drunk unconsciousness.

Maldinado kisses the stranger. Her lips stiffen, quiver slightly. Her body tightens as he moves his arm around her, pulling her closer. She slowly relaxes, lips soften. They linger. They take their time and savor the longest kiss. When they finally pull away to raise the expected toast, they discover everyone else has already finished their wine. She laughs, and he laughs, and they drink together.

Behind them, the tongued-one watches, having watched them from the moment his daughter took the Madar's hand and began to dance. Tears fill Ayson's eyes in this moment of joy for his daughter.

Then the screams begin.

The Adow, rather, Aiya *masquerading* as the Adow, falls to her knees. Faunride crouches beside her, no longer wearing the mask of the assumed First Etabli. Ayson runs toward his daughter who has already left

Maldinado behind as she dashes toward the stage. Chaos! The Adowian Guard converges on the courtyard. Run! Push! Scream!

Faunride removes the mask from Aiya to find her face turned completely red and her eyes dilated. She struggles against him as though suddenly gone mad. Gan searches the crowd in desperation.

"The Red Death!" Someone shouts.

"The Adow is dying!" Another screams.

Gan raises his arms, attempting to quiet the crowd, "No, not the Adow!" He announces more loudly, "She is *not* the Adow!"

The Adow and Ayson reach the stage at nearly the same time, both of them quickly removing their masks. Gan quickly points to them, "Behold, your Adow lives. Silence! *This* is your Adow!"

A hush fills the courtyard. Faunride steps away from Aiya as the Adow takes her handmaiden into her arms. No one utters a word as Aiya dies. When it's over, the Adowian Guard encircles the stage as the masqueraders depart.

But Maldinado cannot look away from the Adow. She deceived him. He kissed the Adow. Only the First Etabli can kiss the Adow! He has lost his honor.

Alarmed, he leaves the courtyard having never removed his mask.

5-Ruby
Special Edition

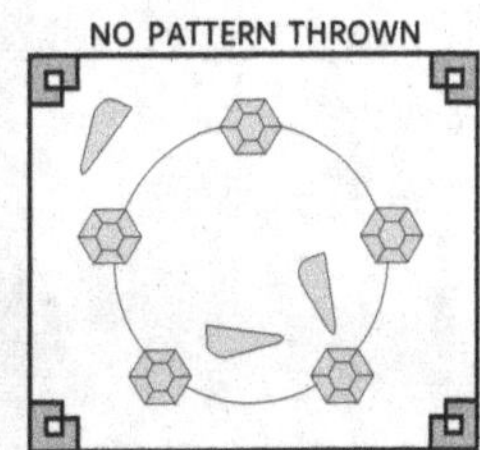

<u>A Record of—*she who served as*—The Adow: H</u>

Moon		Seal
Completion of the Purple Moon		Floating Cr
Completion of the Purple Moon		Hemming T
Shadow of the Purple Moon		River under
Shadow of the Purple Moon		Sword throu
Completion of the Red Moon		Broken Cro
Completion of the Red Moon		Crown of L
Changing of the Silver Moon		Five Crown
Completion of the Yellow Moon		Sword with
Changing of the Blue Moon		Crowned W
Completion of the Green Moon		Crowned Ro
Completion of the Green Moon		Crowned Sw
Completion of the Green Moon		Crown over
Completion of the Green Moon		Two Crowns
Completion of the Green Moon		Crowned Bo
Completion of the Green Moon		Hammer Str
Completion of the Green Moon		Sun Rising
Completion of the Green Moon		Crown betw
Dark Moon		Tiger and C

Months: Erog | Utine | Cil | Flatine | Joone   Date Format: (Gen

Periods: Year = 5 Months | Month = 5 Weeks | Week

The Adow

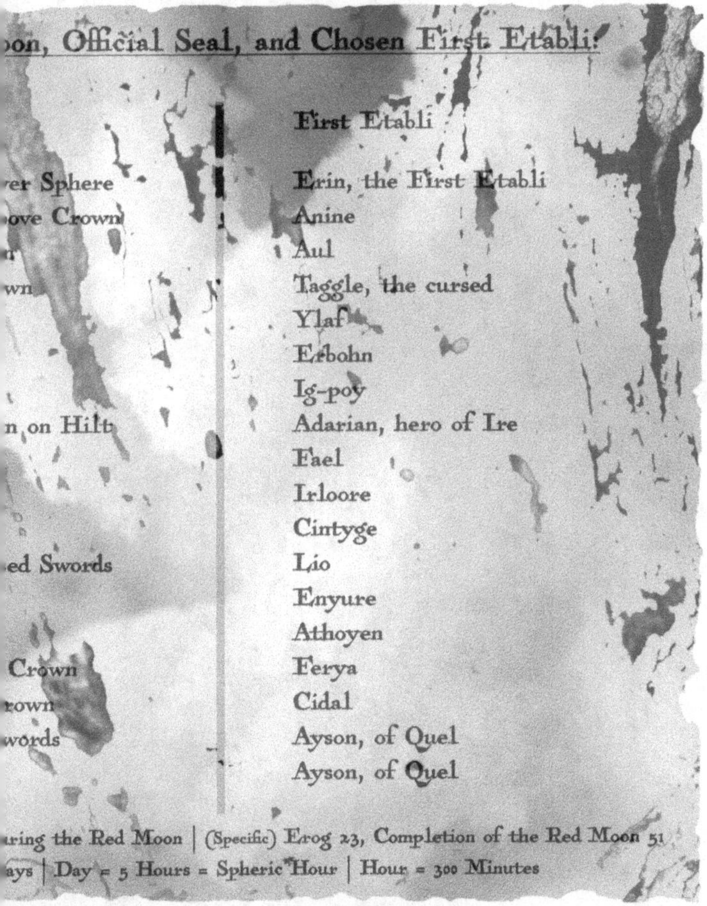

on, Official Seal, and Chosen First Etabli

First Etabli

...er Sphere   Erin, the First Etabli

...ove Crown   Anine

...r   Aul

...wn   Taggle, the cursed

Ylaf

Erbohn

Ig-poy

...n on Hilt   Adarian, hero of Ire

Fael

Irloore

Cintyge

...ed Swords   Lio

Enyure

Athoyen

...Crown   Eerya

...rown   Cidal

...words   Ayson, of Quel

Ayson, of Quel

...aring the Red Moon | (Specific) Erog 23, Completion of the Red Moon 51
...ays | Day = 5 Hours = Spheric Hour | Hour = 300 Minutes

iya takes the silk-wrapped package from Erisyte. He stands before me, half-naked. I wouldn't mind running my fingers down his chest and along every grooved muscle, tightly carved as though Beaug sculpted him. Really, if he didn't already belong to the Overseer...

"May the Sphere protect you," he says with a slight bow.

"And keep you in his light," I respond.

I watch him leave, enjoying the solid movement of his back and shoulders. *If you had to break tradition, mother, why didn't you choose someone like him?* I turn to find Aiya also looking after him, and we share a silent moment and a sigh, "Come, Aiya, we have much to do before the Greeting Feast."

"Open the package first," Ayson sits next to a three-pane window, reading a series of letters he requested upon our arrival.

"What's in the package?" I move to the table where Aiya set it down. The room, though not my favorite in the palace, serves well enough for feast preparation purposes. Well-lit and decorated in heavy green velvet and gold-plated furniture, the space includes a bathing room and several mirrors along the walls. Thankfully, Aiya had the mirrors covered. Better to judge my appearance after I bathe.

"Aiya," Ayson extends a letter toward her. "You need to read this. It's from your distant grandmother."

I remove a white ribbon and unfold the blue silk to reveal a mask and white gown. Nothing more. "What is this?"

"A moment of freedom," Ayson, suddenly behind me, hands me a letter like the one he gave to Aiya, but this one displays the crowned swallow seal of the Adow—she who reigned during the time when Cintyge served as First Etabli. Seal already broken, the letter appears worn with slightly frayed edges and fading, if still legible, handwriting. I glance up from the letter to Ayson, but he doesn't answer my unspoken question, and for once, I don't hate him for his silence. I understand he has gifted me this moment, so I carefully unfold the letter:

Wear this mask to the Greeting Feast, my daughter. Be free of your title for one night. Experience life like never before, and may you return to the feast often. I can offer no greater gift. May the Sphere be with us and keep us in his light.

I lower the letter and Ayson holds me with a gentleness as foreign as the mask on the table, "It should have been your mother giving you this gift, but it's no less significant. The Greeting Feast is a masquerade created as more than a celebration. Aiya and Faunride will take our places tonight. Though I don't envy them." He looks back toward the handmaiden, "You'll be swarmed by everyone at the feast. It's a pitiful sight."

Troq never told me anything about this. Maybe he didn't know. A secret passed down by generations of Adow, now mine to experience. Entrusted to my keeping. I reach for the mask, hold it to my face. I look through the eye slits as though I've discovered a hidden passageway.

"Who else knows about this?" I lower the mask.

"Only Gan," Ayson responds. "He is the keeper of the letters and the masks. From what I know of the tradition, I believe it was his idea."

I again raise the mask to my face. Sometimes, I love being the Adow!

I hug Ayson. A little weird, but I'm so excited I don't care. "Come, Aiya! Now we both have to get ready," I pull her away from her own letter toward the bathing room. She'll be wearing more than my gown tonight, "You're about to become the Adow."

Three hours later, Aiya stands in a corner of the courtyard, barely able to lift a goblet of wine for all the topis surrounding her, and I stand unencumbered beside Gan. Unannounced. Unknown. Free to dance! I don't have to wait long. A topi extends his hand, a warrior by the look of him. He's wearing a golden doublet and matching mask.

Let the masquerade begin.

I consume him. I want to devour him. I haven't been this close to a warrior since Troq died. Faunride refuses to touch me. Ayson can't. This one——*Tasa Ro! Never let me go, stranger.* I dig into his back, rest my head on his chest. *Please, never let me go.*

The music changes, "Then I'm yours to pursue."

Another partner. He stands shorter than me, and he seems intent on crushing my hand. That's enough——I'm done dancing for the moment. I need wine and something to eat. I'm starving! I look for Ayson, or Faunride or Aiya. But no one clings to me. I'm alone. There's no one to fetch me food or wine. For the first time in my life, I am forced to get my own wine!

I walk, almost run, toward the nearest barrel, snag an empty goblet dutifully offered by one of the many taggles carrying trays, and dip it into the dark red wonder of Adarian wine. It runs down my hand, staining the sleeves of my white gown. I don't care. Let it be ruined! I drink the goblet empty and dip two more times before turning my attention to food. I gorge myself on cheese and apples. Sweet bread covered in frosting. Lamb. Goose. More wine. No one serves them to me. Miraculously, I must get it all myself!

The stranger in the gold mask returns. Good. I want to dance. I press my body against his, twirl away, and return. We dance for what seems forever. Then I leave him dancing with another partner. I am his to *pursue*, not keep. Now then, I want to try belladonna root. Where do I find...

Another partner. This one large, not fat or tall, but thick, even for an Adarian. I lean close and whisper, "Where do I get some belladonna root?"

"Look for the mask of the Red Death." He pulls me even closer, "You'll need gold."

Damn! An Adow doesn't carry gold, "I don't..."

He holds a finger to my lips. I say *finger*, but I swear it's at least the size of my arm. "Consider it a gift," he drops a pouch of gold into my hand. Then he leaves. Well, that was too easy. I search the crowd for my father. The tongued-one stands next to Inindu-horse, but his attention lay elsewhere. Hard to say if he played a role. Either way, I'm grateful...and thirsty. More wine.

The Mask of the Red Death greets me at the wine barrel. She wears a plain red mask and a layered black robe. I exchange gold for a single tube of belladonna root. She leaves, lost again to the masquerade. This feels wrong, and altogether delightful. I hurriedly dispense the powder into my goblet and consume the drug before I change my mind. And... then...colors swirl. The costumes of the masqueraders expand, growing more ridiculous. Every mask seems more hilarious than the last. I tumble through a maze of dancing and laughter. My feet never touch the ground! I move from partner to partner with a glee I can barely contain. Did I mention I can't feel my feet, or my face? I dance with everyone and nobody. Hell, I'm struggling to focus on anything. Everything is a blur...

I find myself in the courtyard. Nobody dances. The taggles dispense white ribbons. Everywhere white ribbons. I'm so dizzy. The stranger in the gold mask approaches and wraps his white ribbon around my waist. Yes, stranger. Hold me steady. Let me look into your eyes. Focus...focus on his gray eyes…eyes like Maldinado's eyes. Maldinado! It *is* Maldinado! *Dammit!* Anyone but him.

"No." I pull the ribbon from his hands, "I'll get the wine." And then run away…except I don't run away. This is my night. *My* night. He doesn't know anything about me. He doesn't know he dances with his Adow. Why shouldn't I kiss him? So, I let him hold me in his arms. He presses his lips against mine and, for the first time, I experience life as it should have unfolded. My destiny before my mother ruined everything. Before Quel. I kiss him. Oh, more than kiss him, I linger on his lips…in his arms. Probably, too long. Yes, too long. I slowly pull away, or he pulls away. Whatever, we both pull away and we raise a toast and I drink the last of my wine.

A scream rises. The masquerade ends. Once more, I am the Adow.

5-RUBY
SPECIAL EDITION

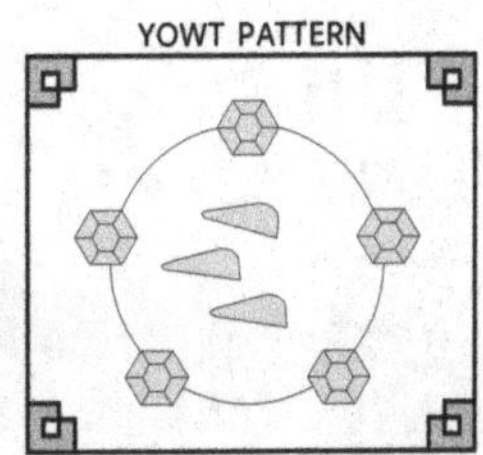

YOWT PATTERN

a taggle's tale

As spoken by a taggle girl who stood on the roof of Goleb's house in Adarian. Her tale began at sunset, two torches illuminating her face and movements, the emotion of both more pronounced by the flickering shadows upon her slender frame. Her voice added weight to the wind, and her black hair blew freely. Only the bleating of a distant goat distracted the audience, but even that eventually faded. Her name was Dellina, daughter of Della, my first love. She spoke in the manner of all taggles, for our story is a journey we share. May the Sphere forgive our mother and remember our father, as revealed in Dsal's vision.

I implore you, speak her name. Speak of Dellina, for she spoke in the manner of all taggles. She told stories, and her words still linger. She lived and we heard her voice. May the Sphere forgive our mother and remember our father.

- DK Vel

$\mathcal{S}$outh of Adarian, not far from the city walls, DK Vel follows his friend Beah down a hillside. An overcast sky sends a cruel mist down upon the taggle boys, leaving their exposed skin and the ground around them slick with moisture. DK Vel, barefoot as always, descends at an angle to keep from sliding down the muddy hill, clumps of mud squeezing through his toes with every step. A scattering of trees provides solid handholds, but the wet bark rips his fingers raw and leaves his knuckles red with blood and strain.

Forgive our mother

Remember our father

The boys head toward a community of taggles where Beah's *Uncle Taggle* lives. A dallic. When they reach the bottom of the hill, they climb over a stone wall and continue down the muddy streets. Familiar images greet them: A baby crawling in the mud, her mother nowhere to be found. Men gathered around a wagon, singing so low that their voices morph into a hum. Thin men, worn and scarred. A woman holds a baby to her breast, as she meanders down the street. An ox follows her, every rib outlined by starvation. A taggle sits in the doorway of his hut, his face painted red, and his eyes closed in meditation. DK Vel recognizes him as the dallic rivac—chosen to pray to the Sphere…repeating the taggle's prayer over and over on behalf of the taggles living in the dallic. The boys bow as they pass the rivac. Then they, too, utter the taggle's prayer.

Forgive our mother

Remember our father

They continue through the dallic, encountering a taggle, bruised and beaten and lying face down in the mud. DK Vel imagines the moment before his death, for in that moment, all taggles discover their destination. They discover whether the Sphere listened to their prayer. If he remembered them or forgot about them. DK Vel decides this taggle went forgotten. He imagines the fear in the man's eyes as he realized his fate…the sudden gasp for air before collapsing in death.

Beah leads DK Vel out of the mist into a hut that has a noticeably large hole in the wall just left of the entrance. The hole provides the only source of light aside from that streaming through various slits in the roof. Here, five taggle boys huddle together, each one has one hand extended with fingers interlocked in a game DK Vel does not recognize. There, an older taggle sits smoking a pipe. Uncle Taggle. Beside him, two women sleep, while a third speaks quietly with three other men—two of them much younger than the third as emphasized by a growing beard. Elsewhere, three girls paint various designs on newly fashioned clay bowls. One of them smiles as DK Vel finally notices her. He finds himself staring at her as though he has never seen a girl before. Certainly, he has never *noticed* one before.

Beah addresses the taggle smoking a pipe, "Uncle, this is DK Vel. We have come for your blessing."

Uncle Taggle puffs at his pipe, smoke drifting from his mouth. A full, white beard covers his face, outlining sallow cheeks. His status as Uncle Taggle means he has lived longer than any other taggle in the dallic, a sign the Sphere still remembers him, "What dallic birthed you?"

"Yenul."

"Does no one bless taggles in Yenul?"

DK Vel shakes his head, "No one."

Uncle Taggle lowers his pipe, "You and Beah must *earn* my blessing."

"We are ready, Uncle. What must we do?" Beah swats at a flying insect.

Uncle Taggle considers the boys for a moment, "Ilion."

The young man with the growing beard steps forward, "Yes, Uncle?"

"Take them with you tonight."

Ilion nods and leaves with a promise to return. DK Vel doesn't notice, having turned his attention back to the girl. She, too, boldly stares at him. A strand of hair covers part of her face. Still, he can see her white eyes—not yellow or bloodshot like most other taggles. Her skin appears unblemished, never bruised or beaten. She looks beautiful.

"Stay with us until Ilion returns," the old taggle offers.

"I am honored, Uncle," Beah bows respectfully.

DK Vel turns from the girl and also bows, "I am honored, Uncle."

They join the circle of boys sitting next to the entrance and, once the game is explained to them, they raise their hands, twist their fingers, and compete with the other boys. DK Vel, however, glances at the girl painting the clay pot, and finds she still watches him. He returns to the game, suddenly eager to win.

Several hours later, the taggles snuggle together in sleep with Uncle Taggle positioned in the middle of a circle of bodies. DK Vel, newest to the group, lies on the outermost perimeter. He can't sleep. By luck or coincidence, the girl's back presses against his chest, her position within the circle, one row deeper, perfectly aligns with the boy's own position. Her name is Della, and he can feel her breath on his hand. Before DK Vel joined the circle, Della slept with her back exposed. Now her hair covers his face like his mother's used to cover it when she would hold him close to keep him warm. He has never slept next to another woman, until now. He closes his eyes, buries his nose into Della's hair, and attempts to fall asleep.

Beah's hand on his shoulder awakens him. His friend motions for him to follow. DK Vel slowly removes his arm from around the girl, quietly rolling away from the greater circle of taggles. He follows Beah to the darkness outside where they find Ilion crouching.

"Say nothing," Ilion takes the lead position, and they silently follow him through the dallic, every step measured. When an Adarian guard comes into view, they fall to the ground and immediately roll through the mud into the shadows of a nearby hut. The guard passes and they are on the move once more. The cold air fails to keep DK Vel from sweating. Ilion doesn't have to say a word for the boy to grasp the nature of their journey. If the guards catch them sneaking around at night, DK Vel will never see Della again.

Another guard comes near, but shadow conceals the taggles and they avoid capture. When Ilion moves again, his pace quickens even as they enter a darker part of the dallic. The growing smell of rotting flesh tells DK Vel they travel toward the open gravesite where taggles are thrown when they die. Every dallic has one, and though they serve as the final destination of all taggles, the living rarely visit. Yet, DK Vel and his two friends soon descend into the mass grave.

"We're safe," Ilion whispers. "The guards don't patrol the grave."

DK Vel can feel the ground shift below his feet, and the distinct clamminess of cold flesh under his toes. He leans against the side of the pit in order to keep his balance as they walk, testing every step before moving forward. His imagination runs wild with the image of a thousand bodies reaching out for him, their hands pulling at him. He breathes deeply to keep from panicking. Then he can hear Ilion rummaging or digging through the bodies, eventually opening a trap door that moans so much the boy feels certain one of the guards will hear them.

"Here, there's a ladder. Be careful."

Ilion helps the boys find the ladder and DK Vel follows Beah down the opening. "You'll find a tunnel below," Ilion secures the entrance with another alarming echo of rust-laden hinges. The resulting darkness proves disorienting. Only the ladder offers DK Vel any sense of reality.

"Where are we?" DK Vel clutches each textured rung like a viper unable to pull free of its intended victim.

"This dallic sits atop an old marble quarry. The workers used these tunnels until they used up all the marble. Then they destroyed or forgot about most of the passageways, but a few remain. We unearthed this one when a taggle hid among the dead above. It saved his life."

"What's down here?" Beah's voice sounds faint, seemingly several rungs further down than what DK Vel assumed.

"The blessing you seek."

When they finally touch solid ground, Ilion leads them down the unseen tunnel toward a glowing light. DK Vel tries to make out his surroundings, but he can only imagine the tunnel as it must have looked years ago with workers moving around performing endless tasks, pausing only to eat or drink. He can almost feel the sense of dread they held on those mornings as they climbed down to face the endless marble. Almost endless. He wonders if they ever met Beaug, sculptor of Adarian. Surely, he must have traveled to the quarry whenever he needed another block of marble. Then DK Vel wonders how many taggles died for that marble.

The glowing light turns into a torch. Ilion takes it in hand and continues through the darkness. Soon, the terrain alters, forcing them to climb over large stones and piles of rubble. DK Vel slams his toe into one of the stones, sending a jarring pain up his leg, and he has to bite his lip to keep from crying out. He continues, gingerly, only to scrape his calf a moment later, and then his chest before Ilion can lead them back to solid footing. Under the dim light of the torch, DK Vel can see a sizable gash on Beah's arm. He avoids looking at his own wounds.

Ilion breaks the silence, "Beah, you want to believe a taggle can be blessed—that life has more to offer a taggle. You want to believe Uncle can give you something the Adow denies you, but you're wrong. There is no blessing for a taggle! Uncle lives in the dallic, same as the taggles who honor him." He stops and turns toward the boys, his face a horror of shadow and light, "So, I ask you, what blessing do *you* deserve?"

"I wish to survive the Torment," Beah responds immediately, defiantly.

DK Vel lowers his gaze, "I seek an Adowian Burial."

"Why do you wish to survive? Why do you seek an Adowian Burial? Because you're taggles and taggles don't survive quests to the Torment. They don't receive Adowian Burials."

"I *will* survive!" Beah slaps his chest with his wounded arm.

"You hope so, yes. You pray for a miracle. But you will die. A blessing from Uncle won't change the fate of a taggle."

DK Vel regains his courage, "Then why bring us down here?"

Ilion turns without answering. The boys follow. When he speaks, again, he doesn't speak to them, "Sanbi, it's me, Ilion." They enter a small room to discover five women—four of them obviously pregnant. The fifth one holds a newborn child to her exposed breast. A taggle mother, yet the ears of the child show no mark. No scars. A pair of taggle ears incredibly untouched by the blade of an Adarian guard. Ilion leans down and kisses mother and child, "This is Beah, and his friend DK Vel. They're here to help. Boys, this is Sanbi." He runs his hand over the head of the baby, "And this is Lay-I, her unmarked daughter."

"I don't understand," Beah speaks the thoughts of both boys.

"Lay-I is your blessing. Deliver her to the Fire of the Sphere, and the Daughters of Oblation will raise her as their own, sparing her the life of a taggle."

DK Vel takes a step backward, "They'll kill us if we're caught!"

"You can't ask us to do this!" Beah protests.

"No. I can't ask you to do it. *You* must make this choice. But you must decide quickly," Ilion takes Lay-I from her mother, holding her in his arms as though…as though holding his own daughter, "Many taggles pray and hope the Sphere will remember them when they die, but when Uncle was still young, he decided he would give the Sphere a reason to remember him; something the Sphere could not possibly ignore. Since then, he has saved dozens of taggles, risking his life time and again without a second thought because he wanted to spare these newborns a terrible life. And the dallic now honors him. We know what he has done for our children. So, Beah, here's your blessing. Give Lay-I a different life, and the Sphere will remember you when you die. Trust me, it's the only blessing a taggle can ever hope to receive."

"No, you're wrong!" Beah points a thumb at himself, "I'm in the Adowian Army. The Sphere remembers everyone who serves the Adow."

"And you'll die as a nothing more than a taggle," Ilion says. "Whether you die in the Torment or risk your life for Lay-I, you'll still die."

"Maybe, but I won't die tonight. Not like this," Beah takes two steps back toward the tunnel.

"Did you come to the dallic for a blessing, or do you only seek to boast about your service to the one who causes our suffering?" Ilion shifts the baby, holding her against his chest.

"Enough! I won't do it."

Sanbi ignores both, turning instead to DK Vel, "Will you save my daughter?"

The taggle boy finds himself drawn in by the baby and her stupid scrambled mess of red hair and her angry-fisted tiny hands and her hope-filled green eyes, "Yes. Yes, I'll take her to the Fire."

"May the Sphere forgive your mother," she says.

"And remember my father," DK Vel replies. "So, how do I get there from here?"

Ilion stands to hand him the child, "This tunnel runs under the walls of Adarian. Once inside, simply head toward the Fire."

Beah stares at his friend, aghast, "Why would you do this? You won't make it. They'll catch you."

Undeterred, DK Vel takes Lay-I into his arms, "Show me the way."

"The night is no place for a taggle." DK Vel freezes, then slowly turns to find a magenta-colored horse and rider. In that instant, the girl in the dallic seems so plain and ordinary compared to the beauty of this creature. He feels somewhat guilty for thinking such a thought, but mostly he stands entranced. Fixated with her beauty. Paralyzed by fear. He attempts to say something, but his lips won't move. Lay-I lets out a cry, no doubt, sensing the danger to her chosen savior.

topi-Inindu slides off Inindu-horse to take the baby into her arms, "This is a yearling. Explain yourself, taggle."

"I served her mother," the boy manages, years of storytelling fueling his mind despite the lack of blood flow to his brain. "But she died just this night, and there is no one else to look after her. I'm taking her to the Fire of the Sphere. Please, she has no family. Let me go."

topi-Inindu holds the baby to her chest and begins to rub her back, "Does she have a name?"

"Lay-I."

She touches the baby's nose with her own nose, turning Lay-I's crying into a gurgling giggle. topi-Inindu repeats the action even as she remembers a time before Adarian's death. A time when Inindu, not some feeble warrior, served as caretaker of the Daughters of the Adow. But that was another time and place.

"I will take Lay-I to the Fire."

As Inindu suspected, the taggle boy runs away without a backward glance, confirming the attempted, and now successful, deception, "Tell me, Lay-I, how did you escape the dallic?" It doesn't matter. The taggles are Gan's problem. Why should she care if they want to sneak around the city? Inindu's never understood the Adow's curse upon the taggles, anyway, certainly not the forced mutilation of their ears. To that end, she inspects the baby's ears once more just to be certain, "An unmarked taggle girl..." The thought would infuriate the Adow. Inindu smiles, "All the more reason..."

She looks up toward the Adarian palace. Inside, the Adow mourns the death of Aiya. More specifically, she mourns the end of a decades-long masquerade—completely self-absorbed. Completely unaware of the world around her. Typical! Inindu touches the baby's nose again, "Yes, all the more reason!"

Inindu delivers Lay-I to the Fire of the Sphere, yet she stops short of entering the sanctuary herself. Instead, she leaves the baby with a Daughter of Oblation, and she promises to return...one day.

Moon	Seal
Completion of the Purple Moon	Floating Cr
Completion of the Purple Moon	Hemming T
Shadow of the Purple Moon	River under
Shadow of the Purple Moon	Sword throu
Completion of the Red Moon	Broken Cro
Completion of the Red Moon	Crown of L
Changing of the Silver Moon	Five Crown
Completion of the Yellow Moon	Sword with
Changing of the Blue Moon	Crowned W
Completion of the Green Moon	Crowned Ro
Completion of the Green Moon	Crowned Sw
Completion of the Green Moon	Crown over
Completion of the Green Moon	Two Crowns
Completion of the Green Moon	Crowned Bo
Completion of the Green Moon	Hammer Sta
Completion of the Green Moon	Sun Rising
Completion of the Green Moon	Crown betw
Dark Moon	Tiger and C

Months: Erog | Utine | Cil | Flatine | Joone   Date Format: (Gen

Periods: Year = 5 Months | Month = 5 Weeks | Week

The Adow

on, Official Seal, and Chosen First Etabli?

	First Etabli
...er Sphere	Erin, the First Etabli
...ove Crown	Anine
...r	Aul
...wn	Taggle, the cursed
	Ylaf
	Erbohn
	Ig-poy
...n on Hilt	Adarian, hero of Ire
	Fael
	Irloore
	Cintyge
...ed Swords	Lio
	Enyure
	Athoyen
...Crown	Ferya
...rown	Cidal
...words	Ayson, of Quel
	Ayson, of Quel

...ring the Red Moon | (Specific) Erog 23, Completion of the Red Moon 51

...ays | Day = 5 Hours = Spheric Hour | Hour = 300 Minutes

hen Troq died, I ran and hid. I cried for days. Then Faunride assumed Troq's role as my protector, so I attacked him. More than once, I beat him with my fists because he wasn't Troq. Faunride would stand there until I pulled away, all the more furious.

When my mother died, I stared at her body, waiting for her eyes to open, her lips to move—waiting for her to tell me what I should do now that they had anointed me Adow. Her body emitted an odor, the smell of death; strange I felt so repulsed by someone who looked so much like me—my reflection. Regardless, her bloodless face withdrew from the world. She lay dead. I transfixed upon her closed, translucent eyelids, waiting for them to open.

Now Aiya has died. I still live because of her, a strange comfort. No, beyond comfort…grateful. She alone gave her life to protect me. Yes, grateful. Horrified. Sad.

She's gone.

Beside me, Ayson snores. The skin of his wrinkled, bald head gathers against a green, silk pillow. My champion sleeps. Aiya lies dead and Ayson sleeps soundly as though nothing happened! I feel a sudden urge to kick him out of bed, but I get up, instead. Faunride stands guard outside the room. Somehow, I knew I would find him here.

"My Adow!" He bows.

I collapse into his arms, "Hold me."

For once, he does.

The next morning, Inindu awakens me by pouring a pitcher of water on my head.

"Tasa Ro!" I'm soaked.

"That takes care of your bath. Now let's get you into some different clothes."

Inindu disappears into the next room. Ayson still sleeps beside me.

This time, I do kick him. He sits up with a start, rubbing his face and trying to figure out what just happened. He looks at me with even more confusion. Inindu returns carrying a blue gown with silver inlay and a series of diamonds dangling from the waist. She tosses the gown at me.

"Why are you here?" I ask.

"I heard you needed a handmaiden." There is a knock on the door. Inindu opens it and takes a serving tray filled with apples from a taggle boy. She closes the door and begins to eat.

Watching Inindu move about the room, watching her talk and gesture, both topi and horse, it's…it's too early in the morning for this nonsense! And I'm soaked!

"Why are you all wet?" Ayson finally notices.

Inindu lies down next to the door, "I gave her a bath."

I pull myself out of bed. My hair sticks to my face. Water drips from my chin, "You're a horribly rotten handmaiden."

"You're not much of an Adow," Inindu devours another apple.

"Who *are* you?" I suddenly realize just how little I know about this magenta goddess. First creature created by the Sphere. Eternal. The whole Adarian dying thing…her tragic love affair. That's it. Troq didn't tell me anything about her, really. Certainly nothing about *this*! "Let me tell you who you are. You're this mythical creature that everyone feels sorry for, and everyone pampers because you've lost your lover. So, what? That gives you the right to judge me? Aiya's dead! My mother is dead—in fact, everyone is dead except him!" I point toward Ayson.

"Hmm…that would solve a lot of problems, wouldn't it?" Something about her tone is frightening, as though she has already plotted Ayson's death.

"She's the one who should have raised you," Ayson retrieves a knife from under his pillow, tosses it to the foot of the bed. "I'm yours to kill, Inindu."

"Why is that your answer to everything?" It's way too early for this! Wait! "What does he mean, *you* should have raised me?"

Inindu bites into another apple.

"She used to raise the Daughters of the Adow," Ayson climbs out of bed and walks to where his armor leans against the wall. He grabs his sword and flings it toward Inindu, "Maybe you'd prefer a sword?"

Tasa Ro! I drop the gown, pick up his sword, and heave it across the room, "If you want someone to kill you, then go find an assassin!"

"She is an assassin!" Ayson retorts.

"*What?*"

Inindu offers me an apple with a coy grin, "A taggle's tale. Completely untrue."

"Seriously, who are you?"

Inindu shrugs and bites into the last of the apples. I'm racing through every ounce of information Troq ever told me about her. He didn't tell me anything about her being an assassin!

Faunride cracks the door, "Is everything alright, First Etabli?"

"We're fine," Ayson replies coolly.

Faunride hesitates, making eye contact with me before finally closing the door.

"I'm your eternal sister, my Adow," Inindu stands, horse and topi rising together, their combined presence a sudden force against which I find myself contending. She picks up the gown and holds it against my shoulder, apparently, intending for me to take it from her, "I trust you know how to dress yourself?"

In truth, I've never dressed myself, but I'll be damned if I'm going to admit that to Inindu just now. I grab the gown and head into the bathing room, slamming the door behind me. *What just happened?* I collapse in a fury, strands of wet hair sliding slowly down my neck and cheeks. I turn the gown over in my hands attempting to find the buttons.

An hour later, I'm sitting in front of my vanity while Inindu runs a brush through my hair as though hacking through a forest, "Ouch!"

"Every Adow has the same knotted hair."

"You don't have to be so rough. Ouch!"

"I stopped being gentle after the third Adow. It's better for both of us if I just rip through it."

"What was she like? The third Adow. Did you raise her?" She who reigned during the time when Aul served as First Etabli. I don't know anything about her. What were any of the Adow like? Did Inindu raise them all? Adarian's death must have driven her away from the Adow, leaving me with Troq and Faunride. Inindu stops brushing and I turn to face her before she can start again. I'm certain my head is now bleeding.

Inindu looks into my eyes as though seeking remnants of the third Adow's spirit behind my own. *Is she there, Inindu? Do you see her?* Ayson, sitting on the bed and dressed in full armor, leans forward to hear Inindu's response.

"She loved to dance," Inindu turns me back around and cuts into my hair with the brush. "You remind me of her in the way you danced last night."

Last night…last night felt incredible…and then… "I don't want to talk about last night. Ouch!"

"She was a quiet Adow. She kept her bedroom filled with Nelic Stems. They smell like smoke, but for whatever reason that was her favorite flower. She told me once their scent reminded her of our father…she was the last Adow to have ever seen the Sphere."

"Wait! She *saw* the Sphere?" I turn again and take the brush from her. If she saw the Sphere, she must have spoken with Him.

"She told me she did, and the two Adow before her."

"Have you ever seen the Sphere? What does he look like?"

"Our Father and I have never exactly…gotten along," Inindu takes the brush back and begins anew. "Don't you keep a taggle around to tell her these ancient stories, Ayson?"

"Haven't you heard?" Ayson asks. "The Adow cursed the taggles. They get a little nervous whenever she's around."

"I didn't know taggles told stories," I've never even heard a taggle speak, let alone tell a story.

Inindu turns me around. I guess there's no more hair for her to yank out, "You're a poor excuse for an Adow."

"And you're no handmaiden," I run my fingers over my throbbing head.

Faunride enters the room with a bow, "The preparations are ready, First Etabli. Aiya's Final Cleansing will begin upon your arrival."

Aiya is dead.

I take and hide the brush in a vanity drawer. I look in the mirror. Aiya looked like me. My mother looked like me, too. Now they're both dead. I touch the blue velvet of my gown, trace the intricate embroidery around the neckline.

I see Faunride watching me in the mirror. Our eyes meet for a moment before he turns away. That's the second time in one morning he has looked me in the eye. Faunride. The guard who insists upon formalities! My Faunride! And last night, he willingly held me…

"So, tell me, Ayson," Inindu exits the room ahead of us. "Have you ever died protecting your Adow?"

Assassin or not, there is much to like about my sister, and much to learn.

5-RUBY
SPECIAL EDITION

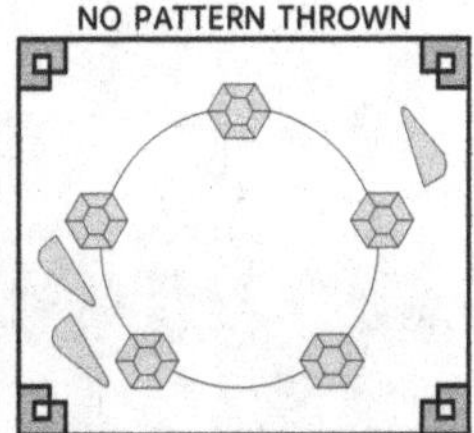

NO PATTERN THROWN

a taggle's tale

As told by a taggle man who traveled with three warriors from Catareb, making it the first known instance of a taggle tale spoken while in motion, or rather, without the benefit of a stage. The warriors kept the taggle's hands tied, a common practice, these days. He struggled to breathe as the result of a previous day's beating, but he told his tale with every ounce of strength he possessed and, by all accounts, as told by those taggles who traveled with him, these are the last words uttered by the man. His name was Phire. I met a boy named Phire in Lor. Eager to hear my tales, he spent several months following me everywhere I went. I told this same tale often, in those days, leading me to believe the boy and the man were the same.

I implore you, speak his name. Speak of Phire, for he spoke in the manner of all taggles. He told stories, and his words still linger. He lived and we heard his voice. May the Sphere forgive our mother and remember our father.

- DK Vel

ingle-level, square clay buildings fill the inner city of Adarian, otherwise known as Chance. Doors and window frames display vibrant colors in shades of blue, red, yellow, or green. The rooftops of each building serve as a collective culinary marketplace. Under the roofs, taverns provide visitors various games of chance and strategy, or if they prefer, rooms for lovemaking. Though many topis visit this part of Adarian, only a few actually inhabit the area. Scholars have long believed the town somehow ensnared in the struggle between the Sphere and Morlac. They say it offers Morlac his only connection to the land. That is what the Scholars say.

Maldinado calls it home.

His sister, Nataline, and her two daughters live here, the only home he cares to visit since their father's murder. As for their mother, Breline— now a Daughter of Oblation—she resides at the Fire of the Sphere. She made a vow, after losing her husband, that she would never leave the four walls of the sanctuary. She has kept her vow. So, Maldinado visits her whenever he returns to Adarian, but he makes his bed at his sister's home.

He sits on the edge of this bed, holding his head between his hands. He can hear Hintor and Nataline murmuring in the kitchen as the smell of sausage and warm breakfast rolls waft in the morning air. No doubt, the yearlings still lie asleep, but they will wake soon enough.

The Madar stands to look out the window. Mornings in Chance typically pass quietly, but that, too, will change. Aiya's final cleansing will occur later today, and after the ritual burning of her body at the Fire of the Sphere, most of the gathered crowd will journey to Chance for a celebration. The Adow, too. He touches his lips. He scratches at his beard.

He kissed her.

A smile cracks through his black whiskers, "Tasa Ro! I kissed her."

Maldinado watches two taggle boys move down the empty street. Chance used to house a collection of the dead and diseased, before Gan transformed the inner city. Now the bones of the dead serve as ornamental pieces seemingly displayed throughout the inner-city: Skulls, used like vases, showcase multi-colored flowers. Full-size skeletons stand guard, dressed in bright colors and skillfully posed in oddly unnatural positions. Bones fashioned into wind instruments. Bone furniture. Bleached bones and painted bones dominate the colorful sculptures of Chance, eschewing the traditional marble-gray of Adarian architecture.

"I kissed her!" Maldinado mutters.

DK Vel and Beah pass by the home of Nataline, the former visiting Chance for the first time. The wonderful colors remind him of the beautiful creature who took Lay-I from him: Inindu. Beah told him stories about Inindu when he returned to the dallic that night.

"Maybe seeing Inindu was my blessing," DK Vel jumps up onto an ankle high marble ledge that encircles a display of painted skeleton warriors, all of them posed as though dancing.

"Your blessing was that you survived," Beah follows behind his friend as they complete the circle. Then they continue their journey, "I didn't think I'd ever see you again. I told Ilion as much, but he said you would return."

"I've never been so scared in my life."

Inindu enters the inner city. Her lover, so often the subject of Beaug's work, does not dwell amongst the skeletal sculptures of Chance. She can find no sign of him. No reference. If Adarian's likeness exists here, it remains unknown or unnamed, for the inner city does not celebrate a single death. They celebrate death, itself, and all who have died. As such, they always have a reason to celebrate in Chance. As for Inindu, she arrived early for the celebration, and just in time to avoid the requisite visit to the Fire of the Sphere. Indeed, she refuses to enter the Sphere's dwelling place. Let the Adow and her First Etabli tend to Aiya's burning ceremony.

Music rises from a side street, drawing her toward the sound of happiness. Adarian loved music and dancing. He loved watching *her* dance. Inindu holds her magenta hair against her nose. So long ago. His scent has nearly faded. Once, her lover's enduring essence smelled strong like lilac or warm honey, but now, even a peeled potato floating in cold broth would overwhelm what remains. She misses him, but she knows he will return to her one day. He promised. He promised her he would return.

She enters a large square where hundreds of Adarians dance in a flurry of brightly colored gowns and gyrating instruments, a pleasing and welcome noise. Once, Inindu helped Gan transform Chance. She lived here during the Completion of the Red Moon, and again during the Changing of the Silver Moon. Yes, she walked these streets and she danced here. Nothing has changed. She remembers this song and this dance, and the music still consumes her.

In this same area, in the same square, an assassin enters one of a dozen overflowing taverns. He orders beer and sits down at a crowded table, one laden with fruit, meat, bread, and cheese—and several of the most amazing breakfast rolls he has ever tasted. Streamers hang from the ceiling. Confetti litters the floor, piled against the walls and bar. He takes a drink and waits for a scarlet to approach him. When she does, he follows her upstairs.

The unoccupied room contains a single bed. No sheet or pillow. No invitation to stay overnight. The scarlet starts to undress before the assassin closes the door. Afterward, she leaves the room with a jingle of coins. Behind her, the assassin lies naked on the bed. He listens to her fondle his gold until it fades into the broader sounds of the tavern. Sounds of merriment. So much laughter and chatter. He wonders if he should stay in Chance and live a different kind of life. Eventually, driven by a craving for more breakfast rolls, he gets dressed and heads downstairs.

On the rooftop above, Maldinado and Hintor oversee a yearling's game of *Blind Goat*. Kaletine and Belur take turns wearing the necessary blindfold. Hintor spins them around one or two or three too many times before setting loose in a mostly staggering, often failed, attempt to retrieve a blue ribbon from Maldinado which they must then tie around a goat's neck all while maintaining their balance. For the sake of the yearlings, Hintor and Maldinado have altered the rules as compared to the version they normally play. Warriors of the Adarian 45th don't use ribbons, they throw knives. Once killed, they cook and serve the goat with a hearty toast to the proud champion.

"I'm getting hungry," Hintor pulls a knife from his boot. "Perhaps I should go next?"

"Don't you dare kill Silar!" Belur runs to embrace the goat, "She's the only goat we have!"

Kaletine lifts her blindfold, "Uncle Hintor!"

But Maldinado wraps her with the blue ribbon to keep her from charging at her uncle, "Mmm…I bet your mother could fix us a nice stew when she gets back."

Both yearlings, falling headfirst into the ruse, burst into tears, horrified by the thought of eating their animal friend. Realizing their mistake, too late, Maldinado and Hintor do their best to then console the yearlings, insisting they only meant it in jest. Still, it takes several minutes to calm them down and a promise to never again force Belur and Kaletine to play such a cruel game.

DK Vel watches all of this unfold while he holds the goat. With the game now over, the taggle boy returns to his perch atop the tavern balcony where he and Beah can watch the scene in the street below. There, he finds fear and wonder. He sees Inindu dancing.

The crowd surrounds her. The music seemingly absorbs her…absorbs the two taggle boys, too. topi-Inindu moves over and under and around Inindu-horse. She lies back over back, slides up to the neck. Hair and mane blend together as one. topi-Inindu wraps her arms around Inindu-horse's neck and swings down to the ground, falling like a banner lowered after battle. She continues to her knees, prostrating before Inindu-horse. Then she rolls to embrace Inindu-horse's back leg. She rises and ducks and twirls and falls, but Inindu-horse doesn't move—as though a god and topi-Inindu the devotee.

DK Vel and Beah watch wide-eyed as Inindu then falls out of her white gown. Oblivious, or unconcerned, topi-Inindu raises her arms and wrapping them around Inindu-horse. The boys lean forward with adolescent lust and innocent curiosity. She is completely naked! The street moves with life, a wave of sensual dancing and unhindered jumping and chaotic movement. Some of the dancers match the rhythm of the song and some don't—but everyone moves. And, well, Inindu is naked!

She looks up toward the boys, making eye contact with them, if only for a second. Did she notice them staring? DK Vel quickly turns away in embarrassment. He taps Beah on the shoulder and motions for him to follow, but his friend doesn't leave. Beah stands mesmerized by the scene in the courtyard below. DK Vel sneaks another peek. A moment later, he again stands and stares.

Behind the taggle, Kaletine and Belur, goat closely in tow and now escorted by their mother, descend the stairs to the tavern below. Nataline has returned from her morning deliveries to various taverns around

Chance.

Maldinado, no longer tasked with looking after the yearlings, scans the rooftops, "This is where the Adow will come. If the assassin is still in the city, this is where he'll strike."

"I doubt it. He'll be too distracted by Inindu," Hintor points.

The assassin, however, does not watch Inindu. He sits in the tavern below eating his fourth breakfast roll. He listens for a distinctive stirring in the crowd that will signal the Adow's arrival. His has a simple plan: Maneuver through the crowd until he finds himself dancing alongside the Adow—then kill her.

He watches as two yearlings leave the tavern along with their mother who holds a rope tied to the goat behind her. He orders another beer and one more breakfast roll. Two bites later, a cheer rises in the street. Morlac has blessed this assassin. He leaves the tavern and shoulders his way into the street.

"I never knew such a place existed," the Adow says.

"Adarian is full of secrets," Ayson feels nervous. Even with the Adowian Guard spread throughout the crowd, and with Faunride beside him…how can he possibly protect her in this crowd, "This is a bad idea. We should head back to the palace."

"I agree, First Etabli," Faunride walks ahead of them, struggling to clear a path.

Confetti covers the sky, thrown from every nearby rooftop as the Adow moves through the street. Ribbons. Sweets. Beads. What they don't toss at her, they perch on poles. Skulls. Melons. They bob above the crowd as though heads of giants. Shouts merge with the joyful screams of hundreds of Adarians.

The Adow begins to move in rhythm with the music and joy, "We can't leave yet. Where's Inindu?"

"She'll be in the center of the square, no doubt," Ayson sighs.

"Lead the way, Faunride!"

Maldinado curses, "Furmec Ro! He could hide anywhere in this lot!"

"Any one of them could be an assassin," Hintor agrees. He points to the crowd now gathered around them on the rooftop, "In fact, we could be standing next to one." Little Birty, less than two feet away, dances with a scarlet and appears altogether too engaged in the effort, "Well, maybe not him."

"Look, she's here," Maldinado watches as the Adow enters the square. She's beautiful even from this distance. His lips begin to tingle, recalling the taste of her kiss, "May the Sphere be with her."

"And keep her in his light." Hintor looks along the rooftop to where DK Vel and Beah still stare at Inindu, "Taggle! Two beers!"

DK Vel jumps at the command. He pulls Beah with him as they disappear into the tavern below.

"I've never seen anything like that," Beah sounds breathless.

"We'll never see it again if we don't pay attention," DK Vel responds. "The Adarians didn't bring us here to stare at naked topis." He takes two beers from the bar counter where another thirty sit filled and waiting, "She *is* beautiful, though."

"Taggle!" Another patron yells.

DK Vel hands both mugs to Beah, "Take these. I'll take care of him." The taggle moves toward the patron…

…even as the assassin moves closer to his target, nimbly maneuvering through the square and the jostling crowd. His hand rests on the knife at his side…

…while Ayson holds the Adow against his chest, one arm around her waist. He shoves his way through the crowd, perhaps a bit more forcefully than he should, but better than the alternative. Too many Adarians have tried to dance with her—all of them drunk and carelessly risking their lives! Faunride leads the way to Inindu only to then turn with embarrassment when he finally finds her. Ayson, too, looks away. Around them, some stare, others sway along.

The assassin stares.

"You're a wonderful dancer, Inindu," the Adow grins.

"How was the burning ceremony?"

"The decorations were nice. Aiya would have been pleased."

"Do you plan to stand there all night, or are you going to dance?"

The Adow looks down at her blue gown, gathering it in her hands, "It's such a nice gown. I think I'll keep it on a bit longer." She bends to grab Inindu's white gown, and then tosses it toward her not unkindly, "I trust you know how to dress yourself? I'll need you before dinner. Don't stay too long."

Inindu lets the gown fall.

"Ayson, I think we've stayed long enough," the Adow whirls and follows her First Etabli through the crowd...

...and the assassin follows the Adow. Unknown. Unseen.

a taggle's tale

As spoken by a taggle boy in the middle of a field north of Adarian. A great deal of wind forced the boy to contend with the rustling bloodgrass, but he proved the master of his voice. His booming, powerful telling captured the audience in a manner that kept their attention. They formed a circle around him, but rarely did he turn his back on any of them for too long, for he paced the entire radius. He stood tall for his age; his face darkened by a spattering of hair not yet turned into whiskers. His name was Beah, my friend.

I implore you, speak his name. Speak of Beah, for he spoke in the manner of all taggles. He told stories, and his words still linger. He lived and we heard his voice. May the Sphere forgive our mother and remember our father.

- DK Vel

"She can't do this!" Hintor raises his arms in a helpless plea, "What about the yearlings?" He stands to pace the kitchen.

"She's the Adow. She can do whatever she wants," Nataline calmly sips a cup of ginger tea. "The yearlings will stay with my mother."

Maldinado, leaning against the door frame with his arms folded, suddenly shakes his head, "No! I won't allow it."

"It isn't your decision to make, Maldinado. You've said yourself I'm the best cook in Adarian. Apparently, the Adow agrees. Besides, we could use the money. You can't support us forever."

"He doesn't have to support you. I'll send you everything I have," Hintor returns to his chair at the table. Then he leans forward with an idea, "Marry me! We'll move to Plenrid and take over my father's farm."

Nataline puts her cup onto the table, "Now is not the time to speak of marriage."

"I forbid it! I don't want you anywhere near Dragon's Torment," Maldinado says.

"Me too!" Hintor affirms.

"Forbid? Do you think I didn't forbid Kanbis from dying? Do you think wives throughout Adarian don't forbid their husbands from going off to war? But do we say anything? No, we line the streets to say goodbye with a cheer. We hold our husbands as they die in our arms. We tell our yearlings it will be alright."

Nataline stands to retrieve the teapot from an orange-tinted clay oven, wipes the tears from her eyes. She looks around at the brass pots, wooden spoons, cast iron pans…the jars of various spices, bags of flour, sugar—her knives hanging from hooks on the wall. She'll have to pack all of it including the cutting board Kanbis made her for their first anniversary, ragged with splinters around the edges. Her tin measuring cups, dented and deformed. She could use a new set, but it would throw off her measures. The set of bowls Kanbis brought back from Yenul…she wipes her cheeks, settles her gaze once more upon the two warriors who have forbidden her to cook for the Adow. *Forbidden*! *Her*!

"I can't protect you and the Adow!" Maldinado says.

"You're afraid I won't come back? Do you think death is something you can forbid? Whether I'm here or there, you can't control my fate," Nataline replies.

"I'll protect her," Hintor says. "You worry about the Adow."

"You won't have to," Maldinado leaves the kitchen. He walks outside past a laughing, hunchbacked skeleton; through the streets of Chance; and straight toward the palace of Adarian. *She can't do this*!

Faunride enters the room with a bow, "First Etabli." Ayson reads in one corner. Inindu and the Adow sit near the bed. "The Madar of the Adarian 45th requests an audience with his Adow."

"Come for another kiss, no doubt," Inindu fidgets with the buttons at the back of the Adow's red gown.

"Let him through, Faunride," the Adow responds.

"My Adow," Faunride bows out of the room.

Ayson grabs his sword from the table and moves toward the door. A moment later, Maldinado enters and kneels, his eyes finding the Adow with her back turned to him. The Madar's look does not go unnoticed by the First Etabli who stands over him. He could rightfully kill the Madar for touching the Adow—for kissing her.

"You're interrupting my preparations, Madar," the Adow says without turning around.

Maldinado stands, "Forgive me, my Adow. It's about your cook. There's been a mistake."

Inindu starts combing the Adow's hair, but the Adow turns and grabs the brush. Inindu shrugs and moves to the window. "I fired the cook, didn't I?" The Adow moves the brush gently through her hair.

"Teyo has found a new one, my Adow," Ayson replies.

"My sister," Maldinado waits for the Adow to make eye contact, but she doesn't look at him. "She has two yearlings."

The Adow finally does meet his gaze, but he finds no warmth in them, "Her family status does not concern me, Madar. Your sister will serve me. We have nothing more to discuss."

"You can't..."

Ayson gestures with his sword, "You may leave now."

Maldinado stares at the Adow a moment longer. The Greeting Feast feels like a distant memory. The Toast of Sark—her kiss. Clearly, they meant nothing to her. "My Adow," he bows and turns.

"Oh, there is another matter," the Adow beckons him back. "We leave for Dragon's Torment at dawn. Gather your warriors and report to Faunride. The Adarian 45th will serve as an extension of my Guard. If we encounter dangers in the Torment, you will be the first to face them. I believe that was your request, was it not?"

"The Adarian 45th is honored," Maldinado closes the door behind him as he leaves.

"Nicely done," Inindu says. "You can put your sword away now, Ayson. Our Adow won't need your services. It seems she has a new sword to play with."

DK Vel and Beah follow Maldinado, Hintor, Nataline, and her yearlings up the steps to the Fire of the Sphere. Behind them, wet streets reflect flames from the large fire atop the sanctuary. The Fire of the Sphere. Even as early morning brightens the city around them, DK Vel wonders if Lay-I survived. Did she find a better life? Inside the Fire they find two hallways that lead to a series of rooms on either side of an inner sanctum. Maldinado leads them to the left, where his mother resides along with the rest of the Daughters of Oblation—separated from the Sons of Oblation to the right. He reaches the iron gate and speaks to the Daughter who approaches.

"We're here to see Breline. I'm her son."

"One moment."

The Daughter of Oblation disappears around the curved hallway. DK Vel looks up at the towering ceiling, with its painted panels depicting scenes of creation, battle, and death. Most of them prominently display the Adow or the First Etabli, but some of the scenes originated from the painter's imagination. Torches line the hallway, shifting light and shadow across each panel, providing the illusion of movement within each painted scene. One of these scenes captures Adarian's death at the Battle of Ire. The Adow holds his body in a traditional representation, but in the smoke behind them DK Vel discovers a dark pink image the painter has all but concealed within the chaos of battle. There is no mistaking that image, or who it represents. Inindu stands in the shadows same as when the boy first met her in the streets of Adarian. When she took Lay-I from him.

The iron gate opens and Breline emerges wearing a white robe and golden sash. In her arms she carries a bundle of blankets wrapped around a baby. Kaletine and Belur run to greet their grandmother and the newborn. Breline squats down so the yearlings can get a better look, "The Father of Oblation gave her to me. I suppose that makes her your aunt."

She made it! DK Vel elbows Beah, but he doesn't have to tell him about Lay-I. He can see her for himself.

Maldinado and Nataline keep their distance, delaying their goodbyes, knowing their mother will cry. Breline looks up at them both with a look of resigned disapproval. Then she turns to Hintor, "I suppose you intend to leave me as well?"

Hintor nods, "Someone has to look after these two."

Breline passes Lay-I off to Kaletine, "Gentle now. Hold her head like this," she guides the yearling's arms until satisfied with the resulting cradle. Then she walks over to Hintor and gives him a hug.

"May the Sphere protect you, Hintor."

"And keep you in his light."

She wipes the tears already streaming down her cheeks and turns to Nataline, "It isn't enough that I give my son to the Adow—now she takes my daughter, as well?" Nataline falls into her mother's arms. They exchange no words, their combined tears communicating everything they have to say to one another. Finally, Breline lifts her daughter's chin and gives her a kiss on the forehead. Then Belur is hugging her mommy's leg. Nataline picks up her daughter and together they join Kaletine, who stands holding Lay-I. Nataline embraces both of her daughters even as Breline embraces her son.

"Protect her," Breline whispers.

Maldinado holds her head against his chest, kisses her hair, "I will."

5-RUBY
SPECIAL EDITION
NO PATTERN THROWN

This tale originated in the Adarian dallic, first told during the Great Snow, as a warning to those who would seek the comforts of this life rather than devote their lives to the Sphere, for many taggles died in those days. According to Adarian tradition, Dsal Tiger has a short tail and black-striped, orange fur except for the patches of white around three of his paws.

I heard this tale from Beah's Uncle Taggle. Listen to these warnings and let Dsal Tiger guide you to the Sphere.

- DK Vel

Dsal Tiger

Dsal Tiger walks the streets of Adarian. Snow falls around him, gathering on his back and making him cold. He searches for fire that he might warm his paws and thaw his frozen whiskers, but the empty streets offer him no fire. Only statues.

Dsal Tiger stops at the base of a marble tree, "Do you have any fire?"

The marble tree shakes its limbs, sending a torrent of snow downward, "I do not have fire. My wood does not burn."

Dsal Tiger paws longingly at the cold and lifeless tree. He lowers his head and leaves the marble tree. No one else walks the streets of Adarian. The snow quickly conceals his footprints, hiding his traveled path; and the blinding storm blinds him to his path ahead, leaving him to wander from one side of the street to the other, never walking in a straight line.

Then Dsal Tiger stumbles onto a marble river, "Do you have any fire?"

"I do not have fire," the marble river says, "for we parted long ago and have gone our separate ways."

Dsal Tiger again lowers his head in sadness. He tests the marble waters, but the surface has frozen over. His paws grow numb. He has lost much of his strength. So, he leaves the river in search of fire. There, in the distance, he sees a marble flame. He manages to navigate the storm. Forcefully taking every step until he stands nearly frozen beneath the fire, "Do you have any fire?"

The marble flame wavers in the howling wind, "I am the flame that burns forever. I *am* fire."

Dsal Tiger encircles the flame, searching for the perfect spot to lie down, eventually choosing to curl up at the base of the statue. Though the marble flame offers no warmth, Dsal Tiger doesn't move. He has found his fire. He closes his eyes and slowly freezes to death.

5-RUBY
SPECIAL EDITION

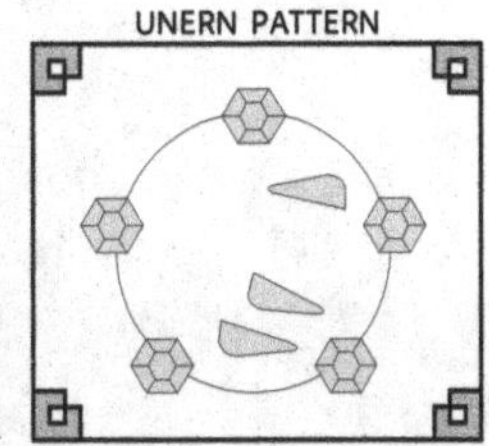

DRAGON'S TORMENT

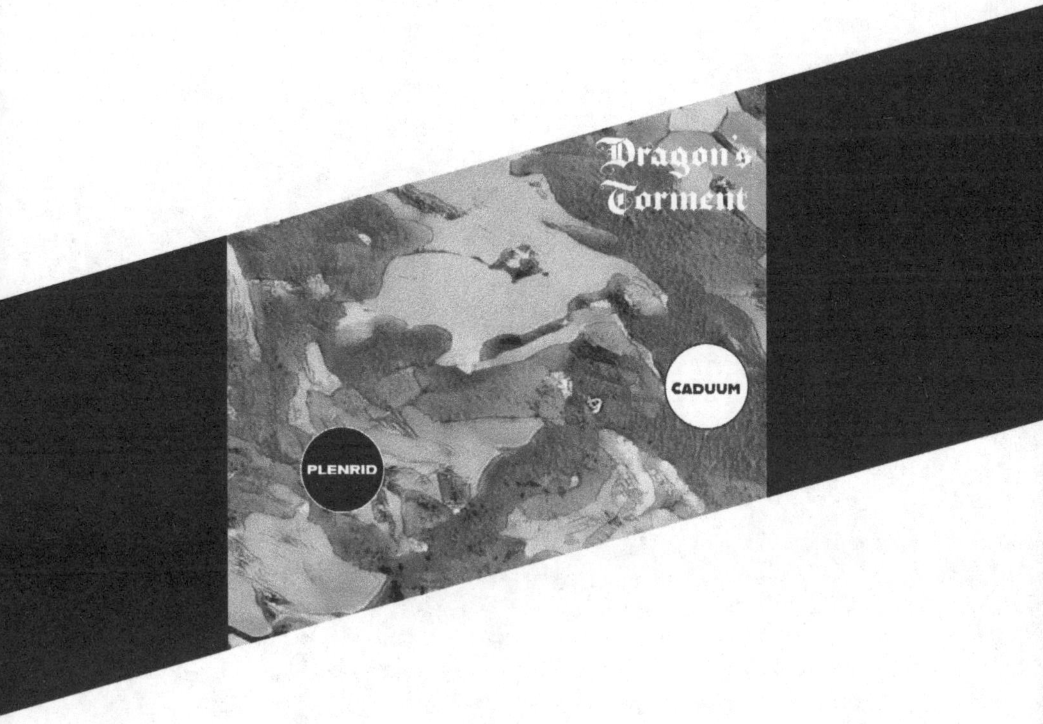

he wind started when the Rorne tribes disappeared. I was not yet fully grown, but old enough to travel with my father for the first time. We sat in the wagon he had filled with crates of plums, red grapes, rhubarb; sacks of potatoes and onions; a chest full of fashionable jewelry and several articles of clothing my mother had sewn. I felt anxious and believed what my friends told me, thus I expected to see wild-haired tribesman mounted on monsters from the shadows. Instead, we stopped in a quiet meadow with enough balor trees to provide shade, but not enough to hide the approach of either party. My father, one of eleven tradesman who waited in the meadow that day, hoped to return with a haul of furs and salted meat. We arrived during the early morning hours on the designated date. When midday turned to evening, we made camp. Still, we waited. After dinner, I heard the first rustling of leaves. As night fell, I felt the force of the wind imploring us to leave. We stayed two more days, but the Rorne tribes never appeared, and we could no longer stand against the wind. We left one tradesman behind, but he never returned. We sent two more tradesmen. They, too, went missing. Finally, we stopped traveling to Dragon's Torment. But the wind never ceased.

from The Known and Unknown History of Dragon's Torment

a taggle's tale

As spoken by a taggle boy in Dragon's Torment at dusk. He climbed onto a boulder and stood high above all the other taggles who had gathered to hear his tale. As we gazed up toward him, we marveled at how clear the night sky seemed, and how many stars we could see. The taggle boy paused for a noticeable length of time before beginning his tale. In contrast to his red hair, which glimmered at the edges, darkness concealed his face. Indeed, he had climbed high enough above us that the fading back-light of the sky cast his whole body into shadow. In this manner, he allowed the wonder of the moment to transform into horror, quite effectively enhancing his tale before ever speaking a word. His name was Edran, Hiate's apprentice.

I implore you, speak his name. Speak of Edran, for he spoke in the manner of all taggles. He told stories, and his words still linger. He lived and we heard his voice. May the Sphere forgive our mother and remember our father.

- DK Vel

$\mathcal{C}$aduum serves as the entrance to Dragon's Torment. It began as a trading post for the Rorne tribes, but the Rorne have not journeyed to Caduum since the Completion of the Yellow Moon. The buildings, neglected and battered by the winds out of the Torment, have begun to lean and crumble, some of the buildings collapsing completely. Rubble in the wind. Nobody cares because nobody travels to Caduum, anymore. Only those born here remain in the town, and they don't dare wander the streets. Instead, they reinforce their walls and hide behind locked doors. They stare out their windows at the ghost-like images that haunt this dying town.

Hiate the blacksmith fixes on an approaching figure. His apprentice, Edran, shakes with fear.

"'Tis the wraith of yer father come to fetch you, boy," Hiate teases. He looks at his apprentice who stands slightly in front of him, holding a mostly fashioned sword with both hands. "Wraiths won't be bothered with weapons. Yer sword be more useful on an anvil this night," The blacksmith looks back to the street. Blown dirt and brush swirl in the air, creating imaginary figures and shadows in the night—probably nothing, "Seems he's left us, yearling. Come back to the forge. We have swords to fashion for the Adow and her Army."

Still, the red-bearded blacksmith peers out into the street and whispers, "And pray yer father has forgotten about you."

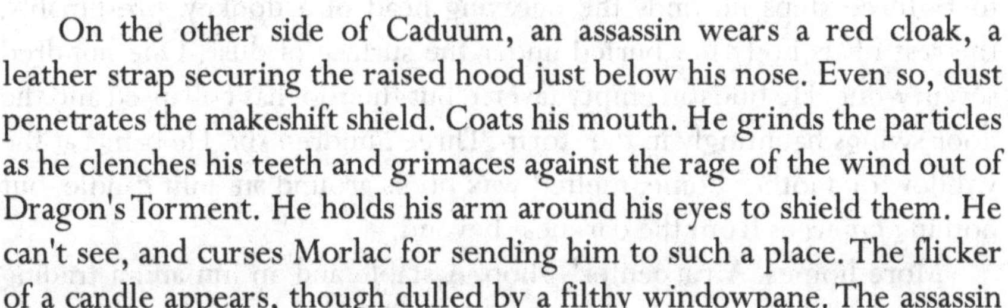

On the other side of Caduum, an assassin wears a red cloak, a leather strap securing the raised hood just below his nose. Even so, dust penetrates the makeshift shield. Coats his mouth. He grinds the particles as he clenches his teeth and grimaces against the rage of the wind out of Dragon's Torment. He holds his arm around his eyes to shield them. He can't see, and curses Morlac for sending him to such a place. The flicker of a candle appears, though dulled by a filthy windowpane. The assassin dismounts and leads his horse toward the light until it vanishes.

Another light. He walks toward it until he stands looking through a six-pane window. The hood of his cloak gathers against the glass, forming a barrier from the wind, providing his bloodshot eyes with some welcome relief. He searches for signs of life. Someone appears from an inner room wearing a white gown, black hair hangs loosely about her shoulders. In her hand she holds a silver brush with wilting bristles, and as she reaches for the candle the assassin notes a small, milky-white birthmark on her forearm. Then their eyes meet. She doesn't scream. She stares at him as though faced with a vague memory. The assassin leaves the window in search of a door, but he finds the wooden entrance reinforced by iron, made to stand against the winds of the Torment. He knocks, but his pounding fails to illicit a response. Nothing more than a whisper in the storm. He returns to the window only to find darkness.

Frustrated, he turns and leads his horse down the street until he hears the sound of wood splitting, followed by the terrible cackle of a shattering building. He flinches, deftly moving away from the sound. The horse yanks against the reins he holds, pulling away and running away.

"Tasa Ro!" He rubs his now rope-burned hand.

Another light flickers to reveal an old topi behind an older window. Short, white hair protrudes from his head in erratic clumps. His throat looks about the size of his nose. His eyes look past the assassin into the hardly visible streets of Caduum beyond. The assassin waves, hoping to garner his attention, but the old topi fails to notice. Never turns his head. The assassin follows his gaze, but he finds nothing in the street behind him. He turns back to the old topi, motioning once more, but ultimately, he can detect no change in the topi's demeanor.

The assassin leaves him to his visions. No other lights appear. No more signs of life. The wind howls around him. Caduum all but disappears in a storm of dust, leaving him disoriented, so he counts his steps. At thirty-two steps the remains of a wooden cart force him to step to the left. At forty-three steps he finds the decaying head of a donkey, presumably, the rest of its body lies buried under the surface of dust. One hundred seventy-one. He finds an empty tavern, but the roof has collapsed and the door swings hauntingly in the storm. Three hundred six. He bangs at the window of another home, melted wax pools around an unlit candle, but nothing emerges from the darkness beyond.

More homes. A carpenter's shop. A stable and an inn and a trading post—all of them destroyed by the wind. Then he notices the glow of a forge, hears the pinging of a blacksmith's sledge. The workshop appears undaunted by the wind, made from stone piled atop stone and reinforced by wide strips of wrought iron. It has several holes for windows, but no glass, allowing the wind to flow freely through multiple openings and providing ventilation for the forge. It also has an entrance…and no door.

The assassin enters and waits just inside the shop. He watches the blacksmith draw out the rough shape of a sword, lengthening the metal with the peen of his hammer, raising and lowering the hammer in smooth, even strokes. A full beard matches the thick red hair he has pulled tight behind him. His muscular frame carries the weight of his extensive—and expanding—waist. A taggle boy with identical red hair kneels behind him, taking inventory of a pile of seemingly already-completed swords.

"Eighteen," the boy announces confidently.

Hiate doesn't stop hammering, "Fetch me more Dragon's ore." The taggle leaves just as Hiate notices the assassin, "You'll not find what yer seeking here, demon. The Torment be the only comfort for you." Hiate continues to hammer, keeping one eye on the assassin.

"There is nowhere else to go," the assassin raises both hands to reveal empty palms, suggesting he presents no danger to the blacksmith. "I've searched the entire town. No one would open their door."

Hiate stops hammering, "There's no door can keep the wraiths away. You be no demon."

"No, and I'm not a wraith, either," he removes the strap from around his cowl, allowing it to fall and revealing a mask of dirt around his eyes.

The blacksmith measures the assassin, "Have you any scars?"

The assassin smiles, "Is that how you greet everyone?"

Hiate sets the hammer on the anvil and pulls up his left sleeve to reveal a scar that wraps around his forearm near the elbow, "'Tis the only way to prove yer still alive in Caduum. When wraiths appear, they be missing all former scars."

The assassin reveals a scar on his right leg, "A Catareb tavern…I was young and mostly drunk."

The taggle boy reappears from a back room, carrying an armload of Dragon's ore. His red hair hangs loose and gathers at his shoulders. When he sees the assassin, he drops the ore, fetches a sword, and charges. The assassin quickly unsheathes his own sword, but Hiate moves to block the taggle's path.

"Calm yerself, Edran," Hiate reaches out and pulls the sword from the taggle's hand. "'Tis flesh and blood before you."

Edran stops, "Have you any scars?"

Hiate pats the boy on the head, "We've already discussed such matters, boy. Go, fetch broth and beer. 'Tis a more pleasant way to spend the evening than swordplay."

Edran leaves and the assassin sheathes his sword, "Where I come from, taggles are killed for such behavior."

"No doubt we'll all die soon enough. Come, sit." Hiate points to a row of metal chairs extending from the stone wall, "Tell me what you saw in the streets just now."

"Nothing," the assassin says. "I saw nothing out there."

Hiate smiles, "Stay for a few more nights and you'll be seeing wraiths. My own father visits every third morning, just before the sun arrives."

The assassin removes his cloak and sets it on the metal chair, exchanging it for the resonating heat of the forge. A lather of sweat soon coats his brow and pools at the base of his throat, "Why does he visit you?"

Hiate laughs, "'Tis a fair question for certain, but one I've not thought to ask." He points to an iron chest on the ground behind him, "He comes through the doorway and walks to that chest. Then he disappears. Never says anything. Never even looks around."

"What's in the chest?" The assassin asks a little too eagerly.

"Nothing," Hiate looks back toward the assassin with a suddenly suspicious stare. "I never understood my father when he be alive. 'Tis the same in his death. I used to avoid him, but now he's a welcome part of my morning, same as Edran fetching the ore."

The assassin continues to stare at the small, blackened chest. It looks severely damaged, dented and rusted, and he can find no visible lock. Edran appears, carrying a wooden tray with bowls of broth, three goblets, and a pitcher of beer. The taggle sets the tray down and hands the assassin his portion.

Hiate notices the confusion on the assassin's face as he lifts the bowl and goblet, "Broth first, then the beer—like this." The blacksmith raises the bowl to his lips and proceeds to drink. A stream of broth runs over the edge of the bowl and down his chin. After consuming the broth, Hiate raises the beer in a toast, "May the Sphere protect you." Then he guzzles it down.

"And keep you in his light," the assassin raises his own bowl and feels the warmth of the broth flow down his throat, followed by the rawness of the beer.

Edran joins the toast, "May the Sphere protect you." He drinks the broth, but when he reaches for the beer, he finds it missing.

"And keep you in his light," Hiate gulps down the beer and laughs at the apprentice. Edran gives him a look of irritation, places the empty goblets and bowls back on the tray, and sulks away.

As the night winds consume the apprentice, the assassin sees a new figure appear—if only for a moment. He searches the night to no avail, "Did you see that?"

Hiate looks at the assassin, "'Tis a wraith you've seen?"

"It…it looked like my father."

"Didn't I tell you? Stay in Caduum and you'll see yer father, yer mother, and the Sphere himself. 'Tis what I said, yes?"

The assassin walks over to the doorway to better investigate the night winds, "How did your father die, Hiate?"

"'Tis a mystery," Hiate points toward the forge. "I found what was left of his body in the forge. My father was a…" Hiate continues with his story, but the assassin only half hears him. He searches for the wraith of his father, struggling to see anything in the street. The assassin nods as Hiate nears the end of his tale, "So, did he ever leave Caduum?"

A look of longing passes over Hiate's face, "No, a smithy be cursed in that regard. Only our work travels the land. We have too much be needing our attention at the forge." Hiate turns back to his hammer, "Which serves to remind me the Adow's army approaches while I be raising and lowering my jaw instead of my sledge. There be a bed in my home for you. I won't be needing it tonight. We all serve the Adow in some fashion, don't we?"

The assassin smiles as he retrieves his red cloak, "Yes, we all have our duties."

Edran returns to take the assassin to his room where, a moment later, he sits on the bed listening to the muted sounds of the forge and hammer. He rubs at his stomach. The broth and beer slosh around, a not-so-subtle warning of the nausea he will soon endure. Again, he curses Morlac for sending him to such a place, for sending him here to wait for the Adow.

Moon	Seal
Completion of the Purple Moon	Floating Cr
Completion of the Purple Moon	Hemming T
Shadow of the Purple Moon	River under
Shadow of the Purple Moon	Sword throu
Completion of the Red Moon	Broken Cro
Completion of the Red Moon	Crown of L
Changing of the Silver Moon	Five Crown
Completion of the Yellow Moon	Sword with
Changing of the Blue Moon	Crowned W
Completion of the Green Moon	Crowned Ro
Completion of the Green Moon	Crowned Sw
Completion of the Green Moon	Crown over
Completion of the Green Moon	Two Crowns
Completion of the Green Moon	Crowned Bo
Completion of the Green Moon	Hammer Str
Completion of the Green Moon	Sun Rising
Completion of the Green Moon	Crown betw
Dark Moon	Tiger and C

Months: Erog | Utine | Cil | Flatine | Joone   Date Format: (Gen

Periods: Year = 5 Months | Month = 5 Weeks | Week

The Adow

...on, Official Seal, and Chosen First Etabli:

	First Etabli
...er Sphere	Erin, the First Etabli
...ove Crown	Anine
...r	Aul
...wn	Taggle, the cursed
	Ylaf
	Erbohn
	Ig-poy
...n on Hilt	Adarian, hero of Ire
	Fael
	Irloore
	Cintyge
...ed Swords	Lio
	Enyure
	Athoyen
...Crown	Ferya
...rown	Cidal
...words	Ayson, of Quel
	Ayson, of Quel

...uring the Red Moon | (Specific) Erog 23, Completion of the Red Moon 51

...ays | Day = 5 Hours = Spheric Hour | Hour = 300 Minutes

find the wind unbearable but welcome the sight of Caduum. After weeks of traveling through nothing but open fields of bloodgrass, it's nice to see some semblance of civilization, perhaps, the last we will encounter. Dragon's Torment looms large over the town, every peak serving as a barrier and a warning. A warning I choose to ignore. Thousands of warriors will soon overwhelm this mostly forgotten town because I've led them here under the guise of a quest, the promise of a reward. The result of a hastily remembered story.

Maldinado appears behind us, the wind dampening the sound of his horse. I swear he hasn't stopped moving since we left Adarian, and I find myself watching his coming and going with great interest. No one has ever invested so much energy into my well-being, not even Troq. His warriors swarm the land: scouting, guarding, reporting. He constantly gives them directions, constantly communicates with them. I wouldn't have so many scars if Ayson demonstrated half the ability Maldinado displays. He reins in beside Inindu, his black hair whipping across his face and his incredible eyes. Oh, his gray eyes…and, *oh*, he sees me staring.

Fortunately, his attention turns back to Inindu, "Have you ever visited Caduum, Inindu?"

"Not since it was abandoned. They built it as a base camp with an intentional lack of hospitality. No one lives here now except ghosts."

"My scouts haven't reported back. Something doesn't feel right," Maldinado leans forward in the saddle. Again, our eyes meet, though he speaks to Ayson, "First Etabli, it may be wise to camp here until they return."

"I disagree," Faunride responds tartly, noticeably irritable since I recruited Maldinado to lead us into the Torment. "My Adow…" That's another thing! He has started addressing me directly ever since we left Adarian, "Despite its lack of inhabitants, my reports suggest we will find no shelter in Caduum. Something we could all use before we enter the Torment."

"No, I would definitely avoid seeking shelter in Caduum," Inindu says. "It's as likely to cave in on us as protect against these winds."

"I've heard similar stories, my Adow," Hintor agrees. Noticeably inseparable, I find he and Nataline—my new wonderfully exceptional cook—oddly comforting. "My great-grandfather journeyed here trade a time or two as a yearling. I hear the town nearly collapsed around him."

"It sounds as though there is nothing left of Caduum," I respond.

"Teyo reports, otherwise," Faunride continues. "He commissioned several weapons from a blacksmith who lives in the town, and found numerous buildings still erect."

"A blacksmith?" Inindu asks with interest.

"Forgive me, First Etabli." Maldinado still looks at me as he speaks. "Faunride's information arrived well over two weeks ago. I'm not comfortable moving into Caduum until my scouts return."

"Can we go around it?" Hintor asks.

Inindu shakes her head, "Caduum serves as the only entrance to the Torment. A broken gate, perhaps, but a gateway all the same."

"And have you ever been to the Torment?" Ayson has grown more and more distracted the past few days, ever since Dragon's Torment appeared on the horizon, "What's it like?"

"A veiled question if I've ever heard one," Inindu brushes her magenta hair away from her face. Not a single tangle! The wind moves her hair as though gently folding a napkin while it ravages through *my* hair! I swear I'm carrying a haystack above me. "The answer to your question is, yes, Ayson, you will die in the Torment. Only a few of us are strong enough to survive."

I doubt if *any* of us will survive. Except Inindu. She has survived before. Maybe several times.

"Are the stories true?" Nataline asks with trepidation.

"Ask your taggle," Inindu points to a boy walking behind us, him and a dozen other taggles—a new addition to my entourage at Inindu's and Nataline's insistence.

"Not now," Ayson gathers himself. "Thank you for your concerns, Madar, but Faunride is right. We are better served by whatever shelter Caduum can offer." Then he adds, "As for the stories…may the Sphere protect us."

"And keep us in his light," Nataline finishes piously.

"A useless prayer since I've never known my father to protect anyone in the Torment," Inindu says.

"The Sphere is everywhere!" I don't even know why I said that.

Really, how would I know? He doesn't speak to me and I've certainly never seen him.

"Have you ever heard the story of Dragon's Torment?" Inindu chides.

Of course, I um…haven't. *Tasa Ro!* "To which story do you refer?" Surely there are several stories or versions of one story. Hopefully? Please don't tell me it's the story about the five wolves. Does she know about Troq and the story of the five wolves? Yes, Inindu—this quest is nothing but a story Troq used to tell me! It's true. I lied!

"The origin of Dragon's Torment."

Oh, blessings and curses, she doesn't know! "Yes, I've heard the tale, or at least, part of the tale about how the Sphere created the Torment to serve as a prison for Morlac?"

"The god of another world is not so easily contained," Inindu warns. "And my Father did not create the Torment. It was Morlac. The Torment is not a prison. It's a barrier meant to keep the Sphere from entering."

"Blasphemy!" Faunride accuses. "May the Sphere protect us."

"And keep us in his light," Inindu responds, sourly, taking Faunride aback. Again, I'm left to wonder how much I really know about Inindu.

"Why would Morlac want to imprison himself?" Hintor asks.

Inindu flashes a wicked smile, "Perhaps we are the ones imprisoned, and Morlac has managed to escape."

I stare at the outline of the peaks marching across the horizon. Dragon's Torment. Forbidden. Troq warned me. Doesn't the tiger die at the end of the story! Now I've led my entire army to Morlac's doorstep. No, this isn't us on the verge of escape. We aren't prisoners. We're fools about to die.

I sneak a peek at Maldinado, but for once he isn't looking at me. Neither is Faunride. To my surprise, only Ayson pays me any attention. He takes my hand in his and squeezes it as if to assure me everything will be alright.

But, no, that's not how this story ends.

Two hours later, Teyo talks to an old topi who cowers in the corner of a hallway in our temporary home.

"It's no use," Hintor says. "Look at his eyes. He's mad. Probably doesn't even know we're here."

"How could anyone live in such a place?" Nataline wonders as she moves toward the kitchen.

The old topi shakes his head from side to side, muttering, "'Tis a wraith, 'tis a wraith, 'tis a wraith..." His eyes long ago clouded over, now white as his beard. His skin, translucent with age, falls from his bones as though mimicking the white gown pulled over his knees, pooling on the wooden floor at his feet.

Perhaps we *are* the ones imprisoned.

I leave the hallway and enter a large room filled with cobwebs and dust and oversized chairs covered in rough canvas. The cream walls give way to a stone fireplace opposite the doorway. A dark-stained, wooden bookshelf surrounds the fireplace, barren except for three books stacked atop one another. The only window in the room faces the street outside, where I can see Inindu, a magenta blur beyond the white film of glass. She refused to enter a building she believes will collapse before nightfall. I feel a little uneasy myself.

"Have your scouts returned?" Ayson asks.

"No," Maldinado quickly conducts a search for any hidden assassins, and then awkwardly jabs his sword up into the darkness of the chimney. "I've sent out a search party. We'll find them, or we'll find the reason they're missing." He turns from the chimney to look at me, "It's safe, my Adow."

Safe. Yes, I have never felt safer... or more exposed. We enter Dragon's Torment tomorrow. Everyone will die including my beautiful Maldinado. I could save him with a single command. I could tell him this is all a big lie. But the feeling of devastation would prove worse than death. Not just Maldinado. They all believe in me, willingly giving their lives for me. How can I take that away from them?

"Thank you, Maldinado," I have nothing more to say. My thoughts drift to my mother and I wonder if she carried a similar burden when she led her army into Quel. How many died for her because she selfishly chose Ayson over Yenen? It seems our story is the same! Despite everything!

I grab my father's hand. I don't know why... because, apparently, his is the only one I *can* grab! I can't touch Maldinado. Faunride is off seeing to the army. Anyway, my mother used to hold his hand. I always thought the gesture a simple display of affection. Now... I wonder if she held him out of desperation and with an awareness of who she had become—whom I've become. I drag Ayson back into the hallway, and then away from the old topi who still mutters some craziness. We cautiously climb a staircase which, of course, creaks with age—several of the dried-out planks split or badly splintered. I half expect to fall through at any moment, blissfully ending this whole charade, but we manage to reach the top without incident. We find two more rooms, but I'm not in the mood to explore. Ayson follows me into the room nearest the staircase, and I close the door, leaning against it with my back. I still hold my father's hand, and I can't help but notice his bald head now glows, catching the light that seeps past the door behind me.

"What's wrong, my Adow?"

I move into his arms and rest my head against his coarse tunic, "Nothing."

He kisses the top of my head.

No, something is wrong. Everything about this quest feels wrong! "They'll all die because of me," I mumble.

He pulls my chin up so I'm looking straight into his resolute face, "No, they'll die because you have given them a reason to die."

I pull away from him and find my way to the shadowed outline of a bed. It feels good to sit on something other than a horse. Unfortunately, it doesn't offer much padding and I can smell the dust now circulating in the air. When was the last time someone slept in this bed? Seriously, how long has that topi been sitting in the hallway downstairs?

I lean forward onto my hands, letting my eyes fully adjust. The room looks undecorated, containing only the one bed and a small table. How did I ever wind up in such a place? Worse yet, an entire army has followed me here! Sure, yeah, I've given them a reason to die. *Tasa Ro*! I turn back toward my ever-comforting First Etabli, "Is that what you told my mother before Quel? That she gave them a reason to die?"

"No, that's what she told me." Ayson sits beside me on the bed, sending up another dust cloud, "I convinced myself I was the reason so many warriors would die at Quel. I could see it in the eyes of everyone who followed your mother into battle. They may have fought against Yenen, but only because they fought on the side of their Adow. I knew what they thought…what they still think…but your mother…"

"She never did care what anyone else thought," I finish his thought. I mean, there's a reason no one liked her.

"She cared—she cared more than you can imagine. No, I was going to say that your mother wouldn't let me feel sorry for myself. She told me I wasn't the reason they would die. We will all join the Sphere, eventually. I simply gave them a reason to die. In a way, I brought honor to their death." Ayson wraps his arm around me, "The truth is, a warrior doesn't want to die of old age. Look at me—I'm weak. Broken. Old. However you want to describe me, I'm not the warrior I used to be and I find myself leaning more and more on Faunride, these days." The smell of dust fades, replaced by the bitter scent of my father, a mix of cooling sweat and chain mail. "I've been thinking a lot about this quest," he continues. "I'm ready to die. In fact, I want to die! If only to bring honor to you and your mother."

He lifts my chin again, "And when I die, promise me you'll make Faunride your First Etabli. I've seen the way you look at Maldinado. It's the same way your mother used to look at me, so I know you love him, or think you love him, but it doesn't matter. Don't make the same mistake! Faunride should be the next First Etabli, and your mother should have chosen Yenen over me. I realize that now. It was all wrong."

It's true, I do love Maldinado. I think. But the Madar will die alongside everyone else. "Alright," I nod. Faunride will serve as my First Etabli. Faunride, my ever-prudish guardian. Oh, imagine his face when he finally, dutifully, sees me naked.

Ayson pulls me closer, resting his chin on my head, "Anyway, your mother was right, but she was also wrong. I wasn't the one who gave them a reason to die. No one willing dies for a First Etabli, especially one they don't believe in. But it doesn't really matter who serves as First Etabli. I'm certain even Adarian never inspired his warriors to die for him. No, my Adow, you are the reason they follow. They will always follow their Adow. You are the reason they live and the reason they die. If all of those warriors die tomorrow, they'll have died willingly, and because of that they will die with honor."

I have no response, and I'm tired of talking, so I let him hold me. Truth or lies, it all leads to death.

I am their Adow, and this is *my* prison.

5-RUBY
SPECIAL EDITION

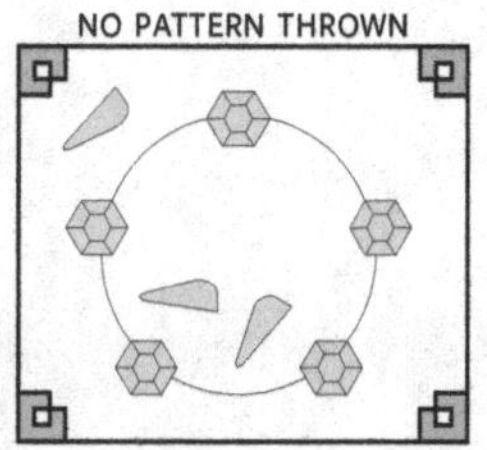

NO PATTERN THROWN

a taggle's tale

As spoken by an old taggle woman to a group of patrons gathered around her fruit cart in the Yenul marketplace. The geyser above the cavern roared in the background, providing a constant presence she used to simulate the winds of Caduum. Hunchbacked and horribly scarred, these looks accentuated her gestures and she exuded energy. At one point, she hurled fruit into the crowd, and at another point she jumped and tumbled around her wooden cart to such great effect that she transported her audience from Yenul into the hell that is Caduum. Her name was Janeel. She did not journey to Dragon's Torment with us, and likely never saw Caduum, but she gathered enough details from those who purchased her merchandise over the years to complete her tale, and I find her telling consistent with what I remember.

I implore you, speak her name. Speak of Janeel, for she spoke in the manner of all taggles. She told stories, and her words still linger. She lived and we heard her voice. May the Sphere forgive our mother and remember our father.

- DK Vel

he assassin moves through the streets of Caduum. Though not his targets, he has already killed two Adarian scouts out of necessity. He would have preferred not to kill them—he let the blacksmith and his apprentice live—but he saw no other option since he needed their armor. Now properly adorned, he moves freely through the natural chaos of wind and dust and the warriors of the Adowian Army who focus instead on constructing makeshift shelters; or they huddle together inside mostly damaged buildings. The few who do notice him think him one of many warriors moving around in the night, and why should they worry about such things?

The assassin searches the scattered encampment for the banner of the Adow. It doesn't take him long to find it as the fools have it waving outside the building where she has taken up residence, announcing her presence and all but inviting him to enter. But his armor means he doesn't need an invitation. He merges with the other Adarian warriors who surround the structure, his unfamiliar features hidden by the endlessly swirling dust.

Maldinado, unaware of the assassin's presence, sits in the kitchen with Hintor and Nataline, "There's one good thing about you serving the Adow. I don't have to worry about someone poisoning her food."

Hintor lifts a spoonful of warm butternut squash, "We don't have to worry about going hungry, either."

Faunride enters the kitchen with two empty plates, "The Adow and First Etabli pass along their compliments and a request for a second helping."

"Of course," Nataline replenishes the plates with generous helpings of squash, chicken, brown rice, and ginger pudding. "Shall I make another plate for you?"

"No, thank you. I'll eat once the Adow has gone to bed," He casts a glance at Maldinado, who chews a mouthful of rice. Then he leaves, returning to his post outside the Adow's bedroom.

"Well, that was odd," Hintor says.

"He's been giving me those looks since we left Adarian."

Nataline sits down at the battered wooden table, "You've been giving him the same looks. The two of you could be less obvious, you know."

"Not to mention the way you and the Adow cast eyes at each other. It's downright nauseating," Hintor scrapes his plate.

"You should talk," Maldinado counters.

Hintor looks up from his plate, then points with his spoon toward Nataline, "We're practically married."

Nataline takes the spoon out of his hand, "We're not married yet." Hintor smiles awkwardly around a mouthful of food while Nataline replenishes his plate, "Do you think Inindu is right about the Sphere not protecting those who enter the Torment?"

"No!" Maldinado responds defensively.

"One thing's for certain," Hintor accepts his plate back from Nataline, "Everyone will offer up a prayer come morning."

"No doubt you'll be the lone holdout," Maldinado says.

"You pray enough for both of us," Hintor grins, but the grin suddenly disappears. "You *are* still praying for me, aren't you?"

Maldinado shrugs his shoulders, "Now that I'm protecting the Adow, I don't have as much time as I did before. It's hard to fit you in."

Hintor appeals to Nataline, but she motions toward the dishes, "I've been a little busy, myself."

"Tasa Ro! Are both of you plotting against me? Really?" Hintor leans back in resignation, "I don't even know how to pray..." Then a thought occurs to him, and he unexpectedly slams a hand on the table, "Breline!" He points in triumph, "Breline is still praying for me."

"One of these days you'll actually have to pray for yourself," Maldinado says.

Hintor fills his mouth with a spoonful of pudding and smiles in response.

After dinner, DK Vel and Beah clean up the mess inside the kitchen, grateful for the respite from wind and cold. DK Vel looks with envy at the food on the table. He hasn't eaten all day. Not for two days. Not since he and Beah split a loaf of bread between them—one they sneaked from a basket they ultimately delivered to the Adow.

He twirls his finger through a glob of pudding and puts it to his mouth, slurping the pudding out from under his fingernail. Beah elbows him in the ribs as a someone walks down the hallway. The warrior ducks his head into the kitchen. He wears Adarian armor, but neither boy recognizes him. He gives them a curious glance, but he leaves without saying a word.

"That was close," Beah exhales.

"I'm so hungry."

Beah begins gathering the dishes, "Tell me a story about Dsal Tiger. It will take your mind off the hunger while we work."

"Alright," DK Vel grabs a wooden bucket and a brush from the corner of the kitchen. "Listen to these warnings and let Dsal Tiger guide you to the Sphere:

Dsal Tiger hunts. He moves his paws over and into snowdrifts littered with fallen limbs from trees long since barren and frozen in death. His fur hangs heavily and gathers in clumps around his legs and chest. Only the soft crunch of the snow tracks his path as he moves through a graveyard of trees.

He sees another set of footprints. His eyes narrow. He nestles his belly into the snow, but he finds no sign of his prey. He follows the footprints until he finds a cricket hanging upside down from one leg, attached to a tree limb, "What do I hunt, cricket? Tell me, and I will not eat you."

"You hunt what follows. You hunt what leads," says the cricket. "You hunt Sumatran."

"Then Sumatran will fill my belly," Dsal Tiger says. "You will live another day, cricket."

Dsal Tiger leaves the cricket and follows the tracks. Snow begins to fall lightly even as a rumbling moves from his stomach to his throat. He sniffs the ground—the trail smells fresh, but still his prey eludes him. He moves his paws over and into snowdrifts littered with fallen limbs from trees long since barren and frozen in death. His fur hangs heavily and gathers in clumps around his legs and chest. Only the soft crunch of the snow tracks his path as he moves through the graveyard of trees.

He sees another set of footprints. He follows the footprints until he finds a cricket hanging upside down from one leg, attached to a tree limb, "What do I hunt, cricket? Tell me, and I will not eat you."

"You hunt what follows. You hunt what leads. You hunt Sumatran following Sumatran."

"Then two Sumatrans will fill my belly!" Dsal Tiger declares. "You

will live another day, cricket."

Dsal Tiger leaves the cricket and follows the tracks. Unseen behind him, a Rorne tribesman——his torso painted with blood he took from the bear and the lion——emerges from hiding. He leaves no footprints, and no sound gives warning as he approaches and encloses his hand around the cricket. Raising his hand to his mouth, the tribesman eats his victim even as he looks down at the tracks of Dsal Tiger in the snow. He smiles and transforms himself into a red cricket. He waits for Sumatran.

Dsal Tiger sees another set of footprints; now three altogether. He sniffs the air, and quickens his pace, causing the accumulated snow on his back to fall away. He follows the footprints until he finds a red cricket hanging upside down from one leg, attached to a tree limb, "What do I hunt, cricket? Tell me, and I will not eat you."

"You hunt what follows. You hunt what leads," the red cricket says. "You hunt Sumatran following Sumatran following Sumatran."

"Then three Sumatrans will fill my belly," Dsal Tiger says. "You will live another day, cricket."

Dsal Tiger passes by the red cricket even as it reverts to the Rorne tribesman. The tribesman pulls a knife from his waist, jumps onto Dsal Tiger's back, and buries the blade into Dsal Tiger's belly. The hunt ends. Sumatran has fallen. The Rorne tribesman smears the blood of Dsal Tiger upon his chest, lifts Dsal Tiger onto his shoulders, and departs from the path Sumatran followed to his death.

Beah smiles as DK Vel finishes his story, but the expression quickly turns to a frown as he notices Inindu standing in the doorway. Horse and topi, two totally separate creatures, yet undeniably united. Her overwhelming presence and beauty fill the doorway. Beah catches his friend's attention, and then DK Vel freezes at the sight of the creature who took Lay-I from him in the streets of Adarian.

"I've been watching you, taggle," the horse speaks the words without a trace of emotion. "You're the one from Adarian—the one with the baby."

"It wasn't me," DK Vel stares at the ground. "I serve Hintor of the Adarian 45th."

"Don't be afraid, boy. I won't hurt you."

"It wasn't me," the taggle insists.

"Don't worry, I'll look after her," Inindu ignores his comment. "Besides, I tend to have a soft spot for anyone my sister curses, though in truth there have been so many over the years that I've lost count. Still, it's easy to keep track of the more obvious curses, and cutting off a chunk of someone's ear certainly qualifies. What's your name, boy?"

"DK Vel."

"Come with me, DK Vel. The Adow has suffered greatly in her education, and it's time she learned a few lessons. She needs a storyteller."

Beah and DK Vel exchange looks of confusion, but Inindu doesn't wait for a response. She simply moves down the hall and past the mumbling, blind topi with an expectation that DK Vel follow, which he does. When she reaches the stairs, Inindu climbs them, horse and topi, without making a sound—as though gliding up the staircase, a stark contrast to the creaks and moans made by taggle boy behind her.

"Open the door, Faunride," she commands the warrior standing beside a closed wooden door. "I have a gift for our Adow."

Faunride hesitates, torn between his desire not to disturb the Adow, and his fear of Inindu. A moment later, he knocks on the door, "My Adow, Inindu wishes to see you."

"There's no need to announce her, Faunride. It wouldn't stop her, anyway," the Adow responds.

Inindu pushes past the guard, "That's true."

She leaves DK Vel at the top of the stairs. He shakes visibly, afraid to enter the Adow's presence for fear of death. "Come along, boy," Inindu beckons. Faunride gives him a glaring look, but otherwise does not prevent the taggle from entering the Adow's chamber.

"I expected to find Maldinado with you," Inindu says with mock surprise.

"That would be improper," Faunride retorts from the doorway.

Inindu looks back at the guard, "Are you still here? Ayson, are you really that incapable of protecting your Adow?"

"Faunride is one of my most trusted guards, Inindu," Ayson responds from beside a four-poster bed covered by a dusty orange-and-brown quilt.

"Yes, but he isn't Maldinado is he, my Adow?"

"You can tell me what you have to say in front of Faunride." The Adow responds a bit tartly.

"No, I can't. I actually need Maldinado. I have news of his missing scouts."

"You found them?" Faunride asks.

"Go, fetch Maldinado," Inindu commands. "If you do it quickly, I may tell you all about it."

The Adow motions to Faunride, who leaves without further comment.

"In the meantime," Inindu continues, "I bring you a gift, my Adow. A storyteller, or as you like to call them, a taggle. Come, boy, tell us a story before this roof collapses on us and Ayson has to run and hide for fear of death." Inindu moves to one side of the room, leaving DK Vel with little in the way of a makeshift stage, her presence making the small room even smaller.

"What would you like to hear, my Adow?" The taggle still shakes, unable to conceal his fear.

"Stand tall, boy," Inindu encourages. "She won't hurt you as long as I'm here."

"That's enough, Inindu," the Adow scolds. "He's scared to death."

"Tell us one of your stories about the tiger," Inindu commands.

The Adow's reaction to the request ranges from surprise to fury. DK Vel lowers his eyes, unsure if he should speak or run. If the taggle feared for his life before, certainly he will die at her next command. Surprisingly, she says nothing, and everyone else waits for him to tell his story. He tries to think of one, but instead, his mind dwells on the image of his severed head rolling on the floor.

"Tell us the one I heard in the kitchen," Inindu persists.

Thankfully, words form, mouth functions, and DK Vel manages to remember the tale he spoke only minutes prior. He begins: "Listen to these warnings and let Dsal Tiger guide you to the Sphere: Dsal Tiger hunts. He moves his paws over and into snowdrifts littered with fallen limbs from trees..." The Adow stares at him with unmistakable horror. The boy pauses, unsure if he should continue. Luckily, Faunride returns with Maldinado in tow.

The Madar bows, "My Adow."

"Not her, *I* sent for you," Inindu begins. "I found your scouts. Their bodies were discovered near the blacksmith's forge. He thinks they were killed by a stranger who stayed with him a few days ago. Hasn't seen the stranger since. Quite the character, this blacksmith—likes to drink broth and beer. You should meet him sometime."

"Another assassin!" Maldinado processes the information, "My Adow, we need to act quickly."

"I agree," Faunride steps in front of the Madar.

The assassin stands guard in the large room downstairs, listening to an old topi in the hallway muttering, "'Tis a wraith, 'tis a wraith…" Then he hears commotion upstairs, and soon afterward Maldinado calls for Hintor. Faunride shouts orders to the Adowian Guards. Warriors quickly appear and await instruction.

"We need to move the Adow!" Ayson shouts.

The Adow descends the stairs into the hallway below, where warriors cram together. Guards surround her, all but suffocating her. More warriors enter through the front door, squeeze into the hallway to receive their orders, and then exit through the back door. Wind blows through the open doors into the crowded hallway, adding dust to the noise and confusion. The assassin moves into the crowd. He draws his sword, but nobody notices because they all unsheathe their swords.

"Someone, find Teyo!" Faunride shouts.

"Hintor!" Maldinado calls.

Ayson, Maldinado, and Faunride surround the Adow, but the undeterred assassin moves ever closer, following two warriors with orders to secure food stores in the kitchen. The Adow looks younger than he imagined. Shorter, too. A new figure appears on the staircase to his right, and the subsequent flash of magenta fully captures the assassin's attention, if too late. Inindu's hair, the long magenta hair of topi-Inindu combining with the mane of Inindu-horse, extends out over the staircase with a wild rage he can barely comprehend. It wraps around him and lifts him into the air above the stunned warriors in the hall below. Inindu continues to wrap and bind the assassin with her hair until completely hidden from view—a spider wrapping her prey.

Then she unravels her hair, revealing emptiness. Without a word, hair and mane retract like two snakes slithering back to rest on shoulders, swaying like it always seems to sway, but no longer hunting. Inindu continues down the steps, "You, too, may want to draw your sword next time we have an assassin in our midst, Ayson. The Adow doesn't need any more scars." Nobody says a word as she exits out the front door, and even the blind old topi no longer sits muttering in the corner of the hallway.

"Who *is* she?" The Adow asks nobody.

DK Vel takes a seat on the stairs. He knows who she is…he knows the stories. The ones Beah told him. Stories rarely told, and always told in secret. Morlac has many assassins, but the Sphere has only one.

Inindu is the First Assassin.

5-RUBY
SPECIAL EDITION

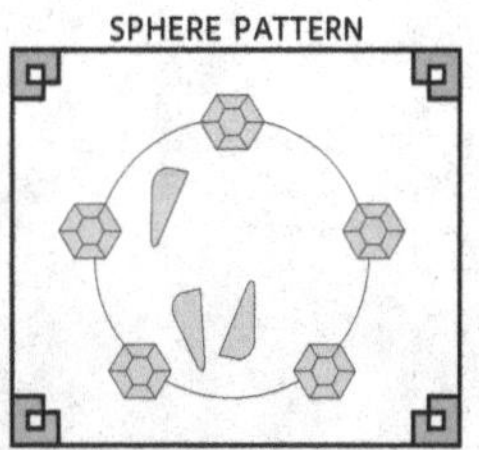

a taggle's tale

As spoken by a taggle woman to her five children. A baby screamed in her arms as blood flowed from the tips of his ears, carved into by the sword of a warrior—a guardian of the Stycral dallic. She held the boy to her breast, but he refused to nurse. The other children looked frightened, just as they had after similar rituals following the births of their taggle brothers and sisters. So, she told them a story, speaking loudly over the crying baby, all the while rocking him back and forth until, finally, he fell asleep. Her name was Ruthee, a woman who gave me shelter one evening. Her brother survived the Torment, only to die two days after his return, beaten by the same guardian.

I implore you, speak her name. Speak of Ruthee, for she spoke in the manner of all taggles. She told stories, and her words still linger. She lived and we heard her voice. May the Sphere forgive our mother and remember our father.

- DK Vel

"'Tis a feast the Dragon be having tonight, boy."

Hiate and Edran stand atop the roof of the blacksmith shop, watching the Adowian Army depart. The rooftop offers them a reprieve from the dust, if not the wind, and it feels cooler than the forge below. The army forms an endless procession of armored warriors marching through the streets of Caduum into the Torment. The pass, known as Dragon's Tongue, presents a steep climb, but it has solid footing.

"Yer trying to scare me into staying," Edran says.

"'Tis an illusion of glory they seek," Hiate says. "But I fear they're heading toward nothing more than a bitter end." He looks around at Caduum, "Though not as bitter as what we be living here."

"We'll need a banner."

"I'll leave such matters to you."

"I've fashioned one with the symbol of a hammer."

"Have you now? 'Tis a good symbol, to be sure." Hiate places his hand on Edran's shoulder, "And what say the others? Will anyone from Caduum be joining us?"

"No," Edran admits.

"We be on our own, then. Fair enough," Hiate nods as he scratches at his red beard. "We'll need the extra blankets from the house, I think. I'll fetch them. Hurry yerself with the horses."

They descend an iron ladder attached to the side of the blacksmith shop. Edran runs off toward a stall around the back of the stone building, but Hiate pauses just outside the open doorway to the shop. The forge still glows, evidence of his early morning work. A metal bucket filled with Dragon's ore sits on the dirt floor beside an unopened iron chest. Several hammers and two sets of tongs hang from the small stone pillar which supports the blacksmith's anvil. His leather apron, along with Edran's, hangs from a metal post just inside the doorway. The ties of the apron blow in the wind. Hiate looks down at his calloused hands, rubs them against his chest, and turns toward the house.

Moments later, blacksmith and taggle ride through the streets of Caduum at a steady canter, their faces all but hidden behind tightly wrapped scarves. Their red hair flows freely behind them, the shock of color suppressed by the dust-filled and circulating gusts. The horses jostle their reins, snorting constantly, but they continue the set pace until, near the edge of town, at the base of Dragon's Tongue, Hiate and Edran catch the Adowian Army—or rather, they join a horde of taggles trailing after the Adowian Army. Hiate dismounts, retrieves a blanket from behind his saddle, and moves to walk beside the nearest taggle boy, naked aside from the brown breech cloth around his waist. No shoes. His hands shield his face against the wind.

"What be yer name, boy?" Hiate shouts. The taggle boy stares dumbly at the blacksmith, "'Tis a blanket and horse I offer you. All I ask in return is yer name."

The taggle bows, "I can't accept such gifts of honor, master."

"Then you have no name?"

"My name is Beah, master."

"Beah…'tis a good name. Beah, take the blanket."

Beah gauges the red-haired blacksmith a moment longer before taking the blanket and wrapping it around his shoulders. Its wool fibers stab at his wind-burned skin.

"We're falling behind!" Edran shouts.

Hiate lifts Beah onto his brown steed and leads the horse forward until they catch up to another taggle. The blacksmith offers her a blanket as well, in exchange for her name: Lyshmee. And then another taggle: Penrem. And another: Vitrec. In this manner, Hiate and Edran climb the mountain pass collecting taggles and wrapping them in blankets.

"Why aren't you with the rest of the army?" Beah asks from the saddle.

"It seemed proper we bring up the rear," Hiate scratches at his beard. "Since we be the last ones to join the quest."

"I like you," Beah states.

Hiate gently squeezes the boy's leg, "Yer a fine boy, Beah. I like you, too."

Hundreds of taggles climb the mountain all around the blacksmith and his apprentice. The Adowian Army marches ahead of them, led by the Adow and her First Etabli. Though the dust of Caduum has subsided the wind remains, flowing down the mountain pass and growing more frigid as the army ascends. But exhaustion soon slows the journey. Warriors, marching under the weight of full armor, fight against the burn and growing stiffness in their legs. Every step weighs a thousand pounds. They begin peeling off layers. Those mounted soon dismount to lead their horses for fear of trampling those traveling on foot. The thin air and cold wind work together to swipe every desperate breath, so by the time the First Etabli gives the command to halt for the night, the army has only journeyed halfway up the pass. Two dozen taggles erect the Adow's tent with a valiant effort, gusts of wind more than once thwarting their efforts.

Afterward, inside the tent, Ayson speaks—or rather, he shouts—at Faunride and Maldinado, "Report?"

Faunride, yelling above the drumming of canvas, proceeds to tell the First Etabli and Maldinado that they have abandoned normal fortifications for fear of losing or severely damaging the other tents, "Only the Adow's tent stands!" Faunride shouts. "The torches make it visible throughout the camp, and it brings comfort to the warriors to know the Adow remains undeterred by the winds of the Torment!"

"Will it hold through the night?" Maldinado asks skeptically.

"It will hold," Faunride responds tersely.

"All the same..." Ayson shouts. "Add some more ropes!"

Faunride exits with a bow and a curious glance as Maldinado joins the Adow who sits staring at a game of 5-Ruby.

"The Begn ruby is naked!" The Madar sits opposite her, "Here, let me show you! It's easier to learn the game with the traditional beginning!"

"What?" The Adow yells.

The Madar holds up a hand, signaling a pause to their conversation. He moves the rubies until aligned correctly, and then he points to the game in triumph, "Easier!"

"You just ruined my game!" The Adow accuses.

Dumbfounded, Maldinado tells her, "That's not how you play 5-Ruby."

"What?"

"That's not how you play 5-Ruby!"

The Adow waves her hand and moves the rubies back to their former positions, "Easier!"

Maldinado stares at the game, "It will be over in two moves!"

"I know!" the Adow says. "And I'm going to win!"

Maldinado looks to Inindu for support, but she sits behind the Adow, brushing her mane and showing no interest in their discussion. Instead, she listens to a taggle boy who tells her a story with a flourish of movement and expression. He turns back to the Adow, "That's cheating!"

"It's manipulation!" The Adow declares. "Cheating implies that I have broken the rules of the game—which I haven't! I am simply manipulating the rubies to represent their future state!"

"Do you even know how to play?" He asks.

"All I need to know is how to win! I've watched enough games to know that!"

Maldinado smiles as a thought occurs to him, "Then you also know it's honorable to place a wager before the tusks are thrown!"

"Alright, what's your wager, Madar?"

"No movement on the next throw!" Maldinado removes five gold pieces from a small leather pouch at his waist and places them before her.

"I don't want your gold!"

"Then what shall I wager?"

"If there is no movement this turn, I will double your gold! If there *is* movement..." She checks to make sure no one watches, "Kiss me."

Maldinado stares at his Adow. Their masks are gone. He has no excuse for mistaking her as his Adow, and she, too, cannot claim ignorance. Maldinado glances quickly around, first at Inindu who still listens to the taggle, then toward Ayson who has his back turned. Then he looks down at the game and decides no movement will occur. It takes years of practice to throw the tusks in the right pattern...the odds favor him, so he accepts with a nod. She smiles, snatching up the three tusks from where they lay in the dirt. Her eyes meet his...her beautiful green eyes. Then Maldinado watches her throw the boar tusks. They hit the dirt and tumble in an awkward manner. The wrong pattern. No movement. She stands and walks away from him to open a small chest, returning with a handful of gold. She opens her hand, allowing the coins to fall on the ground around him. He doesn't move. He can't. He considers her perfect lips and the offered kiss...

The wind takes the tent around them, violently torn from stakes and rope. Without thinking, Maldinado wraps himself around the Adow and takes her to the ground, protecting her with his own body. Wind swirls around them, but the Madar can see the chaos around them as canvas, bedding, furniture, food, and clothing all take to the air, and the vanquished torches give way to a howling darkness.

Maldinado lies atop the Adow, his face against her throat. His nose in her dust-scented hair. Despite the flurry of activity around them, he can only feel her pulse against his cheek. Her hands move slowly through his hair. Someone shouts in the darkness. Her lips...

She pulls him into a kiss.

Then pushes him away as Ayson and Faunride draw near.

"Maldinado!" It's Hintor's voice. He and Nataline had left to prepare an almond stew at the back of the tent.

"Over here!" Maldinado allows Faunride to pull the Adow from his grip. He gets to his knees, grinning despite himself. *She kissed me!*

Further down the mountain, the Adow's tent crashes with terrifying surprise. It flies away moments later, blown again into the night. Hiate and his small band of taggles watch it fly overhead.

"'Tis a wraith," he says. "Nothing more. Finish yer story, Beah."

Beah pulls the blanket tighter around his shoulders and starts again.

Inindu waits for a sorcerer to open the door to his home. Though the Sphere hasn't spoken to her since the day of her creation fifty-one years earlier, she clearly heard his voice this morning when she encountered the sorcerer in the market square. Two words, Kill him.

Turns out the sorcerer lives alone, and when he opens the door to find the magenta haired Inindu standing before him he's dumbstruck... forgets about his magic...can't feel his toes. He stands utterly defenseless before her beauty a moment before her hair lashes out. The sorcerer, a clumsy fool who found power in magic, if not knowledge, dies and his body disappears without a trace. She killed him, her first assassination, on Erog 23, Completion of the Purple Moon 51.

Well done, the Sphere affirms.

Five years later she kills another sorcerer. And again, three years later, when she kills an unsuspecting merchant-turned-sorcerer. Then the topis abandon magic in their search for knowledge. Sorcerers give way to scholars. The Sphere's voice serves a constant companion as Inindu kills hundreds of scholars, singlehandedly driving them into hiding; soon after, topis skilled at politics replace them. They eschew knowledge in favor of status and the Adow adorns these new Scholars with purple robes, inadvertently making them easier for Inindu to identify. But they don't possess the power of the scholars who fled, so Inindu ignores them. She hunts after the true scholars. These scholars prove more cautious in their learning, however, for they know an assassin hunts them and they trust no one…except Inindu. Ironically, they trust the knowledge she possesses. It attracts them to her, rather than her beauty, for she alone has existed since the beginning of time, and when they see Inindu, they see an opportunity to further their own understanding. She witnessed the beginning when the Sphere created the land, and they long to hear her stories, but they soon discover only the taggles tell stories. Inindu shares nothing. Her hair flashes and they die. They all die…except Inindu.

She is eternal.

Hiate scratches at his beard, "'Tis a frightening story, Beah."

"Is she really an assassin?" Vitrec asks.

"There's nothing to fear, Vitrec. Inindu won't kill a taggle," Edran answers.

"How do you know?" Penrem asks.

Lyshmee, the only taggle girl sitting with the group, shakes her head in disgust, "Why would she? None of us will live long enough for her to bother with. Besides, have you ever heard tale of a taggle who is more powerful than a sorcerer, or could out-think a scholar?"

On another part of the mountain, far away from the group of taggles, Inindu shields DK Vel from the wind, her hair stretches and winds tightly around him. The boy can hardly breathe, afraid she will kill him the same way she killed the assassin in Caduum.

5-RUBY
SPECIAL EDITION
NO PATTERN THROWN

Moon	Seal
Completion of the Purple Moon	Floating
Completion of the Purple Moon	Hemming
Shadow of the Purple Moon	River unde
Shadow of the Purple Moon	Sword thro
Completion of the Red Moon	Broken Cr
Completion of the Red Moon	Crown of
Changing of the Silver Moon	Five Crow
Completion of the Yellow Moon	Sword with
Changing of the Blue Moon	Crowned V
Completion of the Green Moon	Crowned
Completion of the Green Moon	Crowned S
Completion of the Green Moon	Crown ove
Completion of the Green Moon	Two Crow
Completion of the Green Moon	Crowned
Completion of the Green Moon	Hammer S
Completion of the Green Moon	Sun Rising
Completion of the Green Moon	Crown bet
Dark Moon	Tiger and

Months: Erog | Utine | Cil | Flatine | Joone   Date Format: (G

Periods: Year = 5 Months | Month = 5 Weeks | We

The Adow

on, Official Seal, and Chosen First Etabli
First Etabli
er Sphere   Erin, the First Etabli
ove Crown   Anine
                 Aul
vn   Taggle, the cursed
                 Ylaf
                 Erbohn
                 Ig-poy
on Hilt   Adarian, hero of Ire
                 Fael
                 Irloore
                 Cintyge
ed Swords   Lio
                 Enyure
                 Athoyen
Crown   Ferya
own   Cidal
vords   Ayson, of Quel
                 Ayson, of Quel
ring the Red Moon | (Specific) Erog 23, Completion of the Red Moon 51
ays | Day = 5 Hours = Spheric Hour | Hour = 300 Minutes

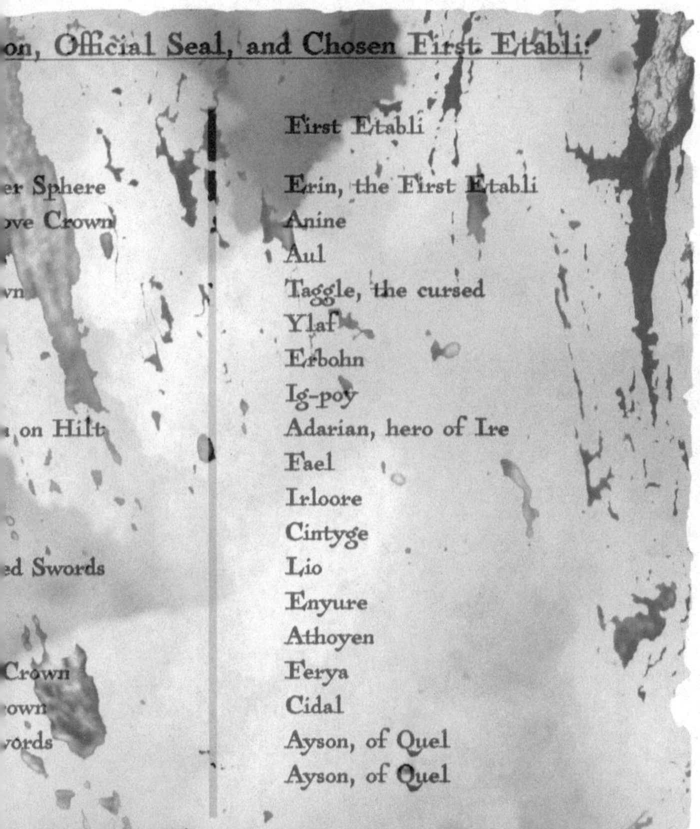

hy the hell did everyone journey to the Torment with me? What do they all hope to find? We made it to the top of the pass. Now what? This only ends one way: Everyone dies. They won't find the Arms of the Sphere because they don't exist! Oh, but they will remember their Adow brought them here…

Ayson takes my hand.

My salvation these last three days, he understands what I must face better than anyone. He had the same feelings at Quel of wanting to run away. He had to endure my mother looking at him, believing in him, just like Maldinado looks at me. The Madar doesn't understand what I'm asking him to do, and my mother didn't understand what she put my father through.

Ayson moves his horse forward and ahead of me. Inindu follows me. Then Maldinado. Faunride. My entire army. At least the wind has turned into a light breeze, and it isn't as cold as I was expecting. The sun shines brightly over red-toned peaks in the distance, leaving only a few pockets of snow to welcome us to the top of Dragon's Tongue which leads to a valley of balor trees, the only known tree in the Torment—fitting it has black leaves.

"What keeps the Sphere from entering the Torment?" Hintor asks Inindu.

"Or Morlac from leaving?" Nataline adds.

"Nothing," Inindu responds. "I said Morlac built the Torment to keep the Sphere away. I didn't say it worked."

I've never seen anything like Dragon's Torment. The balor leaves, though still mostly black in color, shimmer and change shades in the breeze. The ground consists of mostly red dirt with the occasional boulder, also red.

"Where's the nearest water source?" Maldinado asks.

Inindu points toward the peaks, "Five days to the north if we live that long."

"Are we in danger of attack?" Faunride reaches for his sword.

"The scholars live here. They call themselves the Rorne tribes. They'll know by now that we've entered their land," Inindu runs a hand through her hair, which slithers over and around her fingers.

Faunride and Maldinado both motion to and join their respective warriors. The Adowian Guard fan out to my left. The Adarian 45th flank my right. Hintor moves closer to Nataline. Ayson draws his sword.

"Do you even know how to use that thing, Ayson?" Inindu taunts.

My First Etabli doesn't respond. I suppose I should respond for him, but I don't feel like getting into it with Inindu right now. The trees have seemingly swallowed us alive and with the blinding sun…I can't see anything beyond twenty yards. The Rorne could easily hide anywhere and sit waiting to attack these strangers who dare enter their land uninvited.

An eagle flies between the leaves overhead, the first sign of life I've seen since we entered the Torment, and a welcome sight. Something normal. "Are there cities in the Torment?" Admittedly, I've always thought of the Torment in terms of desolation, but the eagle makes me wonder what kind of world Morlac has made for himself. Surely, he would create something like what the Sphere created…

"Yes, but we are a long way from the land of Morlac," Inindu answers.

"Do the Rorne ever cross into our world?" Nataline asks.

Why didn't I think to ask that question? Oh, because I've never thought about the need to safeguard our borders, and I suddenly realize just how little I know about Dragon's Torment. My lack of knowledge seems to be a recurring theme, lately.

Inindu smiles with that grin of hers that tells me she knows more than what she will admit, "The Rorne wouldn't dare enter Caduum." It's the same look she had when she presented that storyteller, the taggle boy who never leaves her side. He walks next to her now.

I wish Inindu would just come out and say she knows what I have done rather than wielding her storyteller in front of me like a sword. She only keeps him close so she can threaten me, but so far he has only told the one Dsal Tiger story. Maybe he doesn't know any of the rest. Maybe he doesn't know the story Troq told me about the five wolves— the reason for this entire mess! Whatever he knows, he's staring at me.

"What's your name?" It seems important. Even if it's just a taggle, I want to know my accuser's name.

"DK Vel," the boy responds with bowed head.

"This is hardly the time for introductions, my Adow," Inindu says. The wind has completely dissipated, but I swear her hair remains in constant blissful motion. I don't know that I ever noticed it before, but since she killed the assassin, or swallowed him, or whatever she did to him, her hair has not stopped moving as if each strand is tasting the air in search of another victim.

"You gave him to me as a present, Inindu. Remember? Though in truth you've kept him all to yourself." Really, she has kept him away from me! Not that I care…but maybe I should. And I can't help but wonder why Troq made it a point to tell me taggle tales. "How many Dsal Tiger stories do you know, DK Vel?" It feels like am I letting this taggle rule over me. So, what if he knows about the five wolves? No one will make the connection between his story and my false prophecy. Go ahead, DK Vel. Tell your stories!

Ayson turns in his saddle, "As it seems we may be heading into an ambush, I'd rather he didn't tell a story."

"Answer me, taggle."

"I've never counted them, my Adow," DK Vel responds.

"My guardian used to tell me a story about a tiger who hunted after five wolves. Do you know it?" So, there it is, out in the open; but if Inindu and her storyteller know anything, they keep guard over their emotions.

"Yes, I know the tale, my Adow."

The impact of his confession feels anything but crushing. Not in the sense I expected, anyway. Instead, the memory of Troq holding me and telling me stories while I fell asleep hits me with crippling force. *Tasa Ro!* My eyes fill with tears, but I manage to keep them from running down my face like a blubbering fool. Still, my voice quivers as I speak, "Tell me that story." Ayson catches the sudden change in tone, but I don't care. I want to hear Troq's story one more time. Inindu gives me a curious look. Fine! Stare! Hey, everyone, look at me!

The taggle begins his tale, but I don't hear his soft-pitch voice. Instead, Troq speaks to me in deeper tones, and I see his face, again—that wonderful white beard I used to tug. I close my eyes, and listen, trying not to have a complete breakdown on the doorstep of Dragon's Torment. But, well, Troq drove me here with his story. I can almost feel his arms around me. The boy's story unfolds exactly the same, as though Troq memorized it from a taggle. Why did you tell me taggle tales, Troq? But then I realize how grateful I am to him that he did share them with me, and I'm glad Inindu has brought this storyteller into my life—though, her efforts to trap me be damned!

"A tiger in Dragon's Torment searching for five wolves," Inindu comments after DK Vel finishes his story. "Strikingly similar to our own situation."

And I'm trapped! I wipe the tears from my eyes and turn to face my judgment, but Inindu doesn't look at me. Instead, she stares at the eagle overhead. One eagle has turned into five eagles, all flying together. Circling together. "That's odd," Ayson notes.

A moment later, Maldinado emerges from the trees. Maldinado, my great and beautiful warrior, instantly sees the tears in my eyes, "Is everything alright?"

"Yes, of course, what did you find?" Ayson answers, not realizing the Madar spoke to me.

I nod. Yes, everything is alright, Maldinado. Nothing to worry about except you worship me, and they worship me, and I've led all of you to your deaths. What could possibly be wrong? Oh, I want to kiss you and run from you all at the same time. Take me! No, I can't! *Tasa Ro!*

"Only more trees," Maldinado answers. "But if there's anyone out there, we'll find them."

Faunride returns. My future First Etabli. A promise made. A promise I will never keep because he will die with everyone else. He looks at me with the same look Maldinado gave me. The same question: *Is everything alright?* No, nothing feels right! Troq is dead and I'm traveling through the Torment. Did the Sphere, who I can't hear, strike all of you blind? We will soon die in these mountains, and it's all my fault. Yes, Faunride, your Adow led you here. I've led you to your death.

Ayson grabs my hand, once more, squeezing it until I start breathing again.

5-RUBY
SPECIAL EDITION

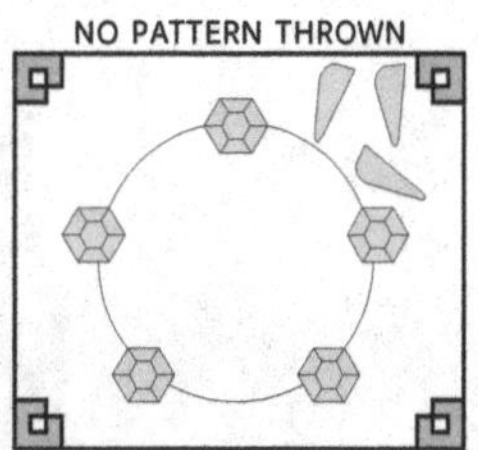

a taggle's tale

As spoken by an old taggle man at the request of his son. The man spoke deeply, almost too low, but the boy listened intently. The man motioned sparingly, typically pointing in the distance, or tracing a circle above his head. His name was my name. I implore you, speak my name. Speak of DK Vel, for I spoke in the manner of all taggles. I told stories, and my words still linger. I lived and you heard my voice. May the Sphere forgive our mother and remember our father.

- DK Vel

aldinado and the Adarian 45th move through the balor trees. He looks skyward, a habit he developed over the past two days when what started as one eagle flying above grew to at least sixty.

"They're more annoying than Brink!" Little Birty grumbles from atop his horse. He looks ahead to where the banner bearer of the Adarian 45th rides, "At least he disappears when I close my eyes!" He closes his eyes to further test the theory, then opens them again with a curse directed toward the eagles, "Tasa Ro! Go on. Find a fish, or something!"

Aside from the birds, however, Dragon's Torment has revealed no other signs of life. The Adarian 45th rides about an hour ahead of the Adow and the rest of the army, and they maintain a distance of at least two hundred yards Faunride and the Adowian Guard who ride parallel to them. If the Rorne tribes await in ambush, as Inindu suggested, they remain well-disguised and extremely patient. Maldinado feels the horse lurch as it begins climbing a good-sized hill. The forest terrain has grown steeper this morning. He again checks on the whirlpool of brown birds above.

"I've never seen anything like it," Gan-Pi, a pimple-faced warrior, rides beside his Rovet and Madar, a position normally reserved for Hintor, who remains with the Adow in order to better protect Nataline.

Maldinado nods, "I get the feeling the Torment will show us many things we haven't seen before."

The Adarian 45th continue to move through the trees in spread formation until they crest a hill where they discover a small village nestled within a clearing in the forest. The warriors draw their swords and close on the village, but it appears whoever lived here abandoned it long ago. Stretched tiger skins, dried and sewn together and laid over balor wood, must have offered shelter, at one point; and an uncommonly large balor tree serves as the village centerpiece. Other than its size, Maldinado finds something else odd about the look of the tree, but any specifics elude him. All around him, warriors aggressively search the empty shelters, but they find nothing of value. Unable to shake the feeling of uneasiness,

Maldinado stirs his horse toward the balor tree. Strange shapes hang from the limbs. *What are those?* He pulls on the reins to find someone has hung eagle feathers in place of leaves. More disturbing, every limb bears the fruit of tiny skulls capping bushels of severed talons. Whoever lived here carefully recreated a balor tree with the remains of a thousand or more brown eagles.

Something shudders at the top of the tree, and a living eagle ascends into the sky, joining the whirlpool of birds above the clearing. Gan-Pi shoots an arrow, but it falls away harmlessly. Maldinado sheathes his sword, and then slaps at something crawling on his neck, but the red cricket avoids death by jumping to his leg. Maldinado flicks it away and motions for the warriors to keep moving.

"Gan-Pi! Report back to the Adow. Tell her about this village," Maldinado orders. He takes one last look at the tree of eagles, and then skyward at the circling birds, "May the Sphere be with us."

"And keep us in his light," Teyo completes Faunride's offered prayer.

The two Adowian Guards watch the birds above for a second longer before returning their focus to the forest.

"Look!" Teyo points to his left where an orange tiger walks parallel to their position.

"Valin!" Faunride calls. A thin but able warrior moves forward, "Our supper has arrived."

Valin rides away with an arrow knocked in his bow. The remaining Adowian Guard, marching in grand procession, stops to watch the hunter aim and release the arrow while remaining perfectly balanced atop his horse. Unfortunately, the arrow strikes one of the trees, sending a now startled tiger back into the depths of the forest.

The warriors cackle and holler at the failed attempt to kill the tiger. Valin rides back to the procession, hanging his head in shame. The Adowian Guard continues its march through the balor trees, shouting insults toward Valin and boasting how they would have killed the tiger if given a chance.

Teyo taps Faunride on the arm, "He's back."

"Yla! See what you can do!" Faunride calls.

The warriors cheer this new hunter with great enthusiasm as he approaches the tiger. He dismounts to draw his bow, but the tiger moves at the last minute, causing the arrow to sail wide. Yla shoots another arrow, but the tiger disappears into the forest, thus the hunter returns under a chorus of insults.

The game continues once more when the tiger returns. Another warrior fails. Then Teyo makes his attempt, but even the master archer cannot slay this beast. No longer amused, Faunride orders the guard to dismount and draw their bows. They wait, more than a few stealing glances at the still circling birds overhead whose seemingly coordinated squawking pierces the silence—one after another, as though taking turns.

Finally, the tiger reappears from behind the trees. Faunride gives the signal and hundreds of arrows fill the air, slapping balor leaf or embedding into tree bark with a thud, but not one of the arrows hits its intended mark. The tiger remains unharmed, so seven warriors, and then a dozen more, draw their swords and charge the beast. The entire Adowian Guard yells after them, cheering their efforts.

"We'll get him for certain!" Faunride yells with enthusiasm.

Beside him, Teyo flicks a red cricket from his arm.

Nataline, too, brushes at her gown, "I've never seen so many crickets."

Hintor points to the forest floor, "They're everywhere."

Ayson looks up at the birds circling above, "There must be a hundred of them now. I've never before seen so much as one eagle in any one place."

"The Torment used to be void of life," Inindu says. "It appears Morlac has added a bit of seasoning to his world," Inindu reaches with her hair toward a cluster of crickets. Snagging one, she pulls it closer to inspect its red body, black hindquarters, and long antennae.

"That's a rather disturbing talent you possess, honored Inindu," Nataline shutters.

She transfers the cricket to her hand, allowing it to jump away, "I have many talents, though none of them include the ability to cook quite so well as you, my dear."

"You are too kind," Nataline bows her head with gratitude.

"What would cause them to gather like that?" Ayson still looks up at the birds.

"I wish they would just go away," the Adow reaches for the First Etabli's hand.

"I suspect they serve as the eyes and ears of Morlac...or the Rorne tribes," Inindu offers. "Yes, likely the scholars. A connection of some sort, and if that's the case, they've gained a great deal of knowledge since last I visited the Torment." Inindu sneers with sudden mirth, "Consider yourself fortunate, Ayson. Turns out, you won't have to bother us with your life much longer."

"Not again!" The Adow scolds. "Seriously, what happened at Quel wasn't Ayson's fault!"

Ayson looks back to his daughter.

She squeezes his hand, "It wasn't your fault."

"There!" Beah shouts.

The taggles travel through the forest of balor trees on bare feet, quietly as the tiger now stalking them.

"I see it, boy. No need to be shouting," Hiate says.

"I've never seen a tiger before," Edran confesses.

Whispers of *Dsal Tiger* move through the group of taggles.

"'Tis one of them hunted in Caduum when I was a yearling," Hiate swats at a red cricket climbing over his beard. "Killed five of us before we finally got him. This one seems bigger than I remember."

"He's amazing," says Beah.

5-Ruby
SPECIAL EDITION

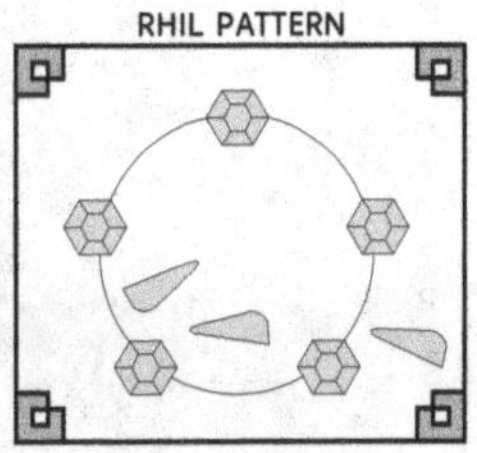

<u>A Record of—she who served as—The Adow: H</u>

Moon	Seal
Completion of the Purple Moon	Floating Cr
Completion of the Purple Moon	Hemming T
Shadow of the Purple Moon	River under
Shadow of the Purple Moon	Sword throu
Completion of the Red Moon	Broken Cro
Completion of the Red Moon	Crown of L
Changing of the Silver Moon	Five Crown
Completion of the Yellow Moon	Sword with
Changing of the Blue Moon	Crowned W
Completion of the Green Moon	Crowned Ro
Completion of the Green Moon	Crowned Sw
Completion of the Green Moon	Crown over
Completion of the Green Moon	Two Crowns
Completion of the Green Moon	Crowned Bo
Completion of the Green Moon	Hammer Str
Completion of the Green Moon	Sun Rising
Completion of the Green Moon	Crown betw
Dark Moon	Tiger and C

Months: Erog | Utine | Cil | Flatine | Joone   Date Format: (Gene

Periods: Year = 5 Months | Month = 5 Weeks | Week

The Adow

...on, Official Seal, and Chosen First Etabli...

	First Etabli
...ver Sphere	Erin, the First Etabli
...ove Crown	Anine
...n	Aul
...wn	Taggle, the cursed
	Ylaf
	Erbohn
	Ig-poy
...n on Hilt	Adarian, hero of Ire
	Fael
	Irloore
	Cintyge
...ed Swords	Lio
	Enyure
	Athoyen
...Crown	Ferya
...rown	Cidal
...words	Ayson, of Quel
	Ayson, of Quel

...ring the Red Moon | (Specific) Erog 23, Completion of the Red Moon 51
...ays | Day = 5 Hours = Spheric Hour | Hour = 300 Minutes

isten!" Ayson pauses, "They've stopped squawking!"

The silence fails to bring me any comfort. The birds have journeyed with us for seventeen days—a constant swirling presence overhead—hundreds of them filling the sky and squawking one after the other in a maddening succession of endless sound. But now, silence.

Ayson moves toward the tent opening even as Faunride enters, "First Etabli!"

"I hear it," Ayson exits the tent with Faunride beside him.

Maldinado moves to protect me, something I find myself resisting. Already, I have Ayson around, and Faunride…the Adowian Guard. Now Maldinado and the Adarian 45th surround me. Whatever happened to having to fend for myself? Ayson used to cower behind me. Strangely, I miss those days. Regardless, these warriors need to remember whom they protect. I draw my sword and move in front of the Madar, feeling awkward and empowered at the same time. Yes, this will work much better.

"Expecting the birds to attack?" Maldinado mocks gently.

"Weren't *you*?" I turn on him, my sword still raised.

"Do you threaten all your lovers in such a manner?" Inindu asks.

That's another thing. Inindu's tone has completely changed with me ever since that taggle boy told his story about the five wolves. I *know* she knows I'm lying. I wish she would accuse me and get it over with instead of taunting me with that added irritating little smirk of hers lacing every comment. Hell, I wish this quest had never happened! And I wish these damned birds would go away and leave me alone!

"Do you suppose they've left?" Nataline looks up as though hoping to see past the tent canvas.

"No," Inindu bites into two apples, horse and topi chewing in unison.

Hintor draws his sword, positioning himself to protect Nataline.

"Not you, too?" Maldinado chides.

"I was just following your lead."

Nataline reaches for the long knife at her side, "I hear something."

I turn around, half expecting an eagle to fly in through the tent flaps. I can feel them, too, like a suffocating awareness. Despite the silence, the birds definitely did not leave. *Tasa Ro!* I sheathe my sword and head outside. Maldinado follows. Of course, he follows! He must protect me, after all. I find my other two protectors, Ayson and Faunride, staring at the sky. I force myself to look. No moon. No stars. Only a mass of swirling darkness. Why don't they squawk? *Tasa Ro!* Say something you stupid birds! Then I hear a tiger's roar off in the distance. I again draw my sword even as both Maldinado and Faunride step in front to shield me. Another roar.

"Why don't they attack?" Faunride asks.

"It's a warning," Inindu emerges elegantly from the tent as though flaunting her unseemly ability to remain calm. "The scholars are telling us to go home. The eagles and tigers speak for them." Inindu reaches for a red cricket with her hair, "The crickets, too."

"Why do they want us to leave?" Ayson asks.

"Because they know they cannot defeat the Adow's Army on their own," Inindu responds. Again, with that smirk! "Which means Morlac will send the Kul, and even the scholars fear the Kul."

"What about you?" Maldinado asks. "Do you fear the Kul?"

Inindu turns to me. Why is she staring at me? "Tell me, Madar, have you ever heard the story of Dsal Tiger and the five wolves?"

"He wasn't there when the taggle told it." Does she plan to accuse me in front of him? Is this the moment she's waited for?

"In the end, the Kul consumes the tiger," her tone sounds almost playful.

"What does a taggle's tale have to do with anything?" Maldinado asks, oblivious to Inindu's game. What game is she playing?

"No, I don't fear the Kul," The playfulness suddenly disappears. "In truth, I came to the Torment to kill her...or be killed."

"*Her?*" Faunride asks.

"Her," Inindu confirms.

I never pictured the Kul as female...or even real. Wait! "What about the five wolves?" I ask, assuming Inindu understands my question. I *need* to know if she understands.

"I'll leave that quest to you, my Adow." Great! What the hell does that mean?

"You can be killed?" Ayson interrupts our cryptic conversation.

Inindu appears genuinely shocked by the concern in his voice. For that matter, I'm similarly taken aback, "We all die, Ayson. Some of us not as quickly as others."

"Have you ever fought the Kul?" Maldinado asks.

"No," Inindu admits. Then she turns to face the oncoming army, "I think I'll go find that blacksmith from Caduum and see if he has any more beer and broth. DK Vel tells me he joined our little quest and now travels with the taggles." She directs her last comment toward me, "You should meet him sometime."

What about the wolves? Are they real? Tell me about the wolves! Instead, Inindu leaves me to the care of my three protectors. She knows, but she doesn't care. Why doesn't she care? *Tasa Ro*! She's as bad as these damn eagles. Squawk already! I sheathe my sword and nearly run back to the tent, startling Hintor and Nataline who apparently took this moment to embrace in a passionate kiss. I no longer find it cute, "Leave me alone!"

They scramble to leave the tent as my three guardians enter. Of course, they followed me. I am *never* alone! I'm completely surrounded and unable to escape…and they'll all die because of me.

Five hours later, Troq holds a younger me in my dreams. I sit in his lap and his white beard hangs over my shoulder, rubbing against my cheek. His tobacco-laced breath flavors every word. We sit together in a velvet red chair beside a silent fire…which doesn't seem quite right.

"Pleeease tell me a story," I beg. "I'm not even tired yet."

"Alright, Ovda. Alright." He kisses my head, "Did I ever tell you how the tiger ate a whale?"

"How can a tiger eat a whale?"

Troq begins his story, his fingers caressing my arm.

The tiger walks along cliffs overlooking an ocean. He climbs atop a large rock and stares into the setting sun. He roars like only a tiger can roar, sending dirt and pebbles tumbling from the cliff face into the ocean below.

A seagull arrives and hovers above him, "Why do you wait, tiger?"

"I wait for that which the sun flees. I await the Kul," the tiger says.

"Then eat me, for you will need wings to defeat the Kul."

The tiger opens his mouth and the seagull flies inside, dying without struggle or sound. The tiger swallows and roars, and then wings form on his back. The sun settles under the horizon, but the Kul doesn't appear.

A ram emerges from the forest behind the tiger, "Why do you wait, tiger?"

"I wait for what the forest hides. I await the Kul,"he roars.

"Then eat me, for you will need my horns to defeat the Kul."

The tiger opens his mouth, allowing the ram to enter and die without struggle or sound. The tiger swallows and roars, and then horns form on his head. The forest behind him shakes in the wind, but the Kul doesn't appear.

A whale rises to the surface of the ocean, sending spray high into the sky—so high that it reaches the top of the cliff where the tiger paces, "Why do you wait, tiger?"

"I wait for what moves in the ocean. I await the Kul."

"Then eat me, for you will need my strength to defeat the Kul."

The tiger opens his mouth. The whale enters and dies without struggle or sound. The tiger swallows and roars, and then his body doubles in size. The ocean crashes against the cliff, but the Kul doesn't appear.

The tiger awaits the Kul. Sun and Moon disappear. Fire burns in the forest. Ocean waves turn to sand. Still the Kul does not appear. The tiger walks along the cliffs. He climbs a boulder and roars, but instead he squawks like a seagull, "I am the Kul!"

The tiger roars again. It's the bleating of a ram, "I am the Kul!"

The tiger roars again. It's the moan of a whale, "I am the Kul!"

Then the tiger's belly erupts, his body splitting in half. From what remains, emerge the seagull, ram, and whale. They watch as the tiger's head rolls and falls from the cliffs...

I awake with a feeling like falling. The tent is dark. Ayson lies snoring beside me. Faunride stands guard, his silhouette barely visible against the canvas.

"My Adow?"

"I'm alright, Faunride."

Yet another lie.

5-RUBY
SPECIAL EDITION

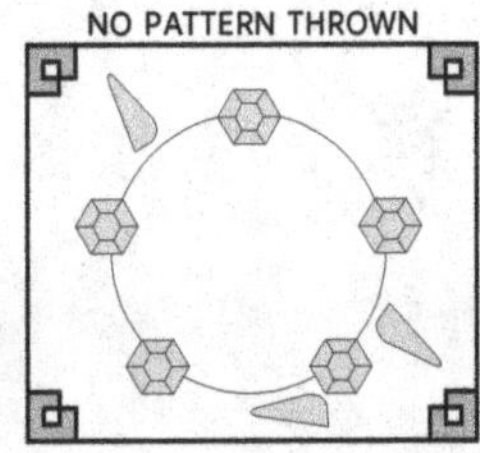

a taggle's tale

As spoken by a taggle boy before the throne of the Adow. He spoke with confidence and with great emotion. He gave a vibrant and, at times, surprising performance, and the gathered warriors, along with their Adow, took careful note of every word. Beyond general interest, they gathered there to learn from the boy. When he finished his tale, they asked the taggle to tell his story again, and again a third time. The boy's name was my name. I implore you, speak my name. Speak of DK Vel, for I spoke in the manner of all taggles. I told stories, and my words still linger. I lived and you heard my voice. May the Sphere forgive our mother and remember our father.

- DK Vel

nindu-horse picks through a pile of red and yellow apples. Topi-Inindu drinks a bowl of warm chicken broth, chasing it with lukewarm beer. Behind her, DK Vel, Beah, Edran, and a circle of taggles lie asleep, huddled together in the manner of taggles. The blacksmith sits across from Inindu, finishing off his fifth round of broth and beer. The eagles still swirl silently above them. The tigers still roar in the distance.

"It won't be long now," Inindu says.

"'Tis the Kul be causing the eagles to grow silent. They can see what the tigers cannot," Hiate pauses to listen for the gentle screech of the red crickets, but he hears only the tiger. "The crickets, too, be sensing the presence of the Kul."

"The tiger is always the last to know," magenta hair reaches for the broth ladle that hangs over a black pot above the fire, filling her bowl before dipping her tankard into an open cask of beer.

"I be creating the tiger for a very specific reason, daughter," Hiate replies. "The tiger 'tis beautiful and independent of this land."

"Like you, dearest father? Is the tiger a representation of the almighty Sphere?"

Hiate scratches at his beard, "The tiger be representing the same as yer beauty, and that of your sister, the Adow."

"A beauty that kills?"

Hiate laughs, "Beauty 'tis a curse, to be certain." Hiate drinks the last of his beer, "My father used to tell me life 'tis covered in ashes, and death decorated in jewels." He looks up at Inindu, "No offense meant to yerself."

Inindu smiles knowingly, "You never had a father."

"As true a statement as ever there be. I'm alone. Well, I was alone." He points toward Edran, "The boy keeps me company. The two of us now one family just as I created yerself to be one creature made from two. And yer sister. Adow and First Etabli be joined to produce one heir."

"Yeah, that isn't working out so well," Inindu-horse crunches into another apple.

"She be free to choose her path, same as yer free."

"You mean she's free as long as she worships you."

"Not everyone be worshiping me. I hear Morlac has his share of followers."

"Thanks to me, you mean."

"Thanks to yer decision to ignore me."

"I was busy with Adarian."

"Adarian was never meant to be yers, daughter."

"We agreed not to discuss him, remember?" Inindu snaps. "I needed someone since you've ignored me ever since you created me."

"I haven't ignored you, daughter. You be avoiding me."

"It's not my fault you chose to live in Caduum."

"I wasn't always in Caduum. I be watching you and yer sister since the beginning."

"Yes, her beloved Troq," Inindu reaches for more broth and beer. "I'm surprised she never realized who you were."

"She loves without the need for knowledge."

"She follows without understanding. My sister has never been the brightest star."

"I created her for a very different purpose than yers."

A log shifts in the fire, a loud crack that sends sparks into the air.

Magenta hair reaches for the blacksmith, wraps around his red hair, strokes his beard, "Do you find me beautiful, father?"

Hiate pulls her hair from his face, "In this form I see yer beauty, Inindu, but it does not hide the death within you."

Inindu pulls her hair away, "Then we disgust one another?"

"No, daughter. I still love you."

"Well, I *despise* you," Inindu stands to leave, topi mounting horse. She grins despite herself, "Hiate the blacksmith amuses me, however."

Hiate stands, slightly wobbling as he talks, "Then you will face the Kul?"

Inindu smirks, "Are you asking me, or is that a command?"

"You be free to choose, beautiful creature," Hiate bows with great exaggeration.

"Yes, father, I will face the Kul. And I will hunt Morlac." Inindu heads into the darkness with a final comment, mocking his accent, "I be an assassin, after all."

Hiate watches after her, "Did you hear all of that, boy?"

DK Vel doesn't move for fear of discovery.

Hiate sits down to another round of broth and beer, "Come, boy. It's time you stopped living in fear. I'll not be harming you."

DK Vel opens his eyes, but still refuses to move.

"Does it surprise you to know yer god lives his life covered in the ashes of a blacksmith's forge? To be certain, I live in places others seldom visit," he lies down on his side. "'Tis the reason I travel with the taggles, no doubt. They think you less than desirable, but you be simple and honest creatures."

The taggle boy can't help but think, *Is he going to kill me?*

"No, boy," Hiate says. "If I kill you, there be no one left to tell my story."

The boy sits up, about to say something, but Hiate the blacksmith… Hiate the Sphere has fallen asleep.

DK Vel can't sleep. He stares with horror and wonder at the blacksmith…mostly wonder, and a peace descends upon him. He leaves the circle of taggles to squat in front of Hiate, leaning forward until his face sits level with his god—the red-bearded Sphere.

Forgive our mother

Remember our father

He prays the prayer several times, only a thought at first, and then he whispers it—repeats it—growing ever louder until the blacksmith stirs and opens his eyes to find the boy's face inches from his own.

"What is it, boy?"

"Forgive our mother, remember our father."

Hiate wraps his arm around the taggle, pulling him down into an embrace. The blacksmith closes his eyes, still on the edge of sleep, "I've never forgotten you, boy. I be in every taggle's tale, guiding you, bringing you comfort…"

The Sphere falls asleep with the boy still in his arms.

Three hours later the Rorne attack.

Beah is the first to die. A red cricket crawls over his outstretched fingers and transforms while the boy sleeps, shedding its form and growing in size until blue skin replaces red exoskeleton. Antennae now long, thin black hair. A nose and lips—soon, a full face emerges, covered with deep-set, infected sores. It seems the whole of his body exists in a decaying state, though most of it remains shrouded under black robes. The transformation takes only a moment. Then the creature buries his newly fashioned, infected hand deep into Beah's chest, crushing his heart while he sleeps.

Lyshmee, Penrem, and Vitrec die in quick succession. Their deaths awaken Edran who startles at the sight of the Rorne tribesman. The boy backs away in frantic fear until Hiate appears, smashing his sizable fist into the tribesman's nose. "'Tis the wraiths come to fetch your soul, boy!" Hiate smiles at the disfigured form of the tribesman, "These be having scars, though."

More crickets transform. Hiate barrels into them, taking five scholars to the ground. He rolls and stands at the ready. He puts his hands together, swinging his arms like a club at the closest tribesman. He lowers his shoulder and crashes into another group of Rorne, taking three down to the ground. Then Edran stands beside him, handing his master a sword. The apprentice wields his own blade, fully recovered from his initial jolt.

"Beah!" DK Vel kneels over the bloodless body, unaware his friend lies dead, desperately trying to wake him.

Hiate smashes his sword down onto and into the head of another foe, garnering a look of dread shock under the blood that now coats the tribesman's face, "Hmm, yes, I be killing yer kind since before I could raise the hammer. 'Tis the steel of Caduum you feel, wraith!" Hiate's beard parts in a vicious grin. Then he pulls the sword from the tribesman's head. He kills three more Rorne. Edran kills another. Clunky movements conceal deadly steel, and the Rorne die—seventeen of them pile around the blacksmith and his apprentice.

Hiate slides another tribesman from his sword. But more live. They cover the horizon, unveiled by the approaching dawn; thousands of red crickets now transformed and slaughtering the taggles who don't even fight back. They have nothing with which to fight. The blacksmith drops his sword and moves to DK Vel who still kneels beside Beah's body.

Hiate falls to his knees and pulls the yearling to his chest, "Yer friend be dead, boy."

DK Vel nods, "He asked Uncle Taggle for a blessing. He wanted to survive the Torment. He was my friend. Why didn't you save him?"

"He be in a better place now," Hiate kisses and embraces the head of DK Vel. "'Tis a much better place awaits all of you."

"Why aren't they attacking?" Edran points to the confoundedly complacent taggles off in the distance, "They won't survive!"

"None of them *want* to survive," Hiate looks over the battlefield. "Come, boys. The taggles be finding their peace this day. 'Tis the Adow be needing us now." He pulls DK Vel to his feet, but the taggle resists, "Alright, boy, I understand. 'Tis an honorable thing to be a friend even in death." Hiate kneels down and lifts Beah's body, cradling him against his chest, "Now hurry and let's be off!"

Edran grabs the reins of two horses. They mount and leave the taggles to their fate, Hiate still cradling Beah's body. They navigate the chaos of the waking Adowian Army and the rush to meet a revealed enemy. They pass the lively banners of the Kiel 2nd, Lull 28th, Golesh 41st...

"May the Sphere be with us!" Someone shouts.

"He already is!" DK Vel whispers, uncertain what it really means. His friend is dead. That's all he knows.

Hiate dismounts and carries Beah's body to a forgotten campfire, pausing to wait for Edran and DK Vel to join him. Heat ripples through the air, but the blacksmith doesn't mind. It feels cooler than the forge.

"Shouldn't we bury him?" DK Vel asks.

"'Tis a curse to be buried," Hiate insists. "Say yer peace, boy."

DK Vel places his hand upon his friend's head, unsure how to say goodbye. Though familiar with death, friendship eluded him until now... until Beah, "May the Sphere forgive our mother."

"And remember our father," Edran adds.

Hiate heaves the body into the flames without further ceremony, "Take yer wraith with you, though. I'll not be having you haunt me, boy." He turns away from the fire, "We've no time to watch him burn." But a healer approaches the blacksmith, his white robes covered with blood, "'Tis no place for a healer, but I'll thank you to watch the fire all the same. If I return, burn me quickly. 'Tis a cursed land we roam."

The healer nods with understanding.

A moment later, Hiate retrieves a spare sword from behind his saddle and turns to DK Vel, "'Tis here we part, boy. I need you to take this sword to yer master. Can you do that for me?" The boy nods. Hiate hands him the sword, "You'll find Hintor in the Adow's tent. 'Tis nothing to fear, boy. The wraiths haven't reached him, yet. Take this to him and tell him

Maldinado insists he use Caduum steel. He'll be able to protect you with it." Hiate turns to mount his horse, "Edran and I be finding the Adow."

With that, the blacksmith and his apprentice leave the taggle standing alone. Holding a sword. In the middle of a battlefield. Never did DK Vel envision this moment when he left Yenul in search of an Adowian Burial.

5-RUBY
SPECIAL EDITION

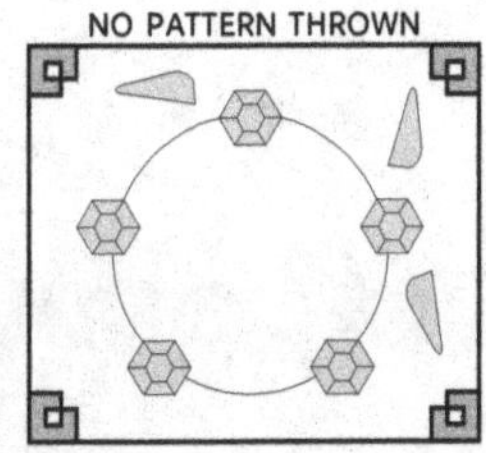

NO PATTERN THROWN

a taggle's tale

As spoken by the oldest of taggle men, his final tale, for his voice grew hoarse with cough and his body weakened as death drew near. He sat in a wooden chair as his audience gathered close enough to hear his garbled words. His inconsistent cadence and labored wheezing proved a distraction, and, by all accounts, his presentation lacked enthusiasm, but spoke with undeniable passion. Those present embraced his remaining life and honored him with their attention. The man's name was DK Vel.

I implore you, speak his name. Speak of DK Vel, for he spoke in the manner of all taggles. He told stories, and his words still linger. He lived and we heard his voice. May the Sphere forgive our mother and remember our father.

- The Adow

aldinado and every other warrior of the Adarian 45th charge into the Rorne like bears crashing into water. Sent in the night to guard the perimeter, leaving Faunride and the Adowian Guard behind to protect the Adow, the site of initial combat occurs a good distance from the rest of the Adowian Army. Maldinado sends his sword through the first tribesman he encounters, and the next. Then he reins in, adjusts his breastplate, and searches for another opponent. An eagle rises. The Madar sees it out of the corner of his eye, but he quickly buries his sword in the belly of another tribesman. An eagle rises. Maldinado hacks downward from atop his horse. He strikes between the head and shoulder of a tribesman. He feels the body collapse under his sword. He shifts and delivers a blow to another tribesman.

An eagle rises.

Maldinado hears a scream, but he doesn't turn. He swings his sword from one Rorne to the next. They don't fight back. They don't even resist! He pulls on the reins. No bodies. All around him, black cloaks lay in circular piles as though the Rorne, rather than fall dead, simply disrobed and vanished. An eagle emerges from one of these puddles with a head jerk. It twists and squirms away from the discarded cloak until, finally free, it gazes at Maldinado. The bird gives a threatening squawk, and then spreads its massive brown wings. An eagle rises.

A warrior screams, drawing Maldinado's attention from the sky. The screaming warrior sits awkwardly atop his horse, staring with horror at the rotting blue hand now sticking out the front of his chest. A Rorne tribesman sits mounted behind the warrior, holding the warrior's still beating heart in his hand. A warrior dies. Maldinado swings downward, hacking away at the approaching scholars. Their robes fall to the ground and eagles rise. A warrior dies. Maldinado jumps off his horse to strike at the nearest Rorne. He follows the cloak until it settles, plunging his sword into the mound. He hits his mark, striking the eagle still hidden within, thus triggering another transformation. The body of the tribesman returns, no longer moving. Dead. Maldinado swings at another tribesman, again waiting for the eagle to appear. "Kill the birds!" He yells.

A warrior dies. Two Rorne extend their hands into and through the back of an unsuspecting warrior. He cries out, but a third tribesman buries his hand in the warrior's throat, effectively muting his scream. A warrior dies. Maldinado adjusts his helmet, raises his sword, and kills a tribesman. In the distance he sees Brink, the banner bearer of the Adarian 45th, "Lucky bastard!"

The eagles descend. They fold their wings and pierce the air and crash into the warriors of the Adarian 45th as though their victims offer no more resistance than what they would feel while passing through clouds in a sun-filled sky. The birds emerge as tribesman, transforming on the other side of the skewered dead, blood dripping from their newly formed hands and, more disturbingly, their uneven teeth. The eagles descend. A gnarled and twisted hand stretches toward the Madar, but he pulls away. His enemy wears a white, patchy beard that exposes the rotting skin of his blistered face between the missing clumps of facial hair. Maldinado strikes him down and waits for the eagle. Instead, a red cricket emerges. Maldinado steps on it. He searches the horizon for the banner of the Adarian 45th which still waves in the distance, "Damn you, Brink! Die already!"

The Madar turns to find Gan-Pi standing beside him, along with Little Birty and five other warriors—their eyes wild with the excitement of battle.

Gan-Pi kisses his sword, "We are in your service, my Rovet."

"For Adarian!" Maldinado shouts.

The eight warriors mount a ferocious and coordinated assault. Two of them strike the scholars while two more wait for the eagles to appear. Two warriors protect the ones who wait, and the final two ward off any eagle attempting to descend. More warriors join and they quickly double in number. Strike! Wait. Kill!

Then the tigers arrive, dozens of them moving in pack formation. They leap into the fray, bringing with them an orange and black striped death to the resilient warriors. Adarians die. One of these beasts slams Maldinado to the ground using its powerful paws to drape over the Madar's shoulders—the bulk of its briny smelling fur forcefully pressing down on his face and chest—but the tiger convulses and dies. Maldinado rolls and pushes the animal off him, retrieving his sword from the belly of the tiger even as it transforms. Adarians die. Another tiger sends Maldinado back to the ground, but this time his sword clatters away from him and across the rocky terrain. He struggles against the significant weight of the beast even as it raises an enormous paw, but Little Birty abruptly severs the paw with a shout, "For Adarian!" The tiny warrior swings through the blow, and then returns to bury the sword in the tiger's chest, setting Maldinado free.

Adarians die. Maldinado retrieves his own swords and it drives into a nearby tiger. He swings downward and cuts into the neck, hacking at it until he completely severs the head. Then something strikes him in the head, and he falls to the ground in a heap. Adarians die. He feels dizzy…disoriented. He sees a tiger running toward him. He should do something. He should… Maldinado rises to his knees and strikes upward with all that remains of his strength. Adarians die. He yanks the sword out and removes his badly damaged helmet. His head throbs. All around him, warriors of the Adarian 45th die. Mauled. Bleeding. Dead. Their bodies surround him. He searches the horizon for the banner of the Adarian 45th, but Brink, too, lies dead. The banner has fallen.

"May the Sphere be with you…" Maldinado says.

No other banner bearer ever lasted so long.

Ayson rides hard after the Adow. Her black hair, like her mother's, flows in the wind. Unlike her mother, however, she wields a sword and yells, "Attack!" She moves past the warriors of the Adowian Army, traveling deep into the enemy forces with little regard for her own safety. Ayson falls further behind. Faunride, too, tries to stay with her, but the Rorne close rank and soon they surround him, halting his progress. Neither one can reach her to protect her. The Adow finds herself alone inside the Rorne circle. Then, a moment later, Inindu stands beside her.

"Where have *you* been?" The Adow asks.

"I was talking to our father."

"This is no time to be praying!"

"Can you think of a better time?"

"Inindu, this was all a lie!"

"This is no time for a confession, my Adow."

"It was a story that Troq used to tell me. This stupid quest is just a stupid story!"

"I know," Inindu responds as the enemy converges upon them and the Adow raises her sword, striking down the nearest scholar. His body bursts into flames. Inindu taunts her sister, "I was beginning to think you'd never learn to use that thing." Her own magenta-colored weapons—ever extending strands of hair—shift and strike like a floating pit of vipers. Slither. Ensnare. Devour. One after another, scholars die. And Inindu savors each death, observing with great curiosity. She has always felt drawn to death…the tightening of eyelids…the void that forms in the pupils. The struggle of the body wrapped in her hair. The stillness. Death. Something she will never experience.

The Adow, on the other hand, obliterates her enemy. Dozens of dead scholars lay burning at her feet, but she does not pause for death's sake. She shows no hesitation in her assault, swinging the sword with a fierceness driven by guilt. She plunges her blade into another scholar and his body erupts in flames.

"My Adow!" Faunride dismounts and sends his sword into the nearest scholar and moves to the next, trying to reach the Adow, but the force of battle pushes him further away.

Even farther back, Ayson also dismounts to find himself surrounded by the Rorne, their diseased hands reaching for him like the beaked necks of hatchling stretching for their first meal. The red crickets swarm and soon crawl over him. He swings at everything and nothing. He stomps and jumps, trying to shake the crickets loose. Then he feels a sharp pain in his arm, causing him to drop his sword. Another stab of pain at his side. The Rorne touch him. Their hands pierce his skin and continue inside his body. He screams. Struggles. He can feel their hands ripping at his body! One in his leg. His shoulder. Black cloaks surround him, swirl around him. A hand touches his heart. He looks down at his chest in a final moment of clarity. The gold of his armor is barely visible under the blood and the red crickets. The hands of the Rorne tighten around his muscles and bones and organs. The red crickets cover his face. The hand around his heart squeezes and Ayson screams, allowing the red crickets to enter his mouth—they slither up his nose and crawl into his ears—quickly silencing the First Etabli's final scream. The hand around his heart rips it from his chest, and Ayson dies. His final thought that of Quel…the Adow as she lay dying in his arms.

Soon afterward, Teyo leads a charge to recover his body. He and several warriors form a circle, protecting what remains of the First Etabli.

Further ahead, Faunride tries valiantly to reach the Adow, but he cannot push through the surge of scholars and, eventually, he must fight simply to protect himself. Across the battlefield, Rorne tribesmen overwhelm the Adowian Army. The last remaining warrior of the Abre 10th lies dead. The Rovet of the Golesh 41st dies. The banner of the Stycral 38th falls. The Rorne attack. Fear moves through the warriors as they witness the brutal deaths of the strongest among them. Five warriors from the Mali 6th flee. Their Rovet sees them, spurs his horse, and runs them down with his spear. When he returns, an eagle skewers his chest and the Rovet falls from his horse. The Rorne push the attack, if not universally successful. Indeed, fifty-seven warriors from the Tesa 89th, wielding swords made by Hiate the blacksmith and Edran his apprentice, kill tribesman along the right flank with each stroke of their gifted swords, so the Rorne fall back and continue their attack on weaker portions of the army. The scholars-turned-tribesman-turned creatures kill far more than they lose, burying sickly hands into the bodies of warrior…and taggle. The cursed taggles show no fear. It doesn't matter. The Rorne squeeze or pierce or maul and the brave die alongside the craven.

Hiate and Edran appear on the horizon, running their horses straight to the front lines of battle. Hiate leaps from his horse, barreling into and knocking three scholars to the ground. He rolls to his feet and promptly buries his blade into two of the three, one landed atop the other, allowing Hiate to spear both at once. He pulls it out and swings at the third whose head falls from his convulsing body. A random hand reaches out for Edran but the apprentice severs it. One of the tribesmen challenges the boy. Edran kills him with one stroke, causing the Rorne to back away…right into the blacksmith. Hiate charges like a wild boar, lowering his shoulder and crashing into the retreating scholars. They fall. They die. He rolls and kills another one. Hiate keeps his thick legs bent, enabling him to stay low and take advantage of his enhanced leverage and a greater sense of balance. He punches. He kicks. He wields a deadly sword and the Adowian Army soon rallies around him, adopting the blacksmith as their new champion.

Blue-faced, black-robed scholars enter the Adow's tent where Hintor stands ready to slay them. He charges with the steel of Caduum in his grasp. Behind him, Nataline wraps DK Vel in her arms as though protecting one of her daughters. She holds a knife in her hand, but more than anything she prays the Sphere will deliver her from this nightmare. Hintor manages to squelch the initial attack. Then he chases the scholars outside. Nataline calls after him, but he doesn't respond. She and the boy can only hear the muffled sounds of battle. Something crashes against the tent behind them, causing Nataline to turn with a start. Nothing. A slumping shadow appears against the canvas, probably a body. Another crash, followed by the squawk of an eagle. The bird rips through the tent's roof, falling in a disoriented heap ten feet from where they stand. Nataline wraps her hand around the bird's head and lops it off with the oft-practiced skill of a great cook, only to then cower away as the eagle transforms into the diseased and now severed body of a scholar.

Hintor returns, makes quick assessment of the scene, and grins, "Not much for conversation, are they?"

"Behind you!"

Hintor turns to find two more scholars. Again, Nataline wraps her arms around the taggle boy to protect him.

Inindu scans the breadth of the battlefield, finding it oddly silent. Yes, warriors shout commands. Eagles squawk. The dying often scream or moan, yet everything feels muted. The Rorne carry no weapon, thus negating the typical clash of swords. The roaring of tigers, though less frequent than other sounds, and perhaps for this reason, somehow rises above the dim silence. But the alarming roar of a tiger does not save Teyo who still stands guard over the First Etabli's remains. Neither does Inindu who sees the tiger leap. Teyo's head strikes the ground with a deafening thud. She watches as the tiger licks his unconscious face, all but removing the helmet as its tongue moves up Teyo's head. When it bites into the warrior's throat, Inindu simply takes it all in with morbid interest. Teyo quivers and dies.

Then the tiger turns its attention to Inindu. But when it charges and leaps, Inindu wraps the beast into her hair. It struggles to free itself from her grasp, but soon enough, the tiger grows calm, slowly relaxes, and stillness replaces life. Death. A great emptiness. Inindu unwinds her hair, but the body is now devoured. Nothing remains in death. She reaches for another scholar just as the sky ignites with fire, scattering and killing thousands of eagles.

The Kul has arrived.

"'Tis a poor place for a creature of such beauty."

Inindu turns to find Hiate the blacksmith walking up behind her, followed by his apprentice, "Perhaps you would like to lead me to a better place?"

Hiate buries his sword in a tribesman's chest and yanks it out, "'Tis the Adow I've come to rescue, no offense meant to yerself."

"Then I will leave you to your purpose, father."

"And I to yer's." The blacksmith looks to the sky and then to the Kul and suddenly grins, "Daughter...may the Sphere be with you."

"Maldinado would be a much more useful companion," Inindu lowers her head slightly. "No offense meant to yerself."

Hiate bows, "None taken."

He and the apprentice leave Inindu, traveling toward the flaming sword of the Adow. Inindu absently reaches for another scholar, shifting her focus from the blacksmith to the creature who descends from the sky. Morlac's greatest creation: The Kul is a yearling consumed by fire. Her pale skin appears and disappears from behind vacillating flames. She has black hair and thin violet lips. No eyes. Nothing visible, at least, which has always bothered Inindu. That, and the swollen eyes of the scholars. Those bother her, too, as though these creatures offered their eyes in sacrifice to a blind god. *Fools!* The scholars bow before the Kul as it settles onto the battlefield. Inindu has never felt inclined to bow to anyone, nor does she have reason to fear, so she gallops toward the Kul without another thought.

The blacksmith and his apprentice finally reach the Adow. She stares out at the Kul with a madness that reveals her otherwise heroic thoughts, "You can't be defeating it, my Adow,"

The Adow turns on the blacksmith with a fire that matches the flames of her sword, "I won't flee."

"You *must* flee," Hiate continues, undaunted. "I won't allow you to be dying on the battlefield like yer mother. Let yer warriors fight for you. Let them die for the honor they seek!"

"I won't leave my warriors!"

"Ovda, you can't be winning this battle," Hiate responds.

"What…what did you call me?" The Adow's flaming sword suddenly extinguishes.

"An old friend of yers asked me to watch after you. 'Twas a warrior named Troq."

"My Adow!" Faunride comes running to her side, pushing past Hiate and his apprentice, "My Adow, the First Etabli is dead!"

Edran motions toward the battlefield, "Master, she's there."

Faunride turns to find Inindu approaching the Kul, "What is she doing?"

"'Tis her purpose to be facing the dark creature," Hiate explains.

But the Adow cannot take her eyes off the blacksmith, "You knew Troq?"

Hiate doesn't respond. His attention remains solely on the scene in the distance: Two champions face one another. He waits and watches.

Inindu doesn't slow her pace, unwilling to delay the proceedings. She simply charges the Kul without concern for ceremony. But then Maldinado appears in front of her, unexpectedly forcing Inindu to come to a halt beside him. He looks battle weary if still obstinate, "The Adarian 45th requests the honor of being the first to attack this creature."

"Spare me your formalities. Go, protect your Adow, Madar!"

"I won't run away," Maldinado starts toward the Kul.

"This isn't your fight!" Inindu moves to stop him, "Protect your Adow!"

"The honor is ours!" He attempts to move around her, but Inindu easily matches his labored movement.

"And what of your sister?" Inindu changes tactics. "Who will protect Nataline?"

Maldinado doesn't turn from the Kul.

"Damn your sense of honor!" Then a vicious thought occurs to her. Inindu looks back across the horizon toward the elevated spot where she last spoke with her father. She can just make out the red beard of the blacksmith, "No, he wouldn't..." But she knows he did...she told him she would rather have Maldinado as companion over the Sphere...and here he stands.

And why shouldn't she take Maldinado with her? The Adow stole Adarian without so much as a whispered apology. Beyond that fact, her sister is a fool. She would choose Maldinado as First Etabli instead of Faunride, thus repeating the cycle her mother began. Such a choice would result in another Quel. She nods toward the blacksmith in the distance, "It seems you will have your wish, Madar, but with one condition: We fight the Kul together." Inindu turns back toward Maldinado, "Take my hand."

He climbs onto Inindu-horse to sit behind topi-Inindu, wrapping his arms around her slender waist. "Do you know why we burn our dead?" Inindu charges the Kul, traveling faster than any horse Maldinado has ever ridden.

"I've never thought much about it," he draws his sword, uncertain what effect it will have on the creature, if any.

Inindu carries no weapon and, strangely, her hair sits upon her shoulders—unmoving and untouched by the wind, "Fire serves as the gateway to another world."

When they reach the Kul, Inindu carries Maldinado directly into the fire, leaping without hesitation.

The Madar and Rovet and protector of the Adow yells, "For Adari..." But his words, and the battle of champions ends abruptly. The Kul consumes both Inindu and Maldinado.

"What is she *doing*?" The Adow watches in horror as Inindu charges the Kul, "Who's that with her?"

"'Tis a brave warrior, to be certain."

They disappear into the Kul, blackness enveloping magenta beauty.

"What happened? I can't see them," Faunride strains to see past the Kul, certain Inindu must have passed through the creature, but he can find no sign of them.

"It was Maldinado..." The Adow answers her own question, "Both of them...now gone...because of me."

"Come, my Adow. We can't be waiting any longer," Hiate sheathes his sword.

"My Adow?" Faunride turns his blade on the blacksmith, "Who is this?"

He bows, "Hiate, a blacksmith from Caduum."

"Inindu told me I should meet you," the Adow mutters.

In the clearing below, the Tesa 89th move to challenge the Kul. The creature consumes them. Then the Stycral 16th. The Kiel 9th. They all die. Having seen enough, Hiate takes the reins from Edran and mounts his horse, "It be time, Ovda." He extends his hand to the Adow, who allows him to pull her onto the back of his horse. The blacksmith looks down at Faunride, "Yer welcome to ride with Edran, fine warrior. At least until we find more horses. I imagine there be some near the Adow's tent, which happens to be our immediate destination."

The four of them ride west, away from the Kul, but not far enough away to avoid the horrors of an endless succession of screams and consuming fire. Warriors die in massive numbers, incinerated while attacking—some attempting to flee. Bolstered by the arrival of their champion, the scholars resume their assault, forcing Hiate and Edran to alter their course if never straying from their destination. They reach the Adow's tent to find Hintor fighting back a horde of scholars. Faunride and Edran assist with the killing even as DK Vel grins at the arrival of Hiate.

"Get some horses," Hiate orders. "It be time to leave."

"I won't leave without Maldinado," Hintor declares. Nataline agrees.

"I'm afraid yer Madar be dead," Hiate informs them.

"Then it was him," The Adow confirms her own suspicions.

"They died with honor," Faunride says.

Nataline falls into Hintor's arms, unwilling to believe her brother is dead, and though Hintor knew this day would come, he finds himself unprepared for the burden of emotion that threatens to break him. He buries his nose into Nataline's hair, fighting back his own tears.

Hiate spurs his horse forward, the Adow still mounted behind him, "There be no time to mourn. Find yer horses and follow me. We've a quest 'tis needs our attention."

"No, Hiate. No more lies," the Adow says firmly as they ride away. "There *is* no quest. It was just a story that Troq told me when he was still alive." She leans her head against his back and starts to cry, "I just want to go home."

"The prophecy you told may be a lie, Ovda, but the story be as true as my beard. There be five creatures in the Torment, alright. They've been waiting there a long time for someone to find them." Hiate pats the arm of the Adow where it curls around his waist, "I suppose it be about time we did just that."

<u>A Record of—*she who served as*—The Adow: </u>

Moon	Seal
Completion of the Purple Moon	Floating
Completion of the Purple Moon	Hemming
Shadow of the Purple Moon	River unde
Shadow of the Purple Moon	Sword thr
Completion of the Red Moon	Broken Cr
Completion of the Red Moon	Crown of
Changing of the Silver Moon	Five Crow
Completion of the Yellow Moon	Sword with
Changing of the Blue Moon	Crowned
Completion of the Green Moon	Crowned
Completion of the Green Moon	Crowned S
Completion of the Green Moon	Crown ove
Completion of the Green Moon	Two Crow
Completion of the Green Moon	Crowned
Completion of the Green Moon	Hammer S
Completion of the Green Moon	Sun Rising
Completion of the Green Moon	Crown bet
Dark Moon	Tiger and

Months: Erog | Utine | Cil | Flatine | Joone   Date Format: (G.

Periods: Year = 5 Months | Month = 5 Weeks | We

The Adow

on, Official Seal, and Chosen First Etabli

First Etabli

er Sphere Erin, the First Etabli
ove Crown Anine
 Aul
vn Taggle, the cursed
 Ylaf
 Erbohn
 Ig-poy
on Hilt Adarian, hero of Ire
 Fael
 Irloore
 Cintyge
ed Swords Lio
 Enyure
 Athoyen
Crown Eerya
own Cidal
vords Ayson, of Quel
 Ayson, of Quel

ring the Red Moon | (Specific) Erog 23, Completion of the Red Moon 51
ys | Day = 5 Hours = Spheric Hour | Hour = 300 Minutes

y Adow, come see," the taggle boy wakes me with a whisper, his shadowed figure barely discernible from the darkness.

"What is it?" I climb out from under the blanket, waiting for my eyes to adjust.

We made camp somewhere deep in the Torment. Hiate pushed the horses hard as possible to get clear of the Rorne and Morlac's beast. I can only imagine what happened to the rest of my army. My greatest champions gone in an instant. What chance do we have to survive such a creature? I look into the starless sky, searching for any sign of the eagles, any sign of the Kul. Nothing. The boy leads me slowly through a dense grouping of balor trees. "What is it, taggle?" But he doesn't respond. Whatever he saw earlier has the boy excited, so I unsheathe my sword. He slows to a stop, and I kneel beside him.

"This is where Hiate disappeared," the boy says quietly. "We were walking together, and then he vanished."

"What do you mean, he vanished?"

"Gone. He was there, and then he wasn't. That's when I saw the light," he points out into the distance ahead.

My sword erupts in flames and I suddenly fear the boy has led me into an ambush, certain Hiate's body lies butchered somewhere nearby. The sword serves as a torch, illuminating the forest around me. I find no signs of a struggle. So, what happened to the blacksmith? I investigate the surrounding area, but I find nothing out of the ordinary. Only the faint light ahead, maybe a mile away. I turn back to the boy. Shadows and firelight flicker across his sallow face and sweaty torso. He stands mostly naked, and his black hair looks as tangled as mine. Why did he wake me instead of Hintor, his master? Does he presume to serve me now that Inindu is dead?

"Before he disappeared, Hiate told me to give you a message," the boy says, as though reading my mind. "He said you'll hear his voice in the stories."

I search anew for the blacksmith, hoping at worst to find his body.

I mean, it feels like there should be a body. It seems like basic manners for someone to leave some sign of their death. Of course, Inindu and Maldinado left nothing behind. *Tasa Ro!* "What kind of…" Hell, I don't even know what I want to say. *Dammit!*

"My Adow, was Hiate really the Sphere?"

"Yes, boy."

Yes, the Sphere took the form of a red-bearded blacksmith from Caduum. Of course, he did…and before that he was my guardian—my storyteller. Did my mother know? And has it always worked this way with the Adow? Oh, is *that* how my predecessors communicated with the Sphere? No, wait, probably the other way around—that is how the Sphere communicates with his Adow.

The boy points toward the light. Right, the light. I lead the boy through the trees, easily navigating a path under the glow of my still flaming sword. The taggle follows me like Ayson used to follow me. He doesn't wield a sword, of course, and he will prove useless if this leads to an ambush. Then again, Ayson would fair no better. And, well, Ayson is dead, too.

It feels like someone just dropped an anvil on my throat and I can't swallow. My father is dead…and Inindu…and Maldinado. *Dammit!* I could use the Madar right about now. I could use more air, too. *Breathe!* *Tasa Ro!* Everything happened so quickly. I didn't…how do we… It doesn't matter. I take several deep breaths, and then I consider returning to camp. Yes, I should probably go back for Faunride or Hintor or both, but instead…well, I'm the one with the big flaming sword.

The light in the distance grows and separates as we move closer, evolving into several different lights without an obvious source. I rule out torches, for I would see reflections or other glimpses of the warriors holding them. I continue to scan the surrounding area as we journey, a helpful habit one must adopt when dealing with assassins and a First Etabli who…will never draw his sword again. *Focus!* Nobody lies in wait, and I find no signs of danger.

We enter a large clearing to discover five sphere-shaped lights aglow and suspended in midair. Perhaps drawn by my own curiosity, or more likely, simply acting the fool, I reach out and touch the closest sphere, wrapping my hand around its smooth and surprisingly solid surface. The warm sphere vibrates as though barely the energy contained within. Then it grows brighter and brighter until the blinding white light forces me to look away, and in that moment, I see the taggle boy prostrating behind me, an unexpected sight if only because I had momentarily forgotten about him. It seems taggles can disappear without ever leaving, though Troq would claim my general awareness of my surroundings has diminished due to lack of training…or do I call him Hiate now instead of Troq…or the Sphere…or *whatever*! I force myself to focus on the prostrating taggle boy. Do taggles typically show this much reverence? The question makes me realize just how little I know about taggles because, well, the Adow cast them from our presence which means I have only ever known one. Specifically, this boy now groveling before me.

Behind me, white light fades to a warm glow, allowing me to turn and see a golden figure in place of the sphere: The sculpted image of a male yearling. The yearling's hair looks like a splash in a pond if somehow captured at the point of impact, a large curling wave of brown hair left suspended above his head; and one curl that hangs down over his right eye. The wildness of his hair reminds me of Inindu's—just as disturbing if less frightening.

I leave the taggle to his worship and touch another sphere. Blinding light and golden figure, same as before, but different. He has a squinting face with eyelids seemingly heavier than what he can bear, aging his otherwise youthful features. I run my fingers across his golden face. It feels warm, almost hot to the touch.

Three more spheres, same as before. Three more golden figures, each of them slightly different. One has a furrowed brow. One displays great sadness. And the last…such innocence, his eyes open wide with wonder. I touch his cheek, irrationally thinking it pliable, but it feels as solid as the other figures. Golden statues. Why? Why place them here in the middle of the Torment? Are these the creatures Hiate said we would find? Are these my wolves? But how? I told everyone a story! I told a stupid story, and now here they stand. Five golden wolves. The five Arms of the Sphere. *Tasa Ro*! We found them. Wait, no, a *taggle* found them. The boy peeks up, his curiosity finally getting the better of his sense of reverence.

"What was it Hiate told you to tell me, boy?"

"That you'll hear his voice in the stories."

"How many stories do you know?" *How many stories did Troq tell me?* Do they all contain prophecies? Why didn't my mother or any of the other Adow tell me these stories?

"I've never counted, my Adow."

But I barely have time to process his response. A presence enters the clearing with enough force to throw me to the ground. It forms a white sphere at the center of the statues. Streams of light pierce the night, extending from the sphere to the Arms of the Sphere with such violence that it sends sparks crackling through the darkness in a thousand directions. I see all of this in a moment, the image forever frozen in my mind. Then I shield my eyes. Gusts of hot air beat against me. A tremendous buzzing fills my ears–vibrations of power I recognize from when I touched the smaller spheres. Can the boy feel what I feel? I can't see him, but I imagine him cowering, so I blindly make my way around the clearing, oddly compelled to reach the boy. To protect him. Is this how a mother feels?

"Boy! Taggle!" I try to remember his name…DK… "DK Vel!" Where is he? I need the storyteller. I need my connection to the Sphere!

"I'm here! I can't see."

I kneel beside him and wrap my arm around him and bury my face in his unwashed hair. *Tasa Ro*! Oh my, he definitely needs a bath…and some clothes, "It's alright. You're going to be alright." I hold my sword at the ready.

"It's him, isn't it? The Sphere?"

"Yes, boy. I think it is."

The presence withdraws, along with its all-consuming light, leaving only the fire from my sword to illuminate the clearing—a feeble substitute.

"Mother?"

"Who's there?" I stand to face the threat.

But I find no danger. A single flame appears, held above the smallish hand of a yearling. Specifically, five yearlings. The golden figures somehow brought to life. The second figure to appear, the sphere I touch, now holds the suspended flame, and the one with squinting features…untamed power resonates from him.

"They're *taggles*," DK Vel points.

I immediately look at their ears. He's right. Turns out, the five wolves of prophecy are, in fact, taggle boys.

Then Faunride crashes into the clearing, "My Adow! The scholars have found us!" Hintor, Nataline, and Edran emerge from the forest behind him, leading the horses.

"Good thing we decided to skip the campfire tonight," Hintor passes a set of reigns to the Adow. "Wouldn't want to give them an obvious light to follow."

a taggle's tale

As spoken by the Adow.

"N o more running," the Adow's sword flares with renewed life. Faunride stands beside her.

Hintor smiles upon seeing the Adow's unique weapon, "It's traditional in Adarian for warriors to exchange swords before a battle."

"Not now, Hintor!" Nataline scolds.

Hintor shrugs and pulls his own sword.

Behind them, forgotten amid the threat, Edran gathers the other six taggle boys to him. He serves as their sole protector, sword in hand. The attack hits them with fury. Horses scatter. Eagles dive. Flames from the Adow's sword leap into the sky, splintering like lightning, searing eagles faster than they can descend. The dead birds transform back into scholars, their bodies falling ungracefully. Still, several of the eagles breakthrough the fire-lightning. Then more. And more. Soon, thousands of them. They billow over and around the fire-lightning like a waterfall obliterating the pathetic flame of a candle. Faunride takes the Adow to the ground, shielding her with his own body. The Adow's sword no longer burns, leaving them all in darkness and enhancing the already deafening noise of the birds. The Adow shouts something at Faunride, but whatever she says goes unheard in the confusion of the attack.

Hintor feels a rush of eagles fly past him, producing a cold wind with a scent of decay. He swings his sword blindly and mutters several unheard quips, but his clumsy attack manages to connect with a thud. The unexpected victim causes his sword to change course, however, and as the eagle, now dead, transforms into a scholar the sudden shift in weight throws Hintor off-balance. Though he follows the tribesman to the ground, he recovers quickly, pulling his sword from the body to once more strike into the night with wide-arcing swings.

The Adow's sword ignites anew. Faunride still covers her with his body, but she has managed to free her arm and now raises her sword to the heavens, illuminating the mass of birds overhead. Nothing seems to exist beyond their piercing cries, glaring eyes, and yellow beaks. "Get off me!" The Adow struggles against Faunride's grip, her rage matching the flames of her sword.

But the flames draw Faunride's attention, for they no longer crackle from bird to bird like lighting. Now the fire rises like a mighty pillar. It rips through sky with brutal efficiency, and only then does Faunride realize the Adow is their only hope of salvation. He cannot protect her. She must protect them. Reluctantly, he releases his Adow.

She rises to fully absorb the attack, but the descending flood of birds part to either side of the flames. They swoop away and return to the sky. Changing tactics, Faunride and Hintor move to the outer perimeter where the eagles fly lowest, and they proceed to hack away, sending bird after bird flailing into the darkness of the forest beyond. Then the flames of the Sword of the Adow abruptly leap onto the blades of Faunride and Hintor. Nataline's, too, and even Edran's, who points his Caduum-forged weapon toward the flames as though intentionally calling them forth or otherwise inviting them. His face certainly shows no surprise, a stark contrast to the aghast expressions of Faunride, Hintor, and Nataline. Thus, five pillars of flame ignite the sky. They fire incinerates a mass of birds, their charred remains turning to ash before they can ever transform. Hintor swings with delightful and unhindered power, "If Maldinado could see me now!" Nataline simply holds her blade aloft, unconsciously reaching out with her other hand to touch the head of the taggle around her leg, DK Vel. Behind her, Edran watches over the remaining taggles. Hundreds of eagles perish. Thousands remain. They circle and swarm, squawking without ceasing. They fly everywhere, appearing and disappearing behind, and through, and around the pillars of flame. Faunride retreats to his Adow, ready to protect her once more, fully aware that he will not rise again if he must take her to the ground. But at least he will die while protecting his Adow.

Abruptly, the eagles flee. The rush of wind fades to silence, along with their deafening squawks. The pillars of fire slowly diminish, giving way to darkness.

Hintor can only hear ringing in his ears and his pupils widen as adrenaline continues to fuel his body, "Run, you bastards!"

"Look!" Faunride points to a red glow emerging above the trees, "The Kul approaches."

"Let it come!" The Adow spits the words, her sword flaring in response.

One of the new taggles steps away from the others. He holds a rekindled flame above his outstretched hand, "Get behind me!"

Faunride looks at the forgotten taggle, stunned by his brashness, struggling to remember all that occurred before the battle, "Learn your place, taggle!"

"Who are you?" Hintor vaguely remembers seeing the boy earlier, "And who are they?" He points to the four boys huddled around Edran.

"'Tis Madic Baltin," Edran replies. "And these be the Arms of the Sphere."

"The five wolves," the Adow confirms.

"Taggles?" Faunride turns to his Adow in alarm.

"Yes, taggles."

"*This* was our quest?" Hintor asks nobody. Then he erupts with rage, "Maldinado died for a bunch of *taggles?*"

"Hintor!" Nataline warns, but she cannot suppress her own feelings, suddenly aware of the taggle boy at her leg. She shoves him with a snarl, "Don't touch me!"

DK Vel releases her leg and quickly, silently, rejoins the other boys.

The flame above Madic Baltin's hand grows larger.

"How is he doing that?" Faunride asks.

"I don't know," The Adow turns back toward the approaching Kul. "It doesn't matter. Nataline, get them out of here."

"My Adow?" Nataline doesn't move, "They're taggles."

"I'm not leaving," Madic moves determinedly, brushing past the Adow to stand in front of her. "This is my purpose."

Faunride reacts to the obvious slight, bringing his sword down upon the offending taggle, but Madic raises his free hand in lackluster response. The sword, as it comes in contact with the taggle's hand, fragments into droplets of water, bursting outward with harmless force. Faunride stares at his now empty hands. Everyone else stares at Madic.

"My Adow," Edran breaks the silence. "You'll not be defeating the Kul with yer sword. 'Tis Madic's task, to be certain."

But the Adow doesn't retreat. In fact, none of them move, for the Kul appears above them. The creature of wind and shadow and fire appears only as a creature of fire against the night sky, a vast mass of swirling flame that fills the darkened horizon.

Hintor wraps his arms around Nataline and holds her head against his shoulder, "Don't look."

"We should run!" Nataline whispers.

Hintor chuckles at the suggestion.

Nataline pushes against him until she can look him in the eye,

"Seriously, take me to Plenrid. I want to be a farmer's wife." The eagles return, emboldened by the arrival of their champion. But they don't attack. They flutter around, circle above, and finally settle into the trees of the surrounding forest, apparently, seeking the best vantage point from which to view the final battle.

Hintor shakes his head, "No, Nataline. I may have been born in Plenrid, but I'll die an Adarian. Your brother made sure of that."

"You're not Adarian!"

"The unbroken circle on my chest says differently."

Nataline smiles despite her fear, both emotions highlighted by the flames of the Kul, now fully ablaze overhead, "In that case, I'll marry you." Hintor stares in befuddlement. Nataline leans forward and kisses his uncertain lips, her tears wet against his nose. He drops his sword, wraps his arms around her, and together they await the Kul.

I feel oddly drawn to these taggles, as though truly their mother, but I did not give birth to them. I did not create them. They are creatures of the Sphere. I touched them, nothing more. I look up toward the Kul and adjust my grip upon the sword. I wield so much power…but not enough. Edran is right. We won't survive. DK Vel wraps himself around my leg, seeking my protection just as he did earlier tonight when the Sphere entered the clearing…which seems like a lifetime ago. I reach down to embrace his head. My storyteller. My link to the Sphere. *I wish I could've heard all your stories, boy. I wish my daughter could've heard your stories.* "It's alright, DK Vel. Everything will be alright."

But I need to do something before we die, "Faunride!" No, I don't have to do this. Yes, I can protect myself. My sword flickers with indecision, "Faunride!" My humiliated protector finally turns away from Madic Baltin, his eyes showing the devastation he feels. No, I don't have to do this, but I extend my sword, anyway, inviting him to take it, "Faunride, It seems I'm in need of a First Etabli."

He hesitates for only a moment. I can't blame him. The Kul, Madic Baltin, the squawking eagles…it's a lot to absorb. Then he hastens to take my sword. The flames extinguish the moment my hand releases the hilt. *Well, that's a little disappointing.* It doesn't matter. This has nothing to do with the sword. *Yes, Faunride, I saw the hurt in your eyes during the Greeting Rituals when I didn't choose you to ride to Adarian.* I won't do that again. He deserves this honor. He deserves to die for me.

I kneel down beside DK Vel and hold him to my throat as the Kul draws near, "Don't worry, boy. I'm here now. Everything will be alright."

Madic Baltin waits for the Kul as though baiting a fish. Though barely perceptible in the darkness, he wears a golden robe, as do his brothers. Beads of perspiration run down the side of his face. With his free hand, Madic brushes the sweat and his unkempt hair made slick around his ears. With his other hand he raises the flame, allowing it to expand upward toward the Kul, toward the face without eyes. The creature continues downward. She does not see or does not fear taggle. Madic's unwavering flame stretches upward until it merges with the fire of the Kul, sliding into her like a fisherman's hook. The Kul stops, suddenly aware of the foreign presence—one she cannot consume. Madic's flame starts to retract, drawing with it the flames of the Kul. Like a net pulling fish from the sea, Madic pulls fire from wind and shadow. The creature howls with a vicious gust, striking at the source of her pain, but the boy continues to gather and pull fire from the Kul. The eagles watch with cocked heads as their champion is drained of her most terrifying threat. Madic draws the larger flame down into the smaller flame until only the latter remains. He keeps it suspended above his palm for a moment longer. Then he lowers his hand and the flame disappears entirely.

Above him, the Kul rages like a wounded animal. She strikes quickly and defensively, consuming the taggle and his companions. She buries them in shadow and chaos. Faunride swings the Adow's sword, but he finds nothing to strike. The wind feels warm, even hot upon his face. Sound is buffered. Breath is taken. Shadow consumes everything. The newly appointed First Etabli lowers his sword and embraces death. But it never takes him.

Madic Baltin stands with his arms extended downward at an angle, hands open. His eyes open to the wind, causing tears to form and stream into his ears. He opens his mouth. He tastes the darkness. Then he devours it. The Kul swirls and funnels down into the taggle's mouth, a maelstrom with Madic at its center. The face without eyes floats helplessly through waves of darkness and shadow, her pale skin swept under the current only to emerge again and then under once more, always encircling her captor. The formlessness of shadow and wind gather toward a single point below.

Madic consumes her, spreading his feet a little wider as the Kul fully enters his body. Then the taggle boy simply closes his mouth.

Squawk.

Madic turns his head to the sound and reopens his mouth. But instead of consuming the birds as he did with the Kul, his body unexpectedly explodes. He erupts with a force that throws everyone to the ground except Edran who somehow remains unaffected. DK Vel opens his eyes to find no trace of the eagles or the balor trees where they perched. The clearing now extends further out by several hundred yards. But instead of the forest, the taggle boy can only see a barrier of fire…and shadow… and wind. The Kul surrounds them, extending overhead to fully enclose them within half of a sphere.

"There be nothing more to fear," Edran says.

"What happened?" Faunride demands.

The Adow stands undaunted, lifting DK Vel whom she embraces at her side, "Are we inside the Kul?"

"No," says Edran. "The Kul be existing in a different form now, her purpose altered."

"And the boy?" The Adow looks around, "Madic Baltin?"

"Madic's purpose 'tis fulfilled. My master created him to be protecting his brothers."

Hintor turns toward the remaining Arms of the Sphere, taggles of varying heights and features. They all huddle around Edran, their expressions ranging from unreadable to a look of terror, but nothing too unfamiliar. Indeed, Hintor has seen similar expressions on taggles before, and he certainly finds nothing to suggest them worth the sacrifice of so many warriors—so many friends. Yet, he cannot deny their frightening power.

"Where is your master?" The Adow asks Edran.

"'Tis a fair question, to be certain. Perhaps he be waiting on the other side of the Kul." Edran begins to walk, "'Tis time we be leaving this place." Edran walks without apparent concern. Neither does he pause before disappearing behind the wall of fire and shadow. A moment later, he reappears. "'Tis nothing to fear, my Adow. Walk quickly through the Kul and you'll suffer no harm." Again, Edran moves in and out of the Kul, "But do not linger or the Kul be consuming you same as it ever did." He disappears, once more, behind the Kul.

Hintor looks around, "Who's next?" No one moves, "Tasa Ro! Why does the Adarian 45th always have to lead?" He retrieves his sword, gives

Nataline a kiss, and boldly enters the strange barrier. His body feels the weight of the Kul immediately, pulling his skin downward as though peeling it from the top of his skull. His eyes close under the force, and his lungs struggle to gather air. His tongue falls to the back of his throat. His stomach collapses inward, legs waver. He can barely keep hold of his sword. It lasts only a moment, however. Hintor emerges from the Kul as though clearing the surface of a lake. He inhales with a desperate gasp, and then exhales with disgust. His mouth tastes like smoke, his tongue feels numb as though burned. He searches for Edran, but he has gone missing, so he takes a moment to calibrate himself. He has entered the forest. It's still dark, but the walls of fire and shadow on either side of him provide more than enough light. They also extend outward from where he stands into the forest and out of sight.

"Tasa Ro! How big is this thing?"

I can't sleep. The walls of the Kul on either side of me feel like a cage, so I sit with my back against a balor tree, resisting the urge to flee. Faunride, still holding my sword, stands guard above me as my newly appointed First Etabli. He stares at the Kul as though waiting for it to take shape and strike. Despite what Edran said, I can't help but wonder if we really are inside the creature. *Are you here, Maldinado? Inindu?* But our camp appears the same as when we left. I can tell the others share my apprehension. Hintor looks out into the darkness, sword raised and holding Nataline's hand the same as he has since we emerged from the Kul. If we have emerged. The Arms of the Sphere sit huddled together in silence. What can I say to them? Madic Baltin seemed so sure of himself. These four seem lost as newborns attempting to stand. I run fingers through DK Vel's hair, his head resting against my leg.

"Will we ever see Edran again?" The taggle asks.

"I don't know," the blacksmith's apprentice never appeared. We searched for him, moving in and out of the Kul several times—not a pleasant experience—but we never found him.

"Will we ever see the Sphere again?"

"The Sphere is always with us, boy." Yes, I believe that now.

"Do you think they have the same powers as the other taggle had?"

I look again at the remaining Arms of the Sphere, a complete mystery to me, "Did Hiate tell you anything about them?" The boy shakes his head against my leg, "Then I think there is much to learn about these taggles."

DK Vel suddenly sits up, causing Faunride and Hintor to react with alarm. But the taggle doesn't look afraid. Instead, he grabs excitedly at my arm, "I found them. I led you right to the Arms of the Sphere. That means I get an Adowian Burial!"

"Tasa Ro!" Hintor curses.

"Yes, boy, you will receive an Adowian Burial when you die," but even as I say it, I realize the implications. I have effectively lifted the curse. DK Vel smiles and returns to where he lay against my leg. Then he sits up again, bringing another reaction from Faunride and Hintor.

"Tasa Ro! Learn your place, taggle!" Faunride steps forward. The taggle cowers in reaction.

I hold up my hand to keep my First Etabli from killing the boy, "His place is with me, Faunride." I guide the boy back to my lap, "Are you always this restless, DK Vel?"

"I just realized...Madic Baltin..." The boy's fear gives way to renewed enthusiasm, "He didn't really die. He saved us. A *taggle* saved the Adow! He will live in that story forever!"

5-RUBY
SPECIAL EDITION
SPHERE PATTERN

This tale originated in Yenul, a bedtime story told by my guardian, Troq, whom I now know was the embodiment of the Sphere, as was Hiate after him. Troq's dark hands held me close to his heart, and I could feel his white beard against my head. He told me many stories about Tiger, tales which I later discovered mirrored those of Dsal Tiger. I always imagined Troq's tiger as white with black stripes. This was the first story he told me, the one he told me most often.

He always began: Listen to my story, Ovda, and may my words forever guide you.

- The Adow

Dsal Tiger

Tiger walks through a valley in Dragon's Torment where he has tracked the five wolves. Many have sought the wolves and never returned.

The bear is dead.

The lion is lost.

The owl has fled.

Tiger remains. He looks around. Sniffs the air. Continues carelessly; breaking sticks as he walks, sending echoes throughout the valley.

Overhead, a falcon draws near, drawn by the loud noise, "Flee this valley," it shrieks, "The Kul approaches."

"Have you seen the wolves?" Tiger calls, but the falcon flies away without another word.

Tiger doesn't flee. He's thirsty. The rain taunts him from a distance. He seeks a river, a lake, or even dewdrops suspended from leaves…but there is nothing to quench his thirst. Finally, at the top of a mountain, above the timberline, he finds a lake. He runs to its edge and lowers his head. The water feels cold as it travels through his body.

A fish appears, causing a smaller ripple in the already rippling waves created by Tiger's insatiable lapping, "Flee these waters. The Kul approaches."

"Have you seen the wolves?" Tiger asks, water dripping from the white fur around his mouth, but the fish has disappeared.

Tiger doesn't run. He's tired. He moves deeper into the Torment in search of a comfortable spot to rest, eventually coming upon a cave. He curls up and falls asleep beside a large rock.

Bats and more bats cover every inch of the cave. "Flee this cave," they squeak, "The Kul approaches."

Tiger awakens long enough to ask, "Have you seen the wolves?" But he resumes his slumber before the bats can respond.

A bear roars.

A lion roars.

But neither bear nor lion appears. Their roars echo from within the Kul, a creature of wind and shadow—a creature now standing at the mouth of the cave. The Kul has come!

Tiger no longer sleeps.

The roar of the bear fades. And that of the lion. Another sound emerges, barely perceptible, seemingly all that remains of the owl, "Who?"

Tiger feels his fur rise along the length of his spine. He growls at the Kul, raising his paw in warning, but the Kul is undeterred. Tiger roars before lunging at the creature, but he finds only wind and shadow. The Kul consumes Tiger. Mostly. A lingering echo remains, joining that of the bear and the lion and the owl.

Flee the Torment. The Kul approaches!

THE END

5-RUBY
SPECIAL EDITION

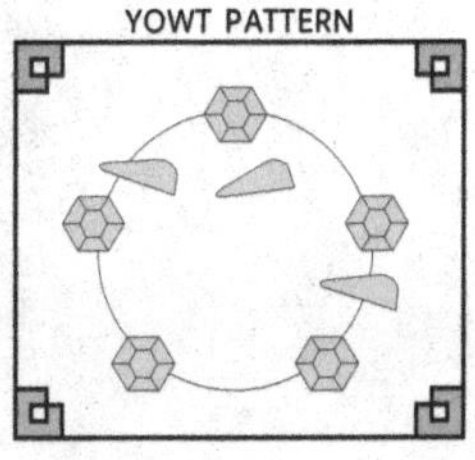

YOWT PATTERN

<u>A Record of—*she who served as*—The Adow:</u>

Moon	Seal
Completion of the Purple Moon	Floating
Completion of the Purple Moon	Hemming
Shadow of the Purple Moon	River und
Shadow of the Purple Moon	Sword thr
Completion of the Red Moon	Broken C
Completion of the Red Moon	Crown of
Changing of the Silver Moon	Five Crov
Completion of the Yellow Moon	Sword wit
Changing of the Blue Moon	Crowned
Completion of the Green Moon	Crowned
Completion of the Green Moon	Crowned
Completion of the Green Moon	Crown ove
Completion of the Green Moon	Two Crov
Completion of the Green Moon	Crowned
Completion of the Green Moon	Hammer
Completion of the Green Moon	Sun Risin
Completion of the Green Moon	Crown be
Dark Moon	Tiger and

Months: Erog | Utine | Cil | Flatine | Joone   Date Format: (
Periods: Year = 5 Months | Month = 5 Weeks | W

…oon, <u>Official Seal, and Chosen First Etabli:</u>

	First Etabli
…ver Sphere	Erin, the First Etabli
…bove Crown	Anine
…wn	Aul
…own	Taggle, the cursed
	Ylaf
…s	Erbohn
	Ig-poy
…wn on Hilt	Adarian, hero of Ire
…r	Fael
	Irloore
…y	Cintyge
…ssed Swords	Lio
	Enyure
	Athoyen
…g Crown	Ferya
…Crown	Cidal
…Swords	Ayson, of Quel
….	Ayson, of Quel

…uring the Red Moon | (Specific) Erog 23, Completion of the Red Moon 51
…Days | Day = 5 Hours = Spheric Hour | Hour = 300 Minutes

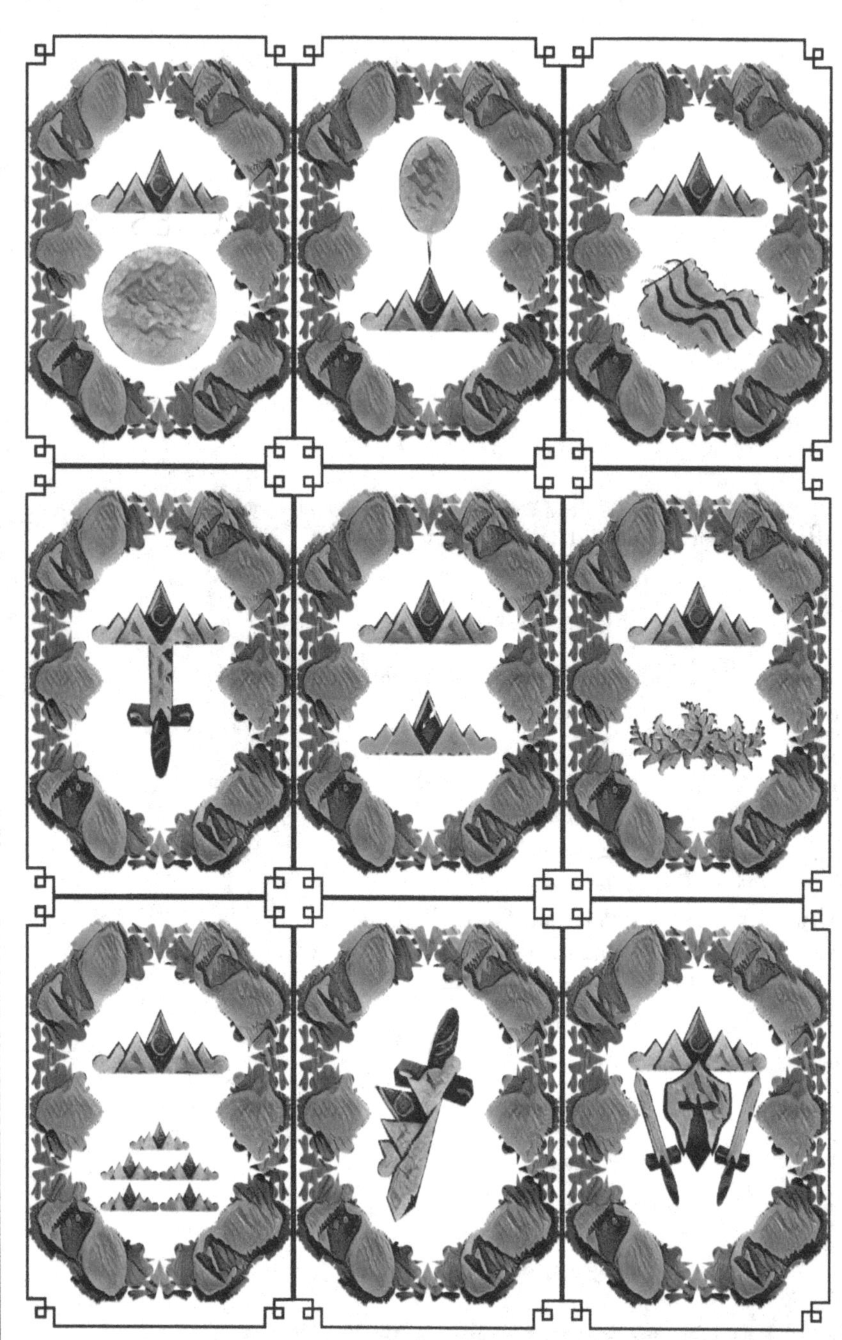

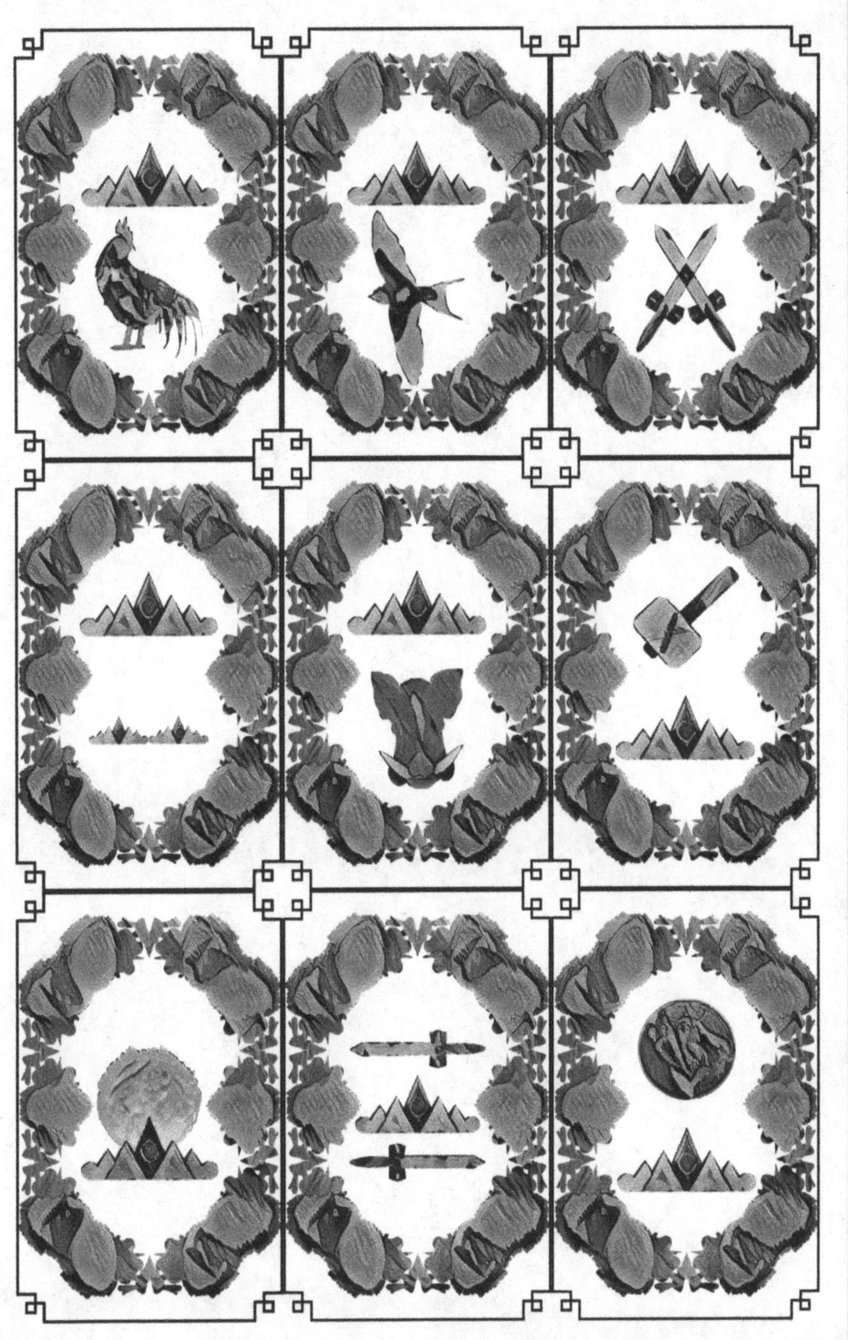

FIVE RUBY
Rules & Game Play

5 RUBY

Great skill is required to land all three tusks within the circle.

Common pieces are small and unmarked. Larger, more ornate tusks designate wealthier players who own and toss their own game pieces.

The Overseer confirms the pattern thrown and collects wagers.

The Unern Pattern is one of several acknowledged patterns.

An average game requires multiple nights and a large supply of ale.

<u>Objective</u>

Align every peach pit to your chosen ruby, and then eliminate any remaining players. To eliminate a player, throw the (3) boar tusks in the chosen pattern of the player; alternatively, all players tied to a *naked ruby*—a ruby without any peach pits aligned to it—are eliminated. (Fig. 1)

(Fig. 1) Example of a Naked Ruby:

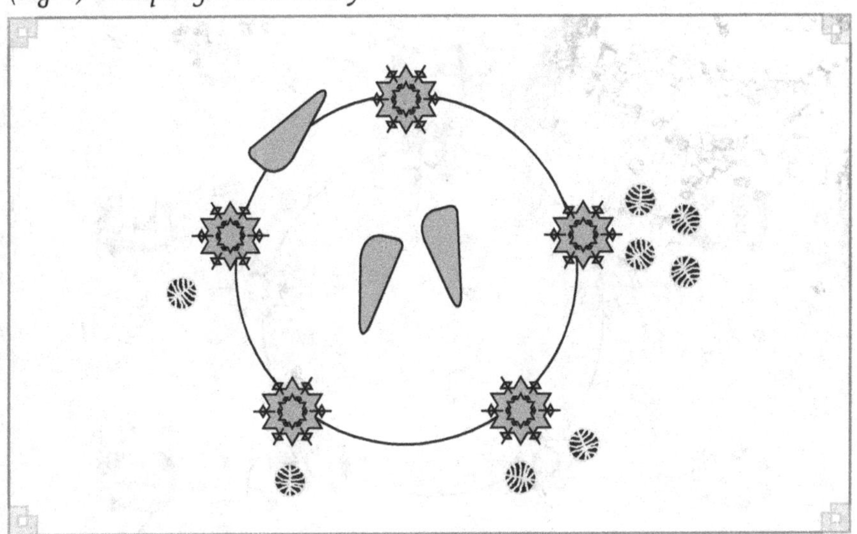

<u>Rules</u>

Each player chooses one of the five rubies to which they will remain tied during game play: (Fig. 2)

        Sphere—Top of Circle
        Rhil—Top Right
        Unern—Bottom Right
        Begn—Bottom Left
        Yowt—Top Left

The oldest player aligned to the Sphere ruby is allowed the first throw, with each subsequent turn determined by age going clockwise around the circle. The players must throw one of the ruby patterns in order to move a peach pit. If the tusks land in the pattern of the ruby they are aligned with, nothing happens. If the tusks land in the pattern of one of the other 4 rubies, the player moves a peach pit to their ruby and they then throw again. If all of the peach pits are removed from a ruby, the ruby is considered naked and the players tied to that ruby are thus eliminated. If the tusks land in the pattern designated by a player as their unique and specific pattern, that player is then eliminated. When 4 of the rubies are naked, the remaining players tied to the last ruby must throw the unique and specific pattern of each of the remaining players to eliminate them from the game. When one player remains, the game is finished.

(Fig. 2) The Five Rubies:

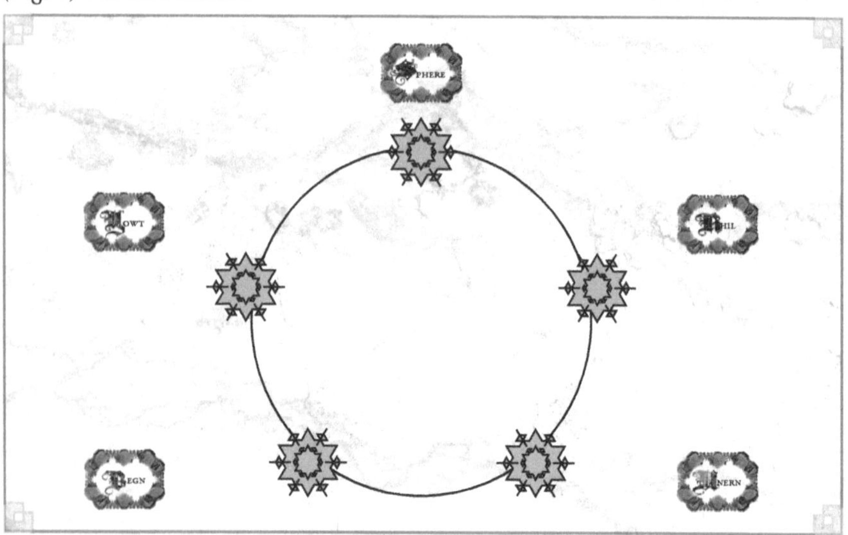

Traditional Beginning

Though variations of the beginning have gained in popularity, the traditional beginning remains the true and most recognized version; and the most honorable as it represents the Sphere. In the traditional beginning, place the five rubies in a circular formation—equal distance apart, with at least two peach pits (players) aligned to each ruby. The three boar tusks are placed in such manner as to be consistent with the diagram below. (Fig. 3)

After placing the pieces, a period of one hour is allotted for players to declare themselves as such, and align themselves with a chosen ruby. This ruby, thus designated, remains attached to the player for the duration of the game. Players must then announce their unique and specific pattern. If the boar tusks ever mirror a player's selected pattern, that player is then eliminated.

(The pattern of the boar tusks shown in the example below is known as the *sermit*. A player may announce this as their chosen pattern, or choose a different pattern.) (Fig. 3)

(Fig. 3) Traditional Beginning with sermit pattern:

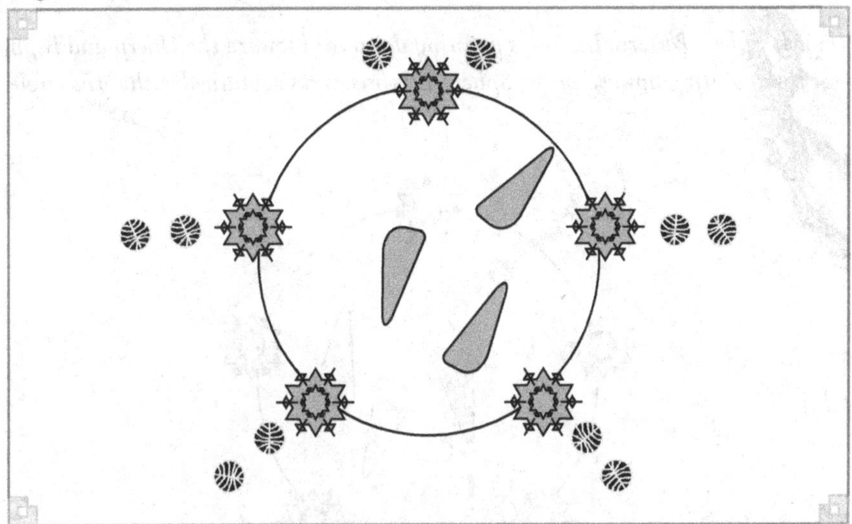

One peach pit is added to the field of play for each active player and, accordingly, the pit is aligned to the player's chosen ruby. Players may align themselves to any of the rubies without regard for even dispersement. (Example: One of the five rubies may have ten peach pits aligned to it while another ruby may only have three peach pits.) A Traditional Beginning, however, requires at least two players, or peach pits, per ruby.

<u>Wagers</u>

It is honorable to place a wager concerning various aspects of 5–Ruby. The following is recognized by the Adow as being acceptable: (Figs. 4-8)

> Specific Pattern Thrown
> Whether Movement of Peach Pits will Occur
> Number of Boar Tusks that will Land in the Circle
> First Naked Ruby
> Prediction of Player Elimination
> Last Ruby (with Peach Pits)
> Last Player Remaining

Any player, non-player, non-participant, or casual observer may place a wager prior to the toss of the first boar tusk of an active player's turn except the active player. A player may not wager on the outcome of their own throw.

To place a wager refer to *Overseer* section. The Overseer, at their own discretion, may establish a minimum and/or maximum wager amount.

(Fig. 4) Sphere Pattern: Two tusks pointing downward toward the Unern and Begn, one tusk pointing upward at the Sphere, all three tusks contained within the circle.

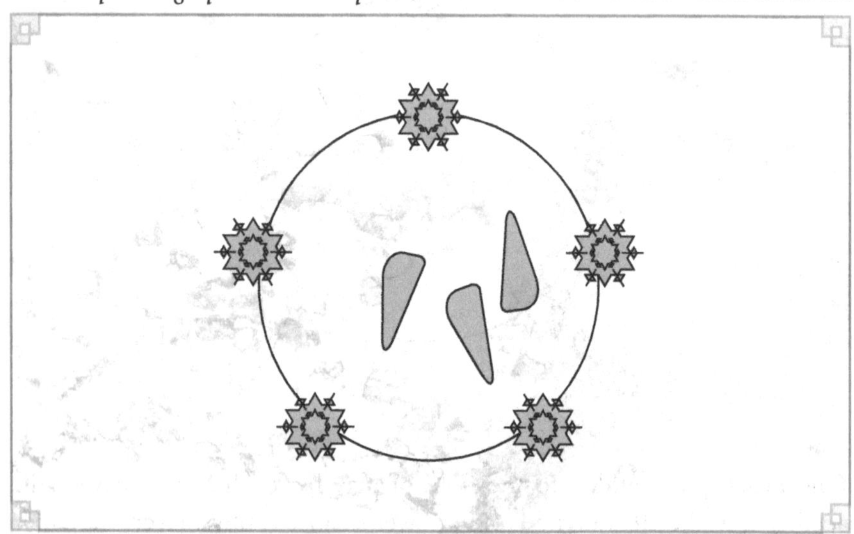

(Fig. 5) Rhil Pattern: Two tusks located within the circle, each pointing toward the other; one tusk outside the circle and pointing away from the circle on the left, or Yowt and Begn, side.

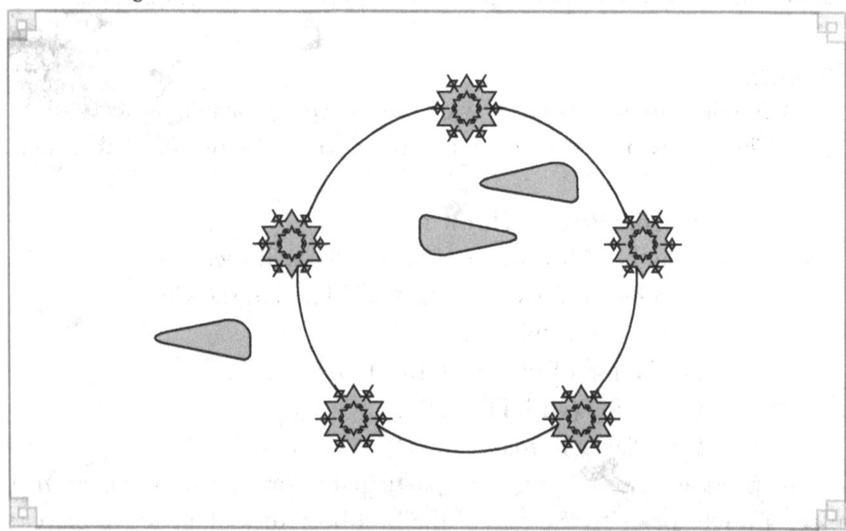

(Fig. 6) Unern Pattern: Two tusks located within the circle, each pointing toward the other; the third tusk pointing toward the Rhil and Unern rubies is also within the circle.

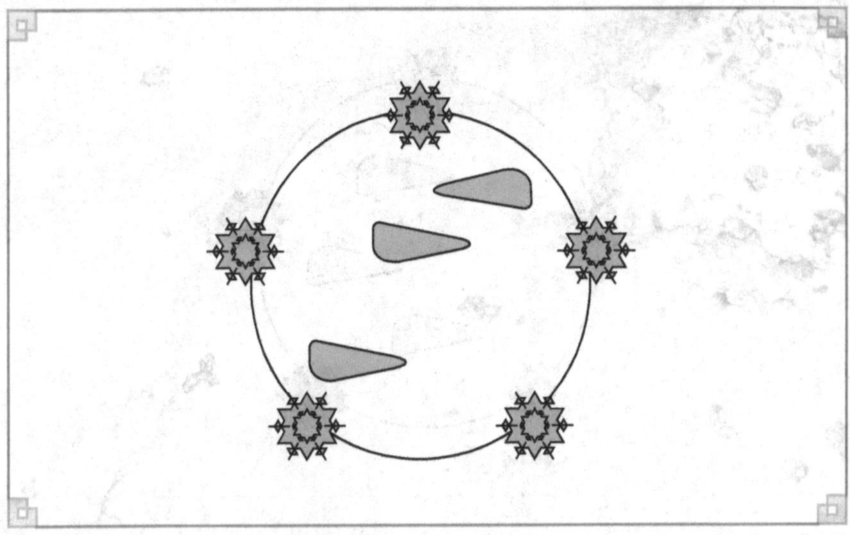

(Fig. 7) Begn Pattern: Two tusks located anywhere outside of the circle, each pointing back toward the circle; the third tusk inside the circle pointing toward the Sphere.

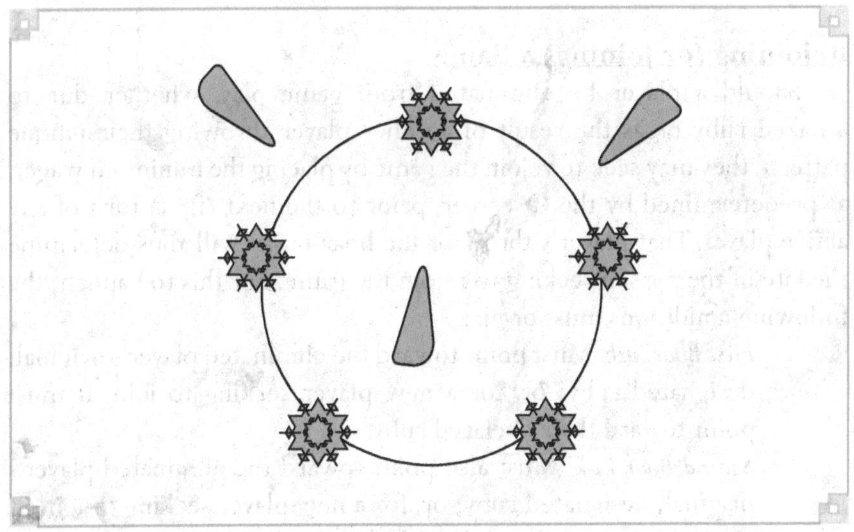

(Fig. 8) Yowt Pattern: All three tusks located within the circle; all of them must face the Yowt ruby.

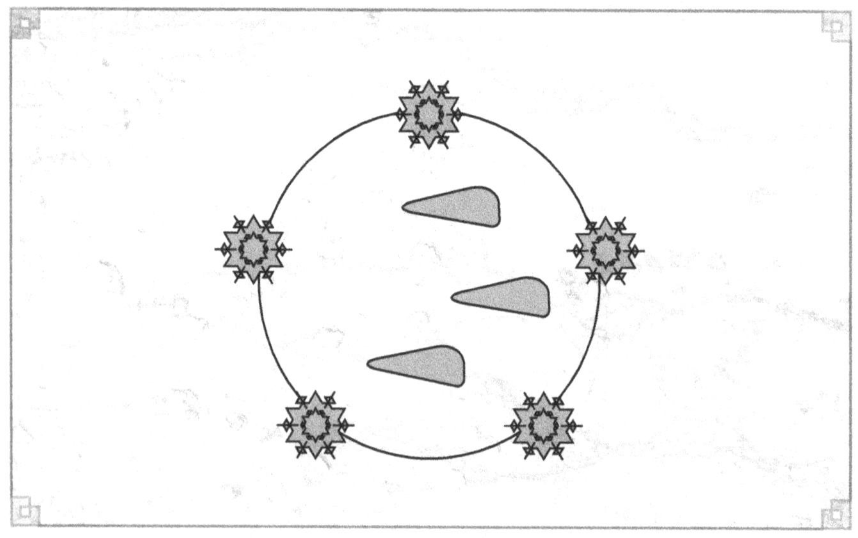

Ruby Patterns

Figs. 4-8 above show the five patterns traditionally associated with the five rubies.

Rejoining (or Joining) a Game

Should a player be eliminated from game play, whether due to a naked ruby or as the result of another player throwing their unique pattern, they may seek to rejoin the game by placing the minimum wager, as predetermined by the Overseer, prior to the next (first) turn of any active player. That player's throw of the boar husks will thus determine the fate of the person seeking to rejoin the game. For this to happen, the following conditions must occur:

> *First Boar Tusk*: Must point toward the eliminated player's original, designated ruby; or, for a new player seeking to join, it must point toward their declared ruby.
>
> *Second Boar Tusk*: Must also point toward the eliminated player's original, designated ruby; or, for a new player seeking to join, it must also point toward their declared ruby.
>
> *Third Boar Tusk*: Must land within the circle.

For the purposes of competitive balance, only the Overseer will know who has placed a wager to rejoin the game, lest one of the competing players otherwise impact or manipulate the subsequent throw of the tusks. Once thrown, the Overseer will announce any wager won and the wagering player may rejoin (or join) the game.

Peach Pits—Assassin

The Overseer will mark the bottom of one of the peach pits with a black "X" prior to the start of the game, and then place all of the pits into a bag or small container. The Overseer will then shake or otherwise shuffle the total number of peach pits in play prior to pulling them out and placing them around the field of play according to each player's selected ruby. Afterward, the Overseer will select five numbers, at their discretion. When the total throws recorded reaches one of the selected five numbers, the Overseer will declare an assassin has entered the game and forthwith flip all peach pits over to reveal the position of the assassin. All players aligned to a ruby where the assassin appears must then toss the boar husks. If the pattern thrown matches their chosen and unique player pattern, the player may remain in the game. If not, the player is eliminated from competition. Once the assassin has completed the kill(s), the Overseer re-hides the assassin by gathering all remaining peach pits into a bag, shuffles, and redistributes them according to game play prior to the assassin's attack.

Should an assassin attack occur during the final stage of game play, meaning all peach pits are aligned to a single ruby, the remaining players must compete in a round-robin format until a round finishes with only one player throwing their unique pattern. Note: If a round concludes without any of the players throwing their unique pattern, the round is forfeit and a new round begins. The last remaining player, therefore, wins the 5-ruby competition.

Peach Pits and Players

Though one peach pit is added to the field of play for every one player who declares themselves, the elimination of a single player does not also result in the removal of a corresponding peach pit. Indeed, the peach pit remains throughout the competition, changing rubies until all peach pits are aligned to a single ruby.

Rubies and Players

A player may rejoin the competition only if their ruby retains one or more of the peach pits. Once the ruby is declared a Naked Ruby, however, all players and non-players aligned to that ruby are eliminated.

Overseer

Players must designate one person to serve as Overseer prior to game play. This non-participant collects all gold and coins wagered. They record each player's unique pattern and, following each toss of the boar tusks, they confirm the pattern thrown which they then announce to the gathered crowd. They verify movement of peach pits and declare a ruby naked. Most importantly, they distribute winnings and serve as keeper of the purse.

Tradition dictates the Overseer receive a minimum of twenty percent of the total purse (the lost wagers) with the remaining portion given to the winner of the competition.

Boar Tusks

Players may supply and throw their own set of boar tusks if shown to, and approved by, the Overseer. If a player does not own a set of boar tusks, or if they prefer not to use their own set, they may throw the common tusks as supplied by the Overseer.

Line of Tossing

Line of Tossing refers to the distance between player and circle, traditionally considered twenty paces as determined by a casual stride of the Overseer. Once designated, all players must toss the boar tusks from behind a clearly marked line of tossing. Should the players momentum carry them over the line of tossing, however, and should this occur while in the act of tossing the boar tusks, the player must forfeit both their current and their next scheduled toss.

Note: A line fault does not prevent a player from placing a wager on other aspects of the game while they wait for their next turn, however, no player or observer may wager anything specific to the line of tossing.

5-Ruby
SPECIAL EDITION

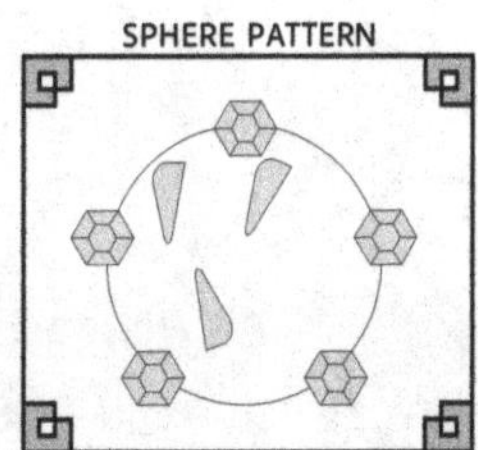

SPHERIC CALENDAR

Completion of the Purple Moon | 260 Years

Erin, the First Etabli | Anine | Aul

Shadow of the Purple Moon | 100 Years

Aul | Taggle, the Cursed

Completion of the Red Moon | 310 Years

Taggle, the Cursed | Ylaf | Erbohn | Ig-Poy

Changing of the Silver Moon | 40 Years

Ig-Poy | Adarian, Hero of Ire

Shadow of the Yellow Moon | 35 Years

Adarian, Hero of Ire

Completion of the Yellow Moon | 75 Years

Adarian, Hero of Ire | Fael

Completion of the Purple Moon | 260 Years

Fael | Irloore

Completion of the Green Moon | 980 Years

Irloore | Cintyge | Lio | Enyure | Athoyen | Ferya | Cidal

Ayson, of Quel

Spheric Moon | 1 Day

Ayson, of Quel

Dark Moon | Present Day

Ayson, of Quel

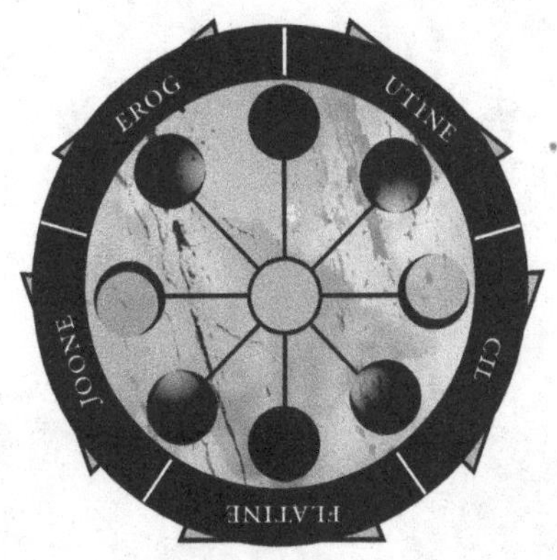

CITIES, RESIDENTS, DIVISIONS, and BANNERS

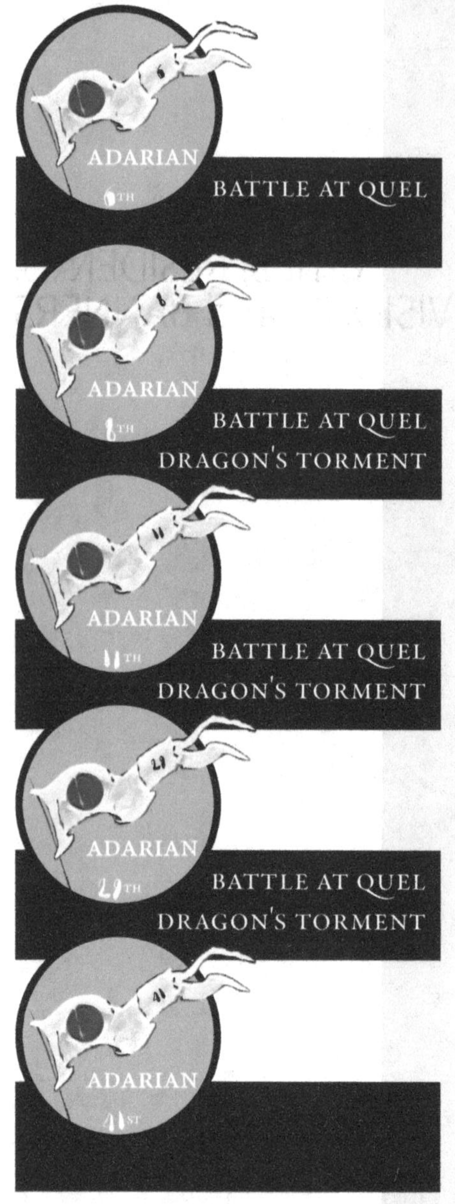

BEAUG
BELUR
BRELINE
DADEN
ERISYTE
GAN, OVERSEER OF ADARIAN
GOLEB
ININDU
KALETINE
KANBIS
LAY-I
NATALINE

BOASTING 161 DIVISIONS, MOST OF ANY CITY WITHIN THE KNOWN LAND, ADARIAN GREEN PERMEATES THE ADOWIAN ARMY. OFTEN REFERRED TO AS THE CITY SCULPTED BY BEAUG, MARBLE SCULPTURES DECORATE EVERY DISTRICT, GIVING SIGHTLESS EYES TO THE FOREBODING PRESENCE OF THIS MAGNIFICENT CITY.

ADARIAN

BIRATE
BRINK
DADEN
DECROME
GAN-PI
HALCROMB
HINTOR
MALDINADO
SHAMLON

THE CITY OF ADARIAN'S MOST HONORED DIVISION AND THE ONLY ONE TO FLY THEIR OWN COLORS INSTEAD OF TRADITIONAL ADARIAN GREEN. TRAVEL HARDENED AND BATTLE TESTED, THESE WARRIORS ARE MOST OFTEN SEEN MARCHING ALONG THE ROAD TO ADARIAN THAN IN THE CITY PROPER.

ADARIAN 45TH

CADUUM
DRAGON'S TORMENT

EDRAN
HIATE

CITY OF WRAITHS AND DESOLATION, MOST RESIDENTS ARE DEAD OR MORIBUND. A CEASELESS WIND BLOWS IN FROM DRAGON'S TONGUE WHICH SERVES AS THE ONLY KNOWN PASS INTO DRAGON'S TORMENT. ORIGINALLY ESTABLISHED AS A TRADE OUTPOST, CADUUM NO LONGER WELCOMES ANY LIVING CREATURE.

CADUUM

Beah

Della

Dellina

DK Vel

Ilion

Janeel

Jin

Koyo, mother

Lucen

Lyshmee

Penrem

Phire

Ruthee

Sanbi

Taggle, father

Treth

Tuloo

Vitrec

Cursed by the Adow, Taggles sleep on dirt or hay and live in a Dallic—located outside the city and so marked by a tiger banner, a figure the Taggles have taken to calling Dsal Tiger. Taggles serve all Topis regardless of banner, though few Topis, if any, know a Taggle by name.

TAGGLES

GOD OF ANOTHER WORLD WHO STANDS IN OPPOSITION TO THE SPHERE, MORLAC'S WORSHIPERS REMAIN IN DEEP SHADOW; SOME HAVE EMERGED AS ASSASSINS WHO SEEK TO KILL THE ADOW. MOST OF THE LAND BELIEVES MORLAC IMPRISONED WITHIN DRAGON'S TORMENT WHERE THE RORNE STAND GUARD.

MORLAC

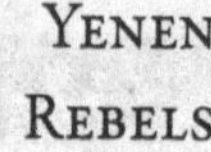

QUEL

BATTLE AT QUEL

QUEL

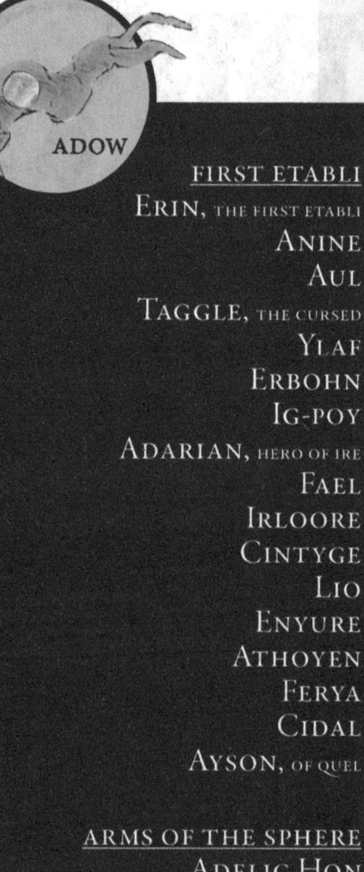

FIRST ETABLI
ERIN, THE FIRST ETABLI
ANINE
AUL
TAGGLE, THE CURSED
YLAF
ERBOHN
IG-POY
ADARIAN, HERO OF IRE
FAEL
IRLOORE
CINTYGE
LIO
ENYURE
ATHOYEN
FERYA
CIDAL
AYSON, OF QUEL

ARMS OF THE SPHERE
ADELIC HON
DISEN T'LADE
MADIC BALTIN
PEL F'RUTE
SOL PEDANTIC

ADOW
AIYA
AYSON, OF QUEL
DAUGHTER OF THE ADOW
FAUNRIDE
GILVAN
PWAX
OG
TEYO
TROQ
VALIN
YLA

YENUL, CITY OF THE ADOW, LIES BENEATH LAKE YENUL WITH THE LAKE ITSELF SUSPENDED ABOVE A SERIES OF CAVERNS WHERE RESIDENTS LIVE—AND THE PALACE WHERE THE ADOW MAKES HER HOME. THOUGH YENUL DOES NOT FLY ANY COLORS, IT PROUDLY YIELDS TO THE BANNER OF THE ADOW.

YENUL

ABRE
ADARIAN
LOR
LULL
CADUUM
CATAREB
MALI
PLENRID
CHANCE
DALLIC
QUEL
RIN
ELE
GOLESH
SORSE
STYCRAL
THE FIRE
IRE
TESA
YAWEH
KIEL
KILAR
ADOW
(YENUL)
YOKUR

KNOWN LAND

GLOSSARY

5-RUBY | A common high-stakes game consisting of tossing boar tusks toward an outlined circle. Often played to pass the evening, or turn a profit.

ABRE | (ĂB-rāy) | City—Located near the western coast line.

Abre10th | (ĂB-rāy) | Division of the Adowian Army. Journeyed to the Torment.

ADARIAN (city) | (ă-DĀR-Ē-n) | Major City—Known for its marble sculptures displayed throughout. Named after Adarian, hero of Ire.

Adarian 6th | (ă-DĀR-Ē-n) | Division of the Adowian Army. Fought in the Battle at Quel. Suffered complete annihilation three-days prior to the final assault on the city.

Adarian 8th | (ă-DĀR-Ē-n) | Division of the Adowian Army. Fought in the Battle at Quel. Generally considered brutes.

Adarian 11th | (ă-DĀR-Ē-n) | Division of the Adowian Army. Fought in the Battle at Quel. Strategists.

Adarian 29th | (ă-DĀR-Ē-n) | Division of the Adowian Army. Fought in the Battle at Quel. Known to capture and torture prisoners regardless of age or gender.

Adarian 41st | (ă-DĀR-Ē-n) | Division of the Adowian Army. An embarrassment to the city of Adarian. Gan, Overseer of Adarian, hasn't allowed the 41st to leave the city since they mistakenly shot a barrage of arrows into the ranks of the Yakur 3rd at the Battle of Ire.

Adarian 45th | (ă-DĀR-Ē-n) | Division of the Adowian Army. Fought in the Battle at Quel. The city of Adarian's most honored battle division. Journeyed to the Torment.

ADARIAN, HERO OF IRE | (ă-DĀR-Ē-n [hero of] Ī-r) | Deceased. First Etabli for she who served During the Completion of the Yellow Moon under the seal of the Sword with Crown on Hilt. He died in the Adow's arms; first to die in battle - first to die protecting the Adow. Revered. Also, the subject of many works of art; the majority of which portray him in the moment before his death.

ADELIC HON | (ă-DĔL-ĬK HĂHN) | A name from prophecy. Also, separately, nephew to Troq.

ADOW | (ă-DŎU) | A title passed down and used as name when referring to she who rules the known land. A queen-like figure. Born with the title of *Daughter of the Adow*, she who reigns assumes title and throne of the Adow upon the death of her mother. The Adow (the collective that is the singular) have ruled from the Completion of the Purple Moon to the current Dark Moon.

[*also*] **Oracle** when speaking prophecies as given by the Sphere

ADOWIAN ARMY | (ă-DŎU-Ē-n) | General term for the warriors who assemble from across the land and follow the Adow into battle.

ADOWIAN BURIAL | (ă-DŎU-Ē-n) | See Glossary of Rituals and Traditions.

ADOWIAN DECREE | (ă-DŎU-Ē-n) | Formal decree issued by the Adow. Each decree is numbered and recorded for historical purposes.

ADOWIAN DECREE 1575 | (ă-DŎU-Ē-n) | "We seek the Five Arms of the Sphere. All who are able must journey to Dragon's Torment—to death or glory. An Adowian Burial awaits the one who finds the Five."

ADOWIAN GUARD *or* **GUARD** | (ă-DŎU-Ē-n) | Twenty warriors hand selected by the First Etabli to protect the Adow wherever she may wish to walk, rest, or ride. From these ranks will the Adow choose her (next) First Etabli.

ADOWIAN PROPHECY | (ă-DŎU-Ē-n) | Recorded prophecy as spoken by the Adow in her role as Oracle of the Sphere.

ADOWIAN SEAL | (ă-DŎU-Ē-n) | The chosen symbol of the reigning Adow, for most, variations of a crown.

AIYA | (Ī-yŭh) | Maidservant to the Adow.

ANINE | (Ā-nēn) | Deceased. First Etabli for she who served During the Completion of the Purple Moon under the seal of the Hemming Tree above Crown.

ARMS OF THE SPHERE | Five figures from a prophecy spoken by the Adow: Madic Baltin, Pel F'rute, Sol Pedantic, Disen T'lade, and Adelic Hon. The prophecy serves as a quest to seek the five.

    [*also*] [**the**] **Five** when speaking in general terms.

    [*also*] [**the**] **Five Wolves** | Characters from a story as told by Troq to the Adow, and how she often refers to the Arms of the Sphere when ruminating on Adowian Decree 1575.

ATHOYEN | (ĂTH-O-YĪN) | Deceased. First Etabli for she who served During the Completion of the Green Moon under the seal of the Crowned Boar.

AUL | (ĂLL) | Deceased. First Etabli for she who served During the Shadow of the Purple Moon under the seal of the River Under Crown.

AYSON, OF QUEL | (Ā-sŭn) | First Etabli for she who served During the Completion of the Green Moon under the seal of the Crown between Swords.

    [also] First Etabli for she who serves During the Dark Moon under the seal of the Tiger and Crown.

BALOR TREE | (BŎ-lōr) | A type of tree. The only kind found in the Torment. Easily identified by its shimmering black leaves.

BATTLE AT IRE | The last great war prior to the Battle at Quel. Revered as the location where Adarian, First Etabli, died protecting the Adow.

BATTLE AT MALI | A lesser battle before the Battle at Quel. A terrible loss for the Adowian Army.

BATTLE AT QUEL | General term used to describe a five-year battle between Yenen and the Adow; though it included multiple cities across a large portion of the known land, and ultimately ended with the destruction of Quel and the deaths of both Yenen and the Adow.

BATTLE AT STYCRAL | A lesser battle before the Battle at Quel. Here, Decrome beheaded the Rovet of the Stycral 12th.

BEAH *OR* **TAGGLE** | (BĒ-ŭh) | A taggle boy. Friend to DK Vel.

BEAUG | (boh-G) | Deceased. Master artisan. Sculptor of Adarian. Responsible for most if not all significant artwork across the known land.

BEGN PATTERN | (BĀN) | Pattern in 5-Ruby: Two tusks located anywhere outside of the circle, each pointing back toward the circle; the third tusk inside the circle pointing toward the Sphere.

BEGN RUBY | (BĀN) | Bottom left ruby in 5-Ruby.

BELLADONNA ROOT | In small doses, this powdery substance is Adarian's drug of choice. Typically poured into wine and ingested. Lethal in large doses.

BELUR | (bāy-LŪR) | Adarian resident. Daughter of Kanbis and Nataline. Niece of Maldinado

BIRATE *OR* **LITTLE BIRTY** | (bī-RĀT) | An aspiring topi warrior of the Adarian 45th eager for advancement. Short. Nickname: Little Birty.

BLIND GOAT | A yearling's game. Participants take turns wearing a blindfold and attempt to first retrieve a ribbon and then tie the ribbon around a tied-up goat. Prior to the attempt they are spun around, making the task all the more challenging as the participant struggles to maintain their balance.

> [*also*] **BLIND GOAT** [*Adarian 45th version*] Warriors of the Adarian 45th substitute knives for the prescribed ribbon. Once killed, the goat is cooked and served with a toast to the champion. Some participants will toss the knives, thus inviting the gathered audience to participate in the game at their own risk.

BLOODGRASS | Red-tipped grass that grows across the Adarian region. The bright red coloring gives the illusion of fresh blood; seemingly all that remains of the ghosts of warriors fallen in battle.

BREAD AND STEW | A tavern located in Lor.

BRELINE | (BRĀ-LĒN) | A Daughter of Oblation. Mother of Maldinado.

BRINK *OR* **LUCKY BASTARD** | (BRĒ-nk) | The stout Banner Bearer of the Adarian 45th. Brother-in-law to Gan.

BROKEN TUNNEL | An unfinished tunnel in Yenul known for it's marketplace.

CADUUM | (CĂH-DŌM) | City—Entrance to Dragon's Torment. A city of wraiths and ceaseless wind. Originally built as a base camp when trade with the Rorne began.

Caduum [*1st*] | (CĂH-DŌM) | Division of the Adowian Army. Journeyed to the Torment. First division by default since they are the only division from Caduum to march with the Adow.

CATAREB | (CĂT-a-rĕb) | City—Located near the center of the known land just northwest of Plenrid; conquered by Yenen prior to the *Battle at Quel*.

CHANCE | Inner-city of Adarian—Known for its colorful architecture, [*topi*] bone and skeletal sculptures, and rooftop marketplace. Place where Nataline resides.

CIDAL | (SY-dle) | Deceased. First Etabli for she who served During the Completion of the Green Moon under the seal of the Sun Rising Over Crown.

CIL | (SĬL) | Third month of the spheric calendar.

CINTYGE | (SĬN-TĬJ) | Deceased. First Etabli for she who served During the Completion of the Green Moon under the seal of the Crowned Swallow.

CHRONICLES OF YENUL [or other city] | A recording of the names of the topis who reside within the city; also, their profession.

CYLEN TREE | (CĬ-lĕn) | A type of tree.

DADEN | (dāy-DĔN) | Adarian warrior.

DALLIC | (DĂWL-ĬK) | The term used for the dwelling place of taggles located beyond the city walls. Typically, a mud pit offering little more than a hut as shelter and an open grave where the dead gather. Every dallic is heavily guarded to prevent taggle newborns from going unmarked.

DALLIC RIVAC | (DĂWL-ĬK rī-VĂK) | A taggle chosen to continually repeat the taggle's prayer on behalf of those taggles living in that particular dallic. Highly respected by all taggles. Identified by the red paint on their face.

[*also*] **RIVAC** when speaking in general terms.

DAUGHTER OF THE ADOW | (ă-DŎU) | See Adow.

DAUGHTERS OF OBLATION | Worshipers of the Sphere who have committed themselves to a life of service and to the ministry of the Fire. Often, caretakers of orphans.

DECROME | (DĀY-crŭm) | Rovet of the Adarian 45th. A flat-nosed warrior with overly long arms. Known more for his courage than his compassion.

DELLA *OR* **TAGGLE** | (dĕl-LĂ) | A taggle girl with unusually white eyes and unblemished skin—healthy in appearance. Member of Uncle Taggle's adopted family. Commonly identified as DK Vel's first love.

DELLINA *OR* **TAGGLE** | (dĕl-LĪNĂ) | A taggle girl. Daughter of Della. DK Vel notes she had a slender frame, black hair, and a throaty voice.

DISEN T'LADE | (DĪ-SĬN tŭh-LĀD) | A name from prophecy. Also, separately, cousin to Troq.

DK VEL *OR* **TAGGLE** | (D-K-vĕl) | A taggle boy. Storyteller.

DRAGON'S ORE | Consumable fuel source favored by Hiate for its ability to burn evenly and produce the concentrated heat required to forge metal objects. Mined from Dragon's Torment. Deep red in color before burning.

DRAGON'S TONGUE | Pass leading from Caduum into Dragon's Torment. Steep, but offers solid footing.

DRAGON'S TORMENT | Mountain range. Cursed dwelling place of Morlac.

[*also*] **[the] Torment** *or* **[the] Dragon** when speaking in general terms.

DSAL TIGER | (DĬ-SŎL) | The figure of Dsal Tiger varies greatly depending upon the dallic where the taggle was born, ranging from Kiel where he is portrayed as white with black stripes, to Ire where he is described as being all black, more panther-like. In Caduum, Dsal Tiger is described as having two red eyes. His fur is white, and he has a single black stripe—a scar on his left side reaching from shoulder to hindquarters. In Adarian, Dsal Tiger is orange with black stripes and has a short tail and three white paws. No matter his physical appearance, however, Dsal Tiger is always depicted as a tragic figure and sardonic sage who never emerges the victor. Instead, his tales serve as warning that they may guide the listener to the Sphere. (Traditional tales may or may not include other characters such as rabbit, owl, wolf, or bear among other creatures.)

EDRAN *OR* **TAGGLE** | (ĔD-rĭn) | A taggle boy. Apprentice to Hiate, the blacksmith. Known for his red hair.

ELE | (ĔL) | City—Located near the center of the known land just northwest of the *Lake of Seven Cities*; conquered by Yenen prior to the *Battle at Quel*.

ENYURE | (ĕn-YĒR) | Deceased. First Etabli for she who served During the Completion of the Green Moon under the seal of the Two Crowns.

ERBOHN | (ĔR-bŏn) | Deceased. First Etabli for she who served During the Completion of the Red Moon under the seal of the Crown of Leaves.

ERIN, THE FIRST ETABLI | (ĔR-ĭn) | Deceased. Original First Etabli who served During the Completion of the Purple Moon under the seal of the Floating Crown Over Sphere.

ERIN'S FIRE | A flower with red pedals and a white center that floats on the water. Prevalent on *Lake Yenul*.

ERISYTE | (ĔR-ĭ-SĪT) | Consort of Gan.

EROG | (ĔR-ŭg) | First month of the spheric calendar.

ESHION | (ĔSH-Ē-ŏn) | Rovet of the Stycral 14th.

FAEL | (FĀY-ĕl) | Deceased. First Etabli for she who served During the Changing of the Blue Moon under the seal of the Crowned Warrior.

FATHER OF OBLATION | Worshiper of the Sphere who has committed himself to a life of service and to the ministry of the Fire. Head of the Fire and leader of the Sons and Daughters of Oblation.

FAUNRIDE | (făhn-RĪD) | A member of the Adowian Guard. Succeeded Troq as chosen protector of the Daughter of the Adow.

FERYA | (fĕrh-Ā) | Deceased. First Etabli for she who served During the Completion of the Green Moon under the seal of the Hammer Striking Crown.

FIRE OF THE SPHERE *or* **[the] FIRE** | A place of worship. Home to the Sons and Daughters of Oblation who tend to the fire that ever burns high above the city.

FIRST ASSASSIN | Mythical slayer of those who seek to ascend to godhood—those who dare challenge the Sphere. Whereas Morlac deploys many assassins, the Sphere has need of only one.

FIRST ETABLI | (Ē-tăb-LĒ) | Consort and Protector of The Adow.

FLATINE | (FLĀ-tēn) | Fourth month of the spheric calendar.

FURMEC RO | (fĭr-MĔK-rōh) | A vile curse rarely used, and never in polite company.

GAN, OVERSEER OF ADARIAN | (GĂN) | Caretaker of Adarian. Powerful ruler-type, second only to the Adow in political power. Old, dreadfully old. Lover of Erisyte.

GAN-PI | (GĂN-PĪ) | An pimple-faced warrior of the Adarian 45th.

GALINOR | (găl-ē-NŎR) | Considered a leader amongst the sorcerers.

gefor | (gĕ-FĬR) | A chamber pot.

GIEEL | (GĪ-ĒL) | A character in *Misdeblue*, an ancient tale.

GILVAN | (gĭl-VŬN) | An Adowian Guard with straw colored hair and a missing front tooth.

GOD OF ANOTHER WORLD | Term used when referencing Morlac.

GOLEB | (GO-lĕ-b) | Resident of Adarian. DK Vel notes his rooftop served as the place where Dellina told a taggle's tale.

GOLESH | (GO-lĕ-sh) | City—Part of the seven islands that comprise the *Lake of Seven Cities*.

Golesh 13th | (GO-lĕ-sh) | Division of the Adowian Army. Part of the Adowian Army seeking the Arms of the Sphere in Dragon's Torment.

Golesh 41st | (GO-lĕ-sh) | Division of the Adowian Army. Journeyed to the Torment.

Golesh 47th | (GO-lĕ-sh) | Division of the Adowian Army. Journeyed to the Torment.

GUBYER | (GŬB-yr) | A traitor whom the Adarian 45th tracked down in Nelic Mountains.

HALCROMB | (hăl-KRŬM) | Grey-bearded warrior of the Adarian 45th. Father of Shamlon.

HEALER | Someone skilled in mending wounds and comforting the sick.

HEMMING TREE | (hĕ-MĒ-n) | A type of tree.

Hemming Tree Forest | (hĕ-MĒ-n) | Geographic forested area located along the southwestern coast line.

HERALD | Learned speaker of words, often the only means by which a topi may hear, for example, an Adowian Decree.

HIATE | (HĪ-āyt) | A red-bearded blacksmith. Resident of Caduum.

HINTOR | (HĬN-TOR) | A farmer from Plenrid. His friendship with Maldinado allows him to serve in the Adarian 45th.

IG-POY | (ĬG-PŎĪ) | Deceased. First Etabli for she who served During the Changing of the Silver Moon under the seal of the Five Crowns.

ILION *OR* **TAGGLE** | (Ī-lĕŏn) | A taggle. Member of Uncle Taggle's adopted family. Lover of Sanbi and, perhaps, father of Lay-I.

IRLOORE | (Ĭ-LŌ) | Deceased. First Etabli for she who served During the Completion of the Green Moon under the seal of the Crowned Rooster.

ININDU | (Ĭ-nĭn-DŌ) | A single creature comprised of topi and horse. The horse speaks, but the topi is mute. Sister of the Adow. Once, caretaker of the Daughter(s) of the Adow. Created by the Sphere at the beginning of time. Eternal. Jaded lover of Adarian, Hero of Ire.

[*also*] **topi-Inindu** *or* **Inindu-horse** when referring to one portion of the creature that is Inindu.

IRE | (Ī-r) | Coastal City—Known for the *Battle of Ire*. Death place of Adarian, hero of Ire.

JANEEL *OR* **TAGGLE** | (jă-NĒL) | An old taggle woman. DK Vel describes her as a hunchback, and horribly scarred, but full of energy. He also notes she did not travel to the Torment.

JIN *OR* **TAGGLE** | (JĬN) | A taggle woman. DK Vel notes her wide brown eyes sparkled and burned - indeed they conveyed vibrant emotions.

JOONE | (JŌ-nē) | Last month of the spheric calendar.

KALETINE | (kăl-ĕ-TĪN) | Adarian resident. Daughter of Kanbis and Nataline. Niece of Maldinado.

KANBIS | (kăn-BĬS) | Deceased. Former husband of Nataline.

KIEL | (KĪ-ĕl) | City—Located inland near the southern coast.

Kiel 2nd | (KĪ-ĕl) | Division of the Adowian Army. Journeyed to the Torment.

Kiel 9th | (KĪ-ĕl) | Division of the Adowian Army. Journeyed to the Torment.

KILAR | (KĪ-lăwr) | City—Part of the seven islands that comprise the *Lake of Seven Cities*.

KOYO *OR* **MOTHER** | (coy-YO) | Gave birth to the taggles after an affair with Taggle, the cursed, producing the only male offspring of any First Etabli.

KUL | (KŬL) | A mystery.

LAKE OF SEVEN CITIES | A large lake containing seven island cities including Yenul where the Adow resides.

LAKE YENUL | A lake held above the cavernous entrance of Yenul by ancient magic. An ever active geyser erupts into and forms the underbelly of this lake.

[*also*] **BLOOD LAKE** [*common*]

LAY-I *OR* **TAGGLE** | (LĀY-Ī) | An unmarked taggle baby with red hair. Born in secret and hidden from the dallic guards. Daughter of Sanbi and, perhaps, Ilion.

LEET SOCNO | (LĒT SŌK-nō) | A banner-like marriage token designed by the bride, and then placed over the couple's intertwined hands. After the ceremony, it is hung above the couple's bedroom door.

LIO | (LĒ-OH) | Deceased. First Etabli for she who served During the Completion of the Green Moon under the seal of the Crown over Crossed Swords.

LOR | (lore) | City—Located near the edge of the known land.

LUCEN *OR* **TAGGLE** | (lew-CĔN) | A taggle boy. DK Vel notes the boy told stories with uncommon maturity and a surprisingly deep voice.

LULL | (LŬL) | City—Located near the western coast line; conquered by Yenen prior to the *Battle at Quel*.

Lull 28th | (LŬL) | Division of the Adowian Army. Journeyed to the Torment.

LYSHMEE *OR* **TAGGLE** | (lĭ-SH-mē) | A taggle girl.

MADAR | (MĀD-r) | A blood inheritance. Formal leaders of battle divisions. Detested cowards who quietly hide in their luxurious tents while Rovets lead their warriors into battle.

MADIC BALTIN | (mă-DĬK bal-TĬN) | A name from prophecy. Also, separately, brother of Troq.

MALDINADO | (MŬL-duh-năw-DOH) | Madar of the Adarian 45th. Friend of Hintor. Brother of Nataline. Son of Breline. Maldinado means *wrath of the Sphere*.

MALI | (MĂW-lē) | City—Part of the seven islands that comprise the *Lake of Seven Cities*.

Mali 6th | (MĂW-lē) | Division of the Adowian Army. Journeyed to the Torment.

MARDTBREN | (MĂWR-T-brīn) | A farmer from Plenrid. Father of Hintor.

MISDEBLUE | (MĬS-duh-blō) | An ancient tale about two anonymous lovers, Tenush and Gieel, filled with whimsical and witty dialogue;

ultimately, a hopeful tale often recited and, on occasion, performed onstage.

MISTAN *OR* **TAGGLE** | (mĭ-ST-ăhn) | A taggle girl. Granddaughter of DK Vel.

MORLAC | (more-LĂK) | God of another world. A castoff disciple of the Sphere.

NATALINE | (NĂ-tă-LĪN) | Adarian resident. Sister of Maldinado. Daughter of Breline. Wife of Kanbis. (Deceased) Mother of Kaletine and Belur.

NELIC MOUNTAINS | (NĔH-lĭk) | Mountainous area separating Adarain and Tesa; the southern foot of Dragon's Torment.

NELIC STEMS | (NĔH-lĭk) | Flower found in the Nelic Mountains. Known for their smoke-like odor. A favorite of she who served as the third Adow.

OG | (ŎG) | A member of the Adowian Guard.

OVDA | (ŭh-V-dŭh) | [short for *of the*] Troq's nickname for the Daughter *of the* Adow.

OVERSEER | Entrusted with the governance of a designated city, as appointed by the Adow.

PEL F'RUTE | (Pĕhl fŭh-RŌT) | A name from prophecy. Also, separately, brother of Troq.

PENREM *OR* **TAGGLE** | (pĕn-RĔM) | A taggle boy.

PHIRE *OR* **TAGGLE** | (FĪ-r) | A taggle boy known to have traveled with DK Vel. Died with his hands tied, a captive on the road from Catareb.

PLENRID | (pl-ĔN-RĬD) | City—Farm land. Hintor's home. Located near the center of the known land just northeast of Stycral; conquered by Yenen prior to the *Battle at Quel*.

PWAX | (fŭ-WĂCKS) | A member of the Adowian Guard.

QUEL | (qu-ĔL) | Destroyed City—Known for the *Battle at Quel*.

RHIL PATTERN | (r-ĬL) | Pattern in 5-Ruby: Two tusks located within the circle, each pointing toward the other; one tusk outside the circle and pointing away from the circle on the left, or Yowt and Begn, side.

RHIL RUBY | (r-ĬL) | Top right ruby in 5-Ruby.

RIN | (r-ĬN) | City—Part of the seven islands that comprise the *Lake of Seven Cities*.

RIN 9th | (r-ĬN) | Division of the Adowian Army. Fought in the Battle at Quel.

RORNE TRIBES *or* **[the] RORNE** | (ror-NĔ) | Mysterious native tribes inhabiting Dragon's Torment.

ROVET | (ro-VĔT) | A warrior who has proven himself in battle. Division leaders, but not the *formal* leaders of each unit. That title belongs to the otherwise detested Madars—a blood inheritance. While the Madars quietly hide in their luxurious tents, Rovets lead their warriors into battle.

RUTHEE *OR* **TAGGLE** | (rū-THĒ) | A taggle woman. Mother of five children. DK Vel notes she once gave him shelter, and further mentions her brother who survived the Torment only to die from a beating two days after his return, beaten by the same guard who carved into the ears of the youngest of Ruthee's children.

SANBI *OR* **TAGGLE** | (săn-BĒ) | A taggle woman. Lover of Ilion. Mother of Lay-I.

SCARLET | A prostitute.

SCHOLAR | Someone devoted to books and understanding the mysteries contained therein; also, recorders of prophecy as spoken by the Adow. Identified by their purple robes.

SHAMLON | (SHĂM-lŭn) | Red-haired warrior of the Adarian 45th. Son of Halcromb.

SILAR | (SĪ-lăr) | Name of the goat owned by Kaletine and Belur.

SORCERER | A pompous sect of society given to vocal and frequent complaints. Good for amusing tricks, but generally useless in a battle. Identified by their black robes.

SORSE | (SORE-se) | Coastal City—Located along the southern coast.

SPHERE | (s-FĒR) | God.

SPHERE PATTERN | (s-FĒR) | Pattern in 5-Ruby: Two tusks pointing downward toward the Unern and Begn, one tusk pointing upward at the Sphere, all three tusks contained within the circle.

SPHERE RUBY | (s-FĒR) | Top ruby in 5-Ruby.

SPRINGS OF MIST | Geographic region located in upper northwest.

SOL PEDANTIC | (sole pŭh-DĂN-TĬK) | A name from prophecy. Also, separately, uncle to Troq.

SONS OF OBLATION | Worshipers of the Sphere who have committed themselves to a life of service and to the ministry of the Fire.

STYCRAL | (STĪ-crŭl) | City—Located near the center of the known land just southwest of Plenrid; conquered by Yenen prior to the *Battle at Quel*.

Stycral 12th | (STĪ-crŭl) | Disgraced division of the Adowian Army.

Fought with Yenen against the Adow in the Battle at Quel.

Stycral 14th | (STĪ-crŭl) | Division of the Adowian Army. Journeyed to the Torment.

SUMATRAN | (sū-MŎ-trĕn) | Archaic name for tiger.

SWORD OF THE SPHERE | Name given to the sword the Adow carries, yet never wields in battle.

TAGGLE | (t-ĂG-le) | A descendant of Taggle, the First Etabli who betrayed the Adow, identified by the scars given to all taggles—their pointed ears carved into and made round at the tip as they exit the womb. It's the mark of their bloodline, the curse given to them by the Adow because Taggle had an affair with Koyo, producing a male yearling. They're allowed to live because of their father, but their ears are a sign to all that their birth, their life, is not recognized by the Adow. They're not topis. They're taggles. Oddly, they are the keepers of story, great orators allowed to share their tales with everyone but the Adow–never the Adow, for although a select few are chosen to serve the Adow directly, they are forbidden to speak in her presence.

TAGGLE, THE CURSED OR FATHER | (t-ĂG-le) | Deceased. First Etabli for she who served During the Shadow of the Purple Moon under the seal of the Sword through Crown. He betrayed the Adow when he had an affair with Koyo, producing a male yearling. Father of the taggles.

TAGGLE'S PRAYER | (t-ĂG-les) | Tattooed markings on a taggle's knuckles which translates as follows: *Forgive our mother* [Koyo], *Remember our father* [Taggle, the cursed].

TAGGLE'S TALE | (t-ĂG-les) | An oral story as spoken, with minimal performance elements, by a taggle; often considered the only true value of a taggle. Few topis will dare tell a story in public for it is considered beneath them as proper members of society. Thus, and though the taggles serve as protectors of story, a taggle storyteller is not a position of honor.

TASA RO | (t-ĂSĂ-roh) | A common curse muttered or shouted when someone feels perplexed, vexed, or otherwise finds the moment entirely out-of-sorts.

TENUSH | (tĕ-NŌSH) | A character in *Misdeblue*, an ancient tale.

TESA | (tĕ-SA) | City—Located near the edge of the known land.

Tesa 89th | (tĕ-SA) | Division of the Adowian Army. Journeyed to the Torment and wielded swords made by Hiate the blacksmith.

TESHA | (tĕsh-Ă) | Warrior in the Rin 9th. Wounded at the Battle at Quel.

TEYO | (TĀY-oh) | A member of the Adowian Guard.

THREE HORNS TAVERN | A tavern located in Yenul, its main decoration a full-sized bronze sculpture of a three horned ram. It is also the only structure in Yenul erected using timber.

TOPI | (to-PĒ) | Those descended from the Adow.

TRETH *OR* **TAGGLE** | (TR-ĕth) | [an] Uncle Taggle. DK Vel notes the Uncle lived in the Abre dallic and spoke slowly and with great patience, allowing the audience to absorb both the rhythm of his voice and the meaning of his words.

TROQ | (TR-ŎK) | Deceased. Former guardian of the Daughter of the Adow. A member of the Adowian Guard.

TULOO *OR* **TAGGLE** | (tŭh-LŌ) | A taggle man. DK Vel notes the man told his story with minimal physical movement.

UNCLE TAGGLE | (t-ĂG-le) | Term given to the oldest living taggle within any given dallic.

UNERN PATTERN | (Ū-NRN) | Pattern in 5-Ruby: Two tusks located within the circle, each pointing toward the other; the third tusk pointing toward the Rhil and Unern rubies is also within the circle.

UNERN RUBY | (Ū-NRN) | Bottom right ruby in 5-Ruby.

UTINE | (Ū-TĪN) | Second month of the spheric calendar.

VALIN | (vā-LĬN) | A member of the Adowian Guard.

VITREC *OR* **TAGGLE** | (VĪ-trĕk) | A taggle boy.

WORSHIPER OF MORLAC | (more-LĂK) | A sect of topis who secretly worship the god of another world, actively seeking to kill the Adow who serves as the voice of the Sphere—a god they despise.

YAWEH | (YĂ-wē) | City—Part of the seven islands that comprise the *Lake of Seven Cities*.

YEARLING | (yēr-lēng) | A child topi.

YENEN | (YĔH-nĕn) | Rebel leader of the uprising at Quel. Formerly, a member of the Adowian Guard.

YENUL | (YĔH-nul) | Royal City—Home to the Adow. Comprised of a series of extensive tunnels and enormous caverns located beneath the *Lake of Seven Cities*.

YLA | (Ē-lă) | A member of the Adowian Guard.

YLAF | (Ē-lŏf) | Deceased. First Etabli for she who served During the Completion of the Red Moon under the seal of the Broken Crown.

YOKUR | (YO-cure) | City—Part of the seven islands that comprise the *Lake of Seven Cities*.

Yokur 3rd | (YO-cure) | Division of the Adowian Army. Fought in the Battle at Ire. Mistakenly attacked by the Adarian 41st.

YOWT PATTERN| (y-ŎWT) | Pattern in 5-Ruby: All three tusks located within the circle; all of them must face the Yowt ruby.

YOWT RUBY| (y-ŎWT) | Top left ruby in 5-Ruby.

GLOSSARY OF RITUALS & TRADITIONS

ADARIAN GREETING RITUALS | Reserved for when the Adow visits Adarian. A test of the Adow. A rite of passage consisting of twenty-four greetings with five hours between each one. The greetings are precise in verbiage, dress, and ritual, and any slip of the tongue or gap in protocol brings perceived weakness upon the Adow. The rituals end with a masquerade and several ribbon dances that lead up to the Toast of Sark when all participants choose a partner to kiss before toasting the Adow's arrival.

[*also*] **Greeting Feast** or **Tenth [other number] Greeting** when

referring to a specific portion of the greeting rituals.

[*also*] **[the] Toast of Sark** a popular alternative name since the Toast

of Sark serves as the most popular and widely attended portion of the

rituals.

ADDRESSING THE ADOW | It is tradition for a speaker to address the First Etabli unless the Adow initiates the discussion.

ADOW IN BATTLE | The Adow's sword, the Sword of the Sphere, remains sheathed. No Adow has ever used the sword. One of the Adow–the one who reigned during the time when Fael was First Etabli, whose seal was a Crowned Warrior–is known to have practiced swordplay in her early years. But even that Adow never drew her sword in battle, and most Adow are never taught such maneuvers. She may enter battle wearing ornamental armor or, as is more often the case, don a traditional white linen blouse with golden doublet and matching trousers. The Adow does not fight in battle, for she has an army, a royal guard, and a chosen protector to fight for her.

ADOW'S APPEARANCE | All Adow share a likeness to one another. It is how they are identified as chosen by the Sphere, confirmed as his chosen ruler.

ADOW'S JUDGMENT | (Occurring on the battlefield) Should the Sphere approve of the Adow's actions, and those of her warriors, light will emanate from her body and she will rise above the battle for all to see, signifying an end to the war; a symbol of either imminent judgment or pending victory for the warriors below.

ADOWIAN BURIAL | A burial ceremony attended by the Adow. Rare. Considered the highest of honors. Upon death, a funeral procession travels the land, stopping at every city for a five-day celebration of life before returning to Yenul where they burn the body in the Fire of the Sphere. Traditionally reserved only for the Adow, and for her First Etabli, only one other, Beaug, sculptor of Adarian, has received such an honor.

BEGGARS | Charity toward beggars in the form of food or token is considered honorable, and the greater honor when giving to the point of personal sacrifice as when someone gives bread to a beggar, and then must fast for lack of food.

BRANDING OF THE ADARIAN 45TH | Warriors of the Adarian 45th are branded as part of their initiation, leaving an unmistakable sphere upon their chest.

BROTH AND BEER | A favorite drink in the Caduum region. The broth, typically chicken flavored, is served in a bowl and consumed in whole prior to quickly drinking the goblet of beer in its entirety. A messy drink, most cannot complete both with a dry chin unless they dawdle which otherwise defeats the spirit of the quickly-gulped drink; or keep from retching afterward which speaks to the competitive nature of the drink. Considered a test of character. Rarely consumed alone.

CADUUM WRAITHS AND SCARS | Those who live in Caduum will greet strangers with a question, "Have you a scar?" In a city where wraiths often appear, residents prove they are real by displaying their scars—inflicted by self or happenstance, for in death all wounds are left behind with the body.

CHANCE—INNER-CITY OF ADARIAN | Once a place used to collect the dead and diseased, Gan, Overseer of Adarian, transformed the inner-city of Adarian into a colorful, exotically morbid, and risqué night destination. The bones of the dead serve as ornamental pieces. Full skeletons—posed unnaturally and often with mouths open in laughter—guard every doorway. Chance serves as Adarian's default celebration destination following a Final Cleansing, boasts a rooftop marketplace above countless taverns, and generally ignores questionable behavior whether of the lecherous or devious sort. Most scholars consider Chance ensnared in the struggle between the Sphere and Morlac, some of whom suggest it serves as Morlac's only connection to the land.

CHILD OF THE ADOW | Known as the Daughter of the Adow, this child serves as the only child of the Adow; a child gifted to the land by the Sphere, thereby granting the Adow a form of eternal life as spirit passes from mother to daughter with the former's death. Inindu once served as formal caretaker but now a chosen warrior looks after and guards the Daughter of the Adow.

[*also*] **Daughter of the Adow**

CHOOSING A FIRST ETABLI [ALSO] **DEATH OF A FIRST ETABLI** | Upon the death of a First Etabli his Adow will select one of the Adowian Guard to assume the role of both protector and consort. Once the Adow passes from one (old) body to the Daughter of the Adow's (new) body, she is able to, again, bear children with the First Etabli of her (prior) choosing serving as the father.

CLEANSING RITUAL | It is customary for those who worship the Sphere to undergo a cleansing on the fifth day of each month. This cleansing requires the worshiper to seek isolation so they may better focus their attention upon the Sphere.

CONDEMNING THE ADOW | Those who dare condemn the Adow while in her presence will quickly loose their head courtesy of the Adowian Guard. Their body will hang on display in the marketplace, and their name stricken from the Chronicles of Yenul [or other city].

CURSING OF THE BANNER BEARER | Adowian warriors are encouraged to openly mock, ridicule, or otherwise curse their division's banner bearer as it forces them to first find the lucky bastard and then follow them. In this manner, a heartily shouted and repulsive curse serves to unify and embolden a highly skilled division such as the Adarian 45th who, by all accounts, take great pride in their creative contumelies.

DEATH AND BURIAL | The body of a topi is burned in a ceremony conducted at the Fire of the Sphere. A taggle is dumped in a mass, open grave located within every dallic, denied the fire in one final curse.

DEATH OF A MADAR | As the only member of a battle division not required to fight in the actual battle, many a Rovet (or other warrior) has killed their respective Madar. These two titles, one earned with blood on the hands (Rovet) while the other (Madar) is passed down to those with shared blood, routinely cast diatribes at one another and seek alliances within the division—one through intimidation, one through manipulation. If the balance of power shifts toward the Madar, the Rovet is usually quick to take action and remove his only political threat within the ranks; thus placing a typically weaker heir into the role and better securing his grip upon the division.

DEATH OF A ROVET | (Occurring on the battlefield) The banner bearer moves the banner in a full circle five times.

EXCHANGE OF SWORDS | An Adarian tradition. Warriors exchange swords with a promise to exchange them again at battle's end. A promise to survive.

FASTING RITUAL | It is customary for those who worship the Sphere to partake in a midday fast spanning five hours; and which occurs every fifth day.

FIELDS OF BLOODGRASS | Grass fields near Adarian, each blade said to represent a drop of blood for every Adarian warrior who has died in battle.

FIRST CLEANSING | An observed isolation ritual conducted on a yearling's first birth celebration. The yearling is placed in the center of the attending family and friends, none of whom may embrace or touch or otherwise acknowledge the yearling's presence for five-minutes. After the ceremony, the yearling is celebrated as having survived their first cleansing.

FINAL CLEANSING | The burning of the dead conducted at the Fire of the Sphere. This topi ritual is then followed by a celebration of life for the departed.

FIRST ETABLI'S SHIELD | Display's an engraving of Erin, the First Etabli's head and torso.

GENERAL DISLIKE OF SCHOLARS AND SORCERERS | Honor is gained in battle and through service to the Adow. Those who seek an easier lifestyle, however, may choose to pursue scholarly studies or practice the craft of magic, but they will forever face public scorn, loathing, and ridicule. For some, it is worth the price, and well, they do have their moments of brilliance to ease the shame.

GUARDING THE ADOW | Twenty of the best warriors across the land are selected to serve in the Adowian Guard, and serve until death. The best of these warriors (typically) serves as First Etabli, as chosen by the Adow, and the next best warrior serves as guardian and caretaker of the Daughter of the Adow. The Adowian Guard work as a unit to scout, secure, and guard any area where the Adow may reside or travel; providing a constant sphere of protection. As for the First Etabli, he never leaves the Adow's side; similarly, the guardian and caretaker of the Daughter of the Adow never leaves her alone—both serve as a symbol of the ever-present Sphere, however, when the mother's spirit passes to the Daughter of the Adow the guardian and caretaker will remove himself from her side, thus allowing the First Etabli his rightful place beside the Adow.

KISSING OF GAUNTLETS | An Adarian warrior's tradition of kissing the back of their gauntlet in honor of their fallen brothers.

LEECHES | Commonly used by the healers to treat open wounds.

MADAR'S THRONE | Customarily made from silver.

MARK OF THE ADARIAN 45TH | Each warrior in the Adarian 45th boasts a circular mark burned into their chest; an act of initiation.

MARKING A TAGGLE | All descendent's of Taggle, the cursed, are marked at birth by removing the upper portion of the newborn's ears. To prevent a taggle from escaping the mark, therefore, each dallic is heavily guarded and every expectant mother closely watched.

ORACLE OF THE SPHERE | The Adow serves as voice of the Sphere. A group of scholars record her spoken prophecies.

ORPHANS | Battle comes with a cost and, as a result, many yearlings are left at or brought to, the steps of the Fire. These orphans are raised by the Daughters of Oblation.

PRAYER RITUAL | It is customary for those who worship the Sphere to offer prayers five times each day: 1. A prayer of gratitude offered upon waking 2. A prayer for guidance offered after first meal 3. A prayer of silence offered at midday, listening rather than asking 4. A prayer advocating for others offered after the last meal *and* 5. A prayer of contemplation offered before sleep.

RED DEATH | Anonymous distributor of belladonna root known only by the mask they wear which is customarily red and without adornment. They attend every feast and festival in Adarian and are aggressively, if secretly, sought after by those in attendance. A simple exchange of gold for powder occurs, and then they disappear. Known as "Red Death" due to the lethal risk and symptoms associated with an overdose which cause the heart rate to rapidly increase before suddenly slowing and stopping; also a red rash seemingly bursts forth as though boiling atop the skin, and the victim further suffers from hallucinations and loss of balance.

[*also*] [**the**] **mask of the Red Death**

SALUTATIONS | It is customary to greet a fellow topi with *May the Sphere be with you* which solicits a response of *And keep you in His light.*

SCHOLARLY ATTIRE | It is customary for a scholar to identify themselves as such by donning a purple robe.

Sleeping taggles | The taggles huddle together while sleeping with the eldest positioned in the middle of the circle of bodies and the youngest, or newest to join the circle, lying on the outermost perimeter of the circle. Newborns sleep at their mother's breast until they are old enough to endure the cold air that nighttime brings at which time they take their proper place within the circle. The taggles snuggle against or hug the body in front of them, and it is not unusual to find themselves embracing a cold body come morning.
[*also*] **taggle sleep circle**

Sorcerer's Attire | It is customary for a sorcerer to identify themselves as such by donning a black robe.

Speaking to the Adow | It is customary to address the First Etabli unless the Adow initiates the discussion.

Taggle Gravesite | Each dallic contains an open mass grave where taggle bodies are thrown when they die. Though it serves as a final destination it is rarely visited by those who still live, and never patrolled by dallic guards which has allowed more than one taggle to escape by hiding amongst the dead. Rarely covered, these mass graves harbor rotting flesh, ancient bones, and myriad diseases.

Uncle Taggle | A term of respect given to an old taggle. Since few taggles see old age, they are considered remembered, or blessed, by the Sphere. A spoken blessing from Uncle Taggle, therefore, is considered good fortune.

Wedding Ceremony | The banner-like Leet Socno is designed by the bride, and then placed over the couple's interlocked hands. After the ceremony, the couple places the Leet Socno above their bedroom door.-

AUTHOR

Chad Michael Cox was only five years-old when his grandpa, a police officer known for crafting stories, handcuffed him and left him in a holding cell as punishment for ending a sentence with a preposition. He worked off his debt to society by diagramming sentences for his mother, and then was forced to accompany his father during visits to local bookstores—a tradition Chad sustains with his own (three) children.

Having grown up under such literary hardship, he continued to torment himself by studying Writing, Literature, and Publishing at Emerson College. If this wasn't bad enough, he married a girl and built her numerous bookshelves and together they accumulated a wonderfully large library and also five cats. Now, he tortures other people's children as a contract writer for Iowa Testing Programs at the University of Iowa.

5-Ruby
Special Edition

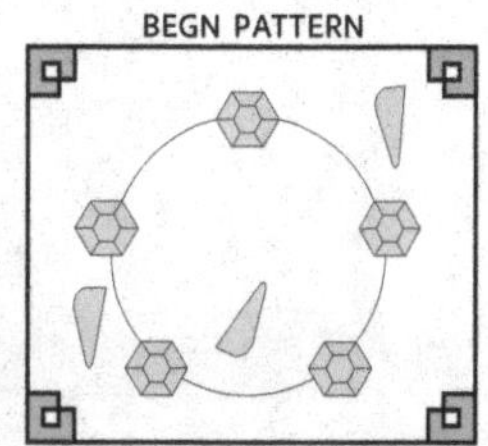